ASHLEY

DRAGONFLIES AND DREAMS

JUDITH ASHLEY

Windtree
Press

CONTENTS

Windtree Press

http://windtreepress.com

Publisher's Note: This is a work of fiction. Names, characters, places, and incidents are a product of the author's imagination. Locales and public names are sometimes used for atmospheric purposes. Any resemblance to actual people, living or dead, or to businesses, companies, events, institutions, or locales is completely coincidental.

Book Cover by Christy Caughie www.gildedheartdesigns.com

Ashley/Judith Ashley – 1st Edition

Print ISBN 978-1940064574

Ebook ISBN 978-1940064581

❁ Created with Vellum

ACKNOWLEDGMENTS

My village for *Ashley* includes the people listed in the dedication as well as Sarah Raplee and Diana McCollum my co-authors of *Love & Magick: Mystical Stories of Romance* who spent time talking with me about the emotional aspects of serious disease and the reality of denial. The #RCRWFTB group and the Goal Writing Challenge group for helping me keep my tush in the chair and my fingers on the keyboard.

And last but not least, Dr. Rui Li, who took time from her important work with her breast cancer patients to answer my questions about treatment options when the patient refuses what is recommended, in this case a mastectomy. I took notes and have done my best to accurately depict Dr. Li's information. Any errors are mine.

1 - THE WEDDING CANCER

Fremont, Oregon
August 1, 2004
Lammas

The vine-covered pergola provided some shade for Ashley Kenner, who stood within the bower watching her children. Amanda, her youngest at six, tried to shinny up Daniel O'Donnell's leg. He leaned down and scooped her up. Squeals of delight filled the air. The boys, Art Jr. or Artie, the oldest at twelve and Anthony, nine, flanked him, staying close enough to hear every word he exchanged with Matthew, the groom, and Michael and Jackson, who sported newly-wed glows.

Daniel, Jackson's closest friend, perched Amanda on his shoulders and reached out to pull the boys closer. To her, her sons stood taller when included in the men's conversation.

While she wouldn't have missed Diana and Matthew's wedding for the world, it was a challenge, a painful one at that, to see her children loved and accepted by a man who was not their father. They soaked up Daniel's, and for that matter, Michael, Matthew and Jackson's attention like children without a father. The truth was, they did have a dad, a dad who had changed over the past five years, a dad who now ignored them.

Ashley stayed partially hidden observing the post-wedding celebration. Diana, her dark brown hair in its traditional page boy, was radiant and it warmed her heart to see her circle sister so obviously in love—and loved in return. It had been a hard road for D to accept Matthew's love. A smile played on her lips, her eyes crinkled—*the horror of it all, Matthew being eight years younger.* She caught a glance pass between bride and groom, saw Diana's flush and Matthew's grin.

They aren't the only ones who've found happiness. Lily and Elizabeth have found their soul mates in Jackson and Michael. All three of my circle sisters struggled with their fears before they found their way to love. She turned away from the festivities. Studying the gold Victorian gazing ball amid a plethora of flowers, she breathed in the scented air from the multi-hued blooms.

The pergola's seating faced both open-sides. She took the two steps and sat on the bench, facing away from the merrymaking. Tears welled. Her power animal, the dragonfly, clutched in her fist, she fought them back. *Not the time to tell anyone the cancer is back.*

Stiffening her spine, Ashley rose and turned back to the celebration. *I've been through this before. I can manage. I will manage.*

"Ashley, where have you been?" Diana wrapped her in a warm hug. "I was looking for you. The Circle wants to spend a few minutes together before everyone takes off."

When Ashley looked around, it was clear that several people had left—in fact, as she took inventory, everyone had left except The Circle and their family members.

"Just doing some thinking," she replied in her soft Southern drawl. People familiar with the various inflections from the south always knew she was from Alabama. Even after a dozen years in Fremont, anyone who heard her speak would know she was from the south.

"Is everything all right?" Diana asked.

"How could everything not be all right, D? I'm surrounded by the light and energy of love."

"You looked a little sad or maybe pensive." Diana linked her arm with her younger circle sister as they walked across the lawn. "Matthew, keep an eye on the children, please," she called out as they passed the group of men.

"Don't worry," Daniel answered and grinned. "Us guys got it covered."

In the house, they found the others gathered in the great room connected to the kitchen. The windows along one side looked out into the backyard. Ashley picked a seat where she could see her children. Not that she was concerned for their safety. It just fed her heart to see them so care-free, so happy, soaking up the men's attention.

"The seven of us won't be together like this until Samhain," Sophia said. Her long brown hair curled for the occasion, was pulled back from her face spiraled down her back. She looked from one woman to the next, connecting briefly with everyone. "I know we had our Ceremony two days ago and spent time sharing our plans and dreams for the next little bit, but the reality is, the seven of us won't gather together until we celebrate Samhain in Ireland with Elizabeth and The Lady."

Ashley listened intently as one-by-one everyone said a few words about their plans. Diana and Matthew were leaving in the morning for their honeymoon—two weeks at the coast.

Hunter, her chestnut hair pulled into a classic ballet dancer's bun, shared, "In addition to my end of the summer recital coming up in a couple of weeks, I've added a full complement of morning classes to my afternoon and evening schedule." Her turquoise eyes serious, she added, "I want the money available for Logan to attend the college of her choice. This way I can put the fees for these classes in savings."

"I'll be working in Seattle a lot of the time on this special project for my boss," Gabriella said, hazel eyes shining. "It really is a big deal for this company to send a technical writer from Fremont there. They do have tech writers but they like something about my work, so I'm going." She tugged a strand of her auburn hair that had come lose from the clip holding it in an upswept style. "In fact I'm cutting my trip to Ireland short and traveling directly from there to Seattle."

"However long you can be with us is a gift," Elizabeth said, reaching over to hold Gabby's hand. Her violet blue gaze was warm with friendship. With her free hand she brushed a strand of her naturally curly dark brown hair back over her shoulder.

Ashley's feelings were mixed as Lily, Gabriella, Sophia and Elizabeth excitedly chatted about leaving in the morning for Ireland. Last year's trips to Ireland held special memories for both her and the kids. With her husband, Art, being so unpredictable of late, last night she'd finally decided, if possible, she'd send the children. They loved the horses and Hunter's daughter, Logan, would be there—but when the time came for her to speak she said nothing about a change in plans.

"Y'all be sure and eat a few of Seamus' scones for us." She licked her lips and sighed in mock distress. "They are the best ever with his fresh butter and jam."

The women came together, arms wrapped around each other's waists, breathing in the calm certainty of being a part of something bigger than they were as individuals. A shiver traced through her. Ashley stepped back and rubbed her arms with her hands.

"Are you cold?" Lily asked. Her blue eyes reflected the concern in her voice. She had fixed her blond shoulder-length-hair in an elegant French twist.

"No," Ashley replied. "Don't know why but I got goose bumps just then. Gram always said something about someone walking on a grave when that happened."

Lily put her arm around Ashley's waist and together they walked out into the backyard. "You are taking care of yourself, aren't you?"

"Course I am," Ashley said, looking over at her children. *Never been able to look someone in the eye and lie.*

"You seem to have lost a little weight," Lily commented.

"Just been a busy summer is all. Yard work added to house work and keeping up with three kids. School starts in a couple of weeks and I'll slow down a bit. Got Mandy signed up for first grade. She'll get to go to school and come home with her brothers."

"That's great. You'll have the day to yourself. Do you have any idea what you're going to do with it?"

"Not really. But I'm sure I'll stay busy," she said, keeping her gaze on her kids who were still hanging around the men. "Guess I need to round up my kids and get home. Still have dinner to put together for Art."

Lily pulled Ashley into a gentle embrace. "You are in my prayers, you know."

"And I appreciate it. I really do." Ashley leaned back and looked Lily in the eyes, "And y'all are in my prayers, too." She slipped away and strode across the lawn to where her kids still gathered around Daniel.

"Gotta go," she announced.

"Do we have to?" Art Junior asked.

"But Mom," Anthony whined.

Amanda just clung more tightly to Daniel's neck, burying her face in his shoulder.

"Come along you rascals," Daniel's voice was gentle but firm. He began herding the children toward the door. "Your Mom said it's time to go, so guess what?"

"It's time to go," her sons chorused.

"That's right," he said giving each boy another quick ruffle of their hair and pat on their back as they started toward the car.

Ashley grabbed her purse from behind the chair where she'd tucked it upon arriving. Keys in hand she led the way to her 1988 Ford sedan. Doors open she stood back to let the heat from the day escape before leaning back in and rolling down the windows.

Daniel lowered Amanda into her car seat and buckled her in.

Where did he learn to do that?

Amanda, her arms still around Daniel's neck gave him a smacking kiss on the cheek. He rested his hand on her shoulder for a second before stepping back and gesturing to the boys to get in.

"Artie, you're in back on the way home," Ashley reminded her oldest as she rounded the car. She caught a glance and a handshake between Daniel and Artie and then Daniel and Anthony. She slipped behind the wheel and started the motor. "Seat belts?"

"Yeah, Mom," her boys chorused.

Easing from her parking spot between two cars across the street from Matthew and Diana's house, she checked her rearview mirror and glimpsed Daniel standing in the drive, his tie and jacket gone, watching them pull away.

Ashley stuck her hand out the window and waved, noting in the rearview mirror he waved back. A longing swept over her as she drove on. *When was the last time Art watched the kids and me drive away and waved? Stop thinking in that direction, Ash.*

She filled her mind with what she had to do over the next few hours: dinner for Art, watering the plants. *Perhaps the kids can do it.* A soft smile tipped her lips as the image of her kids with a hose in their hands tripped through her mind. *Which is better. Doing it myself or doing another load of laundry.* She added to her mental list: supervising the children getting ready for bed and setting things up for breakfast. *Even if Art doesn't get home in time for dinner, he'll expect breakfast.*

Art's car wasn't in the drive.

She stifled a yawn as she pulled into the driveway. Weariness weighed her down. Weariness from a long day; weariness from the stress of what was to come; weariness that she was once again the only one taking care of the kids.

The children piled out of the car and trooped into the house. *He may not be here to help with the kids, but at least he supports us.* Their last fight was about the time she spent with The Circle and his drinking. *At least he agreed if he'd been drinking he wouldn't drive and I agreed to have breakfast and dinner ready for him.*

They'd also agreed if he'd been drinking and the kids were up, she'd come and get him and if they were in bed, he'd sleep on the couch wherever he was. *What was I thinking when I agreed to that? Don't know where my brain's been recently. No, Ash, you do know. It's been worrying about that lump.*

Ashley went into the bathroom, shut and locked the door. Her hand went to her left breast and probed quickly finding the lump. Tears rained down her cheeks, dampening her favorite flower-print blouse. "What am I going to do?" she whispered.

Turning on the faucet, she splashed cool water on her face and patted it dry. "You're going to take care of things, just like you always do," she said to the grim-face in the mirror.

*P*ictures of quiet lakes with rolling hills of green in the background were in this examining room. *I think I like the ocean waves crashing on the rocks better.* Ashley pulled the front-opening gown closer, shifting to find a more comfortable spot. *Don't know why your fussing, Ash. There's no comfortable spot on an examining table.*

"Mrs. Kenner, Ashley, it's good to see you today," Dr. Burton said, her smile welcoming, her voice light.

"Good to see you too, Doc." Ashley was in hyper-vigilant mode so noticed the incongruence. The oncologist's eyes showed concern but her manner was positive.

Dr. Burton stood next to the table. "Let's see what we've got here." She lifted Ashley's left arm up and angled it so it rested across the table above her head. Methodically she pressed her fingers in a pattern across Ashley's breast. Finding the lump, her eyes closed and she manipulated the lump as if seeing it through her fingers. Finished, she closed the gown and lowered Ashley's arm to her side. "It isn't big but the mammogram and ultra-sound indicate it most likely is cancer. Assuming that's what the lab results say and with your history, I'm recommending a mastectomy. Once we get the pathology report back we can tailor the rest of your treatment for best results."

Her brain blanked.

"Ashley?" Dr. Burton said.

A cold numbness encased her. Ashley heard Dr. Burton's voice but couldn't speak.

Mastectomy?

"Ashley?" Dr. Burton said, her hand gently shaking her patient's shoulder.

Ashley reached for the dragonfly pendant hanging from a chord around her neck. Griping her totem hard, the points of the wings pressed deep. She welcomed the pain. The numbness faded but no words came.

Another voice registered. Ashley forced her eyes open and focused on the worried faces of Dr. Burton and Amy, Dr. Burton's nurse.

Terror ripped through her as the numbness left and her brain started functioning. Even though she knew there was a tumor a part of her had hoped, had prayed it wasn't—had hoped and prayed it was benign. Her first bout with breast cancer had been fairly straight forward: radiation, surgery and chemo. Of course all treatment options had been discussed so she knew what having a mastectomy entailed. Only in nightmares had she ever confronted the possibility of having one.

This time, almost five years later, she'd never thought she'd have to have a mastectomy—radiation, surgery, chemo. Those were the treatment options she was prepared to face.

Like a tropical shower that hits with no warning, tears fell. All she wanted to do was curl up in a ball and stay there until it all went away.

A warm hand stroked her arm. "How can I help you right now, Ashley?" Dr. Burton's soft voice asked.

"Just make it all go away," Ashley sobbed. Now on her side, her knees drawn up to her chest, with one hand she clung to Dr. Burton's hand, the other clasped her dragonfly totem. "P-p-please just make it all go a-a-away. A-a-art won't ever understand. He'll l-l-leave me and I-I-I won't be able to take care of my kids."

"Ashley," Amy said in a no-nonsense tone incongruent with her soft touch. "You know there is counseling available and a support group for husbands."

"But last time he refused to even talk to you, Dr. Burton. He wouldn't read anything you sent home to him. He didn't help with the kids or the house or anything," Ashley said. She struggled to sit up, to look her doctor and nurse straight on. "It took months and months before he even touched me. And that's only been in the dark."

Her stomach clenched and she thought she'd lose control of her bowels. "He's always been so proud of how I look. After last time, that changed. If I have a m-m-mast-ectomy… ."

"That is your best chance for survival, Ashley," Amy said, her mouth open to say more.

"This is a lot to take in," Dr. Burton said, casting a quick glance in Amy's direction. She held Ashley's hand and gently squeezed. "Let's finish the work-up. We can do a needle located biopsy and confirm if it is a recurrence of the previous cancer or a new one. We'll also review the amount of radiation you had last time and know exactly how much, if any, you can have this time.

"I have a cancellation next Friday, August 13th. We'll do the biopsy then and talk about options."

Tears streaking her face, her voice wobbly, Ashley asked, "Can you just remove the tumor then?"

"No."

Bile rose in her throat and Ashley thought she'd vomit.

Amy handed her a bag and patted her shoulder.

"We need to complete the tests, talk, have a plan and then move forward. You need to seriously consider the treatment options available to you not only in terms of your life expectancy but also the impact on your daily life. Amy will see you have some reading material so you know your options.

"As I said before, when the cancer has reoccurred, the recommended treatment is a radical mastectomy. If radiation is not a treatment option, even more so," Dr. Burton rested a hand on her shoulder the other on her arm.

"Take one day at a time," she said, in a calm voice Ashley found comforting. "Read the material over and we'll talk next Friday. It will be your decision how to proceed. It will be my job to make sure you understand the risks associated with your choice."

"I appreciate what y'all are doing, really I do." The wall clock in the examining room reminded her of another reality in her life. "I need to get home. My neighbor's watching my kids but they're a handful for her." Ashley exchanged the tissue Amy held out for her for the emesis bag and swiped her eyes.

"We'll let you get dressed then." Dr. Burton squeezed her shoulder before she and Amy left the examination room.

Ashley scooted off the table. She gave herself a stern talking to while she dressed. "You've been through this before, Ash. Maybe Art won't leave you. Maybe pigs fly. How can it get any worse? If he leaves, how can I support us? I haven't worked since we moved here. My job skills are rusty and if I have a ma—if I have that surgery, it will be months before I'd even be able to work."

She paused before shuffling her feet into sandals. "I hope Betty can watch them next Friday."

Her throat tightened and a sour taste filled her mouth. "What'll I tell the kids? The truth will frighten them." Bands of tension crossed her head and met up with the iron bar across her shoulders. Her head throbbed. "I've got to tell them something."

She folded the gown and placed it in the center of the examining table. "They're older now. We can get through the weekend even if Art isn't around to help out."

Gathering her purse she opened the door. "I don't really need all that much time to recover from the biopsy. Gotta look at the positives, Ash. That's the only way you'll get through this."

Ashley's hands and knees shook. She stood in the doorway, touched her dragonfly and took a deep breath. Grabbing her car keys from her pants pocket, she stepped into the hall. On her way out she picked up the envelope with the literature she was to read and confirmed her appointment for next Friday.

Back in her car, she sat, staring at nothing. The only one of The

Circle in town was Hunter and she was busy with an upcoming end-of-the-summer recital.

Adrenaline rushed through her and her heart pounded at the sound of the sharp scream of a car alarm. *At least my kids are old enough to fix a sandwich and take their bathes without me hovering.* Starting the car, Ashley inched out of the parking spot.

Her mantra all the way home: *I can do this! I can do this! I can do this!*

3 - WHEN IT RAINS IT POURS

Sunday, August 29, 2004

*A*shley trailed behind her children as they ran into Sophia's house. She imagined them tearing through the family room and out into the garden. They knew Logan was there: Hunter's car was in the driveway. Now that she had arrived they were all there except Elizabeth, who remained in Ireland with her husband Michael.

Logan and the children were out in back. Movies next to the television and VCR were available if they got bored and restless with the outdoor games. One-by-one the women smudged as they entered Sophia's sacred space, her living room. The altar cloth was gold, the center filled with the green Galway crystal bowl Elizabeth had brought from Ireland last year. Lavender wands and various miniature shafts of grains tied with bright autumn colored ribbons overflowed the bowl's rim.

Ashley added her pouch of protective stones to the altar, placing it in the West—the void. Their altars were always spectacular and this was no exception. While Hunter and she included items from Fremont, the others added new energy with rocks and candles from around Michael's stud farm. Lily added a beautiful card with an iridescent dragonfly on the cover. *My power animal.*

"I saw it and thought of you," Lily said. "It's yours to take home. I don't mean to pry, but you seem a little down. Maybe this dragonfly can help."

"It already has." She leaned over and hugged her circle sister.

As the Connemara marble rock passed from hand to hand, Ashley listened intently to where everyone was in her life. *My worst fears came true when I told Art about the cancer. He just packed up and moved in with a couple of buddies.* Shoulders slumped. She sighed. *In some ways it's easier with him gone. If I'm careful, the kids and I can manage as long as he keeps supporting us.*

The green-veined rock in her hand, she paused and let the warmth heat her cold fingers. She'd drifted a bit but caught enough to know everyone was catching up from being gone four weeks.

"School started last week. It's strange having no one at home all day except me. Mandy loves her teacher. She's so proud she can print her name and count and knows her alphabet. I talked to her teacher Friday when I dropped her off. Mandy's making friends and doing good. It helps she can walk home with her brothers. Saves me a trip and gives me a little more time to get that afterschool treat ready.

"Just listening to y'all talk about your time in Ireland brings back so many good memories. My kids still talk about the horses and learning to ride." She took her time, her gaze tracing from one circle sister to the next, "I missed y'all. Hunter and I were so busy we only talked for a few minutes a couple of times while you were gone. It feels so good just having most everyone back here."

As the last person to speak, Ashley set the stone on the altar cloth, the signal this part of their ceremony was complete. They stood and faced North, arms raised in prayer.

"Spirits, Ancestors, Gods and Goddesses of the North," Ashley started. "Thank you for being with us during this time of reconnecting. Until next time. Farewell.

"Spirits, Gods and Goddesses of the West," she continued, turning in that direction. "Thank you for coming from the void to be with us during this time of reflecting on the ties that connect us to each other. Until next time. Farewell."

"Spirits of the South," Hunter spoke up. "Your presence today reminds us of the abundance, the riches we have when together. Thank you for being with us this day. Until next time. Farewell."

"Spirits of the East," Hunter continued. "Your presence here today lights our paths so we more clearly see our way forward as a sacred women's circle. Thank you for being with us this day. Until next time. Farewell."

They hugged, arms around waists or shoulders, touching as many of the others as they could reach.

"Sending energy to Elizabeth," Sophia said.

Ashley pushed aside her worries and concentrated on her circle sister in Ireland. Even after almost ten years, the shift in energy sent a warm glow through her. *Why don't I tell them about the cancer? I will if I really need them. Right now they've all got stuff to catch up on and the kids and I are okay.*

Somehow everyone always just knew when it was time to move on. No one said anything and yet their arms dropped at the same time. Sophia picked up the green glass bowl and altar cloth after they retrieved their altar items.

Lily handed Ashley the card with the dragonfly. "Don't forget, this is yours."

"How can I forget my power animal? It's beautiful," she said. Hugging Lily, Ashley relished the closeness, the caring. When she stepped away, it was to cross the family room to check on her kids and tuck the card in her purse. The kids were fine, sitting around Logan, listening with rapt attention as an obviously wondrous story was told with lots of drama. Amanda's eyes and mouth were round as —*well, as round as the full moon so bigger than saucers.*

She called everyone in dismissing the groans and smiling at the cheers. *Logan must have promised to finish the story.*

Their tradition was to create a "spirit plate" with the foods everyone brought. Amanda watched intently as Sophia put small tidbits of all the foods on a plate.

Amanda's chest expanded several inches when, after the blessing, Sophia asked her to put it outside next to the gazing ball. So very careful of her precious burden, Amanda took the plate outside and gently placed it in a spot in the flowers. Her face blossomed as brightly as the dwarf delphinium when she looked back and saw Sophia's thumbs up sign.

"She seems so interested, I hope you don't mind," Sophia said.

Ashley's eyes brightened with unshed tears. She cleared her throat and swallowed hard. "No, I don't mind. She's curious and I think sensitive to the energies. She talks to me about dreams and visions she has. I just remember Elizabeth's stories about her childhood and I don't want Mandy to doubt herself."

"I can't imagine that happening, Ash," Sophia said, her hand resting on Ashley's shoulder. "You are such a good mother.

"I'll be by this week with bounty from my garden once I get caught up. As you know school started last week so I'm a bit behind there and that comes first. Garden second. Distributing the largesse of the Goddess will get done this week at some point. Extra I'm taking to the 14th Moon Celebration next weekend."

"We'll love every bit you bring us, Soph. I did come by and check that the watering system was working."

"One of the smartest investments I've made. So glad Matthew thought of it last spring when rototilling the garden for me. Now, when they invent something that knows a weed from a vegetable or flower that will be fantastic."

"Thought that landscape fabric did that," Ashley said, a smile on her face, laughter in her voice.

"Helps a lot but it isn't fool-proof. Enough about gardening—I'm hungry, how about you?"

"Sure could use some of the quiche you made," Ashley said as she moved toward the kitchen island where the food was laid out.

Three days later

FROZEN IN PLACE, Ashley remained at the teller window at the bank. *No money in the checking or the savings account?* She managed a "thank you" and moved aside for the next customer.

Art had not deposited his paycheck in the checking account but more to the point he'd withdrawn money from their savings account. The twenty dollars in her purse was enough to get milk and eggs. They wouldn't starve, there was food at house.

In a daze, Ashley made her way to the car. There was gas but barely more than half a tank. *How bad is it? I've got to know.* She stalked back to the bank and asked the teller if she could see the screen showing the activity on her checking account over the last three months.

As she skimmed over the few debits and no credits since the first of July, she saw for a fact that Art had stopped paying rent and utilities the first of July and had not deposited a paycheck since she told him about the cancer early in August.

A dozen eggs and a gallon of milk in her grocery cart, she struggled to control her features and her tears until she'd paid for the items and was safely in her car. With the doors locked and the windows rolled up, she succumbed. *He'd said not to count on him for anything. I just never thought.* Curled over the steering wheel, sobs rattled her body like an earthquake.

Someone tapped on her window and asked if she was all right. She waved them away with one hand and turned the car on with the other. *Got to get this gallon of milk home before it spoils because I don't have money for more.*

Her vision blurred with unshed tears so she drove the side streets home.

Milk and eggs safely stowed in the refrigerator, Ashley marched to the phone and called Art's cell. Not that she expected him to answer. She didn't but it was turned off and she couldn't even leave a voice mail message. "The party you are trying to reach is unavailable right now. Please try again later."

"You bastard! You freaking bastard!!! What about your kids?" she screamed at the phone. "How could you do this to your own flesh and blood?"

The door burst open and her kids rushed in. Their bright smiles and excited voices gone in an instant.

"What's wrong, Mom?" Artie asked, his arm now around his little sister, a hand on his brother's shoulder.

"Nothing to concern you," Ashley said swiping her hands at her tear-stained face. "Give me a minute and I'll get snacks out for you, okay?"

No one moved.

"You need to change out of your school clothes and into your play clothes. Off with you now." She stood and shooed them towards their rooms. *I can do this. I will do this.* Her hand gripped the dragonfly pendant, the wings marking her palm.

When things calmed down and the kids had changed, she filled the pitcher with ice water, got glasses, cut up apples and took it all out into the backyard. It was a hot day but in the shade of the patio covering bearable.

She explained she had to have a medical procedure in the morning. Since she had to be at the hospital by seven, she had to leave by six-thirty. Betty was going to come over and make sure they got off to school. She'd be here when they got home. If the doctor said so, she'd have to spend the night but she was going to try real hard to be home. "I'll call you if the doctor says I have to stay the night," Ashley assured the children. "Betty will be here and I'll be home before you get out of school Friday."

Artie looked worried.

Anthony asked why Art didn't stay with them. "He has to work," she said in a matter-of-fact voice. "But y'all be prepared. I'm waking you up in the morning before I go. I know your hugs and kisses will be good medicine for me."

Those words brought groans from her boys as she planned.

Amanda, who watched her intently, her forehead puckered in a frown, gave her a hug and a kiss on her cheek. "I got lots more, Mom. Maybe you don't got to go to the hospital?"

Ashley plopped Amanda on her lap and held her. Her daughter snuggled close, her arms around Ashley's waist. Her sweaty little girl smell was like perfume and she breathed in the aroma of life. "I still have to go, Mandy, but your hugs and kisses make everything better."

The next morning Ashley stood in the doorway of Artie and Anthony's room, watching her boys sleep. They looked so young, so innocent.

A tug on her arm, a warm weight against her leg announced Amanda was awake.

"I luv you Mom," Amanda whispered.

"I love you too," Ashley said, her voice soft. Her hand stroked Amanda's hair back from her forehead. "You're up early."

Her daughter nodded.

Ashley waited a few moments more before calling out from the doorway, "Y'all need to wake up now." She waited a moment more. Seeing no movement, she called out again.

Anthony roused first, squinted in her direction, plopped back on the pillow and groaned. "It's still dark."

"No it isn't," she said, walking to the window and pulling aside the curtains.

"Ow! Mom!" Anthony exclaimed. "What are you doing?"

"Showing y'all that it isn't dark out," she said and smiled. "Time to get up, boys. Cereal and milk on the counter. Don't forget to wash up and comb your hair before heading off to school."

A knock on the door. Betty had arrived.

She bent down and kissed Amanda on the cheek, wrapped her arms around her and hugged. "I've got more hugs and kisses for my boys." She laughed as both boys ducked under the covers.

With Amanda at her side, she answered the door. Reminding the kids to behave for Betty, she grabbed her wallet and headed out the door.

The lightheartedness didn't last.

Arriving at the hospital and checking in, she fought the overwhelming urge to vomit. Having eaten nothing since yesterday around noon, there wasn't much to upchuck but that didn't seem to make the roiling swirls of nausea ease.

It had taken some negotiating but she and Dr. Burton had come to an agreement. She'd have a lumpectomy today and in two weeks start chemotherapy: a total of eight treatments over sixteen weeks.

Her regret was—well, she had many of them right now. But beyond the cancer, she was missing this year's Women of the 14th Moon gathering.

Tomorrow Lily, Diana, Hunter, Gabriella and Sophia along with Logan were traveling to the mountains and the land where the 14th Moon would take place. It was the first time she'd missed one since Amanda was born.

The thought crossed her mind that without Betty she'd be in desperate straits. 14th Moon was a special time and she'd never ask one of the others to miss it to watch her kids. *I come from a line of independent women. I know I can do this.*

Monday, September 20, 2004

Wrapped in heated blankets, Ashley's body shook with tremors. They'd had trouble finding a vein for the IV and no wonder. She was cold, dehydrated from vomiting most of the night and tense with nerves. Her right hand reached up to smooth her hair.

In the wee small hours of the morning she'd stood in the bathroom, scissors in hand. She'd almost cut it off. Her waist length silvery blond hair, soft as dandelion fluff was once her crowning glory. Now it was just past her shoulders and although a similar color, was coarser.

She'd brought a book but it lay closed in her lap. *I'm so tired, so very, very tired.* Her eyes closed and she dozed but not so deeply she wasn't aware of the sounds of the nurses going about their business, the other patients leaving and new ones coming in.

Grateful she didn't have to leap up and run out when the chemo treatment was done, Ashley rested. She still had to drive home; the kids would be home from school shortly after she got there.

Sophia had brought vegetables from her garden last night so the fixings for a salad or grilled vegetables to last a week were stored in her refrigerator. She'd inventoried the food in the house and if she was careful, they'd make it for another week or so. What she was out of was meat. *That rat bastard came in while I was at the bank and raided the freezer. He must have got a real kick out of that!*

Anger gave her bit of energy to make it to her car and drive across town to her house. She now had a quarter of a tank of gas. Her head ached just thinking about how she was going to juggle everything.

Why hadn't she said something last Sunday at The Circle's meeting? "Pride," she muttered to herself. "That 'I can do it Carlyle independent pride.'" That was true but there was more to it than that.

Diana was dealing with morning sickness and had been warned about possible complications to the pregnancy. Calling Sophia and Hunter were not options because Sophia taught high school and Hunter had morning yoga and exercise classes.

Last night she'd been scared and sick and worried about the children. She'd called Lily but learned from Jackson she was out with a client. Gabriella didn't answer her phone because she'd already left for Seattle where she'd be working this week.

When Lily'd called her back this morning, she was rushing out the door to get to this appointment. She'd managed to say she'd been up all night sick.

"Take care of yourself, Ash," Lily admonished. "I'll check in on you later in the week, okay?"

"Yeah, that's fine. We'll be okay. Gotta go, I'm too far from the bathroom right now." She'd hung up and barely made it before the dry heaves consumed her.

"Could it get any worse?" Ashley asked herself. "Yeah, it could," she murmured. A notice on the door when she got home said her water was being shut off for non-payment. A voice mail message said her electric bill was in arrears and she needed to make a payment to keep that utility on. Both gave her until October 1st to bring things current.

Her efforts since Labor Day Weekend to track down Art had been unsuccessful. No matter what time of day or night over the last ten days she dialed his number, he never had his phone on. None of his friends had seen him. And when she called his work, she was told he could not be called to the phone. After some pleading, bringing the kids into the mix, the receptionist had said she'd make sure Art got her message. Still he didn't call, didn't come by, no money showed up in the checking account.

Why didn't she just drive to his work and confront him there? She certainly thought about it, thought she'd bring the kids in their most worn and torn clothes, embarrass him into doing something. *He's completely turned away from us. Guess I'm just scared he'll walk away and leave us standing in the parking lot or in the service department.* This was bad but if he walked away from them, that'd be worse, much, much worse.

She'd combed the house, checking the couch and chair cushions, raiding the change bowl she kept on her altar to encourage financial prosperity. Altogether she came up with another ten dollars.

If only I'd done a couple of the house totems, I'd have a few thousand dollars to help get us through this mess. The idea of trying to do a couple now with chemo treatments stretching out in front of her over-whelmed. She wasn't in any shape to call up the energy of the land. Why she barely had enough energy to take care of the basics of seeing to her kids.

In the dark of the night, she fought the urge to curl into a ball and sob or, fist raised in defiance, rail at the unfairness of it all.

Ashley made it to the bathroom just in time. All that was left was bile, but her body didn't care and wrenched and heaved to get rid of it. Weakened, she managed to grab a towel and leaning heavily on the wall, she made it to the living room and collapsed on the couch. From here she could see her kids as they came in the door.

Stretched out, a throw pulled over her, she closed her eyes and rested. *We'll make it. I'm a strong independent woman. We'll make it.*

The picture of Artie standing next to her bed on Labor Day was etched in her mind.

"Dad's gone, isn't he?" He'd shifted from foot to foot, his chin on his chest, not looking her in the eyes.

"Yeah, he is Artie," she'd said and reached out to take his hand.

"Where?" He'd looked up at her, questions in his eyes, in the pucker between his brows.

Even now she didn't know if what she said was right. Should she have lied? Should she have told him the truth?

"I don't know. I can't find him," she said, fighting the tears from her voice.

"So, it's just us?" he whispered, the tension of worry in his stance.

She'd nodded, not trusting her voice to work.

"I can do more," Artie said. "I can fix breakfast so you can sleep, Mom. And, I can help more around the house. Anthony can too."

He'd put his arms around her, patted her back. "We can do this, Mom. I know we can."

"You're right, son, we can do it. We're a strong family. We'll get through this."

"What about the others, you know, Hunter and Sophia and everyone?"

"Sophia brought us food from her garden just the other day. You know there'll be more coming. They're all at the 14th Moon Ceremony this weekend. I'll call them next week if I need to."

"Yeah. I know they'll help out. Like they did before when Mandy was a baby and you were sick."

He'd left her room, his step lighter, her heart heavier—sleep evaded her one more night.

Ashley shifted on the couch, pulled the throw up and tucked it under her chin. A shiver coursed through her from toes to head.

True to his word, Artie had been doing more. While it made all the difference, it was hard to see him step up and try to be the man of the house.

Why was it so hard for her to just call and leave a message for one of The Circle, let them know she was in treatment for cancer? It just wasn't something she could say on the phone. Last Sunday when they'd met, the words stuck in her throat. *Soon, I'll call Hunter or Lily or maybe Sophia.*

She'd lost weight, couldn't sleep and had problems eating even when there was enough food. Right now she wasn't sure if the current waves of nausea were from nerves or chemo. In some ways it didn't matter.

She clutched her dragonfly pendant and waited for her kids to come through the door.

6 - THE SECOND STRING TEAM

$\mathcal{D}$aniel O'Donnell was taking a short-cut through the neighborhood when he spied the three children walking along the sidewalk. Pulling to the curb, he rolled the window down and called out, "Hi guys, want a ride?"

He gave Amanda a hand up to the high-running board and Anthony clambered in behind her. Artie hung back and seemed reluctant to accept his offer.

"It's not that far," Artie said. He stood in the open door to the extended cab making no move to climb in.

"No, it isn't," Daniel replied. "You can walk on home if you want. I can take these two and drop them off."

"I'll come," Artie said and hoisted himself into the cab. As he pulled on his seatbelt, a loud growling grumble filled the small space.

"Why don't I swing by the DQ and pick up burgers for everyone. We'll get something for your mom, too," Daniel said, turning his blinker on to move away from the curb.

A chorus of "yeahs" from the backseat, a heated "no" from the front. *What's going on? Artie's never turned down food.*

He took the turn to take them home instead of the one to the main street and the DQ; groans of disappointment from the backseat, an audible sigh of relief from the front.

Daniel pulled into the driveway and put the truck in park. Before he'd finished that task and turned the engine off, Artie was out of the car and racing for the front door. *What the hell?* First, he steadied Anthony when he almost fell in his haste to jump down from the truck. He put his arms out and Amanda leapt into them. Setting her down on the ground, he wasn't at all surprised when she grabbed his hand.

"Come," she ordered, tugging. "I'm hungry. Ask Mom about the hammurgers."

Daniel stepped through the door and into a level of disarray he'd never believe existed in Ashley's house. He'd only been in the front door a couple of times, picking the kids up or dropping them off but it had always been fairly neat and always clean.

The hall had a jumble of shoes, backpacks and balls from various sports. The couch in the living room off to the right had cushions and pillows at odd angles and a layer of dust coated every flat surface. What had his concern meter's needle flying off the chart was the smell of vomit permeating the air.

Artie marched from the area of the bedrooms; his shoulders back, a serious look on his face.

"Mom's not feeling well so you'd better go," Artie announced. He continued his march to the front door, standing to one side.

"Tell your mom I'm sorry she's not feeling well." Daniel walked out to his truck, got in and drove away—drove to the DQ where he bought cheeseburgers, fries and milk shakes for everyone. *If Ashley's too sick to eat hers, it'll just be a bit more for the boys.*

THE NEXT DAY he waited a half block away outside the school so it would appear he was just driving along when he pulled up to the curb and offered them a ride home.

"Thanks, but we're fine," Artie had replied for all three of them.

Amanda had trudged along with her brothers but had looked back at him a couple of times before Artie said something to her.

Daniel parked his truck a few houses up and across the street trying to decide what to do. Something was definitely wrong but other than Ashley being sick, he couldn't figure it out. He glanced at his wristwatch, pulled out his phone and dialed his friend, Jackson.

"Montgomery Architects," Jackson said on the third ring.

"Where are you?"

"Flew down to Phoenix this morning to meet with prospective new clients. What's up?"

"Something's going on at Ashley's. Thought Lily might have mentioned something to you."

"She's not mentioned anything. Right now she's got two of her people in different hospitals with medical emergencies. She's been traveling back and forth and dealing with a couple of other situations by phone. One of her client's isn't expected to make it so she'll be at that hospital the rest of the day if not all night. You know, Lily. She won't leave if that's the case," Jackson said. "I'll call her and see what she knows. One of us will get back to you."

His phone rang a few minutes later. "She's no idea what's going on," Jackson reported.

"Hell."

"Keep me informed?"

"Yeah, I'll let you know what I find out," Daniel said and hung up. *Guess I'm on my own for now.*

The kids had rounded the corner and were crossing the street to their house when a shiny new red Toyota Camry pulled up to the curb. Amanda and Anthony ran up to the car. Artie held back and then dashed for the house, bursting through the front door. A minute later he was back outside, calling to his siblings or at least that's what it looked like from his vantage point.

Good Lord! His hand on the door, he had it half open before he caught himself. Ashley was in the doorway. It looked like she was barely able to stand. Her hair was—actually she looked a mess.

Art was out of the car, opening the doors, and gesturing—looked like he wanted the kids to get into his car. Ashley was saying something. Artie was trying to pull Amanda and Anthony away.

The neighbor's door opened and Betty came out. An older woman, she looked to be in her sixties or seventies. He knew she watched the kids at times. Betty stalked across the yard, right up to Art. She staggered back when he pushed her away.

That's it. Daniel pulled away from the curb, cruising past the houses until he was across the street. He got out of his truck. As nonchalantly as he could, given the steam threatening to blow the top of his head off, he ambled across the street.

Betty was on her cell phone, he hoped calling 911.

Ashley clung to the door jamb calling to the kids to come in the house.

He stumbled at the curb when Ashley slid down to sit in the doorway, her arms outstretched towards her kids.

Art had Amanda by the arm and was trying to get her in the car. Amanda no longer wanted to get in the car. Arms and legs awhirl, she shrieked her displeasure and reached out to her mom. She put up a valiant struggle as she battled Art but was losing.

Anthony was standing by the passenger door obviously ready to get in. Artie was yelling at him and pulling on his arm, trying to drag him back to the house.

A police cruiser pulled up behind the Camry.

Anthony and Artie stopped struggling. Betty put her phone in her pocket and marched over to Ashley, standing beside her, hand on her shoulder, saying something to which Ashley nodded.

Quiet reigned.

Officer Traynor introduced himself and put his hand out for Art to shake. To do so he had to let go of Amanda. Daniel thought he hesitated a second or two before letting his daughter go to shake hands with the officer. Amanda dashed for the doorway and launched herself into her mother's arms.

Daniel approached. For a moment the idea that maybe he could get back in his truck and drive away flickered, but he'd been seen by the kids, Ashley, Betty, Art and most importantly, the police officer.

"Daniel O'Donnell." He introduced himself and stood back.

"And who are you?" Officer Traynor asked.

"I'm a friend," Daniel replied.

"Fucking my wife," Art accused.

Officer Traynor's eyebrow raised a notch and he waited for Daniel to reply.

"Mrs. Kenner's been sick. One of Mrs. Kenner's best friends is Lily Hughes. Her husband, Jackson Montgomery is my best friend. Mr. Montgomery is out of town and Ms. Hughes is tied up with clients, so I came by to check on Mrs. Kenner and the kids on their behalf."

"Which is why I'm here to pick up my kids. Mrs. Kenner," Art sneered the name, "is too sick to take care of our kids. I even heard she's been evicted and has no place to go. No kids of mine are going to be homeless on the street."

"Now, Art," Daniel said in his most polite voice, "you know Mrs. Kenner and the kids will never be homeless on the street. Why, if what you say is true and she is being evicted, she has a place to stay."

"Where?" Art demanded.

The urge to say "that's for me to know and you to find out" was strong but Daniel fought it back. He knew his jaw twitched and probably the veins bulged at his temple but he held on to his temper, glad he'd tucked his thumbs in his front pockets so they weren't fisted.

Officer Traynor asked a few more questions, getting names, dates of birth, addresses. "You're still married so it really is up to the children right now," he told Art.

"Not for long, she should've been served with the divorce papers this morning. I'm asking for full custody," Art said, a cold smile curled his lips.

Daniel's fingers curled against the jean fabric and he rocked back on his heels.

Officer Traynor stepped to the door and asked Ashley a few questions. He wasn't close enough to hear either the questions or her answers but Daniel knew she said she wanted and could care for her kids. Next Officer Traynor talked to each child individually. Amanda's lower lip quivered and she shook her head or nodded in answer to his questions. Anthony looked ready to cry but he held his chin up and answered with words. Artie glared at his dad while answering Officer Traynor's questions and then stalked back to his mom.

Ashley had struggled to stand to talk to Officer Traynor. She once again sat on the stoop. Betty stood on one side. Artie sat next to her, his arm wrapped protectively around her shoulder. Amanda hung onto Artie's free hand. Anthony, a worried look on his face, paced a small area of lawn half-way between the house and the car.

"Sorry, Mr. Kenner," Officer Traynor said in a polite yet authoritative tone, "the children want to stay with their mom. You have the right to ask for custody in the divorce but the children have the right to stay with their mom until a judge makes a custody decision."

Daniel tensed when Art started toward Ashley and the children. He exhaled when it was clear Art wasn't going to grab anyone.

"We aren't done here," Art snarled at Ashley. "These here are my kids. If you loved 'em, you'd send them along with me 'cause you're dying and they deserve to be with the living." Art spun away and stalked to his car. Ignoring Officer Traynor, who was still there, he peeled away from the curb leaving a strip of rubber on the street.

"I'll keep an eye on things when I'm on patrol," Officer Traynor said to Daniel as he got in his car. He pulled away from the curb talking to someone.

Daniel hoped it was dispatch and Officer Traynor was giving a description of the Camry. He hoped Art got a ticket. He hoped—.

Walking up to the front steps, he bent and picked Ashley up. Her bones poked him. Betty held the screen door open and Daniel stepped in.

"Come inside kids," he said as he moved into the living room. Betty scurried ahead and settled the cushions on the couch. He set Ashley down there and put the throw Betty handed him over her. "Can you stay with her for five minutes?" he asked Betty.

"Of course I can. I can stay for longer than that, if I need to."

"I just need to make a few calls is all," Daniel said.

Ashley turned her face into the back of the couch. Her shoulders shook with silent sobs.

"You kids get your mom a glass of ice water, her heating pad and her sick pan," Betty instructed, shooing them out of the room. The kids hurried off, arguing over who was going to do what.

Daniel stepped outside and called Jackson letting him know what was going on. He said he'd let Lily know.

He called Diana. Matthew answered saying his wife was dealing with "afternoon sickness" but he'd see what he could do.

He called Hunter. Logan answered. Her mom had a class but she'd come over.

He called Gabriella. She was in Seattle at a meeting.

He called Sophia and left a message.

While he was leaving that message, a sleek black Jaguar drove up: Jackson's car. Eleanor, Jackson's mother, got out.

"I have come to do what I can," she informed him in her British-accented voice as she approached.

"I'm grateful for any help," he said and hugged her. He lingered outside a few more minutes filling her in on what he knew which did not include why Ashley was so sick and why Art said she was dying.

"We will not get answers standing out here," Eleanor said.

They started into the house when another car pulled into the driveway and a pickup truck stopped at the curb. Reinforcements had arrived.

Logan popped out of the car, jogged past Eleanor and Daniel and into the house. Matthew got out of the truck.

"Thanks for staying, Betty," Daniel said as he walked her back to her house. "I know you're the one who called the police."

"That officer is my grandson," she said. "I've talked to him about my concerns. Ashley's been a dear friend and neighbor since she moved in. That worthless piece of—well, that husband of hers doesn't deserve the fine family he has. She's well-rid of him.

"I'll keep an eye out for him and if I see him or his car, I'll let my grandson know. He'll let the other officers that patrol this area know what's going on. We'll do our best to keep her and the kids safe."

"We'll all rest better knowing that," Daniel said. He gave Betty a gentle squeeze on her shoulder and a pat on the back. "Ashley may have been a good neighbor to you, but I'm sure you've been a good neighbor back if today's any indication."

When he walked back inside the house, pandemonium reigned.

"Don't you call me that!" Artie screamed at Matthew, Logan, Eleanor and his mom. "Don't you ever call me that again!"

"Hey there," Daniel's loud but calm voice cut through the shouting. "Just so I know, what don't you want to be called?"

"That name," Artie choked out.

Daniel took in Ashley's stricken face and turned to Eleanor and Matthew, who stood side-by-side.

"First name," Matthew said.

"Hey man," Daniel said motioning to Artie. "Let's take this outside and figure something out, okay?" Looking over at Anthony and Amanda, he added, "you guys want to join us?"

Heads nodded. The four of them trooped out to the backyard. Daniel set the kids to pulling lawn chairs into a circle while he went inside for refreshments. *Hell. There's nothing in the refrigerator and the cupboards are pretty bare.* He dug out his wallet and stopping at the sliding door to tell the kids he'd be a minute, he went looking for Logan.

"Here's all the cash I got," he said handing over fifty-five dollars. "Go to the store and get the basics: bread, milk, eggs, maybe some lunch meat, cheese, cereal."

"I'll do food," Matthew said. "Logan can get gas." He handed Logan a set of car keys. "I'll follow you in case you run out before you make it to the station."

Daniel stopped just short of the living room. He heard Eleanor's voice and the soft indistinct replies. *That's under control for now.*

He found various cups and glasses in the kitchen and filled them with ice water, taking them out to the backyard on a cookie sheet. His own ice water in a canning jar in one hand, he gestured toward Artie.

"What's going on?"

"I hate him. Hate what he's doing to Mom. I don't want anything to do with him. I won't be called "that name" anymore." Arms folded across his chest, Artie glared at Daniel. The unspoken "And you can't make me" hung in the air.

"So what do you want to be called?" Daniel decided this was not a battle he could win.

The glare turned suspicious. "What do you mean?"

"Well, if you don't want to be called "that name," what do you want to be called? We've got to call you something—although I guess we can just say "you who have no name" when we want your attention."

The flash of a smile was gone in an instant.

"I want to be called "Rose" because that's a pretty name," Amanda said.

"Amanda's a pretty name," Daniel said.

"Rose is prettier." Amanda's lower lip stuck out.

"Okay, Rose it is." Daniel agreed. "What about you, Anthony?"

"I'm okay with my name," he said slouched in his chair, a foot tapping his impatience.

"Good to know," Daniel said. "So, we've got Rose and Anthony okay with their names. If you don't want to stay you can go and play out here or go inside but—," he cautioned, "let's wait a bit before talking to your mom about these changes, okay?"

The other two jumped up and ran off to the swing set.

Daniel waited, looking out at the yard, noting everything needed watering and the grass needed mowing. *How long has she been sick?*

Having overheard Lily and Diana talk about using silence to start a conversation, he waited. Sipping his ice water, he focused on staying relaxed, relaxed as possible under the circumstances. Circumstances that created a steel bar across his shoulders, rock hard muscles in his legs and arms and added a hyper-alertness he hadn't experienced in a very long time.

Instead of leaping up, instead of asking the dozen questions on the tip of his tongue, instead of acting he sat and waited. Waited for the young boy who he recognized desperately wanting, no actually desperately trying to be the man of the house, to take care of his mom, to watch out for his siblings. *Been there, done that.*

"I thought James would be good," the quiet voice broke through his reverie of memories from his own childhood.

"Know anyone named James?" Daniel asked.

"Not really. A couple of guys at school."

"Is that really the name you want?" *Now why did I ask that?*

"No, but the name I want is taken."

The voice quavered a bit and Daniel made sure he didn't look over to check him out.

"So, "James" is your second choice. Mind if I ask what your first choice is?"

"Charles."

A wrinkle on things that had seemed smooth because "Charles" was his middle name. Of course it was also Lily's son's name. "Yeah, it is sort of taken. Charlie'd probably wonder why you were now going by his name."

"Do you know what your mom's dad's name was? You know your grandpa?"

"Anthony was named after him."

"What was your mom's maiden name, you know before she became a Kenner?"

"Carlyle."

"Some folks name their kids using their mother's maiden name or another family name."

"Maybe "Carl" but not "Carlyle". I don't really like "Carl" that much. "James" is okay."

"James it is then. What about Jim or Jimmy as nicknames?"

"Nah, I'll just stick with James." He scuffed the toe of his shoe on the grass and squirmed in his chair.

"Okay, James, how about this. We'll see how your mom is doing before we spring the news on her. She's having a rough time right now. If it's okay with you, I'll talk to Matthew and Eleanor and see what we think is the best way to tell her of the change. It may be you'll have to step up and talk to her yourself. Okay?"

"Yeah, I can tell her myself," Artie/James responded in a clear energized voice. "What about Anthony and Amanda?"

"You mean Anthony and Rose?" Daniel asked.

A rueful smile on his face, Artie/James stood. "Yeah, them."

"Tell them if you want, but also tell them about not saying anything to your mom just yet," Daniel said. He stood, quashed the urge to pull Artie/James into a tight hug, instead rested his hand on his shoulder. "You did a good job out there, standing up for your mom, James. When she needed you, you were there."

Artie/James' shoulder lifted and he met Daniel's gaze. "Thanks."

"What you need to know though is if your dad took you on physically you'd lose so always call in reinforcements."

"Like you?"

"You can call me but also call 911," Daniel said, his serious tone matching his expression.

"Okay," Artie/James said and smiled.

For a moment they stood and Daniel thought the youngster was going to give him a hug but the moment was lost and he turned away, trotting over to the swing set to inform his siblings of his new name.

Daniel headed back into the house. While he and Artie/James had been talking Logan and Matthew had returned.

"Got it covered," Matthew said putting groceries away.

"Don't worry, Daniel," Logan added looking up from clearing the counters and loading the dishwasher.

Passing the laundry closet, he heard the washing machine going—another good sign.

At the entrance to the living room, he stopped. Ashley was still on the couch, being fed small spoonfuls of soup by Eleanor. Her hair had been brushed and her top changed. While there was still dust on most of the flat surfaces, the living room had been straightened up and order restored to the entry hall. *For the second string team, we've done pretty good..*

7 - WHERE IS THAT LEMONADE?

"One more bite, my dear." Eleanor held the spoon over the bowl raising both towards her.

A slight nod followed by a sigh of resignation, Ashley opened her mouth accepting the nourishment. Ensconced in a corner of her couch, pillows fluffed around her back and sides, a purple throw over her legs, Ashley battled between relief and humiliating embarrassment. *OMG.* Any sense of relief was immediately replaced by humiliating embarrassment when she saw Daniel at the living room entrance.

Eleanor pointed to a chair across the room. "Please bring that closer. I don't want to shout."

Daniel did as instructed, shifting the coffee table to one side so he was seated next to Eleanor only a few feet from Ashley who was busy pleating and unpleating the throw.

Eleanor reached over and laid her hand on Ashley's. "Do you want to tell Daniel what's what or do you want me to?" Eleanor asked, patting Ashley's hand.

Silence.

Eleanor used her free hand to gently touch Ashley's chin and raise it until she made eye contact. "You do know he and the others need to know the basics if not the details." She maintained eye contact with Ashley until she nodded. Once she acquiesced, Eleanor handed her a box of tissues, leaned back in her chair and waited.

Ashley, you're strong enough to do this. She relaxed into the pillows and closed her eyes and visualized a dragonfly. *I can do this. I know I can – I just need to start. At the beginning?*

"The cancer is back," she said in a voice that hiccupped on the last word. "I had the biopsy the second week in August and the lumpectomy just before Labor Day Weekend. Chemo? That started yesterday. I'm so-so much-much sicker… ." She turned her face away, burying it in the pillows along the back of the couch.

"Art, he's left the kids and me," she said her words muffled by the pillows. "Took our savings." Her shoulders shook with quiet sobs.

"I can go from here, if you want?" Eleanor offered.

Ashley nodded.

"That is only the tip of the ice-berg," Eleanor said in her brisk voice. She reached out again and took Ashley's nearest hand, holding it in both of hers. "Art hadn't made the rent payment for several months, hadn't paid the utilities either. So they are being evicted on the first and electricity and water are being turned off about then unless she can make a hefty payment on the bills.

"They've been living on what food was in the house and whatever Sophia brought by from her garden."

Eleanor was interrupted by a loud knock on the door.

"Got it," Matthew said striding down the hall.

Mumbled voices at the door. Moments later Matthew appeared in the doorway. "Someone's got some papers for you, Ash."

"We've been expecting you," Eleanor said to the man now standing next to Matthew.

"Are you Mrs. Kenner?" the man asked, disbelief in his voice.

"Of course not," Eleanor replied with disdain. She rose to stand next to Ashley, her hand on her shoulder. "This is Mrs. Kenner."

"Are you Mrs. Ashley Ann Carlyle Kenner?" the man asked coming into the room. He opened a folder and took out a picture, holding it up, looking from it to Ashley and back again. Shoving the papers at her, he added, "You've been served. You have thirty days to respond."

"I'll show you the door," Matthew said nodding in that direction.

Daniel stood and, thumbs tucked in his front pockets, waited expectantly.

The process server turned and left.

"I'm quite glad that's over and done with," Eleanor said returning to her chair. "I can't think of any other shoes to drop, can you, Ashley?"

"What's that all about?" Matthew asked, leaning on the door frame.

"I believe those are divorce papers," Eleanor answered. "So, if I have this right Art has set things up so Ashley has no utilities and is evicted as a way of getting custody of the children."

"Utilities are being shut off and she and the children are evicted on the first," Daniel summarized for Matthew. "Oh yes, and the cancer is back, she's doing chemo so that's why she's so sick right now."

"Bastard." Matthew strode the few steps to the front door, opened it. "Don't see anyone around," he hollered back inside. He locked the screen and front door before returning to the entrance to the living room. "Kids'll need to stay in the backyard and someone needs to take them to school and pick them up."

"I'm staying the night," Eleanor informed them. "I can take them, but that leaves Ashley alone and I don't trust Art."

"I'll pick them up, walk them into the building, make sure they're okay," Daniel offered. He moved to the foot of the couch and tapped Ashley's foot. "You need to call the school and let them know there're problems and if anyone other than Matthew, Eleanor, or me comes to pick them up, you want the police called."

"You need to call Ms. Lawford," Matthew said. "She's a great attorney. Probably still in her office." He pulled his cell phone out of his shirt pocket, punched some buttons and then handed the phone to Ashley.

"Ms. Lawford," the business like voice answered. "Hello? Hello?"

"I…"

"Who is this?" Ms. Lawford demanded.

Eleanor took the phone. "Ms. Lawford, I'm Eleanor Montgomery. You were the attorney who helped Diana Pettybone."

"What can I help you with, Mrs. Montgomery."

"Actually we're calling on behalf of Ashley Kenner. The twenty-five word version is her husband has not paid rent, utilities, emptied their bank accounts and has just had her served with divorce papers. He is asking for full custody."

"And why is Mrs. Kenner not speaking with me?"

"Ashley's breast cancer has returned and she's been ill from the chemo. Art's non-payment of rent and utilities has resulted in water and electricity being turned off in less than two weeks. She and the children are being evicted at the same time."

"I will need to see her. She'll need to sign papers, etc.," Ms. Lawford said in her brisk tone.

"She is very weak right now. I believe she hasn't been eating much if anything so her children are not hungry."

"No food in the house?"

"There is now because Mr. Houston went grocery shopping, but before that? Very little. Mainly vegetables from the garden."

"Address?"

Eleanor gave the attorney the home address and phone number as well as her cell phone number. "I will be spending the night to help Ashley and see that the children are ready for school in the morning." She nodded as Ms. Lawford continued talking. "Yes, I'll pass that on. We will see you at nine."

Hanging up, Eleanor handed the phone back to Matthew. "Well, she is quite the powerhouse."

Eleanor fluffed Ashley's pillows, sat next to her on the couch and held both her hands. "Ms. Lawford will be here at nine in the morning so you do not need to go to her office. She wants you to call the school today and leave a voice mail message if no one answers. Tomorrow you are to send a note with the children, telling the school that you will confirm with them every morning between nine and ten who will pick the children up. You are to ask them to allow the children to gather in the office until your designee shows up to collect them."

"I can move a couple of things around tomorrow and take them to school as well as pick them up," Daniel said.

"That's settled then." Eleanor marched from the room calling to the children. She returned with paper from a school notebook and pen. "Here you go, dear. It doesn't have to be long. Short is probably better," she said, handing the paper, pen and a couple of magazines that would suffice as a desk to Ashley.

"I know the principal," Ashley said, squirming to sit more upright. "I'll write directly to her." She added her phone number under her signature and then added a P.S, inviting a call if there were questions.

Matthew's cell phone rang and he stepped from the room.

Eleanor's phone rang. "It's Lily, dear. I'll step out and talk to her. I'm sure you don't need to hear the drama repeated over and over." Following her own advice, Eleanor left for another part of the house.

Ashley's gaze met Daniel's. "Thank you. Without y'all I don't know what we'd have done."

"You've got a strong circle of women friends surrounding you. Eleanor, Matthew, Logan and I are their back-up, the second string team."

"You did a first string job today," Ashley said, her voice shaky as the adrenaline she'd used to write the note to the school faded.

"What I don't understand is why you haven't said anything, you know called one of the others?" Daniel said, leaning towards her. "It didn't have to get this bad."

"I thought I could handle everything." She sighed. "Sunday when I knew I needed help, Lily was busy with clients, Gabriella was out of town, Hunter had classes, Diana was sick and Sophia was trying to catch up at school." Her cheeks flushed, she pleated the throw across her legs, her voice barely audible she said, "I know it sounds stupid now but I didn't want to bother them, to ask them to stop what they were doing and come take care of me and the kids."

The sound of excited children's voices drifted down the hall.

"Logan and Matthew are taking care of dinner," Daniel said to fill the silence that had turned awkward.

"I'm blessed to know my kids'll have full bellies tonight," Ashley said, her eyes filling with unshed tears. "I'm very blessed in so many ways."

"Just so you know and aren't blindsided, your kids have a couple of things they want to do. I think they'll try talking to you tonight, before bed." Daniel paced to the window and looked out.

"Will you give me a clue?"

He turned from the window, caught her eye, and said, "Artie refuses to answer to that name, at least not right now. He's in favor of being called 'James'."

Ashley's eyes widened, her mouth formed an 'O' as the memory of her son's earlier angry words about 'that name' poked her memory. "Is that all?" she asked in a trembling voice.

"No, Amanda wants to be called "Rose"," he added matter-of-factly.

"What about Anthony?" She took a deep breath, steeling herself for what else was to come.

"So far he's good with it." Daniel crossed the room to the foot of the couch. "Artie has a lot of anger towards his Dad and if he was here and heard me call Art his dad, he'd be furious," he said leaning toward her. "If you can accept that's where he's at right now, he may change his mind when things settle down. He's really upset with the way Art has treated you."

"I may slip up from time-to-time," Ashley said in a quiet voice. The children were coming down the hall towards the living room.

"Tell them the truth and work out how they're going to respect-fully remind you," Daniel said just as the children pushed and shoved each other coming into the room. "Just so you know," Daniel said to the three children lined up next to the couch, "I mentioned something to your mom about your names. But, you two" he pointed to Amanda/Rose and Artie/James, "have to take responsibility and talk to her about all of this on your own. If it isn't important enough to you to talk to your mom about it, then your original names stand. Got it?"

Artie/James put his hand on Ashley's shoulder and Amanda/Rose climbed up on the couch and snuggled against her mom. Anthony took the chair closest to Ashley and held on to her hand.

"I'll leave you to it," Daniel said, leaving the room and turning toward the kitchen.

"So what's going on," Ashley asked. She raised her hand to pat Artie/James' hand and then tugged him around so she could see him.

"I don't want to change my name," Anthony said vehemently.

"Then you don't have to," Ashley responded.

"I want to be called Rose. It's a pretty name," Amanda/Rose said giving her mom a kiss on the cheek.

"It is a pretty name," Ashley replied, kissing the top of her daughter's head. "You do remember your name is Amanda Rose, right?"

Amanda Rose nodded.

"I think I can remember to call you Rose most of the time," she said. "If I forget, you can remind me, okay?"

Artie/James had moved to the foot of the couch, his mulish "no one can make me" look on his face.

"Why don't you two go check on dinner," Ashley said to Anthony and Rose.

Once both children left the room, she patted the couch next to her. On shuffling feet, her oldest son came over and with a sigh from the depths of his toes, sat.

"Any particular reason you picked James?"

He shook his head and looked away toward the front window.

She reached out and guided his face so she looked him in the eyes. "You must really be angry at your dad to do this," she said, watching his reaction to her words.

"I don't want him to be my dad," he said in a shaky voice. "I don't want to be like him at all."

"Your name don't make you like him," Ashley said.

Daniel appeared in the doorway. "Come in," she invited. "I think my son needs a man's perspective. He thinks he's more likely to turn out like Art if he keeps his name. What do you think?"

"What makes a man who he is comes from the decisions he makes every day. It has nothing to do with what his name is, what he's called," Daniel said, his hand resting on Artie/James' shoulder.

"I want to be called James."

"I want you to know I'll love you with all my heart no matter what name you go by, James," Ashley said in a tear-stained voice. "Always know that."

A firm knock on the door at straight up nine announced Ms. Lawford. Daniel had shown up at 7:50 shepherding the children through the last few minutes of getting ready, out the door and off to school. He'd called from the school office and she'd talked to the principal. Everything was arranged. Her children would wait in the school office until Daniel picked them up. The principal assured her the children would not be released to their father without her consent.

Eleanor ushered the attorney in to the living room. A fresh pot of tea sat on the coffee table along with a plate of store-bought cookies, small plates, napkins and cups.

"I will be in the kitchen," Eleanor announced fussing with the arrangement of food. She straightened, looked Ms. Lawford in the eye, and said "Take care of her and the children." Spine straight and chin high, she marched from the room, her footsteps echoing on the hardwood floors.

Another knock.

Eleanor made her way to the front door and greeted whoever was on the other side. Ashley and Ms. Lawford smiled when Diana appeared in the doorway.

"Oh Ash, I'm so sorry I couldn't get here yesterday. My functional hours are in the morning. By one p.m. my head is in the toilet or I'm too dizzy to be much use." Diana's hand rested on the slight mound of her stomach. "I don't remember being this sick with Bill."

"You sent Matthew, my dear," Eleanor said. "He did very well in your place."

"I'm sure that's true," Diana said, her quiet smile a reflection of her calm demeanor. "He's very resourceful."

"He is the one who mentioned Ms. Lawford," Eleanor said.

"And I'm very pleased he did so," Ms. Lawford interjected in a brisk, business-like tone. "I do have appointments so my time to talk to Mrs. Kenner is limited." She looked expectantly at Eleanor and Diana who quickly excused themselves and went to the kitchen.

Ashley heard the sounds of the tea kettle being put on the stove and figured Eleanor and Diana were fixing themselves tea and cookies —or at least tea.

"First things first." Ms. Lawford's voice brought her back to the conversation.

"My children," Ashley began.

"Protecting your children is a priority, Mrs. Kenner," Ms. Lawford said. "But the first thing is "Do you want me to represent you?"

"I don't know that I can afford you," Ashley said. "I really have no money."

"I thought that might the case, so I drew up the papers based on that." She shifted and showed Ashley legal papers. "Right here," she said pointing to a paragraph half-way down the page, "it says I will be paid when the divorce is final and that you owe me nothing prior to that."

She patted Ashley's hand. "He has money, Mrs. Kenner. He has filed for the divorce. He can pay for it all."

"He wants the children." Ashley's voice shook and her white-knuckled fists clenched around her cup.

"I want world peace," Ms. Lawford said, shuffling papers. "Doesn't mean I'll get it. All that aside, what I need to know from you right now is whether you want me to represent you in the divorce."

"Yes, I'd be ever so grateful if you would," Ashley murmured.

"Sign here." Ms. Lawford indicated the spaces for her signature.

As she signed her name, it occurred to her she was at a turning point, a point from which she could not retreat. She waited expecting nausea, tears or even hysterical laughter. She felt none of those feelings. What she did feel was a deep sense of relief.

"Now that that's done. Do you have any documents showing what monies he's taken off with?"

"I have papers on the end of the coffee table. Eleanor helped me pull things together." Ashley picked up a sheaf of papers and handed them to Ms. Lawford.

"Perfect." She tapped them together, clipped them with a paperclip and slipped them into her briefcase. "Divorce papers?"

Ashley's legs were like old rubber bands, stiff and brittle—about to break, but she forced herself to stand. She took a few steps, teetering like a toddler, just learning to walk. Ms. Lawford's hand on her elbow steadied her.

"You could just tell me where they are or we could ask Eleanor to get them?" Ms. Lawford said, her gentle voice concerned.

"You're right, I could, but I never even looked at them. Eleanor did and told me what they said." Ashley continued to shuffle across the room, stopping at the entrance to the hall. "Eleanor?" she called out.

"I'm right here, dear," Eleanor replied, coming from the kitchen area. "What do you need?"

"I'm figuring you didn't throw them in the trash or burn those papers," Ashley said, hanging on to the molding for support.

"No, Ash, I didn't. Do you want me to get them now?"

"Ms. Lawford wants to see them," Ashley said, moving on into the hall. "If you'll excuse me, I need to use the bathroom."

Diana came into the hall and gave Ashley her arm to steady her as she continued to the bathroom.

"I'll get those papers," Eleanor said, disappearing into another room. Within a few minutes she appeared, papers in hand and gave them to Ms. Lawford.

"Aah, I know this firm," she said with twinkle in her eye. "I'll let them know I'm representing Mrs. Kenner and we're counter-suing. That'll get their attention.

"Let Mrs. Kenner know I'll be in touch. And do make sure I have a current address and phone number for her. It isn't nice to disappear and your attorney not know where you are."

"What about the children staying in the same school while all this is being sorted out?" Eleanor asked.

"Mrs. Kenner needs to talk to the principal and follow the district policies. There are exceptions made so children remain in the same school rather than moving multiple times during a school year."

"When we know where she'll be living, I'm sure she'll talk to the principal and we'll make sure you know her new address," Eleanor said as she accompanied Ms. Lawford to the door and unlocked it.

"Keep the door locked, the children in the house or backyard if it is fenced, and they must be accompanied to and from school."

"I don't think that will be a problem." Eleanor opened the front door and stood to the side.

"Oh, and I don't think Mrs. Kenner should be alone. When he realizes she's going to fight him, he is not going to be happy. She's not strong enough to fight Mr. Kenner off."

"No, she is not. His treatment of her over the last few years has been abominable. We've even seen Ashley with bruises on her arms. While she's never said where she got them, it was obvious to several of her friends that Art had grabbed her hard enough to leave marks."

"Thank you for that additional information, Mrs. Montgomery. I'll be in touch." Ms. Lawford stepped briskly out the door and to her car.

Eleanor closed, locked the door and went to check on her charge.

WHILE ASHLEY RESTED on the couch after her visit with Ms. Lawford, Diana and Eleanor changed her bed and did a load of laundry. Around eleven, Diana fixed a large salad and Eleanor made a plateful of sandwiches. When that was done, they checked again on Ashley. Since she felt much better, they brought her a cup of tea.

A knock on the front door at eleven-thirty announced more visitors. Diana set the food out on the table while Eleanor answered the door.

Before Ashley could stand, she was surrounded by Lily, Hunter and Sophia, her circle sisters. Gently helped to her feet, they wrapped her in warm hugs. Hunter and Sophia on each side, she was escorted to the table in the kitchen.

Everyone grabbed a plate and helped themselves to sandwiches and salad. A carafe of coffee and another one of tea were already on the table.

It may seem like a life-time ago since she'd spent time with her circle sisters but in reality it was less than two weeks. So much had happened it was as if her body and soul had been buffeted by a super storm—a cyclone or a hurricane.

In the silence, there was an undercurrent of expectancy, of waiting for her to eat something. A nibble of lettuce, a bite of tomato, she picked up her sandwich and set it back on the plate.

Ashley was grateful when Eleanor, who sat next to her, stepped into the void, anything to fill the silence and give her more time.

"It seems that Art has not paid the rent or utilities in some time. Water and electricity are being turned off on the first. The eviction notice gives Ashley and the children until then to vacate the premises. In addition he cleared out their bank accounts and has filed for divorce. I think that sums up that part of your life fairly well, don't you?" Eleanor turned to Ashley who only nodded.

"The other part of the problem is, and I want you to remain silent for one full minute when I'm through," she admonished the other women, giving each a stern look until she got nods of agreement, "is… . Eleanor placed her hand over Ashley's, before going on.

"You see… oh my, this is much more difficult than I thought it would be." She squeezed Ashley's hand, her words rushed out. "The cancer is back. Ashley's had a biopsy, a lumpectomy and started chemo Monday. She is having a great deal of difficulty. What I mean by that is her first treatment was extremely hard on her."

All Ashley wanted to do was slide off her chair and curl up in a ball. She did appreciate Eleanor asking everyone to wait a full minute before saying anything, except now the silence was excruciating.

Hunter was the first to speak. "And when did you plan on telling any of us about this crap going on in your life?"

Ashley looked up at her circle sister because she couldn't tell from her tone of voice if she was mad or sad. *Both. She's got fire and tears in her eyes.*

"Is there a reason you thought you couldn't talk to us?" Sophia asked with a studied calmness.

Ashley didn't even try to answer that question, figuring everyone would have something to say and she'd figure out the best way to explain when she'd heard everyone out.

"She knew I was battling morning sickness at all hours of the day and night. Gabby's out of town. Hunter, your classes are full. Sophia is behind and catching up after being in Ireland and Lily is living between two hospitals dealing with clients," Diana said. "Is that a pretty good summary?"

Ashley nodded, wiped the wetness from her face with the back of her hand, and forced herself to look at each woman at the table. "I knew y'all had things going on in your lives. I hoped I could manage without bothering you."

"When did you know the cancer was back?" Sophia asked, her tone telling Ashley she expected an honest answer.

"I found the lump a few days before Diana's wedding. I saw the doctor the next Friday, then had the biopsy that confirmed it was cancer the Friday after that.

"Thursday before Labor Day Weekend I had the lumpectomy. I was doing okay and would have called on you for help after 14th Moon—when I went to get money for groceries on the first and realized there was no money in the checking or savings account, I just…," her voice trembled and even after taking a deep breath she couldn't go on.

With effort Ashley stood and left the table, holding on to the kitchen counter and the wall, she made her way to the bathroom off the hall just in time. The little she had eaten was lost, her retching easily heard through the thin hollow-cored door.

"It'd be a tight fit, but they can use the little house," Lily offered, "or they could stay with us. Again, a tight fit, but we'd make it work."

"Matthew and I could fit them in also," Diana said.

"Before you go any further, I want to inform you of another event," Eleanor interrupted.

"What more could—?" Hunter's question was left unfinished when Eleanor waved her hand.

"Art wants full custody of the children. He tried to abduct them yesterday after school. Fortunately, her neighbor Betty called the police and Daniel was in the area and happened by. Artie, in particular, has been—and I do not say this lightly—traumatized by Art's behavior. He refuses to be called Artie and has chosen the name "James". Amanda now wants to be called "Rose" which is her middle name. It's quite a mess Art's made of everything."

"Anything else we need to know?" Sophia asked.

"Daniel described the scene with the police officer, Art, the kids and Ashley as hell. Art was yelling and saying that Ashley is dying. He also said she couldn't take care of herself much less the kids, where did they think they were going to live—things of that nature. The police officer talked to the children who all said they wanted to stay with their mom. However, Daniel did say that Anthony seems much more ambivalent about staying with Ashley.

"Ms. Lawford said the children need to be escorted to and from school. And, Diana knows this already, but it deserves repeating— Matthew was wonderful yesterday. He bought groceries, fixed dinner, and most important, got Ashley on the phone with Ms. Lawford who came by this morning. Logan was equally marvelous," she added addressing Hunter. "She got gas in Ashley's car and kept the children busy as well as helped catch laundry and housework up. None of you would have believed Ashley even lived here if you'd been by yesterday."

The bathroom door opened and Ashley leaned against the doorframe. "I'm s—"

"Do not apologize, Ash." Lily rose from the table. "Let's get you settled back on the couch. I suppose we could carry you, but I'd rather not have to."

With Lily on one side and Hunter on the other, Ashley shuffled back to the living room and her place on the couch.

"For now, here's the plan—" A knock on the door interrupted Lily's sentence.

Eleanor answered and preceded Daniel into the room. After greeting everyone, he said, "Wanted to check and make sure everything was okay."

"We have the outline of a plan but would welcome your input," Lily said to Daniel who nodded. She turned back toward Ashley, leaned forward and spoke directly to her.

"We will arrive Friday after school, pack everything up and move you to the little house. You will have the office area for your bedroom so you don't have stairs and the children can share the upstairs. Personal things will be moved there. Other things put into storage. We'll rent a truck and have it all done in one trip." She sat back confident this was the way to go.

"I've another idea," Daniel said.

All heads turned toward him.

"I'll move into the little house for now. Ashley and the kids can live in my old Victorian. We can convert the back parlor into a bedroom for her. There's a full bath a few steps down the hall. The kids will have their own rooms and there are two guest bathrooms upstairs. When you're better," he said, catching Ashley's gaze, "you can move upstairs to the master bedroom."

"I can't take your house from you. You've put so much work into restoring it—," Ashley started to protest.

"You aren't taking it," he countered. "I'm offering it. I can move things around in the carriage house and it will hold everything here you and the kids won't be using," Daniel added. "I can pack up the few things I need and be out of there tonight."

"No," Ashley said, trying to rise. "No, I can't ask that of you."

Sophia moved next to Ashley on the couch, gently turned her head so she looked her in the eye. "You aren't asking, Ashley. All this is being offered. Your job right now is to accept. When you are better, stronger, we can revisit this arrangement and make changes if needed. At least until you are through with the chemo, this is the best plan for the children. They know Daniel's house—"

"They know Lily's house—"

"Yes, they do. But think about it. Lily's place has one bathroom. You'll have your own bathroom at Daniel's and the children will have their own upstairs. When we ask them which place they'd prefer, what do you think their answer will be?"

Ashley collapsed against the pillows. *Lily and Diana handled all this care and hovering without being ungrateful. Guess it's my turn.* "Y'all think its best?" She took her time, met each woman's eyes and saw their nods. "Guess that's what we'll do then."

9 - FORWARD INTO A DARK FUTURE

Friday Eleanor stood to one side as Lily and Hunter helped a shaky Ashley into the back seat of Jackson's car. Her first job was to drive her to Daniel's house where someone, either Daniel or Matthew, would be there to help Ashley inside. Eleanor's next job was to see her charge settled in the back parlor the men had set up as a bedroom. And, she'd assigned herself a third task—make sure Ashley drank something nourishing.

"She's as settled and comfortable as she'll be," Lily said, standing back and gently shutting the car door. "Thank you ever so much for doing this."

"I am quite happy to be doing this. If you will recall, I met you almost two years ago and at that time I was not driving and walked with a cane or walker."

"I do remember those days and I also know how hard you've worked to build up your strength and endurance."

"Why Eleanor can now be described as "spritely"," Hunter added rounding the car and joining in. "Ready?" she asked Lily. "We want to get there before Diana feels too sick to get home on her own."

"I believe she is taking something new that she has high hopes will calm things down so she isn't so sick," Eleanor said. "Do not tell her she cannot be there," she admonished.

Lily held the driver's door open. Eleanor backed in and after swinging her legs in, buckled her seatbelt. Catching Ashley's gaze in the rear-view mirror, she smiled. "I will do my best to get you home as quickly as possible, but you must let me know if you are feeling sick. Because, while I will do my best to get you home quickly, we can take as much time as we need if that is what is best for you."

With a wave out the window to Lily and Hunter, Eleanor turned the key in the ignition. The Jag's engine purred to life and Eleanor drove away.

ELEANOR PULLED into the back parking area close to the large wrap around deck. The first-floor windows on the majestic three-story-hundred-year-old Victorian reflected the fall garden's flowers; the upper windows the small grove of Douglas firs.

Ashley'd only been here a handful of times when Daniel hosted BBQ's and The Circle was invited. Even though she hadn't seen the entire house, she knew every inch was lovingly restored to its original splendor. A welcoming energy wrapped around her as she eased out of the car.

Both Daniel and Matthew were waiting for them just in case furniture needed to be moved or heavier items shifted. The men stood on either side and supported her as she shuffled toward the house. With effort she made it up one step. Hands at her elbows, they swung her up the next two.

Eleanor trailed behind as Ashley started across the deck. Mid-way she just stopped; the distance to the house and the room beyond insurmountable. Matthew swung her up in his arms and carried her into the house to the back parlor that had been transformed into a bedroom over the past two days.

"She will have a restful view of pots of autumn asters and chrysan-themums, the ferns and hostas under the trees, and from that angle, a slice of sky," Eleanor said as Matthew stood Ashley on her feet next to the bed.

Before she'd picked up Ashley, Eleanor had met with Daniel and asked him to hang a couple of special pictures in the room. He'd hung the one of dragon and damselflies in the space between the windows. Ashley would see it every time she opened her eyes. The one of two hummingbirds hovering over a bank of fuchsias and the one of the vague outline of a lighthouse on a dark promontory were on either side of the bed, easily seen from the overstuffed chair tucked in a corner on an angle to the bed.

Eleanor set a small bag on the chair and took out a well-worn nightgown and robe, a pair of slippers and a small pouch containing toothbrush, toothpaste, hand and face cream. "Let's get you settled," she said to Ashley, shooing the men out and shutting the door. "Do you want to change into this?" she held the nightclothes up, "or stay in what you have on?"

"I'm fine like I am," Ashley murmured curling up on the bed.

"I think I heard Daniel and Matthew leave," Eleanor said, opening the bedroom door. "I'll put these here then." Eleanor tucked the clothing in a dresser drawer. "I will return in a few minutes."

True to her word, within five minutes Eleanor was back. She had a large bowl with a bath towel inside in one hand and a pan with warm water and a washcloth in the other. Tossed over a shoulder was a soft lavender throw. After putting the bowls on the nightstand, she flicked out the throw and tucked it around Ashley. To one side of her charge, she set the bath towel with the bowl on it. "Just in case." She helped Ashley wash her face and hands before taking the pan and washcloth away.

Another trip and Eleanor was back with a hot water bottle which she wrapped in another towel and slipped next to Ashley's feet.

A third trip produced a book, which Eleanor set on the small table next to the chair and a tray with a tea pot and two cups which she put on the dresser.

"Now, my dear, I'm sure you know staying hydrated is important. While I'd be delighted if you drank a whole pot of tea, I will be content if you manage a cup. I did not bring in mugs, only china cups. That should be doable," she said while pouring tea into the cup. Approaching the bed, she help Ashley into a position more conducive to drinking a little of the hot liquid. "Very good," she encouraged when two swallows were down. "Two more and you can rest."

Placing Ashley's cup back on the tray, Eleanor fixed her own cup and settled in the chair with her book.

An hour later, Ashley was resting when a vibration in Eleanor's pocket alerted her to a call coming in. She pulled her cell phone from her pocket and stepped into the hall as she answered.

"Yes, Lily, how are things going?"

"We've got the kitchen packed—pots and pans, staples but there are plates and cups—oh, never mind. We'll bring some things over and sort it out later. Daniel's place is large enough we don't have to worry about it like we would at the little house," she rambled. "How is she doing?"

"You do know you can call and check on her without having something wrong," Eleanor said, a hint of amusement in her voice.

"Yes, I do know that," Lily said and laughed. "So, how is she?"

"Resting. I'm about ready to rouse her enough to have a little broth. My plan is to have her drink a cup of tea or broth every hour or two. That really isn't enough but if she can do that without being horribly sick, that is a good sign. And, I put a call in to her doctor. I'm quite concerned she's still so ill, unable to keep much down. I'm hopeful with the move made and a routine in place, she'll begin to feel better." She sighed. "It is all I can think of right now."

"You're right, keeping her hydrated is important," Lily said. "Things are moving along quickly here with everyone pitching in. Diana has all of the knick-knacks packed and she and Sophia have started on Rose's room. We know all the clothes and stuffed animals are coming. Thankfully we don't need the beds or dressers. Daniel says he's got enough towels and bedding but we are packing that to bring over because with three kids—just want to make sure we've got it covered. Ash doesn't need to be doing laundry in the middle of the night because the kids used too many towels. I know I'm rambling now." Lily said and paused.

"You seem to have all the bases covered," Eleanor said. "I'm going to hang-up now and make a fresh pot of tea. I think a little lavender added to the chamomile might be nice."

"That does sound good. You'll have to let us know how it actually tastes," Lily said. "I'll let everyone here know how she's doing."

"And I will call you if there is something unusual that happens. Otherwise know that all is going along as expected."

A welcome exception to the expected was the lack of vomiting. Even though Ashley was nauseous, she sipped and kept down an ounce or two of tea or diluted broth each hour. At three Eleanor helped her to the bathroom. Closing the door, she stayed in the hallway listening for any thumps that would mean her charge had fallen.

"Eleanor?" Ashley said, her voice barely audible.

"I'm here," Eleanor said, her hand on the doorknob. "I'm coming in Ashley." Eleanor opened the door thankful Ashley was upright. Standing beside her, a hand on her waist, Eleanor turned on the water so Ashley could wash her hands.

"Thanks, I'm a bit light-headed right now."

Eleanor closed the toilet lid and guided Ashley down. "Do you need to put your head between your knees?"

Ashley shook her head and slumped against the toilet tank. "Just need a minute."

"Take all the time you need."

"Mom! Mom! Where are you?" Three voices called out while the clatter of feet sounded on the hardwood floors.

"Your mother is here," Eleanor called out from the bathroom doorway.

Ashley brightened at the appearance of her kids. She sat a little straighter and attempted to look more like her normal self.

Seeing Daniel in the background, Eleanor made a snap decision.

"Children, your mother needs help to get back to bed. Between the three of you can you help her or should I ask Daniel to pick her up and carry her?"

The children clamored, "We can do it. We can help you, Mom."

"I know you can," Ashley said and struggled to stand. "Just give me a minute to get my legs under me," she added as the children swarmed around her.

"Now Rose, you take one side and Anthony the other. James, you stay behind your mother so you can steady her. Just put your hand out if she starts to lean one way or the other." Seeing the children in place, Eleanor stepped into the hall. "I'll go ahead and see that the bed is straightened."

Coming abreast of Daniel, she said, "I thought you were taking the children to the house to help with the packing?"

"Change of plans. Lily said the packing was basically done. Matthew and a couple of my crew were already there to load the things up that are coming here. Also, she and the others thought they'd seen Art drive by a couple of times.

"They're concerned so are dividing things up between two trucks and their cars. Matthew will take a load to the little house and my crew will bring a load here. Unless Art has an accomplice, he'll have to follow one truck or the other. Diana thought he'd follow Matthew since he doesn't know my crew. Diana is going to the little house and then will follow Matthew back to their place before coming here. Gabriella and Sophia are going to the store to get food and Lily is coming here by a longer route."

They'd moved beyond the back parlor door and talked in hushed tones.

"My goodness," Eleanor exclaimed. "They are taking no chances tonight."

"It's hard enough on the kids and Ash as it is. No need to invite a big drama scene with Art."

"No, no need at all," Eleanor said and stepped away. "You are doing a fabulous job there, children." She stood in the parlor entrance while the children helped Ashley up onto the bed and tucked the throw around her.

"Come on up here, you hear. I need a couple dozen hugs and a hundred snuggles," Ashley ordered in a mock ferocious tone.

In an instant the children were on the bed and she was covered with hugs and snuggles. James was the first to scoot back.

"Very good, James," she said an arm looped around Anthony and Rose. "I can see you better when you're at the foot of the bed like that.

"Everyone settled?" Seeing her kids' nod she went on. "Tell me about your day?"

"I'm going off to the kitchen. Call if you need something—or send one of the children to tell me," Eleanor said, walking out of the room.

Daniel led the way to the kitchen, perched on a stool and stared absently out to the deck.

Eleanor busied herself wiping off clean counters. With a long sigh, she slowly shook her head. Dismay colored her voice, "I pray she'll make it. I don't know what will happen to those precious children if Art gets them. He was never my favorite person," her tone held an edge of righteous anger, "but to think about what he's done now. Indeed, I'd never have thought he'd go to such lengths—even see his own children homeless just to rid himself of that sweet woman. It quite boils my blood."

A horn tooted announcing the truck pulling into the back driveway. Daniel got up, went to the door from the kitchen to the deck and walked out. He waved to his two crew in the truck's cab and directed them in backing the vehicle to the deck steps.

The doorbell rang and Eleanor crossed through the great room and formal dining room to the living room to answer it. Lily, Gabriella and Sophia, with arms loaded, stood there.

"Come in, come in." She stepped to the side to let the other women in. "You know where the kitchen is." She gestured down the hallway.

Lily took the lead passing by the back parlor to set the platter of meats and cheeses on the counter. Gabriella added a large bowl of tossed salad. Sophia followed with a bag of specialty breads and her special multiple layer chocolate cake protected in a cake carrier.

"Diana's bringing a pasta salad and Hunter and Logan will be coming along with store-bought ice cream," Sophia said. "Everyone should be here by six."

"We will not starve," Eleanor said. She gestured towards the hall, "Before things become too busy, you may want to stop and say "hello" to Ashley. The children are with her right now, but they will soon be busy taking their boxes to their rooms and unpacking."

"An update would be helpful," Gabriella said.

"She has been able to keep small amounts of liquid down but she feels nauseous all the time and light-headed if she stands. Since getting back here, she's rested perhaps dozing would be a better description. However when the children arrived, she perked up. I know she's putting on her best face for them. I doubt she'll be able to maintain it for any length of time but it is heartening to see that she can do it at all."

Daniel stuck his head in the door. "My guys have unloaded all the boxes. We're leaving them on the deck until we know where every-thing's to go."

"Why don't you send them home, Daniel," Lily said. "We can get them in the house and up the stairs after everyone is here and we've eaten."

He disappeared back outside. A few minutes later the sound of the diesel engine turning over reached their ears and they saw the brake lights flicker as the truck pulled away.

Eleanor stood off to the side as Lily, Sophia, and Gabriella set everything up for a "make-your-own" sandwich bar positioning the cake at the end. Daniel remained outside, his left foot on the lower deck railing, his elbows resting on the top. The view was lovely as his garden's fall flowers were in full bloom. *I doubt he even sees them. He is torn apart seeing her like this, seeing her children worried about her, seeing her worried about everything. Well, he is not alone in his worry. The Circle does not take it lightly when one of their own is in trouble.*

10 - A SPECK OF LIGHT IN THE DARKNESS

When Ashley woke on Monday, the lightheadedness was gone. A robe pulled over her gown, slippers on her feet, she padded into the kitchen. Daniel would be by in an hour to take the kids to school. *I have time to surprise my kids with a bit of breakfast.*

After starting the coffee, she searched the cupboards for mixing bowls and the ingredients to make pancakes. It took two hands to lift the mixing bowl from the cupboard and she almost fell reaching up for the box of pancake mix. Proud that she'd managed without dropping anything, she went to work mixing the batter. Once that was done she checked the cupboards until she found what she was looking for. With effort she set the heavy cast iron skillet on a burner.

The front door opened and footsteps sounded in the front hall.

"Who is it?" she called out picking up a butcher knife and holding it high.

Moments later, Daniel appeared.

"Just me." His left eyebrow raised, a wary look in his eyes, he stayed on the other side of the counter. "I came by early to make sure the kids were up and ready."

"I was just getting ready to go holler, let them know I'm making pancakes," she said lowering the knife.

"You're looking a lot better, maybe even perky," he said, visibly relaxing. "Find everything?"

"Pretty much."

"I'll get the kids while you get the pancakes started," he said. His footsteps retreated down the hall and then started up the stairs.

Ashley busied herself getting plates down and silverware from the drawer and setting the table for four. *The least I can do is fix him breakfast.*

She checked the refrigerator and found milk and butter. The energy she woke with began to fade.

Daniel returned. "They're up and getting dressed. Glad Eleanor suggested they put clothes out to wear today. That sure saved me trying to figure out what Rose should wear." He chuckled as he moved into the kitchen and got glasses down. Pouring milk, he added, "They'll be down in five and hungry as—"

"As all get-out." Ashley smiled. "My kids can put away a good breakfast." The heat on under the skillet, she added a pat of butter and as it melted poured in the batter for the first batch of pancakes. "Coffee should be done," she said as she checked to see if it was time to turn the pancakes over.

The first batch done, the second batch needed another minute when the kids came storming into the kitchen. Their looks of surprise followed by wide grins made the effort to make them breakfast worthwhile. Heart soaring with delight, she thought it might pump right out of her chest with all the love it held.

"Here's the first of the pancakes," she said and handed the plate to James. "Y'all need to share these."

Daniel went to one of the cupboards and grabbed a bottle of syrup.

So that's where it is. I need to remember that. "Here's another four. Daniel, I made some for you too."

"What about you?"

"I promise I'll eat," she said taking another plate down from the cupboard. "See?"

"What I see is an empty plate."

"Well, it won't be empty long." She put a pancake on her plate and added the rest on the one used for serving. She rested against the counter determined to see this through, see her kids off to school, see herself back across the hall to her room. A glance at the clock *I just need to last another ten minutes.*

"Okay kids, clean your plates and get them in the dishwasher. James, you take the lead on that, please. Anthony, rinse out the glasses and when James is done with the plates, put the glasses in on the top rack." Daniel instructed.

Leaning against the counter, Ashley struggled to remain standing. *Just a few more minutes.*

"Rose, do you know how your Mom likes her pancakes fixed? Good, so you fix this the way she likes it and bring it to her in her room."

Daniel rested his arm around Ashley's shoulder, pulling her against his side to give her support as he walked her across the kitchen and hall to her room. "The door off the deck is unlocked so your friends can check on you. Diana will be by around nine and Lily is bringing Eleanor around ten. I'll pick the kids up from school and we'll be home before four. Someone is doing dinner—just don't remember who."

Ashley rested against the door frame grateful she'd fixed breakfast for her kids. Discouraged she couldn't finish the job, she absentmindedly watched Daniel straightened the covers and fluffed the pillows. Gripping his hand, she leaned into him as she made her way across the room to the bed.

With his help, she climbed up and settled down against the bank of pillows at her back. *I got so weak so fast, I'm glad he was here 'cause my kids would've gone to school thinking about how bad I was instead of my fixing them breakfast.*

The throw was draped over the end of the bed, her book was on the table next to the overstuffed chair. He gathered those and placed them next to her. She picked up the throw and flicked it. The soft lavender microfiber material floated down over her feet and legs. She tucked it around her waist.

"Mom, I got your breakfast done," Rose announced in the door way. She held Ashley's plate, the pancake swimming in syrup, in a tight grip. "And I didn't spill hardly any," she announced with pride.

James stood behind her, a rag in one hand, a grin on his face. "Nope, she hardly spilled any at all."

"Wait right here, Rose," Daniel said as he sidled through the door.

"Thanks sweetheart," Ashley said. "You did a fine job."

"It's getting cold," Rose said, her lower lip sticking out, unshed tears glistening in her eyes.

"It's got so much love in it, it can't get cold," Ashley reassured her daughter.

Daniel reappeared with a tray. "This'll make it easier for your mom to have her pancake while in bed." He shifted the tray under the plate and instructed Rose to set her mom's breakfast on it. He leaned down and whispered something to Rose, whose face broke into a beatific smile. The plate clattered onto the tray and Rose dashed off.

When she returned a few moments later she had silverware. Anthony followed with a glass of milk and napkins.

"Perfect. Y'all done a great job fixing my breakfast." Ashley beamed at her children.

"Time to go, kids. School's waiting."

Ashley leaned back against the pillows, the pancake untouched. *Syrup on the floor. However will I get that cleaned up? In a minute. I'll get up and take care of it in a minute.* The last image in her mind as she drifted into the in-between place was of Daniel, one hand guiding Rose who was glued to his side while reminding James and Anthony to get their backpacks and coats because it was supposed to rain later.

A weight was lifted. Ashley stirred and then slipped back into the almost oblivion that comes with dozing. Something warm wrapped around her arms and neck as she floated away.

Whispers seeped into her consciousness but she couldn't really hear what was being said. One voice or two? *I'm not alone...* A dragonfly flitted through her dream-like state, the iridescence of his wings adding light and color to the gray of the hazy place.

She stirred and stretched.

"She's awake."

"I believe you are correct."

Diana and Eleanor were here. "Y'all been here awhile?" she asked, her eyes still closed.

"Not so very long," Diana replied.

"How are you doing, my dear," Eleanor asked. "I hear you were up and about this morning."

Eyes open, Ashley turned her head. Eleanor and Diana sat in the sitting area of the room. A smaller padded chair had been brought in and was on an angle to the overstuffed chair.

"Matthew dropped me off and carried this chair in." Diana gestured to the chair in which she sat. "Not that you asked, but so you know that Eleanor and I did not do this on our own."

"We could have," Eleanor added, a merry tone to her voice. She made a muscle with her arm and tapped Diana's knee with her other hand. "We've become "Mighty Women" according to Jackson and Matthew."

"From what Daniel said, you were "Super Woman" this morning. You must be feeling much better to get up and make breakfast," Diana said.

"Nowhere near Super Woman but considering how I've been, I did all right." Ashley pushed the throw away and shifted to get out of bed. "What time is it anyway?"

"Almost twelve," Eleanor answered.

"Nope, not even close to Super Woman if I make a few pancakes and sleep at least three hours."

Diana stood up. "Yesterday you barely made it to the bathroom and back so I'd say making breakfast—something more than setting out a box of cereal and a gallon of milk—is a pretty big deal."

"And I've got to go, so excuse me while I take care of business." Ashley shuffled her feet into slippers and started towards the door.

"Are you up to a change of scenery?" Eleanor asked also rising.

"Like?"

"When you're through, come into the kitchen. We'll sit in that sunny alcove and have a cup of tea and maybe a bite of something else."

"Sophia sent over some of her peanut butter chocolate chip cookies," Diana said. "You can have as many as you want once you've eaten a little bit of something less decadent and healthier."

"By the way," Eleanor said to Ashley's retreating back, "the syrup is off the floor so there is nothing to clean up."

As she made her way to the kitchen, Ashley's gaze scoured the floor. There was no sign of syrup on the hardwood floors of the hall or the tile in the kitchen. The countertop was clean and the breakfast table clear.

"Y'all don't have to stay with me. I'm okay."

"Which makes staying with you today all the better," Eleanor said in her brisk British accent. "I've tea and sandwiches. We made egg salad and roast beef so you have a choice."

"And we cut them in quarters so they don't look so big."

"Having said that," Eleanor patted the chair next to her, "we are hoping you will eat two of them—more than that and we'll be thrilled, less than that and we may nag."

"But it would be a loving nag," Diana said. "You do know how lovingly your circle sisters can hover and nag."

"I'm well aware of that particular skill we all seem to share," Ashley said settling into the chair between them. "Guess it's my turn to figure out how to be gracious and grateful," she grumbled.

"Indeed, it is your turn," Eleanor said, setting a small plate in front of Ashley and moving the larger plate of sandwiches closer.

Diana laughed. "It appears to be a lesson we are each getting to learn in our own time and in our own way. Lily got to figure it out after her accident. Elizabeth got to figure it out after she came back to Fremont from Ireland."

"What about when she lost the baby?" Ashley asked.

"I think she was grateful for our hovering and nagging—at least most of the time." Diana sighed. "My turn came when I left Dennis." She shuddered as a memory flickered across her features.

"I quite think this is a life lesson everyone has the opportunity to learn at some point. After I fell, I came face-to-face with what a shambles my life had become. My goodness, to think I seldom ever left my apartment unless Jackson and then Lily took me. When I look back on that time, I see it as a blessing. I decided I was going to be my independent self again and the by-product of all that was Lily becoming my daughter-in-law.

"Think about it," Eleanor continued tapping the table with her index finger. "Do either of you really think Lily and Jackson would be together now if not for her accident?"

The three women looked out over gardens resplendent with colorful chrysanthemums and asters. Because of the milder weather, there were still blooming red and pink fuchsias and geraniums. Diana broke the silence. "I would not have Matthew in my life if not for those dark days."

Will that be true for me? Will I look back on this time and see the blessing?

Ashley glanced down at the two quarter pieces of sandwich on her plate. The egg salad looked good so she'd decided to try it. A small bite, chew slowly and carefully swallow—wait at least a minute before the next bite was the oncologist's instructions. She followed the instructions not in the least surprised that the sandwich didn't taste anywhere near as good as it looked—nothing would taste good right now. What was important was to eat, to keep her body nourished.

Diana pushed back from the table. "It's about time to go," she said to Ashley.

"Go where?"

"Remember, your doctor called back on Friday and said she did want to see you today," Diana reminded her.

"Finish your sandwich and tea, I'll get your jacket and a brush so you can take care of your hair in the car," Eleanor said.

BACK IN THAT grey hazy place, Ashley curled on her side on the back seat. The seat belt cut into her side but she managed because the idea of sitting up was more than she could handle. The doctor had pinched and prodded and eventually poked with a needle. Her body sucked up the bag of saline and if she wasn't so exhausted, she might even feel better.

Get used to it, Ash. Unless you stop puking and drink a gallon of fluids a day, you'll get to do this again.

Diana had followed them to the doctors but headed home when she experienced the first wave of nausea.

Light danced across her eyelids. Eleanor had started up the winding road to Daniel's house. *If I sit up I could see the mountains and river.* The idea was exhausting. To do it overwhelmed.

The sound of tires on gravel registered. The car slowed and stopped. The engine off, the door opened.

"Mom?" James' worried voice penetrated her lethargic brain.

"Your mother is just fine, James," Eleanor soothed. "She's very tired because she's been to see her doctor."

"You kids go on in and make sure your mom's bed is fixed up for her. Maybe get her some fresh water."

She opened her eyes to see Daniel hovering over her, his hands on the seat belt buckle. A click and the pressure eased.

"Let's get you into the house." One arm slipped under her knees and the other wrapped around her shoulders as he eased her out of the backseat.

"I can walk," Ashley said in a voice far stronger than she felt.

Daniel set her on her feet, a hand on her arm to steady her. "Let's go then."

I will do this. I will do this. I will do this. Ashley chanted to herself as she carefully made her way across the graveled parking area to the deck steps. She stopped, gathering herself together to make it up the four risers.

"How about this idea," Daniel offered his hand on her elbow. "You lean on me and I'll sort of carry/help you up these steps." He put his other hand out to stay her objections. "Your kids want to share their day at school with you. Are you that mule-headed? Yes, you can do it on your own but then you'll miss that time with your kids."

He stepped away. "It's your choice."

The dizziness attacked. She swayed and reached for him. "I'd appreciate your help into the house," she mumbled. He took her hand and slipped his arm around her waist. When he pulled her close, every cell in her body relaxed and she sank against him on a sigh.

Eleanor had preceded them into the house and was busy putting on water for tea and getting out cookies and milk for the children.

"A wise choice, my dear," she said to Ashley as the two of them came through the door. "The children have invaded your room and are waiting for you. Daniel, when Ashley is settled let me know and I will bring milk and cookies in."

11 - LOST AND ALONE

Ms. Lawford showed up with more papers in hand. Ashley vaguely remembered signing papers last week and knew she was contesting custody but not the divorce. *No way am I giving my kids to the rat bastard.* Not only had he tried to force her to live on the streets, he'd taken the kids and her off his insurance. Her head pounded and her stomach revolted.

Monday while she was at the doctor's being checked out and getting another IV because she remained seriously dehydrated, Ms. Lawford met with the judge.

"Now, where are you keeping your important papers?" Ms. Lawford asked, she thought for the second time.

Ashley shook her head, her expression blank.

"Mr. O'Donnell?"

At Daniel's appearance in the doorway, Ms. Lawford swiveled in the chair and asked him if he knew where any of Mrs. Kenner's important papers were being stored.

"I don't. But if you leave them on the table next to you, I know Lily or one of the other women will."

"That will have to do," Ms. Lawford said, obviously not pleased.

"I think Lily will be here within fifteen or twenty minutes. You'd have time for a cup of tea or coffee," he quickly amended when the frown crossed her face.

"I'll take that cup of coffee."

Ashley's eyes closed but she listened to Daniel crossing to the kitchen, the low rumble of his voice the high accented tones of Eleanor's answer. She struggled not to slip into the gray haze, knowing she needed to be alert when she and Ms. Lawford talked.

The footsteps returned. "Thank you, Mr. O'Donnell."

"Added a couple of Sophia's peanut butter chocolate chip cookies. They are prized around here so if they aren't to your liking, they will not go to waste."

Ashley opened her eyes to see Ms. Lawford take a bite of one of the cookies, her eyes closed and a soft moan escaped. "These should be illegal."

Daniel laughed. "Yep, but those of us lucky enough to get our hands on them are mighty glad they aren't." He turned to leave the room. "I'll let you two take care of business. And, I'll send Lily in when she gets here." He closed the door behind him.

Ms. Lawford wiped her hands on the paper napkin Daniel had left with the cookies and took a final sip of coffee. "Those are amazing cookies. Sophia could buy her own island in the South Pacific or anywhere else with what she'd make if she sold those commercially."

"I don't think she'd be interested. It's just one of those things she does for her friends."

"Mrs. Kenner—

"I'd appreciate it if you'd call me Ashley or Ash. I don't like being called that anymore."

"Understood. I have good news and bad news. First the good news: the judge has order Mr. Kenner to keep you and the children on his insurance, at least until the divorce is granted. The bad news is that while the judge granted you temporary custody, she also gave Mr. Kenner visitation rights. He is allowed to have the children with him from nine to three every other Saturday with this coming weekend starting the visitation schedule. There is also the issue of birthdays and holidays since those are coming up fairly quickly."

A knock on the door before it opened and Lily stuck her head in.

"Oh my, Ash, what's wrong?" Lily dashed into the room to the bed where Ashley held a pillow to her chest, tears streaming down her face.

"The judge says Art can take the children," Ashley's gulped the words out.

Lily, her hand on Ashley's arm, turned a quizzical look Ms. Lawford's way before turning back to her friend.

"Ash, Ms. Lawford ethically can't say anything while I'm in the room unless you say it's okay."

"That is true, Ashley," Ms. Lawford said. "If it is okay with you for me to discuss the details of your case, at least at this time, with Lily Hughes in the room, you need to tell me so, otherwise Lily will need to leave or I will come back another time."

"I-I-It's all right for Lily to know," Ashley said in a little girl voice.

"What I was telling Ashley just prior to your arrival, was the judge granted her sole temporary custody but also granted Mr. Kenner visiting rights."

"I see," Lily said. "And is the judge aware that two of the children refuse to be called by their birth names because of the way Mr. Kenner has treated them as well as their mother?"

Ms. Lawford nodded. "Yes, she is. However, Mr. Kenner's attorney convinced her that Ashley has turned his children against him."

"So no supervised visitation?"

"No, but she is starting out cautious. He'll have the children from nine o'clock Saturday morning until three o'clock that afternoon."

"I'm sure you've asked the judge to assign a children's advocate to talk to them and to advocate for what they want."

Ms. Lawford smiled. "I'd heard you had a background in child welfare."

"Yes, I worked in child protective services for several years but custody issues are similar whether the person of interest is a child or an elderly parent with dementia. It's extremely important, especially in this case, for the children to have a way to communicate their wishes to the judge."

"I have asked for someone to be appointed. Marjorie Muir will be contacting the children at school. She will not take them out of the building but will talk to the principal to see where she can talk to them in private."

"Do you know how soon she can meet with the children?" Lily asked fingers discreetly crossed.

"Not until next Monday."

Ashley sobbed out, "No, you can't do that to my kids."

Ms. Lawford stood. "I will talk to them on my way out and let them know what's going on."

"Thank you Ms. Lawford," Lily mouthed over Ashley's head.

Eleanor arrived in the doorway. "Call everyone. Crisis time," Lily instructed. "Where's Daniel?"

"I'm here. I heard enough."

Angry shouts and Rose's high-pitched wail echoed through the house.

"Stay here with Ashley," Lily ordered. "Eleanor and I will deal with the children, at least until Ms. Lawford has left."

"YOU CAN'T MAKE ME GO!" James shouted at Ms. Lawford who looked stunned. Rose peeked out from behind the couch where she'd managed to stuff herself. Only Anthony stood quietly, distress evident in his face.

"The judge said—,"

"I don't care what the Mother—,"

"James, that's enough," Lily said stepping into the fray. "Rose you need to come out here and stand by me now."

Eleanor crossed the room to the couch and held her hand out to Rose, who grabbed it and hung on to Eleanor's hand and also her pant leg.

Lily walked to the front door. "Thank you for coming, Ms. Lawford. Usually we are better about not shooting the messenger."

"Ashley said you knew where her important papers are kept. These need to be included wherever that is," Ms. Lawford said, handing a thick envelope to Lily.

Lily took the envelope and retreated to stand next to James. Ms. Lawford picked up her briefcase before turning back to the assembled group. "Mrs. Muir will talk to you on Monday at school. You must tell her what you want and don't want so the judge knows your wishes. You are not being ignored. The judge is trying to make sure that everyone, including your father, has their wishes considered."

"No—," James started but stopped when Lily squeezed his shoulder.

"Again, thank you for coming and giving us this information in person. I know it means a lot to Ashley right now."

"I—," Ms Lawford started, shook her head, and turned back to continue on to the front door. "I will let Ashley know if there is any other news."

When the door closed, Eleanor looked out the front windows turning back to the room when Ms. Lawford strode to her car from the bottom step. "My goodness, what a pickle," she said.

Lily rubbed her forehead as if a headache lodged behind her eyes. "I think it is a very large and very sour pickle if we're going to stay with that analogy."

"I won't go," James said his arms folded tightly across his chest, a dark scowl on his face. "I won't and Art can't make me."

"No, Art probably can't make you but he can make Rose and if neither you nor Anthony goes, she'll be all alone with him," Lily said in a reasonable voice.

James' eyes sheened with unshed tears. "It isn't fair."

"No it isn't." Lily let her quiet comment sit in the silence for a minute before going on. "Why don't you want to see Art?"

"He wants Mom to die!" James shouted. "He doesn't care about us. He just wants us to hurt her."

"Why do you think he doesn't want you?"

"We haven't seen him for a long time," Anthony said. "He didn't go to any of my Little League games and he hasn't played catch with me all year."

"He doesn't talk to us. He doesn't ask how school is or what we're doing." James said in a reasonable tone.

"He doesn't like me," Rose said, her voice quivering.

James turned away, head bowed, shoulders slumped.

"Really, Rose?" Lily asked. "You really think Art doesn't like you?"

"He says she's a big stupid mistake," Anthony said.

Stomach churning, the taste of bile thick in her throat, Lily stood frozen in place. "You heard him say this?" She finally managed.

All three children nodded. "He was angry at Rose and told her that himself. Mom tried to tell him to stop but he shoved her and said she was a big stupid mistake too," Anthony reported in a proud-laced voice.

"Here's what we'll do," Lily said. Deciding to ignore Anthony's tone of voice, she put her confident game face on. "I will make sure that James has a cell phone before Friday and I will make sure that Matthew, Daniel and Jackson's numbers are programed in as well as Diana, Hunter, Sophia's and mine."

"What about Mom?" Anthony asked.

"Right now your mom's job is to fight the cancer and get well. Our job," she said and made a sweeping gesture, "is to take care of these other things so she can concentrate on her job. Okay?"

"What'll I do with the cell phone?" James asked coming to stand next to Anthony.

"You are to call one of us or even 911 if you are worried or scared. This isn't a phone to make a call to a friend on. This will be an Emergency Phone only."

Heads nodded and she took it to mean both nodded in agreement and understanding.

"Let's see what's for dinner. And," she called out to the retreating backs of the children as they fled the room, "you need to go see your mom. She needs to know you're okay with things for now."

12 - SACRIFICIAL LAMBS

*L*ily had been watching for him and yet was a little surprised when, at exactly nine, Art pulled into the drive at Montgomery House.

He honked the horn to announce his arrival instead of coming to the door.

Lily pasted a bright smile on her face, stepped out onto the porch and waved.

Art did not wave back, instead he stepped out of his shiny new red Camry, stood with hands fisted on hips and glared.

Originally their plan had Art picking the children up from Daniel's. That plan had been quickly scrapped because Ashley didn't need to get caught up in the drama. This morning after breakfast, Daniel had brought them over to Montgomery house.

"Art is here," she said to the children standing behind her, backpacks at their feet. "I'll walk you out."

Anthony dashed out to greet his dad. James and Rose followed, their feet dragging. By the time Lily and the children were off the porch, Anthony was by Art, chattering so fast Lily only caught a word here and there. He was telling his dad about a spelling test he'd "A'd" in school she finally figured out.

In a soft voice, Lily encouraged the two children to go to Art, being careful not to call him 'your dad' but neither child moved.

"Come on you two," Art ordered, pointing at James and Rose. "I have things planned and I don't want to be late."

Jackson appeared behind Lily. "Plan B," he whispered.

She nodded.

"Artie," Art took a step forward then stopped, pointed at the ground in front of him. "Right now!"

Rose took a half-step, half-hiding behind James, clinging to his hand.

Lily stepped closer in an effort to comfort and support the little girl. Rose's trembling had turned to shaking.

"Amanda!" Art yelled at his daughter who had turned and clung to Lily. "You and Artie—." He took two steps towards them. "Get in the car. Now!" Art's jaw visibly clenched and his eyes squinted.

Lily put her arm around Rose and started forward, half carrying her. "Come along, James," she said in a calm voice as she passed the young man.

"Stop calling him that," Art snapped as she passed him on the way to the car. "He has a perfectly good name. He's Artie and that's all there is to it."

"My name is James," James said. He stood legs slightly apart, hands fisted at his side, staring off at the trees across the road.

Art grabbed his son's arm and jerked him around. "You'll answer to Artie or you'll have the back of my hand to answer to."

"Fine," James said. "Hit me. See if I care. I won't answer to that name ever again."

Lily stepped between the two when Art's hand rose.

"Do you see Jackson over there, Art? He's taping this whole thing. I am taking it to the judge Monday morning. Is this all you want her to see of how it went when you picked your children up?"

The vein on Art's temple pulsed, his jaw clenched and his teeth ground loud enough Lily heard them. He lowered his hand but fisted it on his hip. "Bitch," he said in a voice so soft Jackson's tape wouldn't pick it up.

"I want your word, Art, that you will not harass James or Rose over their names."

"Fine, I'll just refer to them as "hey you"," he said sarcasm heavy in his tone.

"Perfect," Lily said. "Hey you One – is James and Hey you Two is Rose. Got that you two?"

James nodded. Rose still clung, her face buried in Lily's pant leg.

"Time to go. Everyone in the car," Lily said matter-of-factly while moving to the side of the car. "I'll help you get in, Rose," she said patting her on the shoulder.

She smelled the urine before she felt the warm liquid on her foot. Rose sank to the ground sobbing.

"It's all right, Rose." Lily bent down to help her up. "We'll take care of this and—"

Anthony chortled, "The baby peed her pants, the baby peed her pants."

Lily waited a heartbeat, maybe two, waited for Art to step in and stop Anthony's cruel taunt. He didn't.

She did.

"That's enough, Anthony," she said, her gaze nailing the young boy to the ground. "That is enough. Do you hear me?"

Anthony nodded although he didn't look ashamed. Instead he looked over at Art as if seeking his approval.

Art, who looked disgusted, ignored his younger son.

"Give me an address, Art, and I'll bring Rose over in a little bit. It won't take long to change, but I know you're in a hurry," Lily offered.

He looked at Jackson who had moved off the porch to be closer to the action. "I'll wait." He opened the car door and bent to get in.

"Come on guys, get in. We'll wait for your sister in the car," Art said, motioning to his sons.

"I'll help with Rose," James said, opening the front door so Anthony could get in.

Anthony scrambled into the front seat as soon as James opened the door. His seat belt buckled, his backpack tossed into the backseat, a smug smile on his face, he turned to his siblings, "We're waiting, aren't we Dad."

Art reached over and Anthony cringed. "Cut that out, boy," Art growled. "Of course we're waiting." He turned away from Jackson, looked directly at Lily and glared. "What are you waiting for? You said it wouldn't take any time. I don't have all day."

"Let's get you cleaned up, Rose," Lily said, bending down and stroking her back. The sobbing had stopped but she had not unwound from the tight ball she'd curled into. "I'll help you stand up." She wrapped her hand around Rose's arm and gently tugged. "Come along now."

Rose's head hung, her chin on her chest, her hands gripped her elbows, her crossed ankles creating a tight seam at her knees.

Lily's effort to raise her head, look in her eyes, and assure her everything would be okay failed as Rose pulled her chin from Lily's head and closed her eyes.

James approached. His arm around his sister's shoulders, he started toward the house. "Don't be dumb about this Rose," he said. "I'm not saying you're stupid, just that its dumb to stand around in wet clothes. And don't forget our pact. You and me, we're in this together."

Rose leaned into her big brother and with a shuffling gait, went with him into the house.

Fifteen minutes later, standing on the porch, watching Art's car drive away, Jackson pulled his wife into his arms. "You were magnificent, Lily love."

"So were you. I hope it all shows up clear enough for the judge to see what a mistake she's made—scratch that," she said pulling away. "I hope she sees another option may better serve the children."

13 - CAN IT GET ANY WORSE?

"We're having a great time. I'll bring them back tomorrow afternoon," Art had said less than an hour ago, appearing to totally ignore the judge's visitation order. It was three-thirty when Jackson and Lily arrived at Art's. The lawn needed mowing and the flowers watering, but otherwise it was a ranch-style house on a street with other ranch-style houses.

James and Rose were packed and waiting. They scampered out the door and piled into the back seat, as soon as Art answered the door. Anthony was not as ready to leave. He went back inside to find something else he'd misplaced.

After his fourth trip, Art said, "Just leave it. You'll be back soon. I can always bring it to you at school if you need it sooner."

Satisfied with that, Anthony trotted out to the car.

As Lily said good-bye to Art, Anthony's displeasure at being "stuffed" in the backseat was audible. Jackson's voice quieted the complaining.

"Not taping any more today?" Art asked, sarcasm dripping from each syllable.

"We got enough this morning," Lily replied in a light breezy tone. She turned on her heel and strode to the car.

As soon as her door was shut, Jackson's foot was off the brake. Her seatbelt got buckled as they passed the neighbor's house. To stave off any conversation, Lily turned the radio on finding a country and western music station because that was what Ashley often played.

Jackson drove to the back of Daniel's house and parked. Before the engine was off, the back doors opened and the children tumbled out—literally and figuratively. James stumbled in his haste to get out but quickly regained his balance. Rose scrambled out clutching her backpack to her chest as if it were a shield. James grabbed his backpack from the car floor and his arm around Rose ran up the deck steps and into the house.

Anthony slid out on his side, leaned in to pick up his backpack from where he'd shoved it between Rose and himself. Slinging it over his shoulder, he trudged toward the house.

Lily and Jackson remained in the car. Her head rested against the seat, her hand gripped his. His concern communicated by the soothing, slow stroke of his thumb across the back of her hand.

"This part is almost worse than the pick-up time," Lily said with a weary sigh.

"Why is that?"

"I'm sure all three children were on their best behavior: Anthony because he desperately wants Art to acknowledge him and James and Rose to escape Art's wrath. They know they're safe here with their mother, that Ashley will not hit them or humiliate them. It's almost as if she gives them permission to act out."

Another minute of Jackson's gentle rhythmic stroking on her hand, another sigh, this time of resignation before she said, "It's time." She pulled her hand away, unbuckled her seatbelt and leaned over to kiss Jackson's cheek before getting out and heading toward the house.

Hunter and Gabby were in the kitchen.

"Soph's in with Ashley and Logan's upstairs with the kids." Hunter glided across the kitchen and gave Lily a hug. "Rough, huh?"

"Been through worse," Lily replied, "but it wasn't fun."

"An understatement," Jackson added, coming up behind Lily and putting his arms around her. "What can I do to help?"

"We've hung around, not really knowing what to do but not wanting to leave Ash alone and not knowing what shape the kids would be in. We were thinking about getting pizza for dinner. Soph brought her homemade fudge brownies with walnuts and hazelnuts. Anyway we thought it might be a good thing to have everyone together but not make the kids the center of attention. What do you think is best?"

Jackson shifted so he was speaking to Hunter, Gabby and Lily. "Why don't I pick up steaks and hamburger? I'll go by the house and get a couple flavors of my homemade ice cream and a few toppings. Maybe Mother would like to join us."

"Perfect." Hunter spoke up right away. "I've got a fresh pot of tea for anyone who wants it."

Jackson gave Lily a peck on the cheek. "Be back soon," he said and left.

"The kids?" Lily asked.

"James and Rose charged through here and up the stairs like the devil was after them. Not even a "hi" to Logan much less me. I heard verbal crap between Anthony and James, thought Rose was crying, so I sent Logan up to reconnoiter."

"Good idea. Can you call her and get an idea of what's going on?"

"Sure," Hunter replied.

"I'll fix tea and you can join Soph," Gabby said, starting to run water in the tea pot. Once set on the burner, she added, "I'd feel better if I heard something from that room. Way too quiet from my point of view."

Lily stroked the lioness pendant she wore on a gold chain around her neck. The old talisman brought her comfort and clarity. Holding it gently in her hand, she crossed the hall and after a soft knock, opened the door and went in.

No surprises greeted her although in this case she might have welcomed a different scene.

Sophia was on the bed cradling Ashley in her arms. Ashley stared at the dragonfly picture with that unseeing gaze of someone who really isn't here and really doesn't see what's in front of them.

"Hunter's bringing in a fresh pot of tea and cookies," Lily began, the cheerful note in her voice sounded false even to her. "I thought it a good idea to have some nourishment while we decided what to do next."

"That is a good idea," Sophia said, moving around on the bed to sit up more and have better back support. She never let go of Ashley.

Hunter came in the door with a tray with the tea pot, cups, napkins and cookies. She set the load down on the dresser and poured cups for everyone. Taking Ashley's cup to her, she paused when her circle sister seemed to ignore her. "What's going on, Ash?" Hunter asked.

No answer.

"Ash?" Hunter asked again, this time with a light shake of Ashley's shoulder. She set the cup back on the dresser and approached the bed again. Hands on both shoulders, she gently shook her friend while asking in a louder voice, "Ash? What is it? What's wrong?" Hunter shook a little harder, continuing to ask what was wrong.

Tears spilled down Ashley's cheeks. She turned toward Hunter. "They didn't even speak to me when they came in. They hate me."

"This whole thing isn't even about you, Ash," Lily said. "They are trying to deal with spending a considerable amount of time with a man who is their father but who they no longer really know.

"They know you. They love you. And they know you love them—regardless of what they say over the next several days or weeks, you must continue to believe that underneath it all they love you."

"It'll be worse?" Ashley asked her voice quavering.

"Could be worse—not will be worse," Sophia joined in. "I'd expect a few calls from the school, maybe the boys getting into fights on the playground or mouthing off at a teacher. In my experience any of that would be normal behavior for kids caught up in a custody battle. You need to call the principal or send her a note so she knows what's going on."

"I agree," Lily said.

"Here's your tea, Ash." Hunter held the cup out until Ashley took it.

"Gabby?" Lily called out.

"I'm here," she replied.

"You need to hear this too." Lily stood next to the bed, lifted Ashley's face so she could look in her eyes. "Above all else you need to remember you are loved by many. You are not alone on this part of your journey. You are precious to all of us and especially to your children. Do you understand what I'm saying?"

Lily waited, her hand still on Ashley's chin, the free hand stroking her hair and tucking it behind her ears. Her touch skimmed the silvery blond tresses. When she dropped her hand to her side, a wisp of hair clung to her fingers.

"I need to hear your words, Ash."

"I know y'all love me and my kids do too."

Lily dropped her hands to her side.

"It's just that I get so afraid," Ashley said in a quavering voice. She searched the faces of the other women and added in a whisper, "I look ahead and all I see is darkness."

"When you look around this room, what do you see?" Sophia asked.

"I can see out the window to the flowers. There's a chair over there." She gestured to where Gabriella sat. "Actually there're two chairs and a small table."

"Is that all?" Hunter stood at the foot of the bed.

"Pretty much." Ashley sank back against the pillows, her eyes closed.

"Look again." Hunter tapped Ashley's toes. "There's more in this room than that."

Ashley's eyes opened and her gaze traveled around the room. "Well, y'all are here."

"Keep looking." Hunter remained where she stood. "There are things here you've not mentioned."

"Y'all want me to make an inventory of every item?" Ashley's irritation strengthened her voice.

"Nope, I want you to see what's right in front of you, what's here to help you see the light when it feels dark," Hunter replied.

"I'm tired and sick in my body and soul, Hunter, can't you just let this go?"

"I love you too much to let this go, Ash. It's too important. However, maybe Lily or Sophia or Gabby can say this better."

"Where's your medicine?" Sophia asked, coming to stand next to Gabriella.

"On the table by the chairs," Ashley bit out the words. "What…?"

Sophia scooted closer to Ashley and picked up her hand. Holding it so it pointed between the windows, she asked, "What do you see at the end of your hand?"

"One of my pictures?"

"Yes, it is one of your pictures. Why do you think we hung that particular picture in that particular spot?"

Ashley's brow furrowed in concentration before her eyes widened in recognition. "My dragon and damselfly photograph," she said as if seeing it for the first time. "When…?"

"We hung it there before you arrived, right between the windows so you would see it whenever you looked out at the yard, could see it first thing in the morning and last thing at night." Sophia got down from the bed and crossed to the picture, making a small adjustment so it hung straight on the wall.

"So the question is "Where is your medicine?"" Lily laid her hand on Ashley's. "It would seem to me, you'd want the strongest medicine you have with you to support you at this darkest time."

"I don't know where my sacred things are," Ashley said.

"Between us, we do," Lily said. "What do you want?"

"My altar and my jewelry box to start with."

"Your jewelry box is right here," Hunter said, taking the rectangular box from the bottom dresser drawer and placing it on Ashley's lap. "Gabby, let's go looking for her altar box. I think it may have been put in the storage area in the carriage house."

"We'll be back shortly," Hunter called out as she followed Gabriella from the room.

Ashley opened the jewelry box; her fingers caressed the various pieces. She picked up a figured pendant that sparkled in the sun's light. "I can't wear the metal next to my skin anymore."

"Not a problem, I'll find a piece of twine or string in the kitchen and bring back a length of silk cording later," Sophia said. "For now I can hang it from the window latch so it catches the sun," she said, her actions following her words.

"What is this?" Lily asked, pointing to a small wand made up of various stones.

"I wore this all the time when I first had it." Ashley held up the black silken cord. A three inch wand with tourmaline, turquoise, and amethyst stones attached dangled.

"Be right back," Sophia said and left the room.

"You used every means available to you to fight the cancer the first time." Lily sat on the edge of the bed; her fingers stroked Ashley's cheeks. "In some ways you've even more at stake this time around. Think about using all the resources at your command."

Sophia returned with a red-taper-candle in a star shaped holder. Using a match book she dug out of her pocket, she lit the wick. "Until we get some sage and sweet grass in here, this will have to do."

Ashley held out the wand and Sophia held the flickering flame a few inches below it. The heat rose and surrounded the slender pendant. Next she did the same for the dragon and damselfly necklace in the window. Wandering around the room, she lifted and lowered the candle so the heat and light from the flame touched every nook and cranny.

While Sophia worked with the candle energy, Lily left the room, returning with a pot and large spoon. When Sophia finished, Lily started by the door and circled the room beating on the pot. The gong-like noise brought Hunter and Gabriella running back to the house.

"Is everything okay?" Gabriella asked in a breathless voice.

"Everything is getting better," Lily responded. "I can't believe we forgot to keep cleansing this room. If we don't do it daily, it at least needs to be done whenever you go for any treatment."

Ashley met the serious looks of her circle sisters. "I agree. The energy in here is already better."

Lily resumed her place beside Ashley, the pot and spoon on the floor beside her. "Now, your personal totem is the dragon and damsel fly. It's important to surround yourself with their energy, especially when you talk about being in the dark."

"I know," Ashley sighed. "I know y'all are right. As bad as it got the first time around, it was never as bad as a good day this time. I've been so overwhelmed, so frightened." Unshed tears glistened. She shook her head, wisps of silver-blond hair clung to the pillowcase. "What'll I do if—," she paused and cleared her throat, "I mean to say "when" I get well. I don't know—."

Lily interrupted. "First things first, Ash. That's the only way through this. First things first, one day at a time—all those trite sayings that are based on words of truth. The question always is "What can I do Today?" it is never about the future."

"That's what you did after the accident, right?"

"It is. And some days the answer came easily and I handled the day with more grace and gratitude and other days I just made it though and struggled to find any saving grace in the day other than that it was over."

"You had your figurine of the lioness and her cub with you," Sophia said.

"And that picture of the knight-in-shining armor with two ladies. One being helped and the other doing it herself," Gabriella said.

"I did. And I had them both within visual reach. I couldn't touch them with my hands but I could with my eyes."

"When you came home, you were wearing your lioness pendant," Hunter said.

"I was. As soon as the immobilizers were off for any length of time, I wore that necklace again. I also had it on silken cord because that was gentler on my skin. Having my personal totem with me, being able to draw from the lioness's strength helped me through the harder times."

"We each have our own personal totem. One of the highlights of our time together was our ceremony to identify them," Hunter said. "I was so surprised, and yet not, when Stork appeared. One of Stork's attributes has to do with sacred dance."

"Mine's Blue Jay and when I got past the brash, squabbling image, I realized how perfect Blue Jay is for me," Gabriella said. "We have lots of Scrub Jays or California Jays here, but the true Blue Jay, with its brilliant blue color, nifty crest which can be seen as a symbol of royalty, are seldom seen in backyards. Jays are dabblers and wearing my Blue Jay ring reminds me that to be successful in my writing takes dedication and work."

"You know the Blue Bird is mine," Sophia said. "I have a small blue bird ornament hanging on my rearview mirror, a pendant in a pocket in my purse, as well as my favorite scarf with the blue birds flitting all over it."

"That isn't all you have," Lily contributed. "You have them in sun catchers in your windows, figurines in various places in your house. We keep our personal totems around us because they are our "personal totems" and need to travel with us."

"Did you find Ashley's altar box?" Sophia asked.

"There's a stack of things back in a corner that we couldn't easily get to. We'll go back out and see what we can do. When we heard the banging, we thought something was wrong and came running."

Tires on gravel were heard through an open window. Sophia glanced out. "Daniel's here with Matthew. Maybe they can move things so you can more easily get to the Altar Box."

Gabriella and Hunter hurried outside their voices calling out to Daniel and Matthew. The deeper voices faded as the group moved away.

"I'll go start a fresh pot of coffee and put water on for tea." Sophia picked up the pot and spoon and left the room, calling out over her shoulder as she went, "I may even find a fresh batch of brownies."

"And we'd be grateful if you did," Lily said. Turning back to Ashley she asked, "What are you thinking about now?"

"I did forget about my personal totem. I can't believe I did that," she said with a shake of her head. "I—."

"Beating yourself up isn't going to help," Lily reminded her. "The rest of us forgot to keep your space smudged and until today, we didn't think about the importance of your setting up your sacred space. What's important is we've remember now."

"I know I can't seem to get past the burden piece. What would I do, where would I be without y'all?" Ashley stared at the dragon and damselfly pendant twisting in the breeze from the window. "Where will we go? We can't stay here forever."

Daniel stood outside the door, the Altar Box in his arms. He should have stepped forward sooner so Ashley would have known someone was there. He heard the hitch in her voice and knew she genuinely had no idea what her future held.

The clatter of feet on the tile announced the others were in the kitchen and only a moment behind him.

"I can carry something," Hunter was saying to Sophia.

Time to move.

"Give me a few minutes to get this in her room," he called out, hoping it was enough notice for her to compose herself. He angled through the doorway, more for effect than because there wasn't enough room. He figured she'd see more of the box and less of him that way.

Lily reached to take the box from him.

"Naw, it's fairly heavy," Daniel said wanting to keep this special piece of Ashley close to him for a few minutes longer. He was half-in and half-out of the door way. "Where do you want it?"

"I don't know," Ashley said. "I haven't thought that far."

"How about having Daniel put it in this corner?" Lily gestured to the only empty space in the room. "We can find a table or something to put it on later. I think the others are ready with refreshments."

Daniel eased past the end of the bed and set the box where Lily indicated and Ashley agreed. "I can hunt up a table or maybe make something. It wouldn't be too fancy, but I could have something simple made up in a couple of days."

"That would be wonderful," Lily enthused. "Don't you think that would be wonderful, Ash?"

"What?" Sophia asked coming into the room a large tray with cups, plates, and cookies in hand.

Lily was already clearing off the dresser, tucking things into the drawers, making room.

Sophia set the tray on the dresser. Gabriella and Hunter followed with pots of tea, coffee and a pitcher of milk.

"Where's Matthew?" Lily asked.

"He went to collect the kids," Hunter replied. "We're pretty sure that Sophia's brownies will win them over."

The room was full even before Matthew and the kids arrived. Even with a couple of chairs brought in from the kitchen, in order to have room for everyone to sit, the kids were consigned to the bed. Rose snuggled next to her mom. Anthony leaned against the headboard but kept a foot or more away from her. James decided to sit sideways, at the bottom of Anthony's feet, his legs crossed, elbows on his knees.

Daniel balanced a plate with two brownies and a cup of coffee on his knee. *I have to figure something else out. This is way too crowded.* He glanced over at the bed and realized that it wasn't too crowded for Ashley. She looked like a Madonna with Rose tucked against her.

Anthony's sullenness did not dampen the energy in the room. Daniel knew Matthew had talked to the boys and the youngster was still smarting from that. Ashley was his mom and Anthony knew she loved him.

The problem was, Anthony wanted the same kind of love he got unconditionally from his mom—well, he wanted that from his dad. Daniel was a pretty good judge of character and he figured Anthony was due for a life time of disappointment if he couldn't move beyond that.

Art did have the ability to love but that wasn't the same as the capacity to unconditionally love someone. After seeing the love between Jackson and Lily, he knew why he was still single.

It wasn't that Jackson and Lily never had problems or disagreements, but no matter how frustrated Jackson got with his wife—especially around her not closing down her business and spending more time traveling with him or at the very least no longer working with difficult clients—underneath it all, there was a steadfastness to their love, to their commitment to each other. He saw that between Matthew and Diana and when they were around, between Michael and Elizabeth.

He checked back into the conversation realizing he hadn't missed much. Sophia was limiting the brownies to one for the kids and no more than two for Matthew and him. "We don't want you to spoil your dinner," she admonished a big grin on her face.

"What is for dinner?" James asked.

"Jackson's bringing hamburgers and steaks," Lily answered.

"Steaks are just for grown-ups," Anthony whined.

"If you want a steak, Anthony, all you have to do is ask and then tell Jackson or whoever is doing the grilling, how you want it," Daniel stated. "Do we have all the fixings for hamburgers?" he asked turning toward Sophia.

"We do and I've put potatoes in to bake. Gabriella and Hunter are making a tossed salad and when Logan gets here, she's taking the kids upstairs and making sure they have clean clothes for school on Monday."

"I'll check the grill, if you don't mind," Matthew said to Daniel.

"Be my guest."

Sophia, Gabriella and Hunter gathered plates, cups and glasses and headed for the kitchen.

Daniel stood to leave. Lily stayed him with a wave of her hand.

"Are you picking the children up from school Monday?"

"Planned on it."

"Then I think you need to stay for a minute and hear this. Just so you know what's going on."

Daniel sat back down.

"Monday a lady named Marjorie Muir is coming to school to talk to you. Your principal knows and will call you out of class to come to the office. I don't know that you will talk to her there but wherever you talk to her it will be private.

"What's really important is that you tell Ms. Muir what you think and what you feel about what is going on. Her job is to talk to you and be your advocate—do you know what an advocate is?" Not seeing all three nod she went on, "an advocate is someone who stands up for you, who will talk to you, listen to you and then talk to the judge to make sure she knows what you think and feel—what you want. Ms.

Muir's job is to represent you before the judge like Ms. Lawford's job is to represent your mom."

"Why can't we talk to the judge ourselves?" James asked.

"It may be that, at some point, you will be able to but for right now, you'll first talk to Ms. Muir."

"What if I don't know the right answer?" Rose asked in a quivery voice.

"You will always know the right answer because there is no wrong answer," Lily said. "If she asks you what's your favorite ice cream you know the answer to that. And if your answer is different than James' answer, it doesn't make your answer wrong."

"But sometimes I like different ice cream," Rose said, in a plaintiff voice.

"You mean like you've changed your mind?" Lily asked.

Rose nodded.

"That's okay. The next time you see Ms. Muir, you let her know you think something different. Does that make sense?"

"Uh huh," Rose said.

Logan's voice sounded down the hall. "Where are you hiding? I know you're in the house somewhere."

Rose giggled and tried to scoot behind Ashley. Anthony looked at the ceiling and groaned. James slipped off the bed and started toward the door.

"Here you all are," Logan feigned surprise. "Okay guys and gal, we've a job to do before dinner. Heard that Jackson's bringing home-made ice cream to go with those brownies so we don't want to be late."

Rose bounced out from Ashley's side and jumped off the bed.

"Don't jump on the furniture," Ashley reprimanded.

"I didn't jump on the furniture," Rose said as she skipped out the door, "I jumped off the furniture."

The room was eerily quiet.

"She was right, Ash," Lily said, a smile on her face, laughter lurking in her voice.

"That girl catches me up short sometimes," Ashley said.

"She's bright, loving and very tuned in to what her mom needs."

"True," Ashley said, stifling a yawn.

"I'll let you rest up before dinner," Daniel said standing. "If you feel up to it, I've got a chaise out on the deck. We can take out some extra pillows and a blanket in case you get cold" He started towards the door.

"Thank you for everything, Daniel. I think I would like to spend some time on the deck."

He turned back.

"Not now, but I'll give it a try for dinner."

Lily pulled the door shut as they left the bedroom. In the kitchen, Lily let the others know Ashley was considering dinner on the deck.

Daniel continued out to the Carriage House, stopped just inside the door and looked around. It would be easy enough to renovate his Carriage House into a one bedroom apartment. Throw up a few walls, add a shower to the half bath would do it. *Why am I thinking about that? I'm fine in Lily's house.*

Hands on hips he surveyed the place. Over half the space was now stacked helter-skelter with furniture and boxes. His practiced-eye saw a better way to organize everything. *A job for another day.*

He walked over to his work area and poked around in the scrap wood bin, pulling out two pieces of twelve-inch birch. Another hunt and he came up with two more pieces the same size in fir.

He set the planks on his work bench and studied the pieces, seeing the design come to life even while noting each imperfection in the wood. *This will work.*

THE BED DIPPED. Rose climbing up to sit with her.

I need to open my eyes. Ashley focused on her eyes and managed to open them. Rose was leaning over her, peering at her.

"She's awake, Daniel," Rose said, turning her brightest smile on the man.

"Just barely awake. She needs a bit more time." He reached over and plucked Rose off the bed, held her in his arms at eye level and said, "Tell everyone your mom will be there in a few minutes."

As soon as her feet touched the floor, Rose was off. Ashley heard her voice fade as she dashed out the door.

"Let me know when you're ready and I'll escort you," Daniel said.

"Need to stop…"

"Not a problem. Just let me know when you're ready."

He steadied her while she got her balance. She held onto his arm so her steps were firm. After using the bathroom, they went out to the back deck. Pillows and blankets piled on the chaise indicated her place. As she eased down and scooted back, Daniel fluffed and stuffed a couple of pillows behind her.

She had no real appetite but was surrounded by three children bearing gifts of food, who would notice if she didn't eat all of what she put on her plate. Walking this parental tightrope was familiar although not in this particular context.

"Y'all know I can't eat much just yet," she began waiting for each child's nod before continuing. "So, I'm going to take a little bit from each of you and will get more if I'm still hungry. Okay?"

Eventually she saw three nods. Anthony was the first and James the last. His worried look stayed with her as she forced one bite after another down. *Now to keep it down.* She closed her eyes. Dragonflies appeared on the screen of her lids. *Help me. Please help me.* Wings flashed as they darted about. The nausea eased.

When she opened her eyes, her kids were crowded around Daniel. He was leaving. A wave of guilt that he'd been kicked out of his own home washed through her, her dinner churned in her stomach.

"I probably won't see you tomorrow but be ready Monday," he said to the kids. "I'm the one taking you to school." Before he left the deck, he had a special exchange with each of the children. With a wave to the rest of the group, he was off.

Ashley looked around at the remaining people. Diana and Matthew had left at some point as had Hunter and Logan. Lily was now herding the kids into the house because it was time to get ready for bed and tomorrow. Eleanor and Sophia were taking the last things into the house when Jackson approached.

"Do you tend to shoot the messenger?" he asked squatting down to her level.

"Not usually. Why?"

"I've been tasked with making sure you get safely back in the house and either in bed or settled in the big chair in your room."

A smile and a laugh. *I haven't done that for too long.* "No, I won't shoot the messenger. I'm not even sure I can get up from the chaise without help. So, you are safe this time."

Not only did Jackson lift her up from the chaise, lend her his arm as she made her way back in the house, but he waited a discreet distance from the bathroom while she used the toilet and washed up. Back in her room, she opted for the chair.

"Did I miss dessert?" she asked him once she put her feet up on the foot stool.

"Are you up for that?"

"Sophia's brownies and your ice cream? Are you kidding?"

"How much?"

"A couple of bites is all."

"My wife will dance a jig and Sophia will join in when I tell them this," he said.

"Not Eleanor?"

"She'll be clapping the rhythm and I'll be playing the spoons."

The dragonfly pendant lay against her left breast, covering the spot where the cancer lingered. Gently she rubbed it in a circular motion over the area. *I will survive. I will survive. I will see my children grow up and hold grandchildren in my arms.*

15 - THE BALANCING ACT

*D*aniel pulled into the Visitor Parking space near the front door. Distracted with thoughts of Ashley, who had her second chemo treatment today, he almost missed Art's car parked a block away. Even more alert because the car was empty, he strode to the front door and went inside. An angry male voice came from the office—Art.

Not wanting a confrontation, Daniel ignored the sign requesting all visitors check in at the office. He strolled past the doorway and casually walked down the hall to Rose's classroom. Of the three children, it was the closest to the front door. He knocked on the door frame and waited for her teacher, Miss Martha, to acknowledge him before going inside.

Two male teachers with serious expressions hurried down the hallway towards the office.

"I'm here to pick up Rose and her brothers," Daniel said. "They weren't waiting outside or even just inside the front door so I've come looking for them."

"She's in the office, Mr. O'Donnell."

"Seems to be a bit of a ruckus there right now." It was a struggle to keep his shoulders relaxed and his hands unfisted but he thought of the children and that helped.

"I know," Miss Martha said and approached the door looking out and down the hall to the office. "Rose was called to the office about an hour ago for an interview. Since she was pretty upset afterward, she didn't come back to the room but rested in the nurse's office."

"They're my kids," Art was saying to someone. But Daniel was not going to look out to see what was going on and it looked like Miss Martha was staying put also.

"Is there a way to let Ms. Campbell know I'm here without Mr. Kenner seeing me?" Daniel asked.

Miss Martha smiled and picked up a receiver on the room wall next to the door. "Mr. O'Donnell is here in my room." She nodded and hung up.

Ms. Campbell wants you to stay here for a little bit. They called the police to escort Mr. Kenner off school property. Once he's gone, you can get the children and go."

"Good plan," Daniel said, wishing instead he could see the kids now.

Ten minutes later, the phone on the wall beeped and Miss Martha answered it. "I'll let him know."

"It's safe for me to head to the office?"

"Yes. The woman here to interview the children also talked to the police. Mr. Kenner isn't happy but he is gone," Miss Martha said. She stood in the doorway to her room, semi-blocking Daniel's exit.

"We know this is a difficult time what with Mrs. Kenner's cancer and the custody battle. While we do understand and will tolerate the acting out for now, at some point the children's behavior will need to be more directly addressed."

"What's happening?" Daniel asked. He tucked his thumbs in his belt and listened attentively.

"Rose is sullen and uncooperative. She sucked her thumb earlier today and the other children started teasing her. I put a stop to it but she was devastated. Both James and Anthony were in fights on the playground at lunch. Ms. Campbell just took them inside and had them sit in her office while she worked. Of course she left her window open so they could hear everyone playing outside." Miss Martha smiled. "Perhaps not very subtle but the boys were very subdued when they went back to class."

"Thanks for letting me know. I'll pass it on to their mom."

Daniel strode down to the office where he found all three children waiting. "Hi there, ready to go?" He forced a cheery, upbeat note to his voice and plastered a smile on his face. *If they want to talk about it, okay but I'm not bringing it up.* "So, how was school today?" *Hell!* "Got any homework?"

Ms. Campbell came around the counter. "Remember what I said, 'Tomorrow is a new day.' Your teachers and I are looking forward to seeing you in the morning. It might be hard to believe right now, but we'll support you as best we can while your parents figure things out." She nodded to Daniel, turned and retreated to her office.

"Was today a bad enough day that stopping by DQ for an ice cream cone will help?

"I don't feel good," Rose said, dragging her feet and her backpack as the little group moved out into the hall.

"I want one," Anthony said, a bright tone to his voice, a spring to his step.

James trudged beside him. "I don't care."

"Here's what we'll do then," Daniel improvised. "We'll head home and check in with your mom and see what's going on for dinner. Then if ice cream seems like a good idea, we'll come back and get whatever everyone wants. Does your mom have a favorite flavor?"

"That isn't fair," Anthony stormed. "I said I wanted some. You can't just change your mind. My dad wouldn't do that. He'd go to DQ because he said he would."

This is going to be a hell-of-a long drive home.

"Nuh uh," Rose said. "Art didn't keep his promises hardly ever."

"Let's get everyone in the truck," Daniel said hoping to divert the on-coming vitriol. All he got was a minute or two reprieve and then the bickering and arguing was back in full force. He noticed it was between Rose and Anthony. James sat, arms folded across his chest, a forlorn look on his face.

The gist of the argument was Anthony worshipped his dad and would not tolerate anyone saying anything negative at all. Rose, on the other hand, had nothing positive to say and brought up scenario after scenario where Art had lied or hadn't followed through. *She'd be an excellent attorney with that historical memory.*

Thankful the traffic moved freely and the trip home was uneventful, if you didn't count the constant squabbling, Daniel rubbed his throbbing temples once he'd pulled into the back parking area and turned the truck off. It had been a conscious decision not to hassle the kids about the quarreling. His hope had been they'd have worked most of it off by the time they got home—he'd been very, very wrong.

He sat in the quiet cab for a few minutes after the kids had run into the house. As they'd passed the front drive, he'd seen Lily and Sophia's cars and was grateful someone with more experience was on the scene. *Of course they're here. Ash had another chemo treatment this morning.* If the kids carried on like they were in front of Ashley, he didn't know what would happen.

As he came in the back door, he heard what would happen if they continued to war with each other in front of their mom.

"That is enough. You do not, I do mean *not* talk to each other or about your father that way. Not ever," Ashley said in her sternest voice. "Now sit down. No, Rose, you cannot be up here on the bed. All three of you are in serious trouble."

Lily stood in the bedroom doorway. "Daniel's here."

"Well, he better come on in too," Ashley said.

Reluctantly, he entered the room. The children were sitting on chairs. Rose crying. Anthony defiant. James sullen.

"What happened?" Ashley asked.

A glance in her direction and Daniel saw her sickly pallor, her hand resting on her stomach, the sick bowl and towel next to her. It was taking everything she had to sit up and have this conversation with her kids.

"Guess Art showed up and wanted to take the children with him.

Ms. Campbell said "no." The lady who was interviewing them was gathering her things up. Anyway, they were all in the office instead of back in their rooms when he showed up."

"I thought she was interviewing them individually?" Lily asked.

"She did, I think," Daniel replied. "Rose went first and then because she wasn't feeling well, she rested in the nurse's office. Don't know who went next."

"I did," James said. "I didn't feel good either so Ms. Campbell let me sit in her office."

"That lady doesn't know nothing," Anthony started in. "She doesn't understand the pressure dad is under and that it's mom who's making everything so hard. And Ms. Campbell is mean. She made me miss my lunch recess because Johnny Lardbucket tattled."

"Just a minute young man," Ashley interrupted. "You do not refer to one of your schoolmates so disrespectfully. Lucky for you it was Ms. Campbell and not me—

"You're dying. What can you do? You just stay in bed all day or are sick in the toilet."

"That's enough, Anthony. Your mother has done nothing to deserve you talking to her that way," Daniel stepped in front of the young boy. "You need to apologize. Is that clear?" He stayed perfectly still and fairly relaxed given what was going on until he saw Anthony nod.

"I'm sorry," Anthony mumbled, head hanging down, scuffing a toe on the floor.

"Your mother has worked hard to raise all three of you to be gracious, caring, compassionate young people. Try to remember that," Daniel said, as he moved aside.

"Now, I may be interfering and if I am, I apologize, but you three need to go into the kitchen and start on your homework. If you don't have any homework, let me know because I've some chores you can do." He stood next to the door and gestured toward the kitchen. "Go on."

Rose looked over at her mom. "I'm sorry mom. I'll try to be good." She ran out of the room.

James grabbed his backpack up from floor narrowly missing Anthony in the process. "Enough." Daniel barked.

Heads downcast, both boys trudged out of the room.

"Looks like I've got some work to do," Lily said a sparkle in her eye. Hearing Sophia's voice, she said, "not yet." Sitting in one of the chairs, she patted the other in invitation for Daniel to sit.

"Tell us the rest," Lily said.

"James and Anthony were in fights on the playground at lunch today. Rose is sucking her thumb and Miss Martha said the other kids started teasing her. She didn't handle that well. Miss Martha used the word "devastated." She also said they understood and would support the kids as best they could to a point. I didn't ask where that point was.

"The other thing you need to know," he said looking at Ashley, "is that Anthony totally defends his dad saying things like Art has never broken a promise and that all the problems are because of you not him. Rose argued with him the whole way home, countering every positive memory Anthony has with something negative. I just let them take each other on because I thought they'd wear themselves out or run out of things to say. Boy, was I wrong." He looked contrite. "I'm really sorry. If I'd known, I'd have stopped it."

"Live and learn," Lily said. "Sometimes the best course is to let children squabble and settle things on their own. Obviously from what you've said, this isn't one of them."

"What's the deal about the DQ?" Ashley asked.

"I asked them about stopping by the DQ for an ice cream cone. Rose said she felt sick. James didn't want to—of course, Anthony did and I said we needed to come home and check things out and that we could go back later."

"Well, they aren't going back later, that's for sure," Ashley said. "Didn't mean for this to be so much trouble."

"They're great kids going through a rough time. Anthony is being protective of his dad right now and probably knows Rose and James did not sing Art's praises to the lady interviewer."

"Ms. Muir is her name," Lily reminded him.

Sophia appeared in the doorway and motioned to Lily who got up and left.

Daniel stood to leave. "Ms. Campbell told the kids 'Tomorrow is another day' when we were leaving. Funny how a simple saying, this one only four words, has a lifetime of truth in it." He paused at the door, turned back and said. "Got some things to do in my workshop. Need anything?"

"I'm good," Ashley said, her head rested on the pillows, her eyes closed.

On quiet feet he left the room, pulling the door closed behind him.

16 - RESPITE

Sparkling iridescent lights flowed like billowing clouds behind Ashley's eyelids. Her body relaxed into the pillowed softness of the bed as she drifted on the breeze gliding in her mind. Scenes floated by bathed in iridescent blues and greens, pinks and lavenders, yellows and golds, reds and purples. A life review on some level.

Art proposing to her on Christmas Eve on Gram's porch.

Her belly large with James. Art's ear pressed tight; the delight on his face when he felt a foot or elbow rub his cheek.

The pride on Art's face as he carried Anthony to the car when they left the hospital.

He faded from the scenes and her circle sisters came into focus. Rose's birth, celebrations and ceremonies, Women of the 14th Moon gatherings.

Their beloved faces and those of her children hovered around her, shining light into the darkness.

In that place between here and there, Ashley's mind wandered through memories from Gram and her life in Declan, to ten years in The Circle sipping their lessons without judgment. Steadfastness, loyalty, unconditional love, honesty, courage, trust—building blocks in life's foundation if that life is whole and healthy.

Hope beamed from James' face as he coasted through. Hanging on to his hand was Rose. What did he hope for? She'd like to ask but he drifted away toward a shadowed figure. Who?

The shadowed figure wafted in her direction, coming into focus when nearer. Daniel. One arm was around James' shoulder. Rose? He held her in his other arm. All three of them looked happy, like a family should. Where was Anthony? Lost?

Her mind glided away from the question.

Dragon and damselflies flitted through, up and down, back and forth, a second to hover and then dart away. The light caught their wings and added to the dazzling spectrum of color. *I can see in the darkness when they are with me. How did I forget that?*

Her mind glided away from the question.

Darkness rose consuming the memories. Cold numbed her fingers and toes. The cancer leaked from her breast, its tentacles reaching out for purchase in other parts of her body. The anaesthetized feeling spread. *I'm going to die.*

Her mind glided away.

In that place between here and there, that place where battles are fought in the war of life, Ashley's mind hung suspended in time and space. *I'm going to die.*

Tears leaked from the corners of unseeing eyes, traced a path down the side of her face, dampening her hair. *I'm going to die.*

In the distance a sound, a voice calling her name.

In the distance a touch, a hand shaking her.

In the distance a light—

The light flitted from one dark corner to another, leaving a spark of light. Another light joined the first taking a different path, leaving a spark of light. More lights joined in. Her mind filled with sparkling iridescent light. The darkness vanished, the cancerous feelers retreated. Warmth and life spread through her, banishing the deadened feeling.

Daniel's face filled her inner vision. His scent of fresh sawdust, fresh air, and spice tickled her nose. Dragonflies and damselflies danced around him. Laughter and something else shone in his eyes. His hand, held out to her, invited her to join him. *I've dreamed about being with him but...*

The light faded and darkness encroached.

Ashley grasped the dragonfly pendant she wore around her neck. A glow illumined her inner world. *I must remember this...*

"Mom, Mom," Rose's voice penetrated calling her from that in between place. "Mom?"

Ashley stirred but lacked the strength to open her eyes.

"Give your mom a minute, there," Daniel said. "She's been sound asleep. Just needs a minute to wake up."

The glow brightened to a radiant shaft of light. In the center was Daniel, surrounded by her kids. They were saying something and while she couldn't hear their words, she knew in her heart they were calling to her.

If only… . But her will to open her eyes wasn't strong enough to override the lethargy. A little more time to rest. I just need a little more time.

The mattress shifted, a small body snuggled against her side, a small hand patted her cheek. "I'm here, Mom."

She meant to move her arm, to wrap it around her daughter, the darkness encroached.

17 - A LITTLE CRISIS

She was alone and would be for four hours. The children were on a supervised visit with Art. Mrs. Muir had talked to the judge after last weekend and the incident at school. The judge had changed the order to weekly supervised visits. Knowing they would not be alone with their dad had helped James and Rose immensely. While they weren't excited to see Art like Anthony was, they went without sullen glares or tears.

A treat she gave herself was standing in the shower, letting the water run over her skin. There was something about the gentle beat of the spray that calmed, soothed her like nothing else. She did nothing else except stand and let the warm liquid glide over her. It was too exhausting to try to shower with soap and wash her hair.

Ashley glanced down to see the shower pan begin to overflow. She turned the water off before it streamed past the bathmat and out into the hall. The bathmat squished under her feet as she stepped from the enclosure. A large bath towel on the counter was just beyond her reach. *I can do this.* She chanted to herself, taking one step and then another until the towel was wrapped around her. Little rivulets of water flowed from the soaked bathmat.

Waves of exhaustion and nausea passed through her. She swayed, grabbed the counter for support, and stepped off the mat. No new water flowed but what had oozed out of the mat was now creeping toward the bathroom door.

What have I done? Panic raced through her, the adrenaline giving her enough energy to step into the hall. *If I just rest up, I can clean things up.* Sliding down the wall, Ashley sat on the floor curled over her drawn-up knees.

DANIEL PULLED into the back parking area near his workshop. His plan was to work on a couple of projects: one for Lily's house as a Thank You for letting him stay there and the other for Ashley. It had occurred to him he could build something for each of the other women in the circle. *Not sure I could get them all done by Solstice.*

He glanced toward the house. The children were with Art and Ashley was alone. He knew it was hard for the other women to not be there but the decision was that a few hours to herself would be a good thing—"a break from the hovering" Sophia had said.

I need to get some work done in here. Daniel stood in the doorway and surveyed his work area. Lily's screen door was almost done. He still had to paint it but couldn't do that until he decided on the colors. Ashley's project was on his workbench. Still in the initial design stages, it was blocks of wood with sketches. He hadn't gotten it the way he wanted the finished product to look so he erased the marks and started over.

Thirty minutes later, instead of being done, he had very little to show for the time he'd spent. His mind kept wandering, wondering how Ashley was doing. A niggle in the back of his mind said he needed to check on her. He'd ignored it—well, really pushed it away, forcing his focus back on the wood.

Ah, hell. Just go check. You'll be able to concentrate once you do. A decision made, Daniel strode out of his workshop and to the house. Mounting the deck steps, he used his key to unlock the French doors into the kitchen.

All was quiet.

"Stupid idea to come. But now you're here, you might as well check on her, say "hi", and get it over with," he muttered to himself as he walked to the doorway into the hall.

Old habits die hard and he looked to his right to make sure he didn't run in to anyone. Growing up in a small house with a big family had taught him that rule even before he had a driver's license. It took a moment for his brain to process the sight before him—Ashley curled up on the floor in only a bath towel, water seeping out of the bathroom door.

In two strides he was next to her, speaking softly, not yet daring to touch. "Ash? Ash? It's me, Daniel."

"Daniel?" She looked up at him with large liquid grey eyes pooling with tears.

"I'm going to pick you up and take you to your room," he said in a firm, no-nonsense voice.

"I'm sorry...," Ashley shifted as if to stand.

"Don't apologize and don't move. Just let me do this, okay?" He already had one arm around her shoulders, the other under her bent knees.

"I ...,"

"If that's an apology, I don't want to hear it," he said in a voice gruff with emotions.

The front door opened and chattering voices announced the arrival of Sophia and Hunter.

Silence.

My guess is they've reached the hall. "Need your help here," he said as he walked the remaining steps to Ashley's room.

Hunter turned back the bed covers as he stepped through. "Just put her here, Sophia and I'll take care of her."

"Daniel?"

He turned to see her struggle to sit up. "I'm so s-s-s...,"

Swiveling, he returned to the bed, took her chin in his hand and raised it so their eyes met. "Do not," he said. "Let me repeat it 'Do not' apologize. Is that clear? Do you understand there is nothing to apologize for?"

"The shower—,"

"The shower drain plugged?"

She nodded.

"Good to know. I'll have it fixed in no time. You rest." Daniel paused at the door, his head bent, one hand on the casing. "You have nothing to be sorry for, nothing to apologize for, Ash. Just let it go."

He got his tools and cleaned out the drain. What had plugged it?

Hair. Clumps of what used to be silvery blond hair before it got stuck in the shower drain. His eyes watered. He swiped the back of his hand across his eyes and stood. Gathering his tools, he turned and found Sophia standing in the doorway.

"She's resting now. Thank you for taking care of this the way you did. She feels so guilty about everything right now," she said her voice shaky with emotion. "I hope she heard you because she isn't really listening to any of us and guilt is not helping her fight the cancer."

18 - THE SURPRISE

$\mathcal{N}$o one was telling her anything or maybe they just didn't know anything. The kids clambered into the back seat of the extended cab while Daniel half-lifted her into the front passenger seat. She'd never ridden in his truck. *It's like you can see the world from up here.*

Hugs from each of the kids and a kiss from Rose were delivered before they climbed down and ran to the school building. Ms. Campbell waved from the door where she'd been waiting and then followed them in.

Daniel carefully backed up and pulled away from the parking spot closest to the school. It was marked "handicapped". At her horrified exclamation he'd explained he had permission to pull in there to drop the kids off but parked a spot or two over when he picked them up.

"Want a cup of coffee?" he asked as they drove away.

"I'm fine," she replied.

"You didn't answer my question which was whether you want a cup of coffee or maybe tea?"

"Not right now," Ashley answered.

They drove a few more miles before Daniel pulled into a mini-mall and backed into a parking spot. "It's easier to pull out than to back out," he said in answer to her quizzical expression.

Ashley looked around at the businesses but saw nothing even open at this early hour even though there were a few cars in the parking lot.

Daniel opened her door and helped her out.

"Where?"

"It's a surprise, remember? Want to close your eyes so you're really surprised?" he asked.

His mouth grinned but Ashley noticed his eyes were serious.

"I'm good," she said. "Just point me where I'm supposed to go."

He held out his arm, picked up her hand and placed it there. "This way," he said angling his body between her and the shops.

Daniel stopped in front of a store she thought was obviously closed because the blinds were drawn. He knocked three times, paused, and then knocked again.

The door opened and she was ushered into a—she stopped, her mouth agape. "Whaat?" she stammered. She stood on the threshold of a barber shop. Three mirrors with three barber chairs on her left. A man, who she guessed was in his fifties, with dark thinning hair, brown eyes and a warm smile on his face walked towards her.

"Hi Glen, this is Ashley."

Glen grinned and offered his hand. "Glad to meet you." He gestured to the opposite side of the room. When she turned, she saw three elderly men sitting in armchairs, big smiles on their faces. As Glen introduced them, each waved. Otto, Max and Gary were their names.

Totally confused, she looked for Daniel. He stood a few feet away watching her.

"Have you figured out the surprise yet?"

She shook her head.

In two steps he was in front of her, his hand on her chin. "I thought this would be easier than losing it strand by strand. But if I'm wrong, we'll go. No harm done."

"A barbershop?"

"Glen's great at shaving heads. Just look at these guys who for different reasons have gone with the smooth and shiny look. They volunteered to come by this morning so you can see for yourself what a professional job Glen does." He'd stepped to her side and steered her closer to the three older men.

As she approached they stood, reminded her who was who, and invited her to rub their heads 'for luck' they chortled.

Ashley looked back at Glen who stood beside his barber's chair. A couple of steps in his direction and she stopped. *He has kind eyes.*

Her gaze shifted to look at herself in the mirror. She wore a bandana wrapped around her head and tied in front. *Gram used to wear a scarf like this when she cleaned to keep the dust and cobwebs out of her hair.* She touched the scarf, ran her fingers over the smooth cotton surface. *When I take it off, another hunk of my hair will be inside. Maybe...* The memory of the shower drain clogged with her hair was fresh. *Daniel's been so calm, so caring, so compassionate—and this?*

The shadow of a damselfly in her peripheral vision. Decision made.

She took the last few steps to the barber's chair and used the rung to climb up on her own.

"Let's do it this way," Glen said, turning the chair so it faced away from the mirror. "Unless you want to watch."

"No, this way is fine." She focused on Daniel who'd taken a seat next to Gary. "I've got these handsome gentlemen to entertain me while you do your thing."

Otto told some groaner jokes. She heard the snipping of scissors but never saw any hair on the floor.

Gary asked about her kids. The buzz of the razor, the cool metal touch on her scalp told her Glen was doing his job but again, no hair appeared on the floor.

Max told her why they were all there. He'd had cancer and once Glen had shaved his head, he liked the look and had gone with the bald look for a decade. Otto had watched *Anna and the King of Siam* and thought the Yul Brenner look sexy. Of course that had been two decades ago. Gary had his shaved because he was their friend. "We're the three Musketeers—one for all and all for one."

Shaving cream on her head was an interesting experience. "How does it look?" she'd dared to ask.

"You look better than a banana split," Otto said. "And that's our favorite treat, isn't it boys?"

What she didn't do as Glen carefully shaved her head with the straight-edge razor was look at Daniel. If she looked, what would she see? She didn't want to see revulsion nor did she want to see pity. The old guys' faces showed sympathy. Sympathy from strangers she could handle. Revulsion or pity or even sympathy from someone she cared about? No, she couldn't handle that.

The warm towel wrapped around her head, a gentle massage of her scalp, "We're done." Glen announced stepping in front of her. "Ready to see the results?"

She'd seen her head bald before so she nodded, not expecting to be shocked—but of course she was. Tears threatened when she saw her reflection grow as Glen slowly turned the chair so she faced the mirror.

"My hair...," she said in a trembly voice. "I...."

Max made his way across the shop and stood beside her. "Thought maybe it wouldn't be so hard this way?"

She nodded.

"Then you find out its hard no matter how it happens."

She nodded again.

"So it's hard on the one hand but easier on the other."

"I know," Ashley voice still quivered. "But now it's gone and I don't have to wake up to more on the pillow or be afraid to comb my hair." Her laugh was shaky. "Nothing left to comb."

Otto now stood behind Max. "You do know how beautiful you are, right?"

"My hair...."

"Your hair isn't you. Your hair isn't why you are beautiful. Your hair has nothing to do with who you are." Otto shuffled back to his chair. Max followed.

Ashley stared at the stranger who wasn't a stranger in the mirror.

Glen sat in the barber chair next to her. "Don't open for another hour so you've got time."

Tentatively she touched her head, ran her hand over the top from one ear to the other. The soft smoothness of her skin surprised her and she checked all over finding the sensation the same.

She knew Daniel was watching her, had been watching her the entire time. Calling upon her courage, she fingered her dragonfly pendant and caught his gaze in the mirror. "Thank you, Daniel."

Glen got out of his chair and came to stand beside her to steady her as she stepped down. Feet firmly on the floor, she turned to look at the men who'd born witness to her plight. *No, not plight. That implies —maybe that is the best word because this was a difficult situation.*

"Thank y'all for being here and keeping my mind occupied while Glen worked his magic. I'm finding myself fading a bit here—,"

Daniel was on his feet in a thrice, striding towards her, his hand out. "Your chariot awaits," he said in a grand tone and made a sweeping gesture towards the door.

"One more thing," Glen said drawing her attention back to him. He held out three colors of baseball-type caps. "On the house."

"I know pink is the color that represents breast cancer but I prefer the lavender one."

"Lavender it is then," Glen said presenting the cap to her with a flourish.

Ashley took the cap and found a surprise inside—a soft flannel in a contrasting color, dark purple. The sensation on her bald head was like well-worn pajamas when she put it on. Looking at the men when she put the cap on, she asked, "What about this?" she said turning it so the bill was to the side. They laughed. "Or this?" She turned the bill to the back and looked in the mirror. She smiled at that silly look.

"How about this?" Daniel said, turning the bill to the front. "The sun's bright and it'll shade your eyes on the way home."

They were in the truck heading toward the house when the thought struck her. "We walked out without paying?"

"All taken care of before we even got there. If you'd said 'No', I'd have gotten a trim."

She looked at him, seeing his hair was a little shaggy, curling around his ears and over the collar of his shirt. "We could've waited while you got a trim but shaggy looks good on you."

"I don't look disreputable?"

"Nope, not at all. You just look well-used." She laughed at the look on his face, a mix between horror and amusement.

"I am well-used."

"And well-loved." The words were just there and said before it registered how it might be taken. "You know my kids think the world of you," she hastily added a bit breathlessly.

He wanted to ask what their mother thought of him but that was for another day. Yet again he was reminded she had no idea how much he cared about her. It wasn't just her kids. It was the whole package that had worked its way into his heart. A heart that was terrified to love again.

J couldn't and wouldn't say she was glad today was Monday because every other Monday was chemo day. Afterwards she faced a week that started with retching at worst and waves of nausea at best. *And then there's the hovering.*

Her fingers stroked the temporary dragonfly tattoo Rose had put on the back of her hand.

"He'll help you feel better," Rose had said.

What always made her feel better were her kids. She closed her eyes and relaxed against the chair. A damselfly hovered, the iridescence of her wings refracting colors around her inner eye.

Having chemo every other week gave her a full week when she was able to get up and fix breakfast for the kids, wipe off the kitchen counters, straighten her bed, clean her bathroom and oversee homework. Not that she did all of it every day but she did enough that nothing got out-of-hand. Every day of the second week, she saw her kids, talked to them about school, just spent time with them. On those days things were sort of normal.

Last week on an unusually warm day for mid-October, she'd bundled up and sat out on the deck relishing the fresh air and the feel of the light breeze against her skin.

As she focused on relaxing and thinking the chemo was doing battle with the bad cancer cells, her mind drifted back to her kids. In some ways she was glad they spent time with Art on Saturday afternoons.

Mrs. Muir picked them up, supervised the visits and brought them home. Rose liked her and Ashley found she trusted the woman.

It had been hard not to ask about the visits since the kids didn't talk about it. Lily'd said that was normal and natural. *They've Mrs. Muir to talk to on the way back. That will have to do for now.*

20 - CHOICES

The smells from the kitchen enticed and her stomach growled. Plumped up pillows surrounded her, a blanket covered her legs, thick socks her feet. Ashley relaxed on the couch.

Gabriella came into the living room, the abalone shell of smoking sage in one hand, a painted turkey feather in the other. She walked the perimeter feathering the cleansing smoke into, over and around corners and furniture and paying special attention to the large low coffee table in front of the couch. A large silver bowl with a bouquet of chrysanthemums artfully arranged graced the center. Chairs and ottomans were staged in a circle around the table.

"Ready?" Gabriella asked.

Ashley started to take the blanket off, when Gabriella stopped her. "I'll smudge you there if you sit up a little straighter."

The wisps of smoke swirled around her, shapes shifting in the spiral as it rose to the ceiling. She lifted the blanket so Gabriella could feather the smoke underneath, closer to her skin. While she liked the soft rain-like feel of the shower on her skin, she also liked the whispery touch of the smoke as it drifted by.

One at a time her circle sisters came into the living room passing through the smudging smoke Gabriella held at the entrance. Her children, Logan, Daniel and Matthew were joining them this evening. Jackson was out of town.

Diana snuggled into the couch corner opposite her. Matthew took the next seat and held his wife's feet on his lap, gently massaging them. Even though she looked radiant, Diana was having a difficult pregnancy and Sophia was co-teaching her class for her because some nights Diana couldn't make it.

Her kids sat on the floor in front of the couch, using it for a back support. Daniel sat across the circle from her, Sophia and Lily on one side and Logan and Hunter on the other. As each woman had come in to the room, they'd added to the altar.

"We aren't starting with prayers this evening," Lily said. "Gabriella said prayers when she cleansed the space. This gathering isn't about ceremony but about plans. We do have a talking stone, but it will be handed from one to another rather than going around the circle."

Ashley put her hand up. "I'd like to go first."

Lily handed her the piece of rainbow obsidian. Ashley cradled the heavy stone in her hands, rolling it from one palm to the other as she gathered her thoughts.

"I know it's time to make plans for Samhain," she began. "And I know Elizabeth is counting on The Circle to support her first Retreat Center Samhain Ceremony. The kids and I'll be okay. I have my next chemo treatment on November 1, so traveling to Ireland, even if I was stronger now isn't happening. I'll be good enough to take care of myself and my kids and expect everyone to go and have a wonderful time."

Diana reached out for the stone and took her time making eye contact with everyone across the altar from her. "I talked to the doctor yesterday. She said it isn't wise for me to travel that far. I won't be going to Ireland until after the baby is born. So it isn't just Samhain. I'll miss Solstice as well." She turned to Ashley a rueful smile on her face. "I can travel across town so we can plan on creating a ceremony ourselves. That is if you want to."

"I'd love to do ceremony with you on Samhain." Ashley reached for a tissue and dabbed her eyes.

Hunter waved her hand. Diana passed her the stone. "My classes are full. I've been struggling with how I was going to balance everything and now I've another option," she said, her voice filled with energy. "While I'd love to go to Ireland for Samhain, it would be best for me and my business to stay here instead of cancelling a week or more of classes or scheduling the trip so I'm only there on Samhain with a travel day before and after. I could probably do it, but…," her voice took on a reflective tone. "Solstice is different. I scheduled the Winter Recital for December 17th so I can go to Ireland for Solstice."

Sophia took the stone. "Who is planning on going to Ireland for Samhain?" Her hand remained raised and Lily and Gabriella joined her. "I'm assuming Jackson is going? What about Eleanor?"

"Both Jackson and Eleanor are planning on it," Lily replied.

"Life happens to all of us at some time," Sophia said, her voice quiet, her eyes on Ashley and Diana. "My belief is there is always a blessing tucked into even the worst experience Life can hand us. Jonathan's death is my 'worst' but the blessing is I never take my relationships for granted. I make sure I say the words 'I love you' out loud when appropriate and in my mind when not.

"Your Samhain Ceremony will not be the same as it would be if you were at The Manor in Ireland and with The Lady, but it will be exactly what all of you need."

"Because we are not all traveling, I think it best not to use Cauldron funds," Lily stated. "Jackson and I have frequent flyer miles and are willing to share. I'll be in touch with both of you," she said, indicating Sophia and Gabriella with a nod of her head and a wave of her hand. "We'll work it out."

I thought I'd be upset not to go. But staying here feels right. Ashley rested her hand on James' shoulder before ruffling his hair.

"Aw, Mom." James groaned, squirmed away and stood, using his hands to smooth his hair. "Did you have to?"

"Guess I did," Ashley said a wide grin on her face. "Who's next?" she asked Anthony and Rose.

Anthony scooted away, gained his feet, and dashed across the room.

"I'm next," Rose said and wiggled next to her mom. She reached up, took Ashley's hand and placed it on her head. "I'm right here, Mom," she said.

"Yes, you're right where you're supposed to be." Ashley bent down and kissed the top of her daughter's head before finger-combing the curls. *And so am I.*

Ashley wiped down the kitchen counters, stirred the lentil soup in the pot and checked the four cake layers in the oven. Her toes tapped, her arms raised and she did a little dance ending in a twirl.

Strong arms grabbed her as she staggered out of the turn. "You must be feeling pretty good," Daniel said as he steadied her.

Brown eyes lit with laughter warmed her. She shook her head as she said, "Better than I have in months."

A buzzer went off announcing the cakes were done.

"Gotta get this taken care of so we have dessert tonight."

Daniel lifted the soup pot lid and took a deep breath. "This smells good."

"It tastes good too."

"Bet it does." He turned from the stove after replacing the lid. "Need any help with that?"

"Nope I've got it."

"Anything you need me to do?"

"Y'all can help me move furniture in the living room," Ashley said with a nonchalant air not seeing the look of horror cross Daniel's face.

The kids burst through the door, swarmed around Daniel, their lively chatter filling the air.

Cake pans now on cooling racks, Ashley turned to see her kids, excited faces upturned, regale Daniel with what they'd done yesterday with Art. Visits were now every week for four hours. Mrs. Muir was always in attendance. James and Anthony accompanied each other to the bathroom; Art was not allowed to be alone with any of them. When Rose had to use the bathroom, Mrs. Muir waited outside the door so she could still see Art and the boys.

That being said, Art was coming up with things to do that the children enjoyed. Yesterday's activity was a trip on the Fremont Spirit, the sightseeing boat that plied the Willamette River. They were able to see Fremont from the water and that was a new experience. Even Rose, usually more subdued about the time spent with Art, was animated in her telling of the trip.

Her fingers stroked the dragonfly pendant she constantly wore. *I see a pinpoint of light when I focus on being well and healthy but...*

"Time for lunch," Ashley said breaking into the competition to see who could tell Daniel 'the best part'. When the quick lunch of sandwiches with milk and cookies was finished, Ashley started towards the living room.

"Where do you think you're going," Daniel said in a serious voice, his long strides easily catching up with her.

"Moving furniture around in the living room," Ashley replied.

"Kids, need your help. Here. Now."

How does he do that? Ashley stood in the archway to the living room as her kids charged past.

"Your mom needs furniture moved. Who here is strong enough to help?"

Of course put that way, they'll all say 'yes', even Rose. Ashley smiled as three sets of hands and "I can, I can" bounced in the air.

Daniel turned toward Ashley. "We await your command," he said with a bow and sweep of his hand.

The kids giggled.

Ashley smiled and started into the room.

"You can just tell us," Daniel said.

"The couches flanking the fireplace and the love seat from the front parlor brought in. With a fire going, I want everyone close enough to feel the warmth. Diana's bringing a small water fountain and we'll set it up on the table in the corner by the window so we'll all hear it."

"Who's sitting where?" Daniel asked.

"I don't know right now."

"I want to sit with—," Anthony started.

"Y'all need to wait until it's time."

"Dad says you need to make a plan and act on it to get what you want," Anthony said, a dare in his voice, fisted hands on his hips.

"That's one way of approaching life," Daniel said in a positive tone. "What's really cool is that each of us gets to figure out which way works best for us.

"When I'm building something, most of the time I follow the plans but then sometimes I see something in the wood and I follow it. Both ways work depending on the circumstances. What would have happen if we decided to just nail in boards any which way when we were working on Lily's deck?"

"And we're almost done," Rose chimed in turning to Ashley. "I got to pound on nails. Daniel said I done good but I was even better at holding the—," she turned toward Daniel.

"Spacer," he supplied.

"Yep, the spacer thing. I do it really good so all the holes between the boards look the same."

"So that's an example of making a plan and following it." Daniel put his hand on James' shoulder. "What have we done where a plan wouldn't have worked so well?"

James grinned at Ashley. "Can't say because it's a surprise. Right?" He looked to Daniel for confirmation.

"True, it is a surprise."

"Remember when we added chocolate chips to our popcorn on Friday? That wasn't planned," Anthony said. "But it wasn't as good as we figured it'd be."

"So, experimenting always works because if you don't like how it turned out, you know not to do it that way again." Daniel turned back to the living room. "Do you care which couch is on which side of the fireplace?"

Ashley's heart warmed at the scene before her. *He always seems to know just what to say to keep the peace.* "No, it doesn't matter about the couches, but I do want the low round table in the middle. We'll put our altar on that instead of the floor. And, the smaller tables at the end of the furniture. Not sure if we'll stay here afterwards and eat or go into the kitchen.

"While y'all are moving furniture, I'll go get some wood from the pile and stack it—,"

"You will not do that," Daniel said with emphasis. "Make a list of what you want done. The kids and I'll take care of it."

The pit of her stomach soured and Ashley's eyes widened. She'd not ever heard him speak to anyone that forcefully. *OMG I've totally misjudged him. He's just like— Stop it Ash. He's worried about you. That's all.*

"We want to do this for you," Daniel said in a quiet voice. "We...,"

The quiet was broken when Rose took her hand. "It's our present to you, Mom. And you could give us a present back."

"What present would you like?"

"Hot chocolate with marshmallows and some cookies," Rose quickly responded. "We'll be starving after so much work."

"Where did you hear that?" Ashley asked, the darker mood gone.

"That's what Matthew and Daniel always say when they work on something," Rose said, a bright smile on her face. "Don't they, James?"

"Pretty much," James agreed. "Then they go get hamburgers and French fries or a milk shake."

"To keep up our strength," Daniel added, a grin on his face. "So, you aren't being banished to the kitchen, Ash. Just saving us from a run to a fast food place."

"Put that way, I'll go start the hot chocolate. Just so you know, Sophia's cookies are almost gone. We'll have to bake our own if we want more."

"Why don't you have Rose help you make cookies now?" Anthony said. "The men can move things."

She didn't like the way Anthony worked to exclude Rose but now was not the time to fuss about it. Holding out her hand, she motioned for her daughter to join her. "Let's get that list for them and then we'll start making cookies. What kind do you want?"

"Chocolate chip," Anthony said.

"You don't get any say because you're not doing the cooking," Ashley said. She turned back, a smile on her face, "Unless y'all have changed your mind and want to be in the kitchen with us."

ASHLEY LOOKED at their Samhain altar. Even Daniel and Matthew had brought something to add: Daniel a small figurine of a horse and Matthew a glass marble.

The center bowl held a bouquet of chrysanthemums from the garden and instead of greens, she'd used colorful fall leaves from the old silver maple in the front yard. Orange, black, yellow, red and gold candles graced the mantle and wide windowsills whose curtains were tied back with red cords.

Somehow she and Daniel, with Rose between them, ended up on the love seat. James sat with Diana and Matthew and Anthony with Hunter and Logan.

It was Samhain, a time to honor those across the veil and after calling in the directions, they'd started with the naming of their ancestors. The children had wanted to participate so she'd spend some time that afternoon, helping them list grandparents and great grandparents on both sides.

Hearing her name gave her a start. *Was it a sign I'm not going to win this fight?* Her hand automatically fingered the dragonfly dangling on the cord around her neck. She held it out and marveled as the light from the flames flickered across the iridescent colored wings.

Anthony started with Art's name and Logan included Hunter. Did

Hunter feel that jolt? That sense that something bad was going to happen when she heard her name?

Instead of the intense experience they'd all had last year in Ireland, they spent time in quiet meditation before talking about the other side. Diana, Hunter and she had spent some time discussing how to handle this with Rose, who was not yet seven present. The decision to talk about the other side, beyond the veil, heaven if that is what they wished to call it was easily reached.

"I know biologically I had a dad," Logan volunteered. She leaned forward, the snowflake obsidian talking stone, in her lap her expressive hands moving as she spoke. "I wish I'd known him, had memories of him. And, I have no memories of grandparents or great grandparents, aunts or uncles, not even cousins. But I do have a special person on the other side who loves me unconditionally. His name is Jorge. He was a dancer like Mom. It makes a difference knowing someone other than Mom loves me." She gave an embarrassed laugh as she saw raised eyebrows on Ashley and Diana. "You guys don't count." She buried her face in her hands. "I'm making it worse, aren't I," she mumbled into her hands.

Hunter rested her hand on her daughter's bowed back, gave her a gentle pat and tugged her close so her head was on her shoulder. Logan handed the stone to her mom.

"Do you mean the women in this circle are other moms?" Hunter asked.

Logan shook her head and then nodded. "I don't know," she said, her voice quiet with confusion.

Ashley held her hand out and Hunter passed the stone.

"It's one of those loyalty things," Ashley began. "How do you balance loving the most important people in your life? My answer is 'You don't.' Because you don't need to. There's enough love in your heart for everyone. The love I feel for you, Logan, does not take away the love I feel for your mom, Diana or the others and it certainly doesn't leave my kids with less love."

Diana silently asked for the stone. One hand rubbing her extended belly, the other cradling the stone of protection, she added, "The love I feel for this baby does not take away any love I feel for Bill or for Matthew. In fact, the more I feel love for this little one, the more I feel love everywhere in my life."

The piece of obsidian was passed back to Logan who now sat up straight, her hand on Anthony's arm. "It's hard to think about the other side because that means someone I love has died. But it helps me to believe it's a better place and Jorge is at peace and surrounded by the light of love."

She handed the stone to Anthony.

A sullen look crossed his face. He glanced at his mom and Daniel and his face cleared. "I never knew any of my family who died. Dad says my great grandma and grandpa would've loved me 'cause they loved kids. I never met Mom's mom and dad or grandma or anyone. They never came to see us. Only Dad's mom and dad ever did."

Ashley took the stone from her son's hand. She had debated including the kids because Anthony, at least, would tell Art all about it and her fears about what he'd do, how he'd turn this magical time against her roared through her head.

But Hunter wanted Logan to be present and Logan wanted to participate this year. Having her own kids in the circle was a better plan than having them upstairs or worse yet sneaking down the stairs and listening in to bits and pieces.

"I miss my gram the most. She was the wisest woman I ever knew. It was hard to leave Declan and everyone I knew to come to Fremont. But coming here was a dream come true for Art and me. When Gram died, it about killed me not to go back for her funeral. I was so pregnant with Anthony I couldn't fly. Plus I couldn't have left James here either. That was before I knew y'all," she said gesturing toward Diana and Hunter. "But life happens in some ways for a reason." She leaned towards her son as if imparting a secret. "You came a little early, and it would've been hard to have you while on a plane or in an airport." She laughed, a twinkle in her eyes, "It would've been a great story for you to tell when you're older—how you were born on a plane or in an airport.

"What I miss most about my gram is her calm and steady manner.

She seldom yelled, never cussed and always thought the best of everyone until they showed her different. Her flower garden was even more fragrant smelling than Sophia's if y'all can believe that. Sometimes I hear her talking in my ear, reminding me of something she'd told me years ago."

Rose took the stone and stood up. She held a piece of paper. Ashley knew Rose had practiced and practiced and her linage was memorized. Even though she could recite it without the paper, she was determined to 'read' it.

Ashley smiled as Rose held the paper up and began. "I am Rose, daughter of Ashley, granddaughter of Fran, great granddaughter of Ruby, great great granddaughter of Mable. I come from a long line of strong women who done good with their lives." She folded the paper into fourths and walked to the fireplace. "I want to do as good as they did." Rose tossed the paper into the fire and moments later it burst into flame and was quickly consumed. When it had thoroughly burned she continued around the low table and took her place beside her mom. "Did I do good?" she whispered to her mom.

"You did better than good, you did great."

Daniel took the stone and stood to name his male ancestors going back five generations. Since their first names were all "Daniel" that part was easy but he included middle names and for his father and grandfather, a memory. His father taught him how to drive a nail in straight. His grandfather taught him the value of being honest in his dealings with others. He also included his step-father, Horace, a man who taught him the value of hard work.

Interesting. Never knew anything about his family 'cause he never talks about them. It's almost like he was hatched as an adult. Ashley glanced over at Daniel who now sat, an arm slung along the back of the love seat. The warmth of his hand permeated the shawl she had around her shoulders. She might be over the worst of the chemo side-effects but she still always felt cold.

James took the stone and stood. He read from his list starting with her. "I am the son of Ashley Ann Carlyle Kenner. I am the son of Art Kenner. I am the grandson of Fran," he continued through both his maternal relations until he reached Mable and then named Art's ancestors back to his great, great grandparents. "I don't know if I believe all this stuff," he said his gaze on the fire, "but I know Mom does and it helps her so that's good enough for me right now."

He handed the stone to Matthew who remained seated, his arm around his wife. His rich voice carried as he named his heritage back six generations including mothers and fathers. "I'm very fortunate to come from a long line of men who've found the love of their lives and been able to marry them." He leaned over and kissed Diana's temple. "Next year we'll have our baby with us and can add another generation."

Diana took the stone. "I am the mother of Bill and our unborn child. I am the wife of Matthew." She continued back through her grandparents. "I am blessed this day to be in the company of people I love, who show me in so many ways how important I am in their lives. Last year my aunt came to me during our Samhain ceremony in Ireland. It seems like another life-time ago when I look back at what has changed in my life over the last twelve months.

"Change is in the air. I can feel it as much as I can feel my love for Matthew and his love for me. One of the things I've learned this past year is that change, while scary at the time, can hold more gifts than we can ever imagine. In our quiet time, I asked my aunt to come again and speak to me as she did last year. She didn't appear like then, but she did have a message. "Never take for granted there will be another day. Life is meant to be lived today." Matthew's and my lives will be dramatically changed in another couple of months and my promise to myself is to never take a day in my life for granted, to be grateful for each and every life event. This past year has shown me how important that is."

Diana returned the stone to the table and with Matthew's help, stood. She led the closing of the circle, the release of the spirits who'd come to guide and protect them during this Samhain ceremony.

"It's time to eat," she said.

"Here or in the kitchen," Hunter added.

A chorus of "kitchen" indicated a decision had easily been reached.

Ashley held Rose's hand as they walked down the hall. By this time, everyone knew where bowls, plates, silverware and serving utensils were. She had nothing to do but sit with her daughter on the bench along the nook's table.

James brought her a bowl of lentil soup and a plate with salad and bread.

"Thanks, James," she said to his retreating back.

Diana and Hunter sat in the chairs across from her, Logan slipped onto the bench on Rose's other side. "Looks like the women are here and the men are there," she said pointing to the four males perched on bar stools in front of the kitchen island.

"Closer to the food," Diana commented, her gaze lingering on her husband.

"I'd like to spend more time in front of the fire," Ashley said when the food was finished. The men had cleared everything up, put dishes in the dishwasher and leftovers in the refrigerator.

"I would too," Diana and Hunter said simultaneously.

"Usually we stay up until dawn," Hunter added.

"Not sure I can do that," Diana added. "I tire so easily these days."

"How about this idea," Daniel said coming to stand by the table. "It's midnight and there's school tomorrow. Matthew and I can see the kids have whatever is needed for school tomorrow and get to bed. He and I'll hang out upstairs and that leaves you," he gestured to the women around the table, "here to enjoy the fire."

"Good plan," Matthew said. "Come on guys. You, too Rose. Logan?" An arm around Anthony and his other around James, he started for the stairs.

"Rose?" Daniel held his arms out.

Rose and Logan slid off the bench. Rose ran to Daniel. "Do I get a piggy-back ride?"

"Aren't you too big?" Ashley asked.

"Nah, not for a piggy-back ride," Daniel said, swinging Rose up to sit on his shoulders. He turned back to the women. "By the way, Diana, you and Matthew are in the master bedroom. More comfortable."

"I'm sleeping with Rose, Mom," Logan announced.

"I'll bunk with James or Anthony," Daniel said. "Hunter you have the guest bedroom to yourself. And just so you know, Matt and I are getting the kids up and off to school, so you ladies can sleep in."

Ashley changed into a pair of flannel pajamas. Hunter checked on the children and changed before coming back down. Matthew had brought down a nightgown for Diana. Comfortable, the three circle sisters snuggled on their respective couches after building up the fire.

This was a time when the veil between this world and the next was thin, a time for reflection and inner work. Words weren't necessary.

Ashley pondered Logan's words about having no idea who her ancestors were. A shiver coursed through her as an image of what her life would have been like if she hadn't had her Gram over-laid the fire. She shifted on the love seat to better see the flames.

Flames that shifted into shapes.

Shapes that danced through her mind.

22 - A GOOD WEEK AND THEN?

Chemo on Monday, sickly for four days but then, she improved and life was almost normal. The next Monday, Ashley got up, fixed breakfast for the children and saw them off to school. Standing in the doorway, waving to them as Daniel backed his truck around felt—well, it felt right. Next she cleaned up the kitchen and carefully made her way upstairs, checking on each bedroom, picking up a stray sock or two. Wednesday she did a load of laundry. A glance in the mirror she passed in the hallway, showed her face split with a goofy grin. Who knew doing laundry would be a highlight of her day?

Every night she invited Daniel to stay for dinner but unless someone else was there, he declined. Saturday she fixed pot roast and roasted potatoes and vegetables in the same pan. She was going to bake a cake but decided on cookies instead so the children could finish them up if she ran out of steam—which she did—run out of steam, that is. She figured it was the sweeping and mopping of the kitchen floor that exhausted her.

At three in the afternoon, she curled up on the cushions in the kitchen nook, a cup of hot tea cradled in her hand and waited for Daniel to bring the kids home. Ms. Muir had dropped them off at the little house after their visit with Art. She had another appointment and this arrangement meant she didn't have to reschedule it.

I can never repay him for all he's done for us. Her head rested on the window, the cool of the glass seeping through the flannel lined cap she wore. She saw her reflection and reached out to trace a finger around her face. *Just look at this. I have a different one for every day of the week now.* A smile tilted her lips at the clown face decorations on the bright red cap. *Tomorrow I'll wear my dragonfly cap.* Her hand drifted down, stopping at the image of her damselfly pendant. Still sitting, she swayed one way and then the other, mesmerized by the shimmering charm. *I've four more treatments over the next seven weeks. Y'all will stay with me, won't you?* A rainbow appeared on the windowpane looking as if she wore it as a crown.

A car pulled in the back drive. Eleanor was here.

Lily was due back Sunday from Ireland via a house totem trip with Jackson to Arizona.

Diana was on bed rest.

Hunter was putting in extra hours so she could take the time off over Solstice and Logan was helping her out in between keeping up her own studies.

Gabriella was in Seattle again on a special assignment from her work.

Sophia would be by later tonight and again tomorrow. Stacks of papers needed grading before parent/teacher conferences the week of Thanksgiving.

Eleanor came through the door, small suitcase in hand. "It smells delicious, dear." She took a deep breath. "I will be right back."

Ashley heard Eleanor's footsteps down the hall and moments later they returned. "I've a second bag to retrieve," she said in her accented voice. "But I believe I'll wait a minute. There's something I need to do first."

Crossing the room, Eleanor enveloped Ashley in a warm hug, holding her for a long minute before stepping back, her hands on Ashley's shoulders. "That will have to do until I return."

Daniel's truck pulled in before Eleanor reached the door. The children piled out and charged up the deck steps and into the house, their chattering voices called out to her as they ran past.

Eleanor stepped out onto the deck but Daniel had already pulled her suitcase out of the popped open trunk and was approaching her.

"Good to see you." Daniel kissed her cheek.

"It is quite good to be seen," Eleanor replied, a smile in her voice.

"Let me guess, you already brought your other bag in instead of waiting for me?"

"Indeed I did, Daniel. I am not helpless."

"No, you aren't." Daniel gestured Eleanor ahead of him.

They entered into a slice of bedlam as each of the children bombarded Ashley with stories about their day.

"Hold on." Daniel lifted his voice to be heard above the din. "Just a minute, guys." He paused until Rose shot him her disgusted look before he smiled and added "and gal. What about taking Eleanor's suitcases to her room and giving your mom a chance to catch her breath."

"I've got cookie dough made in the refrigerator," Ashley said. "Take care of Eleanor's things and y'all come back and bake some up."

James grabbed the bag from Daniel's hand and charged off, Anthony hot on his heels.

"Rose," Daniel called as she tore after her brothers. "You are needed here."

Moments later Rose appeared in the doorway. "What?"

"Wash up and get the cookie dough out. I'm getting down the baking sheet."

"You have to wash up too," Rose admonished.

"Yes, I do." Daniel turned the water on in the sink. With a foot he slid a stool over. "Come on and wash up with me. No splashing, now," he said and flicked fingers of water at her.

"I can if you can," Rose said in a sing-song voice, flicking him back.

"Stop it," Ashley said. "Both of you just stop. You're making a mess and Eleanor and I aren't cleaning it up."

"So, if we promise to clean it up, Rose and I can make a mess?" Daniel asked a teasing note to his voice.

Ashley shook her head not trusting her voice. Tears threatened and she turned to look out the window. Even in the best of times in her marriage, her kids had never spent this kind of lighthearted time with Art. Her stomach clenched. The tears won, streamed down her face. *What if I don't make it? What if they have to live with him?* One deep breath and then another, she swiped the tears from her face. A third deep breath and they stopped. James and Anthony's voices helped her find the strength to turn back to the kitchen.

"We washed upstairs," Anthony bragged.

"Indeed?" Eleanor marched over and inspected their hands. "You did not do a good enough job to bake cookies, much less eat them," she informed Anthony. "You need to scrub up to your elbows."

Daniel had no idea what had happened to Ashley. She'd turned to look out into the darkening yard. While there was no reflection in the glass for him to see her face, he knew something was wrong. It looked like she might be crying, wiping tears from her face. He'd no idea what had upset her. Taking a cue from Eleanor, he focused on the kids.

He lifted Rose off the stool letting her use one end of the towel as he dried his hands. "You guys can wash up here." He nodded toward the kitchen sink. "Rose and I'll get the cookie fixings out." He opened the refrigerator door and paused. "Okay, Rose, we're doing this together because your mom made enough cookie dough to last a month."

"I've turned the oven on," Eleanor said. She poured boiling water into the teapot and set it on the table. Getting cups and saucers out she added, "The baking is up to the four of you. Ashley and I are relaxing here with a cup of tea. While we will not do the work, we will give you advice—but only if you ask."

Setting Rose on his shoulder, Daniel opened the cupboard above the refrigerator where the cookie sheets were stored. "Might as well get them all out," he said as she reached in and one-by-one handed them down.

Anthony took them from Rose and set them on the counter. James got out the teaspoons they'd use to put the dough on the baking sheets.

"We're going to set up an assembly line." Daniel said organizing the children around the kitchen island, making sure each had two spoons, and setting the bowl a little closer to Rose. "This isn't a contest it's an assembly line. What's the difference?" he asked giving James and Anthony a smile.

The boys puzzled looked showed him a few hints were needed.

"What happens in a contest?"

"You win, you get a prize," Anthony said, a smug look on his face, starting to spoon up cookie dough.

Daniel put his hand out to stop him. "That's right. In a contest, someone wins and gets a prize, but this *isn't* a contest, it's an assembly line."

"I don't get a prize if I win?" Rose asked.

"Everyone wins in an assembly line," Daniel said and patted her shoulder. "A great assembly line of cookie makers makes what?"

"Great cookies?" James asked.

"Yep," Daniel said. "Great cookies and that's the prize. So, what does a great oatmeal chocolate chip cookie look like? We know since your mom made the cookie dough, they will taste amazing, but what should they look like?"

"Is this like making a car or something?" Anthony asked. "Dad says you want to buy a car made at the factory during the week, not on Monday or Friday 'cause the line is—, well, he says the cars aren't as good then."

"Your dad is right," Daniel said. He saw Anthony's face light up, the smug smile back, and he wanted to add something to wipe that smile off his face but he didn't. Anthony was a kid desperate to have his dad notice him. He recognized the feeling having at times gotten lost in the bustle of his large family.

"Mom always makes them the same size and puts them the same space apart," James said and dipped a spoon in the batter. Using the second spoon he scraped the dough onto the sheet.

"That's the secret," Daniel said. "Same size, same spacing will give you the best assembly line cookies in town."

The evening wound down. Cookie baking assembly line style was a success. The kids helped set the table and cleared things off. Daniel, James and Anthony cleaned up the kitchen, loaded the dishwasher and wiped off the counters—assembly line style.

Rose's job was to see that her mother and Eleanor were settled in front of the television to watch Jeopardy and Wheel of Fortune, a plate of the greatest cookies of all time on the table in front of them. She also had to show Sophia into the living room when she arrived.

Seeing Sophia arrive empty-handed, he suspected she'd been tipped off by Eleanor. Another responsibility Rose had was to make sure the guys in the kitchen knew if the ladies wanted anything. She'd made a couple of trips to let them know everything was "hunky dory." She loved the old time phrase and had put her own spin on it by twirling as she said it.

Daniel didn't look forward to this coming week but he knew they were prepared. He'd take the kids to school. Eleanor would take her to her fifth chemo treatment. Between them all, Ashley and the kids would make it through another week. By next weekend, she'd be better and able to take care of herself and the kids with minimum support—until Monday and number six.

THERE'S BEING through it for almost two months, thinking you're prepared and then being hit with a sucker punch to the gut. For whatever reason, this treatment seemed to suck what little energy and life she had right out of her.

Daniel sat in the overstuffed chair in Ashley's room with her in his arms. The thought of her dying from the treatment to save her life, curdled his stomach. His arms tightened, holding her closer. The lemony scent she favored in her soap tweaked his nose. Nothing wafted from her hair—she didn't have any. Worry and doubt assailed him. Was it a mistake encouraging her to have her head shaved? Was it a mistake to have her move into his house? Was it a mistake to be here now, her thin body wrapped in blankets, trembling in his arms?

Eleanor stood in the doorway. "I am so glad you could come. I do not know what I would have done without...," emotion clogged her voice and she turned away.

"Glad I was close enough...," he started but his voice gave him away. When he'd got Eleanor's frantic call for help, he was fifteen to twenty minutes away. He'd made it here in ten long minutes grateful he didn't have a ticket for speeding because he'd certainly been doing that.

Pulling into the back parking area, seeing Ashley on the ground, Eleanor standing helplessly over her an umbrella in one hand a blanket to ward off the worst of the rain in the other. Just thinking about it brought the terror back full force. Heart pounding, muscles straining, he'd leapt from the cab and ran the few steps to the wet heap of life on the ground. She'd collapsed Eleanor had said and she couldn't rouse her or get her inside.

Bending down he'd slipped his arms under her shoulders and knees. He'd tightened his stomach muscles preparing to lift her—she weighed next to nothing. Was she even a hundred pounds?

In the house he'd banished Eleanor to the bathroom to take a hot shower and change into dry clothes. She had once she'd fixed a pot of hot tea and helped him get half a cup down Ashley, helped him get the worst of her wet clothes off, and helped him wrap her up and put a heating pad on her feet. He should put her to bed but the idea of letting her go—his arms tensed.

"Hunter is on her way. Once she is here, we will get her into something warmer and dryer," Eleanor said. "Do you mind? It could be another ten or fifteen minutes."

"I'm good," he said.

"She looks so at ease right now, relaxed and resting. On the ground she looked," her voice trailed off, a slight quaver at the end. "I do not know how to describe it exactly, but I could not get any response from her. I almost called 911 but then thought if you were close and we got her inside—indeed, we could call 911 now. What do you think?"

"Let's get Hunter's take. Right now it's like she's in a deep sleep. She stirs every few minutes, almost like when someone dreams."

"Shall we try a little more tea?"

"Maybe in a bit. I'm worried about her swallowing. She was semi-with us before. Right now, she's off somewhere."

ASHLEY FLOATED IN THE HAZE. The chill in the marrow of her bones lessened. In the distance the dragonflies' wings refracted the light. Their shimmery sparkle beckoned. A part of her knew she should follow them but she was cold and every bone in her body ached. She snuggled into the heat and scent of woodchips that surrounded her. The dragonflies danced, their dazzling iridescence lured.

Indistinct voices called to her through the haze. She was a rag doll being pulled one way and pushed another. Something was pressed to her lips. *What?* More muffled sounds, the pressure on her lips ceased. Where was the heat, the woodchip scent, rest, safety? She tried to find it but in the haze, everything blurred.

A hum in her ear, sound but no words. The woodchip scent enveloped her. She snuggled into the heat as the haze thickened. The dragonflies were gone.

23 - IS IT TIME TO BE THANKFUL YET?

"Only three more treatments, Ashley," Lily said leaning over her friend. So distracted by her other commitments, it had taken Lily several days after returning from Ireland and the trip to Arizona with her husband before she realized how bad Ashley was. She'd checked in every day but Eleanor and Daniel had assured her everything was under control. Now she knew they were putting a positive spin on things.

Lily turned to Sophia and said, "What's your schedule look like?"

"I'm good until next week. Talked to my principal early in the month and got his okay to do it a bit different this year. I've been calling and talking to parents all month, inviting them to meet with me before or after school, and I'll have a flyer on my space telling parents they can reach me by phone and schedule a time to meet in person if they prefer. I may have to dash out, but I think it's covered."

Ashley wasn't rebounding from the chemo treatment on Monday. They'd made an emergency visit to her doctor to see what could be done. An IV later, the nurse wheeled Ashley out to the front where Sophia's car waited and helped her in. Lily fastened her seat belt and covered her circle sister with a blanket before getting into the passenger seat.

Grim-faced, the two women spoke in low tones on the drive back to the house. The engine wasn't even off before Daniel pulled in behind them. He left the motor running as he hopped out and strode to Sophia's car. Opening the door, he reached in and with a gentleness usually reserved for newborns, he picked Ashley up and carried her into the house. Lily jogged ahead and opened the door. Sophia followed carrying purses and bags.

Daniel gingerly placed Ashley on her bed and tucked three blankets around her; a heating pad snuggled her feet.

"Try and get something down her now while she's somewhat awake." Daniel stood in the doorway, his eyes on the still figure on the bed. "She needs something to drink at least before she drifts off."

"She had a bag of IV at the doctor's," Lily said smoothing a hand over Ashley's shoulder.

The sounds of water running and pots or pans clanking meant Sophia was already busy in the kitchen.

"Eleanor would not approve because this is barely tea," Sophia said as she rounded the end of the bed. Climbing on, she slipped her arm behind Ashley's shoulders and eased her up.

Lily matched her stance from the other side and together they sat Ashley up. While Sophia held the cup to Ash's lips, Lily stroked her cheek saying, "Drink, Ashley. You've got to get your strength back." Seeing a little of the liquid disappear and Ashley's neck move as she swallowed, Lily urged another and another. Half the cup was gone, nowhere near enough for her to build her strength up.

"What about broth?" Lily asked Sophia.

"I've some heating on the stove. Can you manage here while I get it?"

Lily nodded, shifting to take Ashley's full weight against her arm. "You need to sit up, Ash. Can you move your arms for me?"

Tears welled in Lily's eyes when she realized there was no response.

Sophia returned with the broth and they went through the same process as they had with the tea except this time, after two swallows, the liquid dribble out the side of Ashley's mouth.

They leaned her forward to make sure no broth remained to aspirate her when they laid her back down. An extra precaution: placing her on her side surrounded by pillows and blankets for support.

"I am thankful I thought ahead and had her sign medical power-of-attorney papers so I can talk to her doctors," Lily said in firming voice. "What happened? How did things get so bad?" she asked Sophia when they were in the kitchen.

"I'm not sure anyone knows why she is having such a hard time now." Sophia poured two cups of tea and put out a plate of cookies. "I'll fix something more substantial in a bit, right now I need comfort food."

"I saw her last weekend and she was doing so well...," Lily's voice drifted off as tears threatened. "How could I... ?" She shook her head in disbelief at the reality facing her. "She might not make it, Soph. She's so weak and she drifts off. She's not "here.""

"I know but maybe she needs to be there, wherever that is, to heal?"

"She isn't holding her own. She's losing ground every day." Lily paced around the kitchen island.

WHERE DOES SHE GO? Lily stood in the doorway to Ashley's bedroom, watching her circle sister. In the ten minutes she'd been there, Ashley had not moved. The doctor's office had called in a prescription for vitamins and Sophia had gone to pick them and a few groceries up. *Thank goodness Soph is here with me. We'd be out of milk and bread before I noticed.*

The clock in the hall struck the hour. The children would be home in thirty minutes or so. The after school plan changed when Ashley wasn't better over the weekend. Rose went to a dance class at Hunter's and James and Anthony were with Matthew on one of his work sites.

Lily returned to the kitchen and fetched a mug of broth. Back in the bedroom, she climbed on the bed to be in a better position to help Ashley into a sitting position. What she and Sophia had discovered was they could put the mug on the night stand and still reach it from the bed. It was awkward but doable.

"Come on, Ash," Lily coaxed. "Sit up just a little more." She stuffed another pillow behind Ashley and as she levered her up another few inches, another pillow followed the first. Once Ash was in a safe position to swallow, Lily held the cup of broth to her lips.

"Time to swallow, Ash. Ash? Come on, Ashley. A little sip is all you need to do right now," Lily continued to encourage Ashley to take a little liquid and swallow again and again. She and Sophia learned to keep towels and a wet washcloth handy as every sip did not get swallowed.

Children's voices announced their arrival. Lily sat back and looked at the mug in her hand. She'd measured in one half cup and it was gone but at least half was on the towel draped around Ashley's neck. *So far we've got about one cup down her. As a last resort we can consider tube feeding.* Lily shuddered at the thought and moved away from the bed taking the towels and washcloth with her.

"Mom, mom," Rose's voice piped over the grumbling of her brothers. "Guess what, Mom?" She scrambled up on the bed, grasped her mother's face, turned it toward her, and spoke. "I did really good with Hunter, Mom. She said I have a dancer's heart." She bounced off the bed and twirled. "See what I can do?"

"Very nice," Lily praised Rose. "I can see Hunter was right. You do have a dancer's heart."

"But Mom…," Rose started.

"Your Mom is seeing you do your twirls in her head. It's called imagination." Lily gave Rose a kiss on her cheek.

"What's that word mean?"

"Imagination is what you use when you draw a picture of something you don't really know, or tell a story and make up people and things they say and do."

"Like Gabby?"

Lily laughed. "Yes, Gabby has a great imagination, and so do you. I've heard you tell your mom lots of stories."

"She used to like my stories," Rose said, sadness in her voice, her face downcast.

"She still likes them. She's just too sick to tell you she does."

"Eleanor said Mom can still hear me, can she?"

"I think she can," Lily said, blinking back tears. "She loves you very much, Rose. I'm sure she listens to you."

After dinner, Lily took Sophia aside. "I've talked to Jackson and the plan is I'm spending the night. You get the bedroom upstairs. I'm sleeping in Ashley's room. I want to see if maybe she's got her nights and days mixed up."

"She's got to be doing some better," Sophia said her voice pitched so the children who'd just charged into the kitchen didn't hear. "We got over a cup of broth and two doses of vitamins down her"

"And I heard her stomach growl the last time we gave her something. If that part of her body is waking up, remembering its purposes, that is a hopeful sign."

~

"How much sleep did you get?" Sophia asked Lily as she shuffled into the kitchen.

"More than I might have and less than I needed," Lily yawned as she answered. "I kept waking up and checking Ash, but I don't think she moved all night. I'm just grateful she roused enough to use the bathroom before you went to bed. Wish we could have really talked to her then."

"I know, all we got was some mumbled answer to our questions. Very frustrating. Do you think we should consider those adult diapers?"

"I'm more optimistic because a part of her feels the need to urinate and knows she needs to get up, so I'd hate to discourage that. What we want is to encourage her doing more. My goal is to get enough fluids into her that she'll need to use the bathroom and maybe then we can talk to her."

They'd decided to catch each other up and discuss plans outside of

Ashley's hearing. The hearing was the last of the senses to shut down when people died, so it made sense that Ashley could still hear people but whether she understood and processed the words was a different matter.

"How are plans coming along for Thanksgiving?" Lily asked. "It's just two days away."

"Diana has permission to come but will have to keep her feet up most of the time. She and Matthew are bringing pasta and a tossed green salad. Daniel is delivering a thirty pound turkey this afternoon and I've got the makings for stuffing. Gabriella is snacks—healthy and not-so-healthy she said. Hunter and Logan are bringing yams and mashed potatoes. I've got pies to make—a pumpkin, apple, and cherry. Jackson insists on bringing a mincemeat pie with a brandy hard sauce and Eleanor is bringing a plum pudding. Oh, and Jackson is bringing two quarts of his vanilla bean ice cream," Sophia rattled the information off.

"It would be wonderful if Elizabeth and Michael were here," Lily said wistfulness in her voice. "I love going to Ireland and spending time with The Lady, doing ceremony in the sacred grove, but—," she paused and sighed. "Now isn't the time to talk about that. Now is the time to concentrate on Ashley. I'm going to check on her and see if I can get another half a cup of broth down her."

Matthew had picked Rose up from Hunter's dance studio. The children were having dinner with Diana and him. It would be take out because Matthew was the cook of the day. Lily was certain the kids would badger him for hamburgers, fries and milk shakes; he'd counter with an argument for Mexican. He'd bring them home around nine. No school tomorrow. They could sleep in, he'd reasoned.

How did I ever manage handling everything without him? She missed Jackson right now. Part of it was because she was so worried about Ashley. The signs were not good. She had been unable to awaken her enough to talk to her. Even when taking her to the bathroom, which was a stupor-stumbling trip, Ash had only mumbled in response to her questions. *If it isn't working, try something else. That's my mantra when working with clients.*

Lily pulled the layers of blankets off Ashley and turned off the heating pad. *She's so thin.* Tears pooled but she blinked them back. Hands fisted on her hips, she surveyed her circle sister. *Did she just move?*

Backing to the doorway, Lily kept her eyes on Ashley. "Soph? Come here, please."

"Wha...," Sophia stopped mid-word.

"Look." Lily pointed to the bed. "She's moving."

"She's cold," Sophia said.

"I know. And she doesn't like it. She's trying to get warm but she can't unless she opens her eyes to see where the blankets are," Lily's quiet voice was audible in the room.

A buzzer sounded from the kitchen.

"I've got pies in the oven." Sophia hugged Lily. "Good job."

When Lily saw Ashley's hand pat the bed, she rejoiced. *She's trying to find the blankets. Instead she's going to find me.* Lily grasped Ashley's hand and gently rubbed its back.

"Ash, you need to listen to me," she said in a quiet but authoritative voice. "I know this is hard for you, but you are a fighter, Ash. You've been through this before and come out a winner. You can do it this time, too. We're all here with you on this fight, Ash. But we can't fight for you.

"You've apart in this battle if you are going to win the war. The Circle—Elizabeth, Diana, Hunter, Gabriella, Sophia, and I need you to win. You have so many people who love you—Eleanor, Matthew, Michael, Daniel—they need you to win. But first and foremost, your kids—James, Anthony, and Rose need you to win. If you can hear me, let me know. You can open your eyes, say something, or even just squeeze my hand."

24 - A THANKFUL THANKSGIVING

Voices called but the haze held Ashley trapped. Cold permeated her marrow and shivers wracked her body. A spot of warmth touched her hand, a place to start.

Ashley held on to the spot. It spread up her arm and back down. Voices. One voice called her name. She knew that voice but in the haze that engulfed her no name came to mind. Another voice she knew. Another spot of warmth: this one on her shoulder.

Names. The voices were saying names. Her name. Anthony's name. Who was James? Who was Rose? Was she supposed to know them?

More voices. Another spot of warmth on her ankle. Small spots on her cheeks and more voices, different voices. Somewhere in the haze she struggled to recognize them, to put a name to the sound.

Strong arms lifted her and heat flared against her softness. The sense of loss when she was settled back on the bed profound.

Gone. All the spots were gone. All the warmth was gone. The cold claimed her, the haze deepened.

Voices.

Warmth. Spots of heat rubbed up and down her arms, held her ankles and massaged her feet. The haze lightened. In the distance she saw the dragonflies. *Where have they been? Why don't they help me?* The flickering iridescence of their wings called to her. Tears spilled down her cheeks.

A warm soft cloth wiped them away.

The haze lifted. The dragonflies flitted in the sunlight. Ashley struggled against the pull of the haze, struggled to follow the dragonflies, struggled to find the heat her body craved.

Voices called to her.

Lily and Sophia's and Daniel and her children's voices were talking to her. *What are they saying?*

Her eyelids were frozen shut.

Small hot hands touched her cheeks, warm lips kissed her nose. *Amanda. That's our game.*

"Lily?"

"Yes?"

"My mom's better. Her nose is warm."

Hands caressed her face, brushed against her nose. "You're right, her nose is warm."

"I'm going to stay right here until she opens her eyes."

Heat snuggled against her side, a small hand rested on her chest. "I'm right here, Mom," her daughter said.

The dragonflies darted, encircling her.

A cup at her lips, warm liquid in her mouth. She swallowed and opened her mouth for more.

"The Goddess is good," a voice she knew said.

The cup was back offering more. She swallowed, the broth warming her from the inside out.

"Our prayers are answered," another voice said.

"Come on kids, let's let Lily and Sophia take care of your mom," the male voice said.

Who?

"Daniel, they need to stay. She seems to be listening now."

Pats on her ankle helped spread the warmth. Tickles on the soles of her feet—she tried to pull them away, didn't she?

"Mom's feet are ticklish," Anthony was saying. "She's getting awake now because the last time we tried it, she didn't move at all."

The dragonflies flew closer, the vibration of their wings thawing her eyelids. They fluttered open.

Amanda's face was closest but at the foot of the bed, Artie and Anthony watched her with expectant looks on their faces. Daniel was next to Artie, a look of relief on his face. She turned her head and saw Lily and Sophia. Sophia's eyes glistened with unshed tears. Lily's face shone with triumph.

"Welcome back," Lily said, bending over to look Ashley in the eyes.

"Where was I?" Ashley asked.

"We don't know. But we are very glad you're back with us," Sophia said, pulling blankets up and tucking them around Ashley and Rose.

"You've been really sick, Mom," Anthony said. "Scary sick. Dad— ow!" He rubbed his arm where James had punched him.

"Boys, that's enough. Your mom doesn't need your bickering and fighting," Daniel said as he laid a hand on each boy's shoulder. He looked over at Lily and Sophia, "I can take these guys out so she can rest if you think that'd be better."

"How about thirty minutes and then check back in."

"We'll go get pizza for dinner."

"Matthew is bringing Mexican take-out. He dropped us off first because he had a work thing to do before he got dinner," Artie said.

"Okay, but we're leaving your mom to rest for a bit anyway. James, Anthony, Rose – you, too." Daniel gestured towards the door.

James, Rose? Dragonflies flashed in the sunlight and the memory of her children wanting to change their names was clear. *Not Artie but James, not Amanda but Rose. How could I have forgotten that?*

Rose slipped from her side, tucked the covers close, and bounced off the bed. The sound of her footsteps racing after Daniel brought comfort.

"Y'all have been real worried about me, haven't you?" Her voice sounded funny, like her throat was coated in rust.

"We have," Lily said, perching on the side of the bed. "You've been out of it, Ash. Non-responsive. You haven't been eating, you've lost more weight and you didn't have any extra to lose."

"Lots of little meals, Ash. A few bits every hour and you'll build your strength up quickly. You're a fighter," Sophia emphasized. "Those children need their mother, they need you!"

"Can you tell us what happened?" Lily scooted to the end of the bed using the footboard for support.

Sophia pulled the chair closer. "We'd like to know so we can help if it happens again."

"I heard voices some time but … fog or haze, sometimes lighter and sometimes darker. So tired, so cold – but tired most of all. My dragonflies tried to lead me out of it but … just too tired," Ashley's voice faded, her eyes closed. "Rest."

"Rest is good, Ash, but the fog and haze is bad. You can't go back there. Your kids need you to stay with us," Lily said massaging a foot through the blanket.

Ashley nodded. "Feels good," she mumbled.

Sophia pushed the chair back. "I'll fix something for her to eat and be back."

"Sounds good," Lily replied. "Now, Ash, I want you to listen to me. Keep your eyes closed, but your ears open, okay?"

A slight nod from Ashley signaled she could go one.

"Focus on my hand. Do you feel it?"

Another nod.

"Concentrate on where I'm touching you." Lily moved her hand from Ashley foot to her ankle and then rested it on her shin. A few minutes later, she moved it again to the other leg. When Sophia came back and held Ashley's hand, Lily let go. Ashley nodded when asked about Sophia's touch and also squeezed her hand.

Thumbs up they signaled to each other and settled in to trade off physical connection with their circle sister.

After dinner the decision as to how to handle Ashley's need for physical contact through the night was solved when Rose announced she was sleeping with her mom. She'd already changed into her pajamas and brushed her hair and teeth—all by herself she'd informed everyone.

After tucking Rose and Ashley in for the night and giving Rose instructions to come and get one of them if her mom needed to get up to go to the bathroom, Sophia and Lily sat in the kitchen another cup of tea in hand.

"I think you need to go home to Jackson," Sophia said.

"He understands," Lily replied. "And I'd just toss and turn and worry. At least here I'll know what's happening. If she's still making some progress tomorrow, I will spend tomorrow night at home."

"Wherever did you get the idea to take her blankets off?"

"It just came to me that if she was comfortable wherever she was, she wouldn't come back to us. I thought it was worth a try. If she hadn't started to respond, I would have wrapped her in a warm blanket after thirty minutes."

"You amaze me with your creativity," Sophia said.

"This may be my area of creativity but yours is in the classroom," Lily responded.

"What would we have done today without Daniel?" Sophia took her cup to the sink, rinsed it and put it in the dishwasher. Taking Lily's cup from her she added it. "Needs to be run tonight," she commented before asking, "How long do you think he's been in love with her?"

"It was love at first sight with the children. I know he was attracted to her but he wouldn't act on it because she was married."

"I remember seeing him with the children last year in Ireland and remarking, I think to Gabby, that I didn't understand why he wasn't married. He sure is father material and most men who are father material make pretty good husbands." Sophia put the soap in the dispenser, shut the door and turned the dishwasher on. The quiet hum in background followed them down the hall and to the stairs.

"Her divorce should be final before the first of the year. No contest except for the whole custody thing," Lily said as they started up the wide staircase.

"I don't know what to make of Art," Sophia commented is a quiet voice. "The children don't seem to mind spending time with him anymore."

"There's a big difference between that and wanting to live with him. Other than Anthony, I don't see either James or Rose in that space. They'd be happier here with their mother or off with Daniel or Matthew—maybe even hanging out with Jackson if he had a hammer and nails." Lily put her hand up to muffle her laugh. "He's planning on spending some time doing just that, said he missed the hammer and nails part of building, that it's been too long since he worked up a sweat."

HANDS IN DISHWATER LILY REMEMBERED, was Diana's mother's cure-all. Two years last month she'd met Eleanor and subsequently Jackson. He materialized behind her, hands tugging her away from the sink. His lips nibbled her neck and the desire he effortless drew from her flared. "Ashley seems much better. Hope that means you're coming home with me tonight." His breath heated the skin behind her ear.

"I may be here all night cleaning up the kitchen if you keep interrupting," she said in a breathless voice. "Jackson," she said exasperated now. "Do something useful if you want me to come home tonight."

Jackson grabbed a sponge and began to wipe off the kitchen island counter.

Lily finished washing the sterling silver and picked up a dishtowel to dry it before setting it on the table. Her mother always said "leave the good silver out overnight" to make sure it was really dry. *Where do these traditions come from?*

Rose pranced into the kitchen, ready for bed. She expected to spend another night with her mom. While Lily didn't think that necessarily wise, it needed to be Ashley's decision.

Shepherding the youngster into the bedroom, she silently asked the question with raised eyebrows.

"One more night is all, do you hear?" Ashley said pulling back the covers so Rose could scoot under.

"You might—,"

"One more night is all," Ashley repeated.

"Okay." Rose snuggled down next to her mom, eyes closed she feigned sleep.

"Good night you two. I'll see you in the morning," Lily said. "And, Rose? Sophia is in the guest room if your mom needs to get up during the night, okay?"

Ashley cuddled her daughter close. "She heard you, at least I think she did," Ashley said with laughter in her voice.

A squeal followed by a giggle erupted from the bed. "Mom, you tickled me."

"Did I? I thought it was the boogeyman because you didn't answer Lily."

"I heard you, Lily," Rose said, a real yawn claimed her. "I love you, Mom."

"I love you, too, baby."

"I'm not a baby," Rose said a pout in her voice. "I'm a big girl. I can do lots of things. Tomorrow I'll show you."

Lily smiled as Ashley rearranged the blankets covering her daughter. *The gifts of the Goddess... .* She turned down the hall and stopped at the living room entrance. "They're doing just fine, Soph. Sleep well. I'll be back in the morning."

His heat and citrus scent announced his arrival. He held her coat open for her. As she slipped it on, he smoothed it over her shoulders, his touch lingering on her upper arms. A gentle tug and she leaned back against his strength. His arms encircled her. *Oh how I wish every one of my circle sisters could find the love I have with Jackson and that Elizabeth and Diana have with Michael and Matthew.*

"I've got the cell phone and charger," James said. "You don't have to worry, I know what to do. Matthew and Daniel have talked to me too." He patted one arm of the sweatshirt tied around his neck. Knowing he had a way to contact Ms. Muir, Lily, Daniel, Matthew or the other people programmed into the phone didn't ease the anxiety he felt at the change in this visit.

Lily hugged him tight. "I know you do." She stepped back and brushed a lock of hair from his forehead. "See you tomorrow."

"See you tomorrow," James said. "Come on," he called to his brother and sister. "Ms. Muir is waiting for us."

Rose took her brother's hand as they went down the steps. Anthony, who'd raced ahead, was already in her car.

"It'll be okay, Rose. I promise. I'll be there the whole time."

~

"Where are we going, Dad?" James asked as they headed onto the freeway.

"It's a surprise," Art answered. "A big surprise. A really really big surprise."

"But—"

"If I tell you, it won't be a surprise," Art snapped and turned the radio on.

James rubbed his stomach where a very bad feeling settled. Ms. Muir and Lily had explained that the judge had said they'd spend the night at Art's because it was Thanksgiving. And Ms. Muir wouldn't be with them because Art'd been a good dad during the supervised visits. James glanced in the backseat where Anthony sat, an angry look on his face and wondered how his sister was doing. The car sped along the freeway. They were past Salem now and still going. When he saw the Rest Area sign, he had an idea.

"Dad, I've gotta go. Can we stop at the rest area?"

"I gotta go too," Rose piped up.

"I don't," Anthony said.

"Make it quick. We don't want to be late for your surprise," Art said, pulling into the rest area. "You go on, Amanda, meet you here in a minute. Come on boys." Art went with the boys into the bathroom.

Upon exiting the rest room, Amanda was nowhere in sight.

"Come on boys," Art said. "Let's get going."

"But Rose?" James started and stopped, the bad feeling intensifying. He'd hoped to use the phone. Ms. Muir told him she'd come pick them up even in the middle of the night if there was a problem. But with Art watching him the whole time he never got the chance. "I mean Amanda, isn't here."

"Gotta be quick or get left behind," Art said opening the car doors. "Now get in."

"I want to sit in front this time," Anthony said, a tinge of whine in his words.

"Fine by me," James said, looking towards the women's rest room. *Come on Rose, please hurry.*

"Artie is sitting in front."

"It's okay by me if Anthony sits up there. I'm good with sitting in the back with Rose, I mean Amanda. I'm going to check on her," James said and started towards the building.

"Get back here, now," Art ordered.

No threat I'll be left behind. And if he does, I'll call someone to come and get Rose and me.

"Is there a little girl in there?" he asked a lady coming out.

"Why yes there is. She's crying but won't tell anyone what's wrong."

"Would you tell her James is waiting just outside the door?"

"Of course. Is there anything wrong?"

James looked back towards the car and shook his head. Nothing felt right but he didn't have words to explain. With Anthony wanting to be with Art, he worried that any adult he tried to talk to would figure it was just a family squabble.

"Let's go." James grabbed Rose's hand and tugged her towards the car. He shoved her in the backseat and climbed in after her.

A smirk on his face, Anthony got in front.

It was dark and the clock on the dashboard read eleven when they pulled into a motel parking lot somewhere in California. Where they were, James didn't know because he'd fallen asleep a few hours ago.

His Dad left Rose asleep in the car but insisted he and Anthony go with him when he registered. Once they crossed the border into California, the bad feeling like being sick got worse.

There was no way they'd be back in Fremont for Ms. Muir to pick them up at noon. What had happened was beginning to make sense: Art telling Ms. Muir he was taking them out to eat but instead of a restaurant, they'd driven a couple of blocks away. Art telling them to put their backpacks in this SUV. Art cruising around another five minutes or so and then pulling back into the driveway.

The bad feeling swelled when they didn't go into the house. Art wouldn't let them say 'hi' to their puppy, Bingo, even though she barked and scratched the door when she heard their voices.

Talking about going on an adventure, Art'd led them out the back gate and down the alley until they reached the street where this vehicle was parked.

Of course Anthony was excited.

Rose became quieter and quieter.

And he, well he just felt a darkness creeping around him. It reminded him of a new word he'd learned in school "foreboding". That was how he felt. Something bad was going to happen but he didn't know what or when. If he could only figure out a way to use the phone and not get caught he could call and get Rose and him some help.

Anthony? His younger brother wanted to be with Art. If he wanted to come with Rose and him, okay but he knew Anthony would tell Art about the cell phone if he remembered there was one and knew where it was.

They were up and in the car at six. Now he was certain Art had kidnapped them and no one knew where they were.

Art refused to let him sit in back. Rose was sitting behind Art and Anthony behind him. When he glanced back, he'd seen Anthony's hand poke and pinch Rose. She had scooted as far away as possible. He caught her eye at one point, saw the tears and fears and knew it was up to him to do something.

"Dad," James said in a choked voice. "I'm hungry. Are we going to stop for lunch?"

"You had breakfast three hours ago. It'll have to do."

"Well, I also have to pee and I'm tired. If I sit in the backseat, I can stretch out and sleep."

"I'll ride up front with you, Dad," Anthony said his eagerness evident. "I'm not tired."

"Maybe at the next rest area?" James added with a hint of pleading. He'd noticed Rose had her legs crossed and was fidgeting as if she had to go too.

Art put the blinker on and pulled to the side of the road. Cars sped past and the SUV shuddered when a large semi rushed by.

"Get out and go here," Art ordered.

"But—"

"If you have to go that bad, then get out and go here."

James opened the door and slid out.

"Anthony, Rose get out and stretch. If you stand with your back to me, all the people in their cars won't see me."

As soon as Anthony opened the door and got out, Rose was standing next to James.

He bent down and whispered in Rose's ear, "I'll help you as best I can."

She nodded and turned her back to James.

He and Anthony stood side-by-side and peed into the grass on the side of the road. As soon as they'd tucked themselves back in their pants, Art ordered them back in the car.

Rose's frantic look and tear-filled eyes jarred him into action. He grabbed his sweatshirt off the floor, the cell phone still inside the sleeve where he'd tucked it before leaving the house.

"We'll be okay, Rose," he said as he stepped away from the car.

"I said get in the car now!" Art yelled.

"Rose has to go too," James said. "Anthony, why don't you get in front and as soon as Rose is done, we'll climb in back."

Anthony sprang into the front seat. "It's okay, Dad. I'm here."

"I'm going to leave," Art threatened and inched the car forward a few feet.

James didn't budge, his hand on Rose's shoulder, he guided her to the back of the car. Holding his sweatshirt out to shield her as best he could, he helped Rose take off her pants and panties.

"I can't wipe myself and pee dribbled down my legs," Rose said choking back a sob.

"I know. You'll just have to wipe yourself off with your panties and then put your pants on. If Art makes us do this again, we'll be prepared and have tissue or something."

Rose stepped away from the puddle she'd made and wiped her legs with her panties. "You think he'll do this again?" she asked, her quavery voice now held a note of hysteria.

"I don't know. I never thought he'd do anything like this now."

"He's taking us away somewhere, isn't he?" Rose asked as she pulled her pants up.

"Yeah, he is." James put his arm around his sister. "You can throw those panties away if you want—or not. It's up to you."

"They smell like pee. I'm leaving them here."

James helped Rose up, saw that she was buckled in before settling himself in his seat. After he put his seat belt on, he closed the car door. "We're ready to go back here," he said. *I know now he won't leave me, I don't think he'll leave Anthony, but I'm afraid he will leave Rose.*

Without looking at the clock, James knew when it was noon. Art changed. He ordered his sister to get down on the floor and stay out of sight.

James whispered he'd protect her.

Art heard him and threatened to stop and leave her by the road.

Rose curled into a ball and started sucking her thumb.

A block of ice lodged in his stomach and James thought he'd puked.

Anthony, for once, said nothing.

Early afternoon they crossed into Arizona. The desert landscape was fascinating and yet the idea that Rose could be left on the side of the road horrified him. A few hours after Art ordered Rose to stay down on the floor, James unfastened his seat belt and scooted down, sort of curled around her. She shivered as if she'd been wrapped in ice.

Art yelled at him to get back up and put his seat belt on.

James refused. He had his sweatshirt across his shoulders the weight of the cell phone reassuring. What would Art do if he found it? Throw Rose out, tie him up? By now, James' imagination ran rampant with what Art would do if he found the phone.

People were now looking for them. James prayed for the opportunity to make a call. But he didn't even know where they were or if there was coverage. It was too risky to take the phone out and check.

Art pulled to the side of the road to make his threat more real. James didn't budge and said, "Unless Rose can be on the seat also, I'll stay right here." His insides churned with fear and vomit rose in his throat.

"Rose and I can get out," he threatened and crossed his fingers there was cell phone coverage out here in the dessert.

That threat seemed to turn things around. At least Art said Rose could be up on the seat but she had to have a blanket over her and he couldn't talk to her.

New Mexico. It was dark but the sign was lighted. "Welcome to New Mexico". They'd left California and crossed Arizona during the day. Now they only stopped for gas and to use the rest rooms. Art never let him out of his sight. At first when James was careful to include Rose in the process of using the facilities, Art was upset. He relented when he saw people looking at him and then the children. James knew the last thing he wanted was to draw attention to them.

Food came from fast food restaurants' drive through windows. Art never ordered food for Rose but James felt sick enough it was easy to share with her.

Tonight they stopped at a motel connected to a truck stop and restaurant. Art pulled the SUV into a spot between the two buildings. He grabbed James from the back seat and hauled him across the lot to register. No sign of Anthony or Rose this time.

When everyone was asleep, James slipped the cell phone from his sweatshirt sleeve and tucked it in the bottom of Rose's backpack. He didn't try to call because he worried Art would hear him. Why did he move the cell to Rose's backpack? Tonight Art had been really nice to Rose, got her hot chocolate and a cheeseburger. James was even more certain Art planned on leaving her here.

Rough hands shaking him, roused James from a deep yet fitful sleep. *Where am I?* He scrubbed his eyes, opened them as he was jerked to his feet. "Come on," Art said in an urgent yet quiet voice. "We need to get some breakfast and get going."

"What about Amanda?" James thanked his still waking brain for remembering to call his sister by that name.

"She's sound asleep. Sleeps good for her. We'll order food and she can eat it when we're on the way."

Anthony was by the door, holding both their backpacks in hand, waiting for the signal to go.

His sister was deep asleep, her backpack next to her.

The sick feeling swallowed him up and he choked on bile. "I don't think I can eat anything. I don't feel so good. I'll just stay here and when she wakes up we'll come over to the restaurant."

"She can read. We'll leave her a note," Art scribbled something on the pad of paper by the motel phone. "Come along now," Art ordered, dragging him across the room. "We need to get on the road soon." He paused at the door and smiled. "Just anxious to get on the road and I want us all to have a good breakfast. This place has a reputation for great food."

With a last look at his sister, James went along with Art.

DORIE JUDD WATCHED the man and two young boys come into her restaurant. Something wasn't right but she wasn't sure what it was.

"I'll take that table," she said to Pammy. Pad and pencil in hand she approached the booth as the man scooted in next to the older boy.

"What can I get you boys today?" Dorie gave the man her best welcoming smile and made a point not to look at the boys.

"Got to look at the menu first." the man said.

"What about coffee or hot chocolate?" She did look at the boys when she said the last. The older one looked sick and the younger looked excited.

"Please, can we please, Dad," the younger one said.

The dad looked at the older boy, a question arching his left brow.

"Not for me," the boy said. "I mean, no, thank you, ma'am."

"One coffee and one hot chocolate," Dorie said with pencil poised over the order pad.

The man nodded.

"Coming right up."

After serving the coffee and hot chocolate, Dorie stayed behind the counter as the man and younger boy looked over the menu. *Definitely something wrong.* She punched a button on her cell phone and said, "Time for a coffee break." and hung up.

"Looks like two of you are hungry for sure," Dorie chatted as she took two orders. "What about you, young man?"

"He isn't feeling well," the man said.

"Well, I've got a few things here that might help that," Dorie said. "Car sickness is something we deal with all the time around here. Not too many places along this stretch of road to get out and stretch your legs, get some fresh air, and just be still—stop that whirring inside."

The older boy looked miserable as if he was going to cry or vomit or both. "Think about it. Let me get your order in and you can let me know." As she turned away she caught a glimpse of the man jabbing the boy in the ribs with his elbow and saying something. From the look on his face and the way the boy flinched, it wasn't pleasant.

Her cook nodded towards the back and Dorie made her way down the short hall to her office area. Strong arms pulled her aside and familiar lips claimed hers. "Now Dutch," Dorie laughed. "That isn't what I meant when I said it was time for a coffee break."

"What's going on?" Dutch Judd asked, tucking his shirt into his pants and arranging his holster.

"I think we've got a problem," Dorie said, patting her husband's uniform covered chest. "Just wait back here and I'll see if I can get the boy away from this man. I don't know if he is his dad although the younger one called him that."

"I can just go in and ask for identification and stuff."

"Let me try this first."

"Not a problem.

~

JAMES SAT WAITING for the waitress to come back. Her name tag said 'Dorie' and she seemed nice, someone who would see that Rose was okay. He didn't want Art to go to jail. Or at least he didn't think he did. And Anthony? Anthony would hate him forever. When they moved out of Daniel's house they'd be sharing a room and if Anthony hated him that would be really bad.

Dorie returned with Art and Anthony's plates. It looked good but his stomach churned. His hand flew to his mouth as he started to puke.

Wild-eyed, he looked around for some way not to embarrass himself by vomiting all over the table. Paper napkins were thrust in his hand.

"Excuse me, sir, I think the boy is going to be sick," Dorie said to Art.

"What the hell?" Art glared at him. "Stop!" he ordered.

The first convulsion stabbed through him most of it caught in the napkins in his hand.

"Damm it, Artie, I said stop it!" Art surged out of his seat and grabbed for James.

Dorie was issuing orders and people were bustling around.

"Sir, I've got an order in for fresh food. Come along now and let's get you and your son seated at a clean table."

Another waitress approached. "Right this way sir," she said and herded Art and Anthony away.

Dorie leaned in and put her arm around James' shoulder. "Let's get you cleaned up and that stomach settled."

"I'm okay now. I just need to use the rest room."

"Just along that hall," she directed. "Is this yours?" She pointed to the backpack.

He nodded and she handed it to him.

The busboy came up and started clearing and cleaning the table. She breathed in the reassuring odor of disinfectant. Turning back to the counter, she saw the man giving the waitress a hard time as she stood to the side of the booth blocking his exit.

"How can I help, sir," Dorie said, motioning the other waitress away.

"Where's my boy?" Art demanded, standing up and looking around.

"I believe he's in the men's room, washing up and maybe changing his clothes," Dorie said in a steady voice. "Of course there's no extra charge so there's nothing to worry about." She flashed him her best "everything's just fine" smile but he started past her towards the hall to the rest rooms. Turning back to the younger boy she said, "Hi, my name's Dorie. What's yours?" She slid into the seat just vacated by the father, glanced up and smiled her 'thanks' when a fresh cup of hot chocolate was set in front of him.

"Not supposed to talk to strangers," he mumbled.

"Good rule but after what just happened, do you think we're really strangers?"

"Anthony."

"Glad to meet you, Anthony. Long trips can be hard on parents and that makes them hard on kids." She let the statement hang in the air. "You enjoy that chocolate. I'm going to check on your brother and dad."

The shouting began as she stood. Anthony bolted from the booth and darted through the tables to the hall. Dorie followed but at a more leisurely pace.

At the hallway entrance, Dorie stopped and took in the scene before her. Dutch had the father up against the wall his right arm twisted up behind him.

Anthony stood frozen for a second before launching himself at Dutch. Before she had a chance to move, the older boy hollered and tried to yank Anthony off.

Dorie whistled an ear splitting sharp sound.

"Let's take this into the back room. You're disturbing my customers."

James looked over at Dorie and nodded. He let go of Anthony and stepped back. Anthony still clung to Dutch's arm hoping to free his dad.

"Come along, Anthony," Dorie said and gently placed her arm on his shoulder. "Your dad just needs to stop fighting the sheriff and then we can talk this over and sort things out. You can't get on with your trip until things are sorted out."

Dutch's threat of handcuffs stopped Art's struggling. Reluctantly Art preceded the sheriff into the room.

"I want Rose," James blurted out as soon as they were in the back room.

"Your mom?" Dutch asked.

"My sister."

"Where is she?"

"At the motel. I want Rose and I want to go home. I don't want to see Art's surprise."

"The motel next door?"

James nodded. "I don't know the room number but it was on the ground floor. Please, if she woke up she's scared."

"Mr. Kenner?" Dutch stood, arms folded across his chest, feet spread should wide.

Art sat, a defiant look on his face, and said nothing.

"Have it your way," Dutch said.

"We can check with Hiram about the room number," Dorie added.

"Art didn't register all of us." James said, wringing his hands and biting his lower lip.

Dutch looked at Art who glared back. "Not a problem. We'll figure it out."

"They're my kids and I have every right to have them with me," Art accused. "I've done nothing wrong and I'm leaving." He stood and started toward the door. "Artie, Anthony come along now."

Anthony sprung to the door, hand on the knob he looked expectantly from Dutch to Art.

"Artie, we're leaving now." Art strode the few steps to the door and turned. "I said come along now!"

"I'm not going with you. I'm going to get Rose." His stomach churned again, reminding him of the inside of the ice cream maker when Jackson made homemade ice cream except this time he didn't think he was going to puke.

"Fine, we'll get her." Art said and slammed out the door, Anthony in his wake.

Dutch put his hand on James' shoulder. "Don't worry. We'll get your sister, make sure she's okay and finish sorting this out."

26 - LOST

Noon - Art Kenner's House The Day Before

$\mathcal{M}$s. Muir knocked and rang the bell and waited.

No sound or movement from the house.

She pounded on the door and called out.

It wasn't totally silent. Bingo, the puppy Mr. Kenner had adopted from the animal shelter a month ago, whined and cried from inside the garage.

Her watch said quarter past twelve and she'd been at the house a good ten minutes. When she first arrived, she'd noticed the curtains were drawn. What she hadn't noticed was how tightly they were closed. There was no possible way to see inside at all.

Where are they?

Her instincts on high alert, she tramped around the house confirming all doors were locked and all windows covered. Even the window on the back door into the garage had a towel over it.

Back in her car, she pulled out her cell phone and keyed in the non-emergency police number. Her request was for a squad car to meet her at the house. She knew something was wrong. Her never-fail signal was the electric current screaming up and down her spine.

How did this happen?

Art Kenner had written an eloquent plea to have a little more time with his children this holiday weekend—a twenty-four hour visit. That and the fact that James had a cell phone and could call if there were problems resulted in Judge Peterson granting his request.

Ms. Muir had had reservations, vague feelings of unease. She knew unless she could put those vague feelings into words, there was no point in saying anything.

She'd reminded James three times to call her if there was a problem. She'd told him she'd come in the middle of the night if he called. Something was terribly wrong.

When the police cruiser pulled up in front of the house, Ms. Muir's fears did not abate. The officer seemed pleasant, but her cool gaze was not. In the middle of briefing Officer Smith as to what the situation was, her cell phone rang. Glancing at the number, Ms. Muir motioned 'just a minute' to the officer and answered. "Ms. Hughes, I'll call you back within thirty minutes. I'm talking to the police right now."

Hanging up before hearing any response, she turned back to the officer. "The only sound I hear is the puppy in the garage. When I call her name, she scratches on the door. As I told you, I've walked around the house and attempted to look in all the windows. Something is not right."

"You sure Mr. Kenner didn't think he had the children until tomorrow?" Ms. Muir noted the skepticism in the officer's tone even though she had her notebook out and duly noted Ms. Muir's information.

"I'm absolutely certain he did not. They are supposed to be in school tomorrow. Furthermore he is banned from the school grounds." Ms. Muir gave Officer Smith the name of the school and the principal's name and phone number.

"I'll take a look around," the officer said.

"I'll call Judge Peterson while you do." Ms. Muir's hands shook as she dialed the judge's home number and her voice shook as she explained the situation.

"Who is the officer with you?" Judge Peterson's clipped voice telegraphed her displeasure.

"Officer Smith."

"Really? Officer Smith?"

"Traditional spelling. She seems very competent but hesitant to break into the house just because they are forty minutes late."

"I'll make some calls," the judge said and hung up.

A pickup pulled to a screeching halt across the street and Daniel O'Donnell jumped out. Matthew Houston piled out of the passenger side. Behind them a black Jaguar parked, Ms. Hughes and Mr. Montgomery already climbing out.

The four marched across the street to where she stood on the sidewalk creating a semi-circle of concerned frustrated adults. When Officer Smith joined them a minute later, Ms. Muir made the introductions.

Of course everyone wanted to break into the house and get the children.

Officer Smith reminded them there was no evidence the children were even inside.

That didn't help. The men swore and Ms. Hughes became well, she became the Lily Hughes Ms. Muir had heard about over the years.

"Stop it right now," Lily ordered the men who meekly subsided. "If you think standing around here swearing is helping, think again.

"Officer Smith, what do you need before you believe you have the legal right to enter the house to see to the welfare of the children?" she asked, her manner professional.

"Well, Ms. Hughes, I've been told the children have a cell phone and can call if there is a problem. No one's received a call." Officer Smith visually checked with each person. "It may be they aren't even here."

"But that's Art's car," Daniel said, his frustration barely in check.

"I've run the plates and he is the registered owner. But that doesn't mean he's inside. They could've walked down to the park or taken the bus to the mall." Her shoulder mic crackled and she excused herself and walked down the sidewalk. Moments later she made a call. By the time she hung up, another cruiser was parked at the curb.

The officer identified himself as Captain Morrison and he stepped aside and spoke quietly to Officer Smith. A fire truck was the next to arrive along with yet another police cruiser.

"Obviously Judge Peterson has gotten through to the higher ups," Ms. Muir observed.

"Straight to a Captain," Lily said in an aside to Ms. Muir. "You've done a great job to get the right people here so quickly.

Officer Smith?" Lily called out. "Ms. Muir and I would like to talk to the neighbors and see if they know anything."

"The police will handle that if needed," Captain Morrison answered.

The captain led the fire personnel around the house. Moments later the front door opened. Captain Morrison stood in the doorway. "The place is empty. No furniture or nothing except for the dog in the garage."

"How bad is the pup?" Daniel asked.

"Desperately needs a bath and food. She's getting some water now. I'm calling Animal Control to come pick her up."

"She belongs to the children," Daniel said. "I'll take her." He returned to his truck and retrieved a large towel. "We can wrap her in this until we get her cleaned up."

"Let's see if we can clean her up here, wrap her in the towel to keep her warm until we get home," Lily suggested starting towards the house.

Ms. Muir remained on the sidewalk with Jackson as Lily marched into the house Daniel trailing behind her. Matthew got tools from the truck and helped the fire personnel secure the back door.

"I've no idea where they are or when they left," she said. "I even drove by late yesterday and saw the car in the driveway. Mr. Kenner had said he was taking them out to eat and then they were going to watch movies. When I dropped the children off, the car was at the curb. When I saw it in the driveway, it never occurred to me... ," Ms.

Muir said her voice trailing off as what may have happened became a certainty.

"It never occurred to anyone that he'd kidnap all the children," Jackson murmured. "Daniel was worried he'd take off with James if he had the chance but no one thought with Rose along there was a chance in hell he'd do something like this."

Lily's laughter rang through the cold November air accompanied by deeper male chuckles. Ten minutes later she exited the house wearing a yellow slicker, water dripping from the hem. Behind her a splattered Daniel carried a towel-wrapped squirming puppy. Taking the yellow slicker off, Lily handed it to one of the firefighters.

"Thank you," she said extending her hand.

"Anytime," the firefighter said shaking it. "Glad it was you doing the dog washing and not me."

"Do you need me for anything more?" Ms. Muir asked Captain Morrison and Officer Smith.

"We need a description of what they were wearing, pictures, etc."

"Of course. I can follow you to the police station—"

"Or," Lily interrupted, "you can come to the house and talk to Ashley Kenner, their mother and Ms. Muir at the same time. I know there are school pictures and some from Thanksgiving we can get developed at one of the One Hour places if we hurry."

After a short consultation with Captain Morrison, it was agreed that Officer Smith would meet them at the house.

"Give us an hour, please," Lily said. "I think it would be better if we," she gestured to the others standing around her, "talked to their mother. This scenario is her worst fear come true. She's been very sick…."

Jackson slipped an arm around Lily's waist and tucked her against him. He put his hand on Ms. Muir's shoulder. "If you don't mind, Matthew can drive your car and you can ride with us."

"Thank you, Mr. Montgomery. I am a bit shaken by all this. I just had this bad feeling but…."

"You couldn't put it into words," Lily added. "It feels like you've failed but you haven't. Something is wrong. I know that for a fact. But

I feel the children are alive and anything that has happened to them can be overcome." She reached past Jackson and took Ms. Muir's hand. "I've been where you are more than once."

Ms. Muir grasped Lily's hand. "I know you have and this isn't the first time for me. I just feel so helpless at first and then it passes. I have notes and descriptions. I always note what children are wearing when I take them on a visit. I can tell Officer Smith what outfits they were wearing down to the color of their socks."

On the way to the house, Lily called ahead to let Eleanor know what was going on and also called Diana asking her to let everyone else know. "If nothing else, Ashley needs your energy and the children need your prayers."

Walking up the front steps, Mrs. Muir saw half hung Christmas lights strung around the porch, the last string hanging loose, swinging in the wind.

27 - A PLAN

Ms. Muir introduced Officer Smith and the two women took charge of the interview. Ashley sat on the couch flanked by Lily and Daniel. Eleanor, Matthew and Jackson took seats nearby. "Do you have pictures of the children Officer Smith can have?" she asked Ashley.

"I know their school pictures are here someplace," Ashley said, her chin quivering and her voice quavering.

"I know right where the packets are," Eleanor announced rising to get them. "I also made a list of the clothes they packed. I only have one copy."

"That isn't a problem," Ms. Muir said. "Officer Smith is the one who will need it so she can include the possible outfits in her description."

"Do you have any idea where Mr. Kenner might have gone with the children?" Officer Smith asked Ashley.

"N-n-none," Ashley responded. "I can't even believe he's done anything like this at all. He's pretty much ignored the kids the last year or so." Her voice trailed off. "How did this happen?"

"Obviously Mr. Kenner had this well-planned," Officer Smith answered. "From what I've gathered the children want to be with you so it's just a matter of time before one of them contacts you. When that happens, you need to find out where they are and let us know immediately. We'll be able to have the local authorities intercede, take them into protective custody and see that they get back here."

Ms. Muir's cell phone rang. "Excuse me," she said rising and leaving the room as she answered.

"Yes, Your Honor?" All heads swiveled to where Ms. Muir stood in the hallway facing away from them. She turned back and returned to her chair, the phone still at her ear. "Yes, just a minute. Judge Peterson wants to say something so I'm putting my phone on speaker.

"Go ahead Your Honor."

"Ashley, please forgive the informal address but I believe you've stated you do not want to be addressed as Mrs. Kenner," Judge Peterson's words had a tinny quality and were issued in a precise, clipped, no-nonsense manner. She continued, "I want you to know we are doing everything possible to locate James, Anthony and Rose and as soon as they are found, we will bring them home. Both the police and Ms. Muir are able to contact me directly. My staff will interrupt any proceedings I may be involved in when we know where the children are. Take heart, Ashley. You have a team of the best working to bring them home."

"Y'all know they didn't want to go with Art," Ashley said, the color rising in her cheeks matching the anger in her voice. "But y'all made them go anyway."

The moment of silence when Ashley stopped speaking was filled by Judge Peterson. "The truth is, Ashley, Anthony has always wanted to go with Mr. Kenner. James has appeared ambivalent. Rose is the one child who has consistently stated she didn't want to go. While I did consider her wishes, she is the youngest.

"Mr. Kenner wrote an impassioned plea asking to see his children overnight during the Thanksgiving weekend so he could show them he was a good dad. I made the decision based in part because Mr. Kenner did have the right to see the children and make amends for his past choices and because James and Anthony did want to spend some time with him."

Judge Peterson paused. When she spoke again, there was an icy edge, hardness in her words. "I want you to know we are and will continue to do everything within our power to find them and return the children to you and Mr. Kenner to my courtroom."

Ashley's mouth opened to reply.

The phone went dead.

"About the cell phone," Officer Smith said. "Who gave it to which child now?"

"It was a group decision," Lily started.

"Lily and I were talking about safeguards and thought a cell phone might be useful. I went ahead and purchased it. We talked to James about who he wanted to be able to call and made sure those phone numbers were in 'contacts' and that he knew how it worked. We also talked to him about using 911 and how he could dial it and yet not actually talk to the operator if he could give information like who he was and where he was," Daniel added.

"We had him practice calling us and charging it so we knew he was comfortable and could handle things under pressure," Matthew continued.

"When they left Saturday, he had it in his sweatshirt sleeve where the arms were knotted together. It was charged but not on. James said he wanted it there so he didn't have to dig in his backpack for it," Lily finished.

"Did Anthony and Rose know about it?" Officer Smith asked.

"We didn't keep it a secret but we didn't include them in the training," Lily said. "Anthony's desperation to win Art's approval was a deterrent because we weren't sure he wouldn't tell his dad. We were sure Art would take the phone away if he knew it was there. Rose hung around while we went over things with James but we didn't have her practice. That may have been a mistake."

"She's bright, my Rose is. She could figure it out if she had to," Ashley said.

"You're right, Ash. And Rose was paying attention," Daniel said. "My guess is they just haven't had the opportunity to call or they would have. Even Anthony hasn't said he wanted to leave you. He's only said he wanted to be with his dad and those are two different things."

Officer Smith stood. "Here is my card with my phone number," she said handing the cards to the assembled group. "If you think of anything or hear from the children, call me immediately."

"I'll see her out," Ms. Muir said and accompanied the officer to the front door.

Ashley stood, walked to the window and watched as Officer Smith descended the steps and got in her police cruiser. Her brow furrowed in confusion because the car didn't pull away. Ms. Muir came to stand beside her. "She's broadcasting the description of the children right now. Next she'll go to the station and have the pictures sent out along with the descriptions to all the law enforcement agencies west of the Mississippi."

"Y'all think he's left Oregon?"

"I do," Ms. Muir said. "With the children with him, why would he stay? The house he was in is empty. While waiting for the police, I called his work. The service department manager said he gave notice and Friday was his last day. He picked up his pay check. I'm sure when they check his bank accounts will be closed." She paused. "Are you sure you've no idea where he might have gone?"

"He has family in Mississippi and Alabama but he hated it there and couldn't wait for us to leave after we were married," Ashley said.

"I'll let Officer Smith know to extend the Amber Alert to Louisiana, Arkansas, Mississippi and Alabama. It can't hurt and it may be he's decided to go home or someplace like home. It wouldn't be the first time."

28 - MEMORIES

*D*aniel brought the landline phone in from his workshop just in case. He, Matthew and Lily were attempting to stay off their phones in case James called. Bile rose in his throat at the vision of the young boy being in trouble and not able to use the phone. *Bastard, I'll beat you to a pulp if you've touched a hair on any one of their heads.* He plugged the phone in, setting it on the coffee table.

Ashley turned from the window, her gaze locked with his. Daniel looked into grey eyes filled with tears, filled with fear, filled with questions. Helplessness and emptiness consumed him. His arms opened and she walked in to his embrace. Fragile, delicate and ethereal described her physically but he knew she was strong, sturdy and substantial.

"You do know you aren't alone," he said, his cheek resting on her cap.

"I know," she said and started to pull away.

"Let me do this, please," he said, tightening his arms a fraction.

She sighed and relaxed into him, let him bear her weight. His heart pounded with exhilaration but the 'what if's' of having a family again stuttered the beat with terror. He loosened his grip and leaned back, far enough to look at her face. The tears were gone but the fear and questions remained.

"Let's sit and see if there is anything else we can think of to do," he said, turning to the others.

"I'll get fresh pots of coffee and tea and some of Sophia's peanut butter chocolate chip cookies. I know they'll help us think better," Eleanor said, heading to the kitchen.

Daniel stayed through dinner, mostly silent but adding a comment now and again. He couldn't imagine the children were okay and not calling. Matthew had brought Diana by. She said the children were okay, frightened but okay. That echoed what Lily said.

Back at the little house, Daniel paced through the rooms in an effort to quell the rage inside. He stopped in the office area staring out. The pattern from the solar lights in the winter-pansy-filled-pots dappled the deck and ground, light from the moon added a shimmering glow. A part of him recognized the eerie beauty but the dark part of him wished for the vacant emptiness of pitch black darkness.

He tapped some papers on the table under the window, drawings of ideas to convert the little house into something roomy enough for Ashley and her children. A twitch in his back, a tick in his left eye, reminded him he had something else weighing on his mind.

Returning to the living room, he slouched on the couch, feet crossed at the ankles and on the coffee table, arms folded across his chest, hands tucked into his armpits. *I don't know if I can handle being there so much anymore. The crisis is past. Eleanor can stay with her and the kids until the treatment is done.*

His head rested on the couch. *I'm having nightmares again and tonight I almost shoved her away. What if.... Don't go there, man. That leads to disaster.* Memories of the worst night of his life swirled just out of sight. *If I close my eyes—Don't.* A scene from tonight flashed. The women were standing in a circle saying prayers and sending energy to James, Anthony, Rose and Art. He couldn't understand why Art was included.

"When people do unspeakable acts of cruelty, of violence, it shows us they are enveloped in darkness. By sending them love and light, it can only help. We want Art to be calm, to think about the well-being of his children because if he does that, the children will be taken care of," Lily explained. "Hate engenders more hate. Hate and fear are our enemies. Love heals and Light beats back the darkness."

"Sounds good," Daniel muttered. "But how do you send love and light to someone who has taken everything good from you? And forgiveness? Hell! Why should I ever forgive the dr—?" He shifted, sat upright, buried his face in his hands. "I'm going mad." He glared at his cell phone, sitting on the table and willed it to ring.

Nothing.

"I could call someone to meet me for a drink. Stupid idea. I don't need a drink to get past this." He dropped to the floor. Arms straight, he lowered his chest to an inch from the floor, rose up on his toes and pushed up. Sweat dripped off the end of his nose, puddled on the floor. Muscles burned and cramped but Daniel persevered, the rhythm of the exercise numbing him from the outside in.

"Is this Daniel O'Donnell?" the masculine voice from a phone number in an unknown area code asked.

"Who's calling?" Daniel responded his voice laced with suspicion.

"Sherriff Dutch Judd."

"Do you have a lead on the Kenner children?" Daniel asked.

"Got 'em right here," Dutch said. "James wants to talk to you first and then Rose. It'll be a bit before the other one can talk. He's on his way though so it shouldn't be too long."

"James? James is that you? Are you okay? And Rose? And Anthony? Where are you? What happened?" Daniel's staccato questions sprayed the phone line like bullets.

"Daniel? How's Mom?" James' worry hurried his words. "Daniel?"

He scrubbed his face with one hand, tears welled. Daniel fought them back but his voice shook when he answered.

"Your Mom's worried as we all are but she's hanging in there." It struck him then that the Sherriff hadn't called Ashley first.

"Dutch wants to talk to you," James said, his next words muffled.

"Mr. O'Donnell, James and Rose are worried about their mom. Said she had a treatment today and thought you'd know how she is.

We can call her next if you think it's all right. Heard she's been real sick with the cancer."

"Where's Anthony?"

"Mr. Kenner took off and Anthony went with him. My deputy caught up with them and is bringing them back. The boy's just fine. Wants to be with his dad, I guess. The other two not so much."

Daniel's mind was spinning. So many people to call. Officer Smith, Ms. Muir, Judge Peterson. He knew once Lily knew the rest of The Circle would get a call.

"Mr. O'Donnell? You still there?"

"Yes, Sherriff, do you have paper and pen handy."

"Sure do."

Daniel strode to his truck and grabbed his organizer. "I've got some names and phone numbers for you."

"Well, now this cell phone has a bunch of them already programmed in."

"Right," Daniel reminded himself to slow down. Rushing right now wasn't needed. "Here are the people to call first. I know Ms. Muir's name is in there and she has Judge Peterson's name and number and also the Fremont Police Officer who is heading the case up." He leaned against the side of his truck his legs buckling as the tension of the last two days leached from his body. "What happens next? Where are the kids going to be?"

"I'm going to make these calls," Dutch answered. "Dorie and me are registered with the state of New Mexico—"

"New Mexico!" Daniel shouted. "They're in New Mexico? That fucking bastard!"

"Mr. O'Donnell, take a deep breath and listen. My wife and I are registered with the state for emergency placements. She is already calling and talking to the county worker here. Now that I've got these other contacts, we'll be making calls and confirming arrangements. I'm sure our state people will want to talk to your judge and all that. In the meantime, the kids are safe. James has the cell phone and you can call and talk to him or Rose or Anthony any time you want. That goes for his Mom and anyone else up there.

"You may want to call him right away when we hang up which we're doing now so I can get the social worker and everyone up there in Oregon on board. Okay?" One of those rhetorical questions the Sherriff was being polite to ask.

"Sorry about blowing up and all. We were all so worried. Never saw it coming," Daniel's voice shook with relief. The kids were okay.

"Call James," Dutch said and hung up.

The phone log had a long list of cell phone numbers so it took him seconds to punch the call button. James answered on the first ring. "Mom?"

"You can call and tell her you're okay. She'll want to hear it from you."

"I-I please, Daniel, will you tell her we're okay? She'll ask me lots of questions and I… ."

"She'll want to talk to you herself. Make sure you're okay."

"I know."

The deep sigh that followed those two words tore at Daniel's heart. His promise to himself last night to keep his distance was already being broken. "I'll talk to her."

"Thank you, Daniel, thank you," a gulp and half sob finished whatever he'd been going to say.

"Daniel? It's me, Rose."

Another tear-stained voice in his ear, words wrapping around his heart. "I'm here, sweet pea," his own voice husky, he cleared his throat.

"Come and get me, Daniel, please?"

He could see her big green eyes pleading, the way her brows scrunched when she concentrated on something important, her mouth half-open in anticipation of what to say next to get her way. "I can't—."

The scream shattered the last of his resolve. "Rose, Rose, listen to me Rose. It's important that you listen."

"O'Donnell? What the hell happened? What did you say?" Dutch Judd boomed.

"She wants me to come get her. I told her I can't."

More talking that he couldn't hear, a woman's voice, Rose's hysterical sobs lessened.

"Sherriff? Sherriff Judd? Dutch?" Daniel was yelling into the phone. His crew stopped working and stared, his lead worker started towards him. He waved him away. "I'm okay," he lied.

Walking away from the work site, he listened hard and made out a few of the Sherriff's words. Something about talking to the judge and Ms. Muir; something about everything would work out; something about ice cream. With the last statement the sobs changed to hiccups. Air whooshed from his lungs and he gasped in fresh air.

"Calming down now, she'll be okay. Been hard on her from the bits and pieces I've learned. Not had much time to really talk to them, been trying to let you folks know what's going on. Got to go now and get back to the judge. She's been calling here while I've been talking to you."

The dial tone sounded. *Call back.* He shook his head, strode back to the job site and gave orders to his crew. Everything was moving forward smoothly. "Call me if you need me," he told his lead worker as he strode to his truck. The door closed, quiet reigned. He punched in Lily's number and briefly updated her. "I'm on my way to see Ashley. To give her the news in person and be there when she calls the kids. Let Eleanor and the others know what's going on."

ELEANOR HAD JUST HELPED Ashley into the house from this, her sixth chemo treatment when Daniel's truck pulled into the back parking area. Ashley heard the diesel engine rather than saw the truck as she shuffled into the bedroom and collapsed into the chair, too tired to climb into the bed on her own.

She struggled to stay in the present, to keep the nausea at bay, to keep from puking her guts out. In the dark of the last night, Ashley'd felt her kids were alive but frightened. Her mind ran endless scenarios about what Art might have done. *Has he changed so much he'd hurt his own kids?* That was the question that kept her awake.

She pulled herself out of the past. It was approaching noon and Daniel never came by at this hour. He stood in the doorway, his face unreadable but he had his work boots on. Stunned, she stared at his feet, her stomach revolted and a keening cry escaped her lips.

Eleanor shoved the sick bowl in her lap, put her cool hand on Ashley's forehead. "Daniel?"

"Your work boots are on," Ashley said, trembling, terror streaking shards of pain through her.

Daniel looked down. He never wore his work boots in the house except for right now.

"Ash, it isn't what you think. The news is good."

"Why didn't you call me?" she shrieked. "Y'all could have called me and put me out of my misery as soon as you knew something!"

"You've just got home from your treatment," exasperation laced his voice. "I needed to talk to, to tell you in person. The sheriff called. The kids are in New Mexico."

"New Mexico!?" Ashley screeched. "What—How—"

"Ash," Daniel interrupted, "Sherriff Judd says the kids are okay but they are really upset. You'll need to call them and talk to them and they may—ah hell, Ash, Rose is hysterical and James sounds lost. I haven't talked to Anthony, something to do with he and Art and a deputy. I just didn't want to say all of this over the phone."

Ashley heard the words, knew what they meant but still didn't understand what he was saying. "My kids are okay or aren't they?" She spoke in a calm, quiet manner but her palms were marked by nails digging into them.

"Dutch, Sherriff Judd, hadn't talked to them very much—well, he's been busy letting everyone know—" Daniel stopped at the look on Ashley's face.

"Everyone except their mother." She bit out, her words cold and empty. "Their mother has to wait until everyone else knows and someone comes to tell her in person." Bitterness clawed through her, bile rose in her throat.

The doorbell rang. "I'll get it," Eleanor said.

She heard Lily's voice and another one that was familiar.

Daniel started towards the door.

"No, you can't leave," Lily and Ms. Muir said almost in unison.

Ms. Muir's phone rang. She glanced at the screen and excused herself going into the living room.

"Sit," Lily ordered Daniel pointing to a chair. "We've things to discuss and children to call."

Ms. Muir came in on the tail end and added "And a judge to see at four."

"Why the judge?" Ashley asked a question she wasn't sure she wanted to hear the answer to.

"The children have asked that Daniel come and pick them up. It is highly unusual since I'm already involved and you are their mother to have someone not related make the trip. They have talked to Judge Peterson, well Rose and James have. Anthony refuses to. They know you had a chemo treatment today and are very worried about you. Sherriff Judd said their first question was about you which is why the call went first to Daniel, so he could assure them you were okay."

James coming into her room two short months ago: did they have enough to eat, a place to stay trailed through her mind. *Why would I think he'd stopped worrying? Just because I've seen him laugh and play?* The quiet registered. She blinked and looked around at the four people waiting for her to say something.

The effects of this treatment gnawed at her guts, siphoned her energy. She steeled herself and looked at the others.

"Guess I need to give my kids a call and let them know I'm much better now that I know where they are and that they'll be coming home soon." Her kids needed to hear that message from her, needed to know she was okay and would be here when they arrived.

"Who's got the most battery life on their phone? Got to give those kids a call right now."

AFTER TALKING TO HER KIDS, Ashley collapsed. Too exhausted and sick to make the trip to the courthouse, she talked to Ms. Lawford on the phone. Her attorney attended the meeting as did Lily, Ms. Muir, Daniel and Jackson.

At the end of the meeting with Judge Peterson, Daniel and Jackson had dinner at the little house, leaving The Circle to spend time with Ashley. It wasn't a fancy meal like his friend cooked, but it was food—take & bake pizza from the shop a few blocks away. He had cold beer in the fridge and the two of them downed a bottle along with making a major dent in the pizza.

"Were you surprised when Judge Peterson gave you temporary custody of the kids?" Jackson asked, his fingers idly stroking the tall bottle.

"You were there," Daniel responded. "What do you think?"

"Poleaxed," Jackson said and chuckled. "I think you stopped breathing for at least a minute. Actually I thought you'd argue with her, refuse, bolt and run—something dramatic."

"My first thought was to refuse, next to argue with her and yep, I did think I'd just get up and walk out but then I heard Rose's hysterical sobs when I told her I couldn't come and get her. I don't know everything that bastard did to her, but I couldn't let her down."

"The tricky thing is, as I understand it, Anthony was and is okay with going on to Mississippi with Art. He didn't seem to think there was anything wrong in what they did or what happened."

Daniel swallowed the last of his beer. "I'd like to do something special for James. Dutch said he protected Rose as best as a twelve year old could. Obviously Art wasn't kind to her. Probably treated her more like he did when he first had a visit with them."

"Doubt that. He ignored her for the most part."

"Called her mean names, taunted her—borderline cruel. Ms. Muir stepped in and told him to change or the visit was over. He just ignored her after that. I don't think he ignored her this time." Daniel's hand fisted. "I'll beat the crap out of him if he's hurt her."

"No you won't," Jackson said. "You'll do something far worse."

"What?" Daniel leaned forward, his curiosity and the chance for revenge a light in his eyes.

"You'll parade around in front of him with his sons. He may not care about Rose, but he does about James and will settle for Anthony if James isn't available. You've already got James wishing you were his dad—"

"What?" Daniel, startled by Jackson's pronouncement, pushed back his chair and rose. The chair tipped and crashed to the floor. "What the hell are you talking about?"

"You're not that blind. Those children adore you and you dote on them."

"You don't understand. I can only be their friend from time to time. I can't do anything more." He picked up his chair and gingerly sat on the edge of the seat. Sledge hammers pounded inside his skull. Steel bars comprised his shoulders and spine. The pizza and beer he'd just eaten threatened to make an encore appearance.

"Want to change the subject?" Jackson asked while watching him closely.

"Are you ever sorry you never had children?" Daniel never blinked as he asked the gut-punch question.

Jackson just sat, no outward change, but Daniel saw a flicker of something in his eyes.

"If I thought you really cared about my answer, I'd give one," Jackson said his mild tone in contrast to his tight jaw.

"It's an honest question since you think those kids 'adore' me," Daniel said putting quote marks around the word with his fingers.

"Rose and James are your shadows. Even Anthony wants to be by your side, wants your approval—at least some of the time. They all watch you, listen to everything you say and quote you constantly. I didn't pick that observation out of thin air, my friend."

"They want to be with you and Matthew and when in Ireland with Michael," Daniel started.

"We're different. They want to be with me when I've homemade ice cream or James wants to work on a model. They want to be with Michael so they can ride his horses. They want to be with Matthew if you aren't around. You are their default guy. The one they want to be with all the time.

Daniel listened to Jackson, his stomach still churned, his head still throbbed but the steel bars were gone. "I'm exhausted. Need to call it a day so I can get up and catch that early morning flight."

"I'll pick you up at six and take you to the airport."

"I'll call a cab," Daniel said.

"You get to explain to Lily why I'm not taking you to the airport then," Jackson said as he got to his feet. "I'll help you clean up."

"Yeah, toss the pizza box in the fireplace and the beer bottles in the recycling bin."

"What all are you taking with you?" Jackson asked as he closed the fireplace doors on the now burning pizza box.

"Not much. A couple of changes of clothes for me. Dutch said to bring an empty suit case because they'd bought them a few things to tide them over. His wife washed Rose's stuffed rabbit but he said she won't have anything to do with it. She just sits and rocks, holds on to her backpack waiting to leave from what he says. James stays pretty close to her. Anthony has nothing to do with either of them and is sullen or belligerent to Dorie. Dutch thinks Ashley will have a difficult time with him. Said he's going through that stage where kids act out thinking their parents will send them away. He's hoping to be sent to live with Art."

"Not much chance of that happening. Art's in the jail in New Mexico and will be transferred to the jail up here. Judge Peterson is not pleased with him," Jackson said, an exaggerated shudder emphasizing his words.

"That's an understatement. She's pissed at him and while she has ethics and won't bend the law or anything to get him, she sure won't cut him any slack."

"*D*ddaaaannniiieeelll!"

He staggered back against the patrol car as Rose flew off the porch. Her small arms clasped around his neck, her legs wrapped around his waist, her head tucked into his shoulder. Her sobs dampened his shirt, her shudders evoking deep dark emotions.

"Don't," her words muffled in his shirt when he started to put her down.

"Hey, sweet pea. I'm here. You'll be okay," he said, wrapping an arm around her clinging form.

"James," Daniel reached out to the young boy a few feet away. "Come here and let me get a good look at you." As soon as he was within arm's reach, Daniel pulled him into a side-hug. "Good to see you, man." When he let him go, he ruffled his hair, rested his hand on his shoulder to keep him close by. "Hey, Anthony," Daniel called out when he spied him still on the porch, keeping his distance from both Dorie and Dutch.

Daniel regained his standing balance and keeping eye contact with Anthony walked to the porch. "You've been missed. How are you doing?"

"Okay," Anthony mumbled.

"Let me see." Daniel said.

"See what?"

Daniel managed the steps with Rose still entwined around him and his hand on James' shoulder. "See you up close so I know what 'okay' looks like." He gently squeezed James' shoulder before letting go and reached out to Anthony, who tried to duck away. Expecting that maneuver, Daniel intercepted him and pulled him into a hug. He held him close until Anthony stopped resisting. As he let him go, he tousled his hair. "The hugs are from your mom and the rest is from me."

James stayed close, Anthony did not. Rose, well Rose wouldn't let him go. At one point when he had to use the bathroom, she agreed to let him go but sat right outside the door and glommed onto him as he came out the door. She did turn around when they sat down to eat but would not get off his lap. It was clear she was going with him no matter where he went.

"Come along Rose, it's time for your bath and bed," Dorie said.

Rose tightened her grip on his neck. She'd been dozing and was relaxed against him. She hadn't left his arms except for his couple of trips to the bathroom. When she had to go, he had to go with her. He drew the line at going in the bathroom with her, but he had to talk to her so she knew where he was.

Thankful for his conversations with Dutch as he was driven to the Judd's home from the airport a couple hours away, he had some idea of what Rose had been through and what James had done to protect her.

Daniel had asked Dutch for five minutes alone with Art. Sherriff Judd had firmly rejected that request but counter-offered five minutes with him present. Daniel had declined. Once he'd spent five minutes with Rose, he knew seeing Art was out of the question. There was no way he'd be able to keep his hands off the bastard and sitting in the next jail cell wouldn't help the kids or Ashley.

"Come on, sweet pea," Daniel said and stood. "Time for your bath and bed." He followed Dorie through the house to the bathroom across the hall from where Rose and James slept. She shook her head, her death grip like a vise. "It'll be like when you went pee," he said. "I won't leave, okay?"

"Promise?" Her small hands framed his face turning it so she looked him in the eyes.

"I promise I will not leave the hall."

"No, by the door."

He walked from one end of the hall to the other with her still in his arms. "I'll be here." He gestured from one end to the other.

"I'll sit by the door, Rose," James said.

"No, Daniel," she argued, her lower lip protruding, tears welling in her eyes.

Dorie stood in the bathroom doorway. "Do you want bubbles in your bath or a shower? We got your favorite bubble bath at the store yesterday. You sure enjoyed that last night." Her bright smiled matched her words. "A shower is quicker though so you'll be through and back with Daniel and James before you know it. What'll it be?"

"Let me guess, your favorite bubble bath is dandelion," Daniel said, snuggling her under his chin and breathing deeply. "Nope, not dandelion. It's… ." He took another deep breath, letting it out slowly. *Sweaty little girl who needs a bath smell. Can't joke about that given what's happened to her.*

Rose turned her head and took a whiff of her top. Her nose wrinkled and she looked up at Daniel. "I need a bath," she announced. "Promise you won't leave me." She was so serious, so unsure he'd stay, his heart broke.

Dutch said from the end of the hall. "I'm putting him under house arrest. That means he can't leave the house or he'll be in trouble."

"I don't want him in trouble," Rose said, her voice high with anxiety. "I don't want him in trouble, Dutch, I just want him to stay with me."

"I promise he'll be right here by the door when you get out of that bubble bath," Dutch said. "I'll keep him right here by me." He motioned for Daniel to put her down and although reluctant to let go, she did. "Anthony?" Dutch called out. When Anthony appeared, Dutch said, "You get to stay by the door. Dorie will tell you when Rose is finishing her bath so you can come get Daniel and me. Come along, James."

Daniel wanted to look back but dared not. He listened to Dorie's chatter as she took Rose into the bathroom and shut the door.

"Don't look back," Dutch muttered as they left the hall and started for the living room. "James, you can watch some television or go check on the horses. We'll call you when it's time for you to come in and shower."

James stood in the middle of the room. His movements hesitant and jerky as if unsure of what to do.

"I'm not going any place, James. Just going to step out on the porch with Dutch, stretch my legs and get a bit of fresh air."

"Can I really go out to the barn and see the horses?" James asked.

"Course you can. You're a natural with them. Take a few carrots with you. Only one for each of them now. They'll want more."

James laughed. "I know, leave the bunch by the door and only take one with me when I go up to each horse."

"Smart lad. Now go on with you." Dutch shooed him toward the barn and James loped off.

"Just so you know," Dutch said turning to Daniel. "There's been a delay and you'll be here for a couple of days. Interstate Compact has to approve everything and the social worker on our end can't get out to meet you and talk to the kids until Thursday so it'll be Friday before you can head home."

"Hate to impose. I can get a motel in town, rent a car," Daniel offered.

"No imposition at all. That little girl needs to be with you right now. She hasn't sucked her thumb once since you arrived. Of course she's clinging so tight to you she can't rock. Dorie and me have been real worried about her but she seems to be coming out of it."

"Did Art really plan on leaving her along the side of the road somewhere?" Daniel's dinner churned and nausea rolled through his stomach.

"According to James, Art had left her in the motel and didn't plan on going back for her after they'd eaten. Whenever they stopped

James made sure he stayed out of the car until she got back in because he said Art said he'd leave her because she was too much trouble."

"Of course she heard everything." Daniel's dinner was definitely in revolt. He focused on his breathing and the bile receded a notch.

"Yep, and Dorie's convinced he'd drugged her with something that night at the motel because she was sleeping so sound and seemed so groggy and disoriented when she woke up. Nothing like she's been here," Dutch said.

"Won't change your mind about that five minutes, will you?" Daniel popped one fist in the palm of the other hand.

"Nope, but my offer still stands. If you want to see Art, I'll take you there myself but I won't leave you alone with him."

"Amanda's done," Anthony announced from the doorway.

He heard her screams as he walked into the living room. *My God!* He sprinted for the bathroom.

"Hey, sweet pea," he said, scooping her up. "I'm right here. I'm here, Rose. You're okay."

"You said," she sobbed. "And you weren't here. You p-pr-o-om-mised."

"I did promise, Rose, and I'm sorry I was so slow getting back here. Let me show you where Dutch and I were." He started down the hallway, counting his steps out loud. "Help me here, sweet pea. I know you know your numbers."

The sobbing had stopped, the hiccups too by the time they reached the living room. "Going to make me do all the counting myself?"

She snuggled closer if that was even possible.

Daniel continued counting out to the porch railing. He leaned against it and said, "I was here when Anthony said you were ready."

"I luv you, Papa," she whispered, her arms around his neck, the dampness of her hair cooling his skin and wetting his shirt.

He grabbed the rail post and hung on, knowing if he let go he'd fall into the darkness that seeped closer and closer. Over the years he'd learned to keep himself physically grounded when the memories came. He was very good at superficial relationships and sucked at anything requiring intimacy. "Good with children" was a misnomer.

The worst of his fears were coming true. Rose would not leave him and neither would James. He ended up sleeping in the recliner with Rose tucked against one side and James on the couch. Only Anthony was willing to sleep in his bed. Daniel noticed that Dutch made a big fuss of turning the alarm system on.

He woke to his phone ringing. Ashley.

"What's going on?"

Daniel explained the Interstate Compact snafu and that Dutch figured they'd be able to fly out on Friday if all went well.

"They're missing a week of school," she said.

"They'll catch up over Winter Break," Daniel had assured her.

Rose had woken and he handed the phone to her. "It's your mom and she wants to talk to you. I'm going to go... ." he gestured toward the hall.

She shook her head and glared at him. "You promised."

"What did Daniel promise," Ashley asked.

"He promised he won't leave me," Rose said, her voice firm, glaring at him.

"What do you mean? Where is he going?" Ashley's voice mirrored her confusion.

"He wants to go pee," Rose said indignantly, "without me."

"I want to talk to Daniel, now," Ashley ordered. "Right now!"

Rose handed the phone back to Daniel just as Dorie came in the room. He jumped up from the recliner, thrust the phone at her and headed toward the hall. "I will be back."

Dorie plopped down in the recliner as Rose started to follow. "No, Rose, Daniel has the right to use the bathroom without you right there. Check my watch and see the numbers change. We'll see how long it takes him to get back here, okay?" Without waiting for Rose to answer, Dorie said, "Hi Ashley, did you have a question or something?"

"Is Rose going to the bathroom with Daniel?"

Dorie laughed. "Not that she wouldn't if he allowed it but he does have some boundaries when it comes to this one," she said and gently tickled Rose's side. Rose giggled and squirmed, her eyes never leaving Dorie's watch. "He's her security blanket right now."

"What happened to her rabbit?" Ashley asked.

"Not a story to tell at the moment," Dorie responded, her arm around Rose.

"Is it gone for good?"

"Yes and cannot be replaced and right now not even substituted."

"I called to talk to the children. I miss them ever so much," Ashley said in a wistful voice.

"Rose is still timing Daniel, but James is right here." Dorie handed the phone to James who eagerly told his mom all about the horses and learning how to feed and take care of them.

"Dutch says you have to know how to take care of a horse before you can ride it. You know Michael and Dickens said the same thing. Dutch and Dorie's horses are quarter horses not Arabians."

When Daniel sauntered into the living room, his hair was damp from a quick shower. He had clean clothes on but still sported a day's growth of whiskers. He'd also taken a few minutes to check on Anthony, who was faking sleep. Rose pointed at Dorie's watch and frowned. Dorie whispered something to her and her eyes grew wide. She nodded and got up, took Dorie's hand and they left the room. Dorie winked as they passed.

James was still on the phone with his mom.

Going to find Dutch and see what he thinks of my idea. He nodded to James and kept going out the front door to the porch. The patrol car wasn't in sight which meant Dutch was working. James brought the phone to him and he talked for a few minutes more with Ashley, telling her Anthony was still asleep and Rose was helping Dorie fix breakfast.

Called into breakfast, Daniel decided to wait and talk to Dutch in person. Dorie mentioned he'd be off at one and home by two.

"Best breakfast I've had in a long time," he said and grinned at Rose. "Wonder what the secret ingredient is that you and Dorie put in the pancakes?"

Rose beamed, slid a side-long glance at Dorie, but said nothing.

His freedom was short lived because once breakfast was over, dishes cleared and kitchen cleaned up, Rose was right next to him. Whenever he sat down, she climbed in his lap. She shadowed him down to the barn where James introduced him to the horses. She kept step with him albeit two of hers to one of his, when he went out to an old shed to look at the new litter of kittens. He was thankful when Dorie told them they were too young to leave their mother. For a moment he was going to mention the dog but since none of the children had asked, he kept silent.

As if his thoughts were read, Anthony asked about Bingo. Truly confused, Daniel couldn't answer until Anthony reminded him that was the puppy's name.

He decided to be honest. "When we found Bingo, she had no food, no water and was covered in her own poop because her rope had been caught on a box. We got a bottle of water from my truck for her. Lily washed the worst of the poop off at Art's. Then Matthew took her home and gave her a bath. You can call Matthew and Diana any time and see how she's doing?"

Anthony looked away and Daniel saw the sheen of tears coat his eyes. *Guess I'll add a dog run in the backyard of the little house.*

"Art wouldn't let us take her along," James said, his shoulders slumping with sadness. "When did you find her?"

"Ms. Muir heard her crying when she went to pick you three up on Sunday at noon. But it was a lot later before the police were willing to break into the house to see if you were there."

Three heads swiveled sharply in his direction.

"When Ms. Muir couldn't get anyone to come to the door, she called the police. Then she had to call the judge at home and the judge had to call the police chief, who had to call the precinct captain who then came out to the house and said it was okay to break in.

"Lily called to see why you weren't home and Ms. Muir was talking to the police. Jackson and Lily, Matthew and I headed over to see what was happening. When we got there, we could hear Bingo crying. The police were going to call animal control and have her taken to the animal shelter but Lily talked them out of doing that."

"Bingo gets scared," Anthony said. "She pees on the floor. Dad said she had to stay in the garage unless we were out in the backyard with her." He looked forlorn.

Daniel noticed one of the spaniels seemed to be nearby Anthony and sure enough, the dog came over and bumped his head against his hand for a pet. Anthony dropped down on his knees and hugged the dog who licked his face. *Guess Bingo will be one of the family sooner rather than later.* He had a premonition more complications loomed on the horizon.

THE NEXT COMPLICATION came with the social worker from Interstate Compact. Rose refused to leave the room with her. Anthony slouched in a sullen pout. Only James seemed to realize talking to the woman was essential to their going home and was ready, willing and even eager to talk to her.

Daniel talked to Dutch who'd reluctantly agreed to his plan. He asked the social worker's permission to speak quietly to Anthony while in her line of sight and at her nod, he motioned the younger boy to meet him at the doorway into the hall.

"I've talked to Dutch and once we get everything cleared to leave for Fremont, you can see your dad if you want to. Talking to the social worker is the next step. Up to you though." Daniel said and walked away.

Anthony glared at him. He could feel the animosity strike his back but he didn't turn and Anthony did go with the social worker. Rose still refused to leave the room without him.

Finally a compromise was reached. The social worker would talk to James and Anthony first. When it came time to talk to Rose, Daniel would sit on the porch so Rose could see him through the window. Rose was not happy about that. Dorie talked to Rose and the social worker. He was very sure bribes were involved. Whatever it was, it worked and that was all that mattered.

That evening Dutch took Anthony in to the jail to see Art. Neither

James nor Rose wanted to go. Rose regressed in front of his eyes and physically reattached herself to him. He reminded himself that tomorrow night they'd be back in Fremont and he'd be back at the little house.

A defeated Anthony returned with Dutch. The tracks of tears still marked his face. During bath time, when Daniel had a few moments with Dutch he learned that Art asked after Artie and wanted to know why his oldest son wasn't there.

Art got angry when Dutch said only Anthony wanted to come. The young boy was totally ignored by his dad. Anthony tried to talk to him, asked him questions about how he was doing and if he was okay. Art lashed out at his second son.

Dutch cut the visit off. He'd talked to Anthony on the way home but it hadn't been a good scene at all.

"And Anthony doesn't see that Art's a shithead?" Daniel asked after hearing Dutch's account of the visit.

"Nope, he's devastated that his Dad wants James and doesn't want him. Don't know what it'll take for him to see there's nothing wrong with him. It's his dad who has the problem."

31 - HOME AGAIN

The flight home was an eventful uneventful trip. Rose had reverted to clinging to him. James was his shadow and Anthony had withdrawn into a shell that even Dorie's fudge brownies with ice cream couldn't breach. He made sure Rose had used the rest room in the Farmington airport while Dorie was with them.

The Phoenix airport was another story. Anthony looked like he might bolt, Rose clung to him like ivy to a brick wall and James stayed so close he bumped into him when turning around.

They had thirty minutes between flights. He checked with the flight attendants and with Rose looking frantically around her, was able to get permission for her to use the toilet on the plane as soon as they boarded. First to board, Rose raced down the aisle and a flight attendant showed her how to use the on board facilities.

Settling into their seats was another challenge. His plan was for James to sit in the seat just across the aisle, Anthony in the window seat and Rose in the middle. The problem? Rose refused to get off his lap. It took some talking before the flight attendant convinced Rose the plane could not take off until she was in her own seat. She pointed out that when the seat belt light went off, she could unbuckle her belt and sit with him again.

Rose being Rose, the second the light went off she scrambled into his lap where she remained for the entire trip. James had the choice of remaining in the seat just across the aisle or moving into the seat Rose had vacated until landing. He chose to remain in his seat.

Carrying Rose, Daniel herded Anthony in front of him. James, a few inches from his side, carried his and Rose's backpacks.

It was obvious as the other passengers streamed past them, that the young boy did not want to be here at all. His attempts to talk to Anthony last night and this morning at the airport had all been met with silence or one word answers. He wanted nothing, had no preferences, didn't care. Daniel knew Anthony needed to talk to someone or the darkness would consume him.

Finally they were on the concourse and heading toward the exit. He knew Ms. Muir would be there. Figured Ashley would be also regardless of how she felt. He hoped Lily and Jackson would also show up. He could pass Rose on to Ashley. James and Anthony to Lily and Ms. Muir and he'd have Jackson to hang with as they went to baggage claim and exited the airport. In his grand scheme, Jackson would drop him off at the little house; he'd get a good night's sleep and be ready to roll in the morning. Recliner-sleeping with a six year old on one's chest was not very restful.

Prayers can be answered. As they passed the last security check point, he easily spotted Ashley, standing but with a wheelchair behind her, Ms. Muir, Lily and Jackson and just beyond them, Gabriella, Hunter, Logan and Sophia. A text message last night from Matthew told him Diana was on bed rest again so he was surprised to see Matthew.

Rose did not let go of him. The confusion and pain in Ashley's eyes hit him in the solar plexus and he staggered under its onslaught.

"Let's sit over here." Ms. Muir gestured the group to an area of empty seats a few feet from the path of incoming passengers. She took Anthony by the arm. He resisted but Ms. Muir tightened her grip and moved him along.

James hugged his mom and then taking her hand, walked with her over to where Ms. Muir waited.

Jackson stood next to him, engaging Rose as best he could. She tucked her head into Daniel's neck and refused to look at anyone.

Daniel took the seat Ms. Muir pointed him to. He started to pry Rose's arms from around his neck but she held on tighter. One trick that had worked before was to relax into the seat and let go of her. Within a couple of minutes, Rose had always relaxed and sometimes even let go altogether. *That might be too much to hope for.* His vision of going from the airport to the little house faded as the reality of integrating Rose back with her mom dominated.

He gave Hunter and Gabriella the baggage claim tickets and they went off to pick up the two suitcases.

Logan sat next to him, her soft voice invited Rose to remember a fun game they'd played. "I'm spending the night with you," Logan whispered. "I've got the flashlights and everything."

Rose didn't budge.

Logan forged on with other enticing activities the two of them would do.

Daniel knew Rose listened, was tempted. *Stubborn, stubborn, stubborn.* For his part, he remained seated, relaxed into the cushions, his arms on the chair's arms, talking to Jackson and Matthew who'd kept on top of his crews.

"Rose," Ms. Muir said. "It's time to get the luggage and go home."

Her arms tightened and the little he'd gained was lost.

Lily, Ashley and Sophia stood before him. "Let's go, Rose," Lily said, reaching out to pluck her off him.

"I don't want to," Rose's muffled voice still brooked no argument.

"Daniel has things to do," Lily continued. "He'll come see you tomorrow when he's through work."

"You can help me fix his favorite dinner," Sophia said. "We want to thank him for all he's done with his favorite meal. I'll need your help because I don't think I know what he likes."

"Tell her," Rose ordered.

He shook his head.

"You have to tell her," Rose sat back her small hands on his cheeks, a fierce look in her eyes.

He shook his head.

Tears welled. It occurred to him then she didn't know what his favorites were. He pulled her close and whispered. "I'll tell you my favorites if you'll help Sophia fix them."

"Okay," she whispered back. "Promise you'll come for dinner."

"I promise I'll call you when I get home tonight. I'll call you tomorrow at lunch. And I'll come have dinner with you and stay until your bedtime. Deal?"

"Deal. Pinky swear?" She held out her hand with her little finger extended.

"Pinky swear." Daniel locked his little finger with hers, leaned forward and kissed her on the cheek and whispered "pot roast with carrots and potatoes, green beans, and chocolate cake, can you remember that?"

She nodded, scrambled off his lap and relayed the information to Sophia.

"If that's too hard, a good steak, baked potato, tossed salad and cherry pie with ice cream will work," he added. Standing, he watched Rose climb into Ashley's lap. Sophia began pushing the wheelchair when Rose looked back at him and said, "You come too."

He saluted and started to follow. It felt strange to watch her go off with other people. She'd been appended to him for most hours of the last four days. Relief and loss warred. His eyes blurred and he stumbled. Matthew and Jackson reached out to steady him.

"Looks like it's been rough," Jackson said. "Thought you might call just to talk."

"Nothing to say that I wanted Rose to hear. She's been glued to me since I got out of the patrol car on Tuesday. Either like you saw just now or within her line of sight or sound. The furthest away I ever got was the front porch when she was taking a bath."

"The boys?" Matthew asked.

"James has been my shadow. He's got bruises from where I've stepped on his toes, banged into him, but he loved the horses Dutch and Dorie have so he'd take off for the barn when Dutch was around. And Anthony? Well, he is still desperate to have Art want him."

"What?" Matthew's forehead was bunched in confusion.

"I thought it would be good for him to see Art so he could talk to him. Problem was Art didn't want to see him. He only wanted to see James, who he still calls Artie. He refused to talk to Anthony who wanted to know how he was. It got worse when Art realized James didn't want to and wouldn't come to see him. He went on a rant and Dutch ended the visit right then."

"What a bastard," Jackson muttered, his eyes on Anthony who still had Ms. Muir by his side.

"You can say that again," Matthew added.

"What a —."

"Don't really need to have it repeated, Jackson. Focus needs to be on helping these kids recover from their time with him. He did a lot of damage for having them for so little time," Daniel said.

He walked with the group to the parking garage, made sure he got his suitcase and not the one with the children's things. Gave extra hugs to Rose for getting into her car seat so quickly. Checked with Ashley about calling and saying 'goodnight' to Rose.

"Why don't I have her call you," Ashley proposed.

"Perfect."

"Daniel?"

Ashley's soft voice stopped him in his tracks. He turned around stuck anew by how beautiful she was. Bald underneath her pink cap, angular features not yet fleshed out and way too thin but there was a luminosity, a glow that surrounded her. Grey eyes filled with gratitude met his, her hand reached out and touched his, a zing of energy passed between them. "Thank you for all you've done. I don't think I could have survived this without your help and I know my kids wouldn't be home and doing as well as they are," a rueful smile played on her full mouth, "without y'all being the one to get them."

She stepped forward, reached up and kissed his cheek. "I owe you so much. Somehow I'll find a way to pay you back."

His hands cupped her shoulders. "You don't owe me anything, Ash. We're friends and this is what friends do for each other."

He let her go, turned and walked away. Matthew, who was taking him home, had already gotten his truck and was waiting for him. Climbing in, they took off. The drive was over in ten minutes. When he got out of the truck, Matthew did too. He grabbed Daniel's suitcase and followed him into the house. Five minutes later, Jackson pulled into the driveway. He came into the house with a six pack of Daniel's favorite beer.

"Thought you needed a little company and libation to end the day," he said, opening a bottle for each of them.

"You must be psychic," Daniel said, taking a big swallow. He settled in the chair across from the couch and began at the beginning. "Dddaaaannniiieeelll!"

32 - THE HEARING

December 20, 2004
Fremont County Courthouse

*A*shley kept her face as neutral as she knew how when the deputy led Art into the courtroom. Thankfully the way everything was arranged, she didn't have to look at him. Ms. Lawford sat on her left and Art and his attorney were at the table across the aisle beyond Ms. Lawford.

Behind her were her circle sisters, even Elizabeth. She and Michael had chosen to spend the winter holidays in Fremont because neither she nor Diana could travel. The Circle was strong and knowing she was held in The Light by all six of them gave her a strength she sorely needed.

Everyone in the courtroom rose when Judge Peterson came in, sat when she sat and waited until she spoke.

"First on the agenda is the divorce proceeding between Ashley Carlyle Kenner and Arthur Kenner. I've affidavits in front of me from both parties waiving any and all objections to granting the divorce today." She looked at the two attorneys. "Do you have anything to add?"

Mr. Treeland stood. "Mr. Kenner would ask Your Honor to grant him full custody of his children due to Mrs. Kenner's health."

"Your client should be grateful I'm not terminating his parental rights after what he's done. Request is denied." She picked up her pen and signed her name on the papers in front of her.

"The divorce is hereby granted. Mrs. Kenner's legal name reverts to her maiden name. She is granted custody of the three minor children of this marriage, James, age 13; Anthony age 10, and Rose, age 6. Mr. Kenner may petition the court in six months regarding visitation rights. In the meantime, he may write to the children, send them gifts, etc. through the court. He is to have no direct contact with any of the children until such time as the court deems appropriate.

"Mr. Kenner, I strongly advise once you have finished serving your jail sentence that you seek professional counselling in the areas of parenting, anger management and relationships in general. However, I am not ordering you to do this as I believe for you to become the parent I've heard you once were, you must make the decision to seek help on your own."

The judge handed the sheaf of papers to her clerk, picked up the next file and called Ms. Muir to the stand. Ms. Lawford reached over and patted Ashley's hand.

Ashley turned to see Daniel sitting with Jackson and Lily. He'd been subpoenaed to attend today's hearing. She knew him well enough by now to see he was not pleased to be there because outwardly he appeared disinterested.

"The next matter before the court comes at the request of Ms. Muir acting as amicus curia on behalf of the Kenner children, James, Anthony and Rose. James and Rose are asking the court to change their legal last name to Carlyle or O'Donnell."

Even though she'd been warned something like this might happen, Ashley's heart skipped a beat. The rustle of witnesses and bystanders in the court room conveyed everyone's surprise.

"Ms. Muir, please tell the court the reasoning behind the request," the judge asked the social worker once she'd been sworn in.

"James is frightened of his biological father and at this point in his life does not want any contact with him. In my interviews with James, he has cited the following as his reasons for not wanting the Kenner last name or contact with Arthur Kenner." She then went on to list James' perspective of how Art had treated not just her, their mother, but also each of them. She gave a graphic account of what had happened to Rose on the trip. Ashley searched wildly for some container because she knew she'd be sick any minute. Seeing the waste can under the table, she seized it, hurled the meager contents of her stomach into the detritus and rested her head on the table.

Ms. Lawford asked for a fifteen minute recess, which was granted. Ashley made it to the restroom down the hall before the dry heaves claimed her.

She sat, stunned on the bathroom floor, as Hunter and Sophia wiped her face with cold, wet paper towels. "She wouldn't talk to me about what happened and neither really would James." Dizziness brought her head between her knees.

"Do you need more time?" Ms. Lawford asked.

I am the granddaughter of Gram. I can do this. She held her dragonfly pendant in her hand. A dragonfly pin was on her cap and a small dragonfly fetish was tucked into her bra. She touched each talisman, drawing strength. *The light is at the end of this tunnel. I must believe my dragonflies will see me through this darkness.* With help, she stood and faced her attorney. "I'm ready."

Back in the courtroom, Ms. Muir retook the stand. "I've maintained contact with the children since their return from New Mexico," she told the judge. "Rose was the most affected by the kidnapping. You can see why from James' account of the ordeal. Rose has specifically asked to have Daniel O'Donnell be her 'papa.' She told me clearly she'd never call him 'dad' because that is a bad name." Ms. Muir then went on to list ten reasons Rose wanted Daniel to be her 'papa.'

While she knew the children, or at least James and Rose, were asking the judge to change their last names, she had no idea Rose wanted Daniel to be her father. The idea of Daniel as Rose's parent, or James and Anthony's for that matter, did not bring panic or fear. She knew he'd make an excellent parent, that the children would always know they were loved, that there'd be no favorites.

Ms. Muir left the stand. Seeing Daniel standing before Judge Peterson roused her from her musing. He stood in the space between the attorneys, posture straight, head held high and she noted, hands fisted at his sides as if he was about ready to clobber someone. Something was wrong.

Beyond him, Mr. Treeland was loudly whispering to Art to sit down and shut up.

"Mr. O'Donnell," the judge began. "You have voluntarily moved out of your own home in order to give Ms. Carlyle and her children a place to stay?"

"Yes, your honor."

"You have kept the maintenance on the house up and paid the utilities during this time?"

"Yes, your honor."

"In addition you've been one of several people to assist with the children in various ways such as getting them to and from school, attending school events, teacher conferences?"

"Yes, your honor."

"You are the first person the children called when Sherriff Judd came upon them and you were the person they wanted to come and get them, correct?"

"Only because of their concern for their mother, who had been ill."

"For the record, Mr. O'Donnell, the answer to my previous question is—?"

"Yes, your honor."

"Thank you, Mr. O'Donnell. You may be seated." She paused as Daniel made his way back to his seat. "The Court will take under advisement James and Rose's request for a name change.

"It is the order of this court that Daniel O'Donnell will move back into his own home. The temporary guardianship given to him to retrieve the children will remain in effect."

Art lunged across the table towards the judge. Mr. Treeland grabbed at him in an attempt to restrain him. The guards moved quickly and pulled him back into his chair. "I won't stand for that bastard being around my children. He is poisoning them against me. It's all his fault any of this has happened—."

"One more word," Judge Peterson, shook her gavel in Art's direction, "and I'll have you physically gagged."

"He's been screwing my wife for years!" Art screamed before one of the guards silenced him.

"Ms. Muir will make weekly home visits to monitor the situation. The court will review the living situation in ninety days." The judge rose. "In my chambers, now!" she ordered as she left the court room.

Ms. Lawford asked Ms. Muir who Judge Peterson's verbal order applied to. They waited while Ms. Muir checked. In the meantime, a bound and gagged Art was removed from the courtroom.

"The judge wants to see you," she pointed to Ashley and Ms. Lawford, "and Mr. O'Donnell. She suggests that Mr. O'Donnell bring Ms. Hughes with him."

"Of course I'll come along but I also think Daniel needs some moral support. I don't know about him, but I'm flabbergasted by this turn of events," Lily said.

Matthew and Jackson stood. "Good, one of you may have to stand, but there will be room," Lily added.

Ashley noticed Ms. Muir heaved a deep sigh and knew more than talking to the judge awaited her.

The clerk opened the door to the judges' chambers. Ashley's mouth dropped open and she froze in her tracks. Sitting on Judge Peterson's lap was Rose. Her daughter was animated while regaling the judge with some story. James and Anthony sat in chairs to either side of the judge. Four chairs were arranged in a semi-circle in front.

Nudged from behind, Ashley stumbled forward, caught her balance and stepped to the side. Ms. Lawford took her elbow and guided her to the far chair, leaving room for Ms. Muir and Daniel.

Judge Peterson took one look at the crowd in her chambers, asked her clerk to clear the courtroom and put the closed session sign up. She then stood and ushered everyone back to the courtroom. The court stenographer remained as did her clerk, but Judge Peterson sat back and surveyed the people in front of her.

"Mr. O'Donnell, I sense you are uncomfortable with my order."

"Your Honor, first, it took me by surprise. With Mr. Kenner's accusations I don't think it wise for me to move back in."

"Ms. Carlyle is legally divorced. What can his accusations do?"

"While it isn't true, he already thinks—"

"Yes, he does," the judge interrupted. "I see no downside to this plan. If you do, please share. I can amend the order if you can convince me this is not in the best interest of the children."

James spoke up. "If you live at home, we can finish decorating the house and we can help you take everything down and put them away."

"Your Honor," Daniel began. "I have drawn up some plans to upgrade the house where I'm currently staying, which is owned by Ms. Hughes with a second bathroom and additional bedrooms on the upper floor. I can get my crew—"

"Ms. Hughes?"

"If the house was renovated and the roof raised so another bathroom and a couple of bedrooms were added to that space, it would be more than adequate for the family."

"Do you object?"

"To the work being done? Not really. I do wonder about moving the children to a third school district this year. They all seem to be doing very well in this school. They have teachers who are understanding and accommodating and they've made friends. With all the turmoil they've experienced so far this year... ." Lily's words trailed off when she saw the look on Daniel's face.

Stricken was the word that came to Ashley's mind as Daniel listened to Lily's reasons to delay them moving. She knew Lily wouldn't bring money up because The Circle had already offered to pay the utilities and property taxes. Sophia brought food, Eleanor and Hunter cleaned. Logan helped the kids with homework. Lily and Gabriella gave Eleanor breaks by staying the night. Someone had been there every night since the children returned. Rose woke with nightmares and she knew James came and checked on her during the night.

If Daniel lived in the home, he'd be back in his room upstairs, close to the children. She knew it would ease Rose's night terrors and hoped it helped James and maybe he'd be able to reach Anthony.

"Let's try this for ninety days," the judge said. "I can tell something is going on, Mr. O'Donnell. You don't have to tell me what it is. So I'll ask you this, can you manage for ninety days?" She held her hand up, turned to her clerk. "What's on my docket in ninety days?"

"March 20th is a Sunday, Your Honor. You have time on your docket the Friday before, which would be the 18th or on Monday, March 21."

"If you feel you can manage whatever it is for ninety days, you pick the date, Mr. O'Donnell."

The courtroom was silent. The children, even Anthony, leaned forward expectantly. How Rose managed not to say or do anything was a testament to her desire to have Daniel with them. His face was impassive but still Ashley knew there was something he feared would happen if he moved home. Whatever it was, she couldn't quite put her finger on it, but something was definitely there.

"Friday, March 18th will be fine."

*D*elicious smells assaulted his sleepy brain as Daniel struggled awake. He was in his own bed but not alone. Well, technically he was alone as no one was actually in his room but the door was open a crack and the whispered voices told him both James and Rose were ensconced on the other side.

The urge to snuggle back down and drift off to sleep was strong but he knew the whispers would not go away and within a few minutes one if not both of the kids would be in his room.

"Come on in," he called out, running a hand through his hair, rubbing it along his beard-roughened chin.

The door banged against the wall as it flew open. Rose, the first to reach the bed, scrabbled to climb up but was thwarted because of the height.

"Give her a boost," he said to James and patted the bed.

With one kid snuggled on each side of him, Daniel contemplated, yet again, how different his life would be over the next ninety days. Rose's small hand rested on his t-shirt covered chest, just over his heart. *She's come so far since returning home. I'll talk to Lily and see what's best.*

"What's that I smell?"

"Coffee, I think. Eleanor said you like it best in the morning."

"She's right."

"And cimamun rolls with lots of frosting. Eleanor said we had to be real quiet and not wake you up or we couldn't have any." Her bright green eyes were guileless as she said, "and we was real quiet so we didn't wake you up."

She'll charm the snake charmer. "Okay you two, up and out. I need a shower and shave so I can eat all of Eleanor's cinnamon rolls." He made an exaggerated smacking noise and rubbed his belly. "Yep, won't be any left for the two of you if I get there first."

Squeals and thunks as feet hit the floor, giggles and taunts— normal kid stuff. *If this is how they've been getting up and going in the morning, doesn't look like they need me here at all.* He tossed the covers back and made sure the door to the hall was closed before getting a change of clothes and heading in to the bathroom for a quick shower and shave. *If I do want cinnamon rolls, I'd better get a move on.*

LILY AND SOPHIA sat in Ashley's room munching on cinnamon rolls and sipping tea while discussing what to do for Winter Solstice.

Ashley, propped up in bed, nibbled on a piece of cinnamon roll. "Everybody has accommodated me, the least we can do is the same for Diana. I can do this. I want to do this. If Diana can't be up, then we need to meet there," she said with an air of finality.

"We can see if Logan is willing to be here with your three and Charlie and Bill have come home for the holidays also. I've talked to Charlie and he's okay hanging out here," Lily said.

"Y'all remember last year? It was so magical with Elizabeth's wedding and all. I loved having the children do the spiral dance. Seems this year… ." Ashley's gaze focused on something distant, outside the window.

"Every Winter Solstice Ceremony is special in its own way. Remember our first one?" Heads nodded. "It was wonderful and we were just finding our way then," Sophia responded.

No patter of little feet as the clatter of shoes pounded down the stairs. "Me first," Rose said elbowing James.

Ashley didn't have to see them to know what was going on. A part of her was relieved to hear the sibling rivalry again.

"Y'all stop right now or I'll tell Eleanor not to give you any cinnamon rolls," she called out. "Where's my morning kiss?"

Rose bounded into the room and jumped on the bed. Ashley was expecting her so had her cup of tea already set on the bedside table. Little arms hugged her neck and Rose's exuberant kisses covered her cheeks. "Much better," Ashley said tucking Rose next to her.

"Next?" Her expectant look at her oldest son was met with a sheepish hang of his head. *He needs a haircut.* She patted the bed and James dutifully sat facing her.

She turned her head and pointed to her cheek. "Right here'd be good."

Warily James approached his mother whose cheek was still turned toward him. She might not be her fastest but—

He darted in for a kiss. Danced back and laughed when he saw his mom's fake frown. "You missed," he taunted.

"I'll give you more kisses, Mom," Rose said in a serious voice. "My kisses help you get well."

"Yes they do," Ashley kissed Rose on the forehead. "But the cinnamon buns keep you strong."

Rose slid off the bed and dashed into the kitchen.

"There's enough for you both as well as your brother and Daniel," Eleanor said in her clipped British accent. "Sit down at the table and mind your manners."

Ashley smiled as the vision of her children sitting quietly at the table failed to materialize. Rose would fidget and James would squirm. Deciding to check on them, she got up and crossed the hall to peek in the kitchen. Both children were sitting as still as statues while Eleanor plated and served the breakfast treat. *They're like strangers to me right now. Will they ever fully recover?*

"I'll just take a couple of these with me," Daniel said entering the kitchen. "I want to check on my crews this morning."

"Here is a thermos of coffee just the way you like it," Eleanor said. "Will you be stopping by for lunch or not until dinner?"

"Dinner."

Ashley was back in her room before his response. The backdoor opened and closed. She stood at her window and watched him cross the deck to his truck.

"In case you've forgotten, Sophia, your cinnamon rolls are decimated by this crew," Eleanor said from the bedroom door.

"That's why I brought extra and put them in the freezer. I figured with Rose's sweet tooth and Daniel being here there'd be nothing left for anyone else."

"Back to this evening," Lily said. "I think if we plan on having dinner at Diana's with everyone present, even the children, we can sort things out from there. If the younger ones want to do something themselves, they can easily come back here. Logan, Bill and Charlie all have licenses.

"I'm also suggesting that we consider starting with what we want to manifest with the coming of the light. The younger children may want to participate in that also."

"I'll stop by Elizabeth and Michael's on the way home and talk to E and Gabby. I've a few treats in the trunk for them also," Sophia said.

"I'll call Hunter and Logan," Ashley volunteered.

"I'll call D," Lily said. "I told her I'd teach the first few weeks of her Winter term. Once that baby girl is born, she'll be back in the classroom in no time. I can cross two items off with one call—Winter term and Winter Solstice!"

ASHLEY LOVED the smell of sage, cedar and lavender. A light haze hovered around the ceiling as everyone smudged. *Our first Ceremony with all the children participating. Almost all. Anthony is upstairs watching a television program. Probably for the best because he still wants to be with Art and I don't need him trying to get custody because of this.*

With prayers said, everyone settled in a circle. A few sat on the floor but Diana was in a recliner and she was also. Logan sat next to Hunter who was next to her. James and Rose were bookends to Daniel. Lily, Jackson and Eleanor, Elizabeth and Michael, Gabriella sat with Charlie and Bill who was next to Diana. The circle was complete, or almost so. In her heart she knew Anthony being upstairs was for the best but somehow it still felt wrong.

"Bringing forth a healthy baby is uppermost on my mind right now," Diana began. "While it's true I've had some difficulties because bed rest is not my normal nature, overall it has been an easy pregnancy. I was much sicker with Bill even though I was never on bed rest. Knowing that another child conceived in love will soon join us gladdens my heart."

"Y'all know I've number eight coming up on Monday. It's my last one. Good health which means a strong body and being cancer free is what I want to manifest this coming year." Ashley passed the rose quartz on to Hunter.

"Celebrating Logan's graduation from high school; celebrating another successful year at Twinkle Toes—I want to manifest experiences to celebrate."

Holding the stone in her hand, Logan looked around the circle. "I want to manifest opportunities to share this experience with all of you throughout the coming year." She looked at her mom, "and I'm looking forward to celebrating my graduation and my acceptance into the college I most want to attend."

James nervously shifted the stone from one hand to the other. "Most of all I want my mom to be well." He shoved the stone at Daniel.

"Manifest? My business remaining profitable... ." His gaze jittered around the room not catching anyone's eye.

Rose reached over and took the stone from him.

"I want to manfest Daniel to be my papa. He'd be a really good one and I could live here forever and have a dog because Daniel said Bingo could come live with us when we went home. I want to manfest my own room with a bed for my dog and," her eyes filled with tears and she look right at Ashley. "I want my mom to be well and happy. Daniel would be a good," she paused and seemed to struggle for what to say next. She leaned over to Lily and whispered something. Lily whispered back. "Daniel would be a good husman for my mom, too."

The stillness was palpable. Ashley's horror showed on her face. Daniel looked shell shocked.

Lily put her arm around Rose, gently lifted the stone from her hand. "I thought we was supposed to say what we wished for?" Rose's voice quivered.

"You are supposed to say what you want to happen," Lily said as she hugged Rose, who struggled not to cry. "You did it just right."

With her arm around Rose and the rose quartz in her other hand, Lily began. "What I most want to manifest in the coming year is more time with Jackson. When Ashley is stronger, I've asked her to help me by checking on some of my clients. I know she'll excel at it and I'll have at least an additional day a week to spend time with Jackson."

The stone passed to Jackson who said "I want what she wants." And passed the stone on to his mother, Eleanor.

"I have realized these past few months how important it is to me to feel necessary or needed. I am now offering my services to any of you who need a helping hand. Of course I'll remain with you until you're on her feet again," she said to Ashley. "But sometimes a new mother can use a little help," she smiled at Diana. "It has been awhile since even my youngest grandchild was in nappies but I do believe I remember how it goes."

"Are you offering to travel?" Elizabeth now held the stone. At Eleanor's nod, she continued. "Expect to spend at least the summer and fall in Ireland then because I intend to manifest a little Murphy by the end of June." Her smile radiant, she handed the stone to Michael.

"We're still discussing whether this child," he said, his brogue thick, "will be born in Ireland or here." He reached over and patted his wife's still flat belly. "Whichever it is, your help will be welcomed."

"My manifestation goal remains the same. To become a published author. I can see, when I look back over the years, I'm much closer to my goal. Fingers crossed it will happen this year," Gabriella handed the rose quartz to Charlie.

"I've already manifested my goal. I want to spend more time with my mom and that's happening. It's easier now that I'm in college. And I've grown up some. Dad even knows I'm here and won't be home this year for Christmas. I've meets this spring so it'll be summer before I'm with my Ohio family and only for two weeks because I've got a summer job at the University of Oregon's Summer Track Camp."

Bill took the stone. Held it up to the light. "It's opaque. Never paid much attention before." He cleared his throat. "Finishing my sophomore year in the top ten percentile of my class is what I want to manifest. I'm going back to Italy for part of the summer in a work study program Giovanni and one of my professors worked out. The last half of the summer I'll be in Ireland finishing it up." He grinned. "Not sure you can count on me to change nappies but I'm pretty good at making funny faces for babies."

A serious look settled on Bill's face and he looked around the circle. "One more thing, I'm grateful for the love and support you've given mom and me over the years. I know there were times when I would have lost her or she would have lost me if not for this circle." As he passed the stone to Matthew, he quipped "Us guys should have something like this."

"What I have control over right now is very little in compared to what I want control over. I would like to manifest a wife who is compliant, at least until the baby is born. I'd like to manifest a strong healthy baby who weighs no more than five pounds. I'd like to manifest a baby who immediately sleeps through the night," he grinned up at Diana, who shook her head an amused look on her face. "What I have control over is manifesting my love for this beautiful woman who carries my child and who has given me a young man to be a part of my life."

He handed the stone to Diana, who kissed his fingers before she let him go. "Time for a break. This little one is dancing on my bladder," she said rubbing her extended belly. She shifted in the recliner to sit up straight and started to wiggle forward.

Matthew leaped up. With an arm around Diana's back and holding her right arm at the elbow, he helped her lever up to stand. Holding her tight against his side, he supported her as she started toward the bathroom down the hall. Ashley heard Diana's giggles in response to something Matthew was saying in a mock ferocious voice.

Everyone was up and moving about. Ashley looked for her children. James was silent, hanging back from the other males. Jackson reached out and pulled him in. Jackson, not Daniel she noted.

Rose was sitting on Lily's lap, her head on Lily's shoulder. Eleanor was patting her foot. *I should be comforting my daughter.* And although she believed that, to join Lily and Eleanor, she'd pass near Daniel. Right now she couldn't imagine being able to do that.

Hunter reached over and tapped her arm. "It'll be okay. Lily and Eleanor will make it all right for Rose and Jackson and Michael will do the same for James. Matthew too when he gets back."

"I've no idea what to say or do around Daniel now. I knew from what Ms. Muir said that Rose has these ideas. Just never thought she'd put them out like she did."

"It isn't a bad dream," Hunter said. "It isn't like she wants you and Art to get back together."

"No, that nightmare is probably Anthony's fantasy." Just the thought of being with Art again and her stomach churned, a dark cloud seemed to hang right over her head. She rubbed her dragonfly pendant and the darkness abated. Her stomach remained a bit queasy but she knew she wouldn't puke.

Diana returned, her step a little lighter but still leaning on Matthew's arm. She paced back and forth across the living room. "Don't want my legs to shrivel up and fall off," she joked.

"If your legs shriveled up, you'd be the first pregnant woman in history to have that happen," Ashley said. "When I was pregnant with Rose, I couldn't see my ankles after four months. Well, I didn't have any ankles to see would be more accurate."

Jackson spoke up. "Here's the plan. Logan and Rose are staying with the women. We men are going to Matthew's man cave and do our own thing to call in the light." He glanced at Lily, one brow quirked.

She gave him a thumbs up.

At the bottom of the stairs Michael called up. "Hey Anthony, you're needed down here. All the men are doing manly things in Matthew's man cave."

Ashley heard an answer but couldn't make out the words.

"Wrong answer, man," Michael said. His footsteps on the stairs were quick and light.

"Don't worry Ash," Elizabeth said. "He needs to be with the others. Sitting by himself and brooding or whatever he's doing, isn't healthy."

"I know and there's nothing I can do to make it better. Used to be so much easier," she said, her eyes filling with tears. One slipped over the rim, trickled down her cheek. "Used to be able to kiss the owee and make it well. Those days are in the past with my boys." She looked over at Rose, a smile flickered. "Hope I have a few more years with my girl." She held out her arms. "How about cuddling up with your mom?"

"You're not mad at me?" Rose's lower lip trembled.

"Now why would I be mad? You asked for what you wanted as we all did."

Rose bolted across the room, jumped up and snuggled down beside her mom. "What happens now?"

"Now," Diana said, "we sing."

January 1, 2005

Ashley heard the phone ring, Daniel's deep voice answering, It still seemed strange to hear a masculine voice, to feel the masculine energy of an adult man. He'd been back in his house for twelve days. The easy camaraderie they'd shared in the past was missing and she didn't know why. Daniel seemed distant with her, a brief word, a curt nod. After several days of racking her brain to try to figure out what she'd done, she'd stopped.

Finished with her chemo treatments her job now was to get her strength and endurance back. While the nausea was pretty much gone, she was weak. The old sayings "drug through a knot hole backwards" or "something the cat wouldn't even drag in" seemed particularly appropriate today.

She stretched and got out of bed, wrapping her robe around her and slipping her feet into her wool slippers. Before she opened the door to the hall, a knock sounded.

Thinking it was one of the kids, she called out, "Come on in."

Daniel stood in the doorway. "That was Lily. Matthew called her. Diana's on the way to the hospital," he said.

"I think this will be harder on Matthew than Diana," Ashley said. "She's done this before and he hasn't."

"He's been to all the classes, read books—."

"I know all that. It's just different when it's your wife. Art wanted to be there when James was born. He was at least at the hospital when Anthony came but wouldn't come into the delivery room. With Rose, well with Rose he didn't come to the hospital at all. Just picked us up in front when we were discharged."

"Don't you resent that?"

"Would I have liked him to be there with me? Of course I would. But some men just aren't cut out for the delivery room. Seeing someone you love scream, moan, curse—all the things women are known to do when in labor and then there's the blood, placenta—well, some men can't handle it."

Ashley crossed the hall to the kitchen. Eleanor was making scrambled eggs and toast. "Smells heavenly."

"And you need to eat a good breakfast my dear," Eleanor said with a knowing look in her eye.

"I will," Ashley promised. "Want to gather my brood first."

At the bottom of the stairs, she stopped and called out. "Breakfast is almost ready. And I need y'all in the living room first."

The patter of little feet was more like a stampede as all three children pounded down the stairs, across the entry hall and into the living room.

Joining them, she gestured them into a circle around her. "I've news." She smiled her brightest smile when she saw the worry flicker across James' face and Rose's lower lip quiver.

"Diana has gone to the hospital. Madison Michelle is coming into the world. Isn't that a wonderful gift on New Year's Day?"

"The baby is being borned?" Rose asked.

"Yes, the baby is. Matthew called Lily who called here."

"Can I go and watch?" Rose implored, hands folded as if in prayer.

"No, sweetheart, you can't go, but as soon as Matthew and Diana say it's okay to visit, you can."

"And if your mother isn't up to taking you, I will," Eleanor said from the doorway. "Breakfast is ready and will only get cold if you tarry too long."

"Before we go in, let's hold hands and send a prayer to Diana, Madison Michelle and Matthew that all is well." Ashley held her hands out. Rose clasped one. She waited for James or Anthony to take the other and then complete the circle. There was no surprise Anthony was last but Ashley stayed centered on gratitude that he joined in.

Eyes closed, she prayed. "Goddess who watches over us, we ask that you especially keep watch over Diana as she brings Madison Michelle forth into this world. Stay with Matthew and let him know all will be well.

"Do you have anything else to add?"

"Goddess, tell Madison Michelle she is already loved by her mom and dad and the rest of us," Rose said. Ashley smiled and winked at her daughter. *She is already connected to the sacred. I'm grateful she had that connection so early in her life.*

She checked with her sons who both shook their heads. "Guess it's time to eat." Before letting go, she gave each of her boys' a kiss on the tops of their heads. *My goodness, James is almost as tall as I am and Anthony isn't far behind.*

"Wash up first," she called out. Instead of turning to the back of the house and the kitchen, Ashley turned to the front door. Standing and looking out the oval etched glass she sent another prayer and a bit of energy to her circle sister. *May your labor be short and uneventful. May the joy of welcoming Madison Michelle into your life ease the pain. May Matthew's experience of having a child overcome his worry for you. Blessed Be.*

~

IN THE END, Ashley's prayers were answered. Madison Michele was born just at midnight according to Matthew who had stayed with Diana through her labor. There were a few dicey minutes, he'd told

Sophia who was the conduit this time, but all was now well. He was fervently glad they had not opted for a home birth because somewhere along there, 911 would have been called and Diana rushed to the hospital.

"Dicey?" She heard later from Lily who was the news passer that Diana had been bleeding more than they liked and the umbilical cord was wrapped around Madison Michelle's neck. Because they were at the hospital, while these were considered complications, they were easily handled.

Ashley sent another dozen prayers to the Goddess for being there with Diana and Matthew as they welcomed their daughter into this world. Sophia stopped by with more cookies and pictures of the baby on her cell phone. The scrunched-up red face was framed by dark hair. Madison Michelle did not appear happy to be here. In a second picture, a tiny fist was jammed in her mouth. A final picture showed Diana and Matthew, besotted looks on their faces with their daughter tucked in between them.

Diana and the baby were kept an extra day because of the complications in the delivery and Madison Michelle's refusal to nurse. She was small, weighing in at 4 lbs. 10 oz. but everything was fully formed and functioning except her desire to eat.

Each day she got updates on Diana and the baby. Thursday she talked to her circle sister on the phone. Later that same day Daniel took the kids over to meet the new extended family member.

"I got to hold her," Rose said in an awestruck voice, her eyes dancing with delight. "Diana said I can teach her all kinds of things when she gets older, like Logan does for me. I'm her hon-hon-"

"Honorary?" Ashley supplied.

Rose's head bobbed as she rushed on. "sister," Rose finished in a rush. "D even said I can teach her about the Goddess and lots of things."

"You'll be very good at that," Ashley assured her daughter realizing as she did so that Rose needed no assurance in this area. *She is my old soul daughter. The only time I've seen her discombobulated was when Art kidnapped her. But even as upside down as everything was for her, she's bounced back fairly well. I know so much of it is having Daniel around. Her world is in order, when he's nearby. I wish I knew what is wrong, why he is so distant these days.*

35 - A NEW YEAR

The next week, she put on her Pink Ribbon shoes, a gift from Lily. Knowing a percentage of the profits were going to support breast cancer research made the gift even more special. She wriggled her toes and flexed her ankles. *They're really comfortable too.*

Even though she ate, she didn't seem to gain back any weight and still tired easily. Afternoon naps were a must. She could do the stairs, check on the kids, do a load of laundry but paid a price when she did so.

One of those burst of energy ended with her sitting in the upstairs hall, waiting for the washing machine to finish so she could put the load in the dryer. Too tired to stand and chilled to the bone yet determined to at least finish this task, she'd pulled her blue quilt with the embroidered dragonflies from the pile of laundry and wrapped it around her.

The clatter of feet charging into the house, young voices calling out for her registered. She had a cramp from being on the hardwood floors. Her efforts to stand were foiled by her legs being caught in the quilt and the cramp.

"Mom!" Rose shouted from the top of the stairs, fright etched on her face.

"Daniel!" James called out as he ran down the hall to her. He leaned over and tried to help her stand.

Daniel appeared behind Rose and James.

Opening her mouth to speak, he cut her off.

"Don't apologize," Daniel interrupted. "You can thank me, but *do not* apologize." He lifted her legs, pulling out the quilt trapped under them. "Cool shoes," he said. "I can see the bottom through the soles."

He helped her to her feet and ordered her back to bed, assigning James and Rose as her watch dogs.

"I'll put the clothes in the dryer," he'd said, turning to do just that.

"I'm not tired," Ashley said. Hearing the defensiveness in her voice, she quelled the urge to stick her tongue out at him.

"Okay, but you are going back downstairs. Fix yourself some tea or something," he said, his back to her as he put wet clothes in the dryer.

"I'll start dinner, then." Ashley said as she shuffled away Rose and James as her escorts.

"Already taken care of."

"We're going to D's and see the baby and then get hamburgers and everything," Rose chattered as they went down the stairs.

Ashley fixed herself a mug of tea and curled up in the big comfortable chair in her room. She slipped the shoes off her feet, examining them before putting them on the floor next to the bed. It seemed strange to examine a pair of shoes but the unique design called for it.

Daniel came in, picked up the quilt and flicked it. The light caught and reflected off the metallic threads in the dragonflies as if they were real and flitting around her, reminding her that there is always light when you look for it in the darkness. He handed the quilt to her and she tucked it around herself.

The awkward silence grew. They used to be so comfortable together, always had something to say at least about the children.

Rose and James crowded into the room and the silence vanished.

"Where's Anthony?" she asked.

"He's watching television," James said.

～

AND SO IT WENT. Each day she tried to do a little more and some days that worked and other days it didn't. Since Daniel had moved back, Eleanor didn't spend the night but she was stopping by on her way home from helping Diana just to check in.

Ashley knew she was letting Daniel know what was going on because on her bad days, he came home with a pizza or submarine sandwiches, Mexican or some other takeout meal. She was grateful she didn't have to figure out how to feed her kids without his help.

"You know how sick your mom has been," she overheard Eleanor telling the children. Ashley was resting after overdoing earlier in the day.

"Even though your mom isn't getting more chemo, it is still doing battle with the cancer. There are days your mom needs to rest and let it do its work," Eleanor said.

"She's dying." Anthony said the words as if fact.

"No she's not," James and Rose screamed at him.

"Anthony," Eleanor's voice was firm yet kindly. "Have I ever lied to you?"

There was silence. Ashley wanted to close her ears but couldn't. Anthony was her son and Eleanor, her friend, was fighting for her.

"I see your head shaking so I'll take that as a "no." I promise you this, then. If I find out that your mother is dying, I will tell you directly. Otherwise, you must believe that while she has been very sick and still has bad days, she is not dying. It is her body's way of fighting the cancer."

"Dad says she's dying," Anthony's mulish tone buffeted her.

"In this your father is wrong," Eleanor calmly replied.

"He is not a liar!" Anthony's angry voice pummeled Ashley's heart.

"I do not recall I said Art was a liar," Eleanor continued. "I said he was wrong. People can be wrong without lying.

"Let me explain it this way. When you were first learning the alphabet, did you say it perfectly the first time?"

There was silence and Ashley imagined Anthony mulling this over and most likely shaking his head.

"Of course you didn't. No child does. Does that mean the child lied when the letters were mixed up? Of course not. The alphabet may have been said wrong but the child did not lie."

"Why does Art keep saying Mom is dying?" James asked, his puzzlement obvious in the question.

"I have no idea," Eleanor answered. "All I know is that your mother is not dying. She is sick and those are two very different conditions."

"Art never cared—," Rose started.

"We don't know that Art never cared. There were years when he was a very good husband and father. Some people hear the wedding vows and don't understand that 'for better or worse, in sickness and in health' will ever happen much less be truly awful. It could be as simple as that. When Art and your mom got married, he might never have believed she'd be so sick, that he'd have to be a mom and a dad to all of you."

"When mom was sick the first time, everyone helped out. Dad was hardly ever around," James said.

"And everyone is here to help out this time, also," Eleanor said. "Who would like a cup of hot chocolate and one of Sophia's chocolate chip cookies?"

Ashley relaxed into the pillows, her eyes closed as she drifted off into the haze. *I am blessed with The Circle. And even more blessed to have The Second String too.* She smiled at the name Daniel, Eleanor, Matthew, Jackson and Logan had given themselves knowing that The Second String allowed The Circle to be there for her and also Diana with fewer challenges.

A pair of dragonflies danced through the garden in her mind's eye. The haze beckoned but she stayed focused on her totem, connected to the present.

Ashley mentally cursed too sick to speak. It wasn't the chemo. She'd picked up a flu bug. Where? Maybe something the kids brought home. She'd only been out of the house a few times: twice to see Madison Michelle and twice to Sophia's since her last treatment December 27. And although her hair was making a valiant effort to grow back in, it was patchy. Daniel had taken her back to Glen's for a shave.

Not only was she bald, she was gaunt. No matter what she did, she couldn't seem to gain any weight.

Her hands gripped the sick bowl next to her. When the vomiting ceased, her strength had ebbed. Her grip faltered.

"I'll take that," a familiar male voice said.

A cool cloth stroked her cheeks, across her forehead. "Better?"

"Hmm," she managed.

"Good."

"You'll be surprised to know," Daniel continued. "Madison Michelle is four weeks and one day old. You might wonder how I know this."

She heard the smile in his words as he continued to run the cool soft cloth over her face.

"Well, since you asked," he chuckled and she strained to open eyes with lids too heavy to move.

"The proud dad manages to be driving by whatever work site I'm at at least once a day. Today I was regaled with pictures of M_2's 4th week birthday gift. Want to know what he got her?"

There was a pause and Ashley knew he waited for her to respond. A slight nod.

"Well, it wasn't a car." Daniel laughed and the bed jiggled. "He got her a new mobile. That little girl has four of them now. Her crib is only so big." He chuckled. "I asked him if he could even pick her up through all the dangling swirling—"

The bucket was back in her hands. Daniel helped her sit a little straighter and continued to support her back as her body strained to empty itself. There was nothing left in her stomach but her body seemed oblivious to that and continued to clench and wretch.

"I'll get Eleanor," he said. "I think you need some of that anti-nausea medication." He eased her back on the pillow and left one hand on the sick bowl.

His footsteps faded but she could hear the timber of his voice so different from Eleanor's British one. Footsteps approached. Gentle hands and a voice that soothed.

"This will help, I'm sure," Eleanor said as she helped Ashley turn on her side. Once the suppository was in place, she pulled the blankets up and tucked them around her. "Rest now, my dear. You'll feel better in a bit."

The haze beckoned but Ashley fought going there focusing on the medication being absorbed by her body, the nausea diminishing and the concerned voices coming from the kitchen.

The back door opened and closed. The truck's engine turned over and revved when he gave it some gas. Her imagination heard gravel crunch as he backed out and drove off. She missed him.

Quiet footsteps came to her door. Eleanor. A gentle pat on her shoulder, a bit of fussing with the blanket. "You will overcome this hurdle, Ashley. You will not give up. I know you can do it and so do you."

37 - IMBOLC

*A*shley was still weak. Doctor Burton had prescribed enhanced nourishment drinks and asked her about her stress levels. Stress, the doctor had said, slows the healing and recovery process. She'd assured the doctor she was meditating and doing everything she could to eliminate stress. The reality was she worried constantly about the children, her future, getting well. Even with Lily's promise of work, she didn't see that as something to sustain her, to give her the resources to independently take care of the kids.

Art had been ordered to pay child support but being in jail, he wasn't working so no monies came in. Daniel and The Circle said not to worry, everything was taken care of but that didn't help—as much as she knew they meant those kind words to help, they did just the opposite.

Debt hung over her like a black guillotine. She owed everyone more than she'd ever be able to repay.

Rose, tucked next to her, patted her hand and whispered, "I'm right here, Mom. I won't leave you."

Her daughter's steady presence helped her stay connected. There was something about that child-body pressed close, the little voice in her ear, the small hands stroking or patting, bringing her comfort that brought her back to the present when the haze called.

My old soul daughter. I'm so blessed.

A baby's whimper, a mother's soothing murmur followed by the sound of a baby nursing. *Madison Michelle.* The images the sounds evoked were happy ones.

"I'm still here, Mom," Rose said, her words followed by a soft pat on Ashley's cheek.

"I know and I'm ever so glad."

"If you apologize, Diana Houston, for feeding that baby I'll be very disappointed." A smile tugged at the corners of her mouth. She could just see Sophia standing, hands fisted on her hips, delivering that blister.

"The Circle—," Diana began.

"Is flexible," Lily added. "You can stay where you are and Ash where she is and we can still create a circle."

A hand snuck under the crazy quilt. Hunter she guessed and shifted. Rose had her other hand. She missed the small hand on her cheek but knew another one of The Circle held it. *One of the biggest gifts in my life was checking out that flyer Sophia sent out. I don't know how I would have coped with all this without these women.*

She started to drift into the light as the ceremony began. "Mom, I have to hold the candle with two hands," Rose said in a soft voice, "but I'm still here. Don't go away, Mom."

Diana started the song about calling in the light. She knew each candle was being lit. Sophia would start by lighting her candle from the one on the altar. From there the one to her left would light her candle from Sophia's. Around the circle they'd go until each candle was lit and the last person would light the kindling in the fireplace.

By concentrating, she could tell when one candle was lit from the next. Rose's intake of breath and soft sigh when Hunter's candle wick lit lifted her spirits. *My Rose is a part of this now. No matter what happens she'll always have these women to help her through life.* Tears welled. *Stop it, Ash. You're going to be okay. Just stop worrying and add your energy to the prayers.*

"May The Light be strong in each of our lives," Hunter said.

"May The Light illuminate the darkest corners of our lives," Gabriella added.

"May The Light shine on our path so we can find our way," Sophia said.

"May The Light's glow surround each of us as we go about our day," Diana sang.

"May The Light drive away our dark thoughts so we see the world around us with The Light," Lily said.

"May we always see and know The Light of Love," Ashley whispered in a raspy voice.

"Blessed Be," they chorused.

"Lily, can I say Blessed Be?" Rose asked.

"Of course you can."

"I like how it feels to say it," Rose added. "It feels pretty."

The Light of Love lives in my daughter. I am blessed.

"Thanks, Eleanor," Ashley said. "I couldn't have done it without you."

The two women were in the kitchen putting the final touches on dinner.

"My pleasure, my dear," Eleanor replied. "My being here gives Jackson and Lily a little time to themselves."

"I'd sure be surprised if you don't have flowers or something waiting for you when you get home."

"Jackson always has been thoughtful," Eleanor said, her fingers entwined around a necklace. "He got this for me," she held out a tree of life design with various gems stones on the limbs. She smiled. "He added to the original one that only had Archie and my children. Now I have Lily and my grandchildren, too."

"Lily has a similar one," Ashley remarked.

"Yes, she does. If you will recall, those two didn't hit it off very well to begin with. Jackson was smitten, not that he would have admitted it then, but he so wanted to give Lily something for Valentine's Day but knew she'd balk at receiving anything.

"I think he was rather creative with the trees. Lily's had Charlie and all of you on it. And I had mine. How could she reject a gift like that? Such a clever son." She chuckled as she put the finishing touches on the salad.

"I'll call everyone for dinner," Ashley said and started down the hall. On the small table at the bottom of the stairs, she picked up a bell and rang it. "Coming, Mom," in three different voices followed by the muted thunder of feet. *I'm glad Daniel decided to put a carpet runner in. Those feet make a lot of noise.*

"Dinner's ready. Wash up first," she called out.

Daniel came in the back door. "I want to shower and change."

"Be quick about it and we'll wait," Eleanor told him.

"You don't have—,"

"Daniel, I said be quick about it and we'll wait. Do not stand around here arguing with me. Get on with it," Eleanor said.

Ashley stood to the side as a grumbling Daniel strode past her. The children pressed the stair railing to let him past.

"What's wrong, Mom," James asked, worry evident in his voice, his face pinched.

"Daniel's had a long hard day working. He just needs some time to clean up and right himself," Eleanor said as they settled around the table in the formal dining room.

"Like Dad when he came home from work and wanted to be left alone?" Anthony asked. "Mom told us he worked hard to take care of us and just needed some time to himself and it didn't mean anything."

"Daniel never used to need time when he first got home. He always used to have time for us," James said still worried.

"Doesn't look to me as if you three washed up very good. Take turns in the hall bathroom. Dinner's just about ready. All your favorites because it's Valentine's Day." Ashley laughed as the children chimed in on the last two words. *I'm so glad I started this tradition before things got bad between Art and me.*

"I'm washing upstairs," Rose announced and scurried up the steps.

"Don't you go bothering Daniel," Ashley called after her.

39 - A VALENTINE'S DAY
DINNER AND...

He knew she was outside his door, lying in wait for him to exit the haven of his room. Technically she was doing what her mom said but he was bothered, more so since having lunch yesterday with Jackson when the tables had been turned. He recalled a similar conversation a few years ago when Lily was recuperating from a bad accident at the Montgomery's home.

"What are you getting Lily for Valentine's Day?" He'd asked in part out of curiosity and in part to needle his friend. Today's exchange was pure needling on Jackson's part.

Insert Ashley for Lily is how Jackson's interrogation began.

Then he shoved the kids in his face as if he didn't know they liked him. "Like you," Jackson had sputtered. "Like you?"

A five minute lecture on the difference between 'liking' and 'adoring' ensued. At least Jackson stopped to take a bite of sandwich, chew and swallow which gave Daniel a few minutes to regroup and attempt to leave.

"Not so fast," Jackson challenged. "We aren't done yet."

Can you fast forward back in time? Scenes from another encounter with Jackson, this one in this house. *Why did I ever... .* He sighed, his hand on the doorknob. *It was obvious he was half in love with her so I tweaked him a bit. Came back to bite you in the butt. Won't you ever learn?*

He rested his head against the smooth oak door, his hand still on the knob. *Jackson is right. I'm afraid of being close to a family. It was much easier when Ash was married and off limits. Kids with no benefits and that suited me just fine.*

Daniel straightened, shook his head as if dusting out cobwebs. *Not cobwebs but old memories. I know the kids are hungry, shouldn't keep them waiting.*

He opened the door without stepping out fairly certain the way was blocked by a blond haired, green-eyed waif of a girl. It was.

"Hi sweetpea."

"Hi papa." She bounced up and took his hand. "Dinner is really good tonight. All our favorites. Mom makes us all our favorites on Valentine's Day because she loves us. Eleanor had to help her because Mom is still getting better but we still have all our favorites. Even yours."

"No one knows my favorite," Daniel joked as they started down the stairs.

"Uh huh! I member. You told me and I helped Dorie fix it." At the bottom of the stairs Rose started to skip down the hall towing him along.

"We're eating in the dining room with the good dishes and everything," she announced as she pulled him into the formal room.

"You didn't—,"

"Yes, we did have to wait. Now you're here and we can eat," Eleanor said. "You may sit at the head of the table, Daniel. Ashley, you at the other end. Children, at a formal dinner, people are seated male, female. So, I will sit on this side with Anthony next to Daniel and Rose and James can sit on the other side. James next to your mother and Rose next to Daniel."

Daniel's favorite was the last thing served—desert: triple layer chocolate cake with a chocolate ganache frosting and Bavarian cream filling. Of course it was melt-in-your-mouth-moaning-delicious just like everything else served. *No doubt in my mind Jackson will check in to see how this damnable evening went.*

Everyone was in cahoots or so it seemed to him. The children cleared the table and helped Eleanor put leftovers away and load the dishwasher. Once that was done, they asked Eleanor to come upstairs, check on their homework, tell stories and basically leave Ashley and him alone. He could make his excuses and leave her here at the table. Why he didn't was a thought for another day.

"A fire is laid, I can light it for you," he said, rising from the table.

"That would be mighty nice of you," Ashley said in her soft drawl, the one that crawled under his skin and settled in.

He rounded the table, pulled back her chair and with a light touch on her elbow, guided her into the living room to the couch in front of the fireplace. A strike of a match on the rough brick surface and a flame flared. Within minutes the cheerful crackling of the fire filled the room, warmth radiating from the blaze.

"Y'all know I don't bite," Ashley said patting the cushion next to her. "You see the fire better from the couch than the recliners."

What she said was the truth, so he sat. He called Rose Sweet Pea. Tonight it was the scent Ashley wore. It wreathed around him as if a rope, lassoed and pulled him in.

He slouched on the couch, feet crossed at the ankles and arms at the chest. How he could be tense and relaxed at the same time he wasn't sure but when he checked the urge to bolt and run outside, jump in his truck and drive away it seemed countered by the urge to just be. For now he chose the latter reminding himself he had the keys to the little house and could always leave.

ASHLEY KNEW her feelings for Daniel were not superficial but she hesitated to put a name to them. She didn't think her feelings were all about gratitude for all he'd done but she didn't want to examine them too close. After all who would want a woman with scars inside and out and three kids?

Sitting on the couch, she breathed deep, inhaling the scent of his after shave, a scent that meant she was safe and cared for. *I should know the name.*

He's like a furnace and would keep me warm on the coldest—Stop right now, Ash. You know going there can only lead to trouble. She shifted so she sat sideways on the couch facing him. It was time to talk, to find out what was wrong.

Her courage wavered.

Her hand patted her pants pocket where another dragonfly totem lay. *I'll never get to the bottom of this if I don't say something.*

"I hope Rose didn't pester you too much," she started.

"Nope."

"That's good. I know she can be a pest but she means no harm by it," she forged on.

"She's six, Ash. Of course she means no harm," he said, annoyance showing. He stared into the flames.

"She turns seven next week," she said. Trying for a bit of humor she added, "Has she asked you to marry her yet?"

"No, she asked me to marry you," he said sitting up.

Her face flamed with chagrin mixed with embarrassment. "I'm sorry, Daniel. I'll talk to her."

"Stop apologizing. You aren't responsible for every word that comes out of her mouth or James or Anthony's either for that matter." He heard the exasperation in his tone, scrubbed his hand down his face. "Look," he said turning towards her. "I can handle it." He started to rise.

"Please don't go yet," her soft voice implored.

He stopped mid-rise and sank down on the couch.

"I don't know how to say this, so I'd really appreciate you listening, hearing me out before you take off or say something," Ashley said. At his nod, she continued.

"I've already thanked you and told you how much I appreciate all you've done for the kids and me but there is more. Something has happened since you went to New Mexico and I don't know what it is. I don't know what I did wrong or what the kids did wrong. I don't think you'd be upset with us because of what Art did," she said, watching him intently for any sign that her words had an effect.

"You and I used to talk about all kinds of things. I used to hear you laugh with the kids as if you enjoyed being around them. Since New Mexico, it's like you've gone away even though you now live here," she looked over at the fire and fought the urge to wring her hands. Turning back to him, she went on.

"I thought we were friends at one point. I don't want to lose that friendship. I know my kids adore you and…. . Well, I don't know what more to say except, please tell me what happened. I'll do everything I can to fix it," Ashley said a hint of plea in her words. She stopped, glanced at the fire and then back at him.

"Of course it could just be that it's time for us to go. I'm better now and can manage things at the little house with the kids and all. I will understand if it's as simple as that. It just feels like it's something more…." Her words trailed off.

He sat, stoic. He hadn't moved but had he really listened?

Now what? She's given me an out. Do I take it? Jackson would kick my butt to kingdom come and back again if I lie to her.

He stood and stirred the fire, adding a log.

"I'm thirsty, want something to drink?" he said, stalling for more time.

Ashley popped up from the couch. "What do you want? I'll get it for you."

"I can get my own," he growled and stomped off to the kitchen. He grabbed a beer from the refrigerator and then put it back. *No coffee.* He pulled a bottle of soda from the refrigerator door, ice from the fridge door clinked into the glass. The cold fizz on his dry throat didn't ease his arid mind. Like a desert of blowing sand, words swirled forming a mirage. *What am I going to say? Good night and go up to bed. Coward.*

Jackson's words from the hellish lunch came to him. "She's been through a lot but she's a survivor. You owe her the truth. Trust me on this, she'll think it's something she did or something one of the kids did." *When did he get to be such a know-it-all. Must be Lily's coaching.*

He chugged half the soda, filled the glass with the rest of the bottle. Taking down another glass he filled it with ice water. His gut churning, sweat dampening his shirt, his jaw clenched, he returned to the living room.

After handing Ashley the water, he chose to sit in the recliner. He told himself it was because he could see her better from that angle. And that was true. He easily saw her sharp intake of breath, the rigid way she held herself when he moved to the recliner. The look on her face tore at his heart and he almost moved back to the couch, back to sit next to her.

He'd never get said what needed to be said if she was so close.

Daniel cleared his throat, took another swallow and looked into the coals. Words were a jumble in his mind and stuck in his throat. In desperation he looked over at Ashley, sitting on the couch, waiting for him to speak, to tell her what she needed to do to change things back to the way they were. Jackson was right. She deserved the truth.

He started his story from his childhood weaving a tale of a large and happy family life. His father had been killed when he was seven, his mother remarried when he was nine. His step-father, a widower, was a great guy and loved him and his younger brother and sister as his own. Two more children were born, add that to his three step brothers and he was the oldest of the eight kids.

Even though both of his parents worked to support them, they always had dinner together, even if one of them went back to work or ensconced themselves in their bedroom to finish up whatever was brought home.

"As the oldest, I ended up with more responsibilities for the younger ones, especially the two babies of the family. The youngest a little girl," his voice shook.

"Every summer we had a family vacation," he looked at her without seeing her, lost in the memories of happy times. "We regularly went to the beach for the day or maybe a weekend and some summers it's where we spent the whole vacation. Other years we took road trips to see relatives.

"A couple of years when money was tight, we stayed home. We

might have been at home at night but every day was an adventure with outings to the park, picnics in the yard, going to outdoor concerts and even an indoor movie.

"The year I was twenty-one, I was working construction. We had a deadline to meet and I needed to stay late. I had my own car and told everyone to go on without me and I'd catch up." Unbidden the sob claimed his voice, no words, only choking noises as he struggled to gain control.

"Y'all don't have to tell me everything." Ashley's arms wrapped around his neck and she sat on the arm of the chair. Letting go, she stroked his hair back off his forehead.

His arms wound around her waist pulling her onto his lap. Burying his head in her shoulder he continued, "A drunk driver crossed the meridian and hit them head-on. I heard a traffic report there was an accident, that life flight was being called in, traffic was backed up but it never occurred to me my family was involved."

She held him close, murmured words of comfort, never once saying it would be all right because she knew for him it would never be all right. He'd survived. If he hadn't stayed to work, he would have been with them.

"My youngest sister survived for a few hours. Long enough to get to the trauma center, long enough for the police to pull me over and escort me to the hospital, long enough for her to hold my hand and tell me she loved me one more time. We'd argued that morning, something stupid that siblings do. I'd stormed off to work without telling her I loved her."

"Y'all were able to tell her at the hospital."

"She died within minutes of my arriving and didn't hear me."

"Of course she heard you." Ashley tipped his head and looked him straight in the eyes. "Of course she heard you, Daniel. She either heard you with her human ears or her angel ears. In her heart she always knew you loved her. Don't think for a minute that isn't true.

"Think back to that morning and the fight. Did you stop loving her because of it? No, you didn't. I don't even need you to answer that question because I know you well enough to know you don't just stop loving someone when you are upset with them or don't like what they are saying."

Silence.

Her hand dropped away and he looked at the fire.

Minutes passed. She waited.

Finally she shifted to stand. His arm tightened around her waist.

"I'm sorry for your loss, Daniel. I don't really know how you feel but I can relate a little because when Art took off with the kids, I went a little crazy because they are my life. Why would I still fight the cancer if not for them? But you did live and you've made a good life for yourself. You are loved and respected by many people.

"All I can figure out is you're afraid to have a family again and maybe lose it. Is that it?"

He nodded.

"I'm not asking you to marry me, Daniel. Just be my friend. That's enough. Be my friend and go back to being my kids' friend. I'll talk to them and let them know we can be friends but not a family. They, well Rose, will be disappointed, but if you will be their friend, it'll be okay."

When he didn't reply, Ashley rose. "I'm going to bed now. You need to get some sleep too." She made sure the fireplace screen was in place and the glass of soda in the center of the side table. As an afterthought she pulled the throw off the back of the couch and put it around his shoulders. At the door into the hall, she glanced back.

He hadn't moved.

Ashley walked on and turned off the lights.

40 - TAKING A TIME OUT

*D*aniel shivered awake. Pain streaked through his neck, down his back and shoulders. Sledge hammers pounded in his head. "That's what you get for sleeping catawampus in a chair," he muttered shifting to stand.

Struggling to his feet, he cautiously took a step. Both legs were tingling. "Falling is not an option," he grumbled. A glance at the grandfather clock in the hall showed him the time was five. *At this time of year, even the sun is still asleep.*

Shuffling into the kitchen, he closed the door into the hall before running water to make coffee. He shoved his cup under the first drips and sipped the hot liquid a bit too soon. *Damn!* He muttered, sticking his hand under the ice maker's chute. As soon as he had a cube in hand, he stuck it in his mouth and sucked.

"Shower, a shower will help," he told himself as he climbed the stairs to his room. But a shower didn't help, neither did another cup of coffee, or a cup of the special blend with a double shot of espresso at the coffee shop at the bottom of the hill.

Oh he was awake, awake and almost jittery from the over-dose of caffeine, but the oblivion he sought from his thoughts and their attendant feelings seemed even further away.

A benefit of owning his own construction company was he could do what he wanted. He picked up a hammer and delivered punishing blows to nails. His crew stayed clear, responded when spoken to but did not offer comments much less jokes.

This was a new boss, one they'd never seen before. Over their own lunches one remarked the closest he'd ever seen the boss like this was when those kids were kidnapped. Heads nodded. What had him in such a state now? No one knew and no one wanted to ask.

Daniel knew his crew saw him as a bit off his rocker. *Well, what if I am. What saved me back then was the physicality of work. It'll have to do the same now.*

Thirty-three degrees out but sweat dripped off his nose. His hair plastered to his head, his shirt to his body were the outward signs of the turmoil that raged inside. He drove his crew, taunted them to keep up with him, knew some might quit thinking he'd gone round the bend. And still he forged on. His arms ached, his hands were blistered, his eyes burned and still he worked.

The familiar black Jaguar that parked on the street next to the work site was not welcomed but it wasn't a surprise. The sable-haired, gray-eyed, grim-faced man who got out was also not welcomed but also wasn't a surprise.

"Time to knock off," Jackson said to Daniel's crew. "Be back at the regular start time in the morning. No, make that nine—that'll do, be here at nine."

Daniel glared at his friend but said nothing. The men had stopped working. He didn't have to look around, silence at a construction site was a sure sign no one was doing anything. He glanced at the lead man who stood there looking at him. No one would leave until he said so.

He nodded.

Every man there moved quickly to clean up the work area, stow the gear and high-tail it out of there. In less than ten minutes the crew was gone.

"Buy you a beer or something stronger," Jackson said.

"Why are you here?"

"We're friends."

The hammer slipped from his grip and landed inches from his toes. He was too beat to bend over and pick it up except that was a core principle. Just like cowboys took care of their horses, construction workers took care of their tools. He looked down at the hammer and started to squat down to pick it up.

"I'll get it," Jackson said. "You grab your tool belt and thermos. Meet you at your truck."

Daniel moved slowly as much because his muscles were in total rebellion as he didn't want to hear what Jackson had come to say. *A beer or something stronger isn't going to help.*

Resigned to the inevitable, Daniel stowed his gear and followed Jackson to the little house. He parked in the driveway when Jackson parked on the street and waved him on.

"Shower? I brought a change of clothes just in case," Jackson said, shoving a sack at him.

"Probably would be a good thing," Daniel said. He shot a look of pure disgust at his friend before shuffling off to the bathroom. The hot water eased the soreness in every cell in his body. The air full of steam eased his headache. *If only I could wash these memories down the drain.* He leaned against the shower wall and let the massage jets beat his shoulders and back. *But memories are all I have left of my family.*

The water warmed. Daniel turned it off, got out and dried off. Putting clean clothes on, he wrapped his dirty ones inside his shirt and left them in a corner of the bathroom.

When he walked through the kitchen, he saw a bottle of his favorite whisky, a bottle of his favorite red wine, a bottle of his favorite rum, an ice bucket filled to the brim, another bucket with cold beer and several bottles of mixer all lined up on the counter. Simmering on the stove was Jackson's special marinara sauce. Another pot filled with water to cook the homemade spaghetti waited to be heated.

He continued on into the living room where Jackson was sprawled on the couch with the television on, volume down low. Daniel knew he was watching either the Home and Garden or the DIY network.

"Don't let me disturb you," Daniel said when Jackson straightened and turned off the television.

"Rerun," Jackson said standing. "I'll start the water for the pasta." He paused in the kitchen doorway, "What'll you have?"

"Am I getting drunk?"

"Depends on how long it takes you to wise up."

"Saying I'm stupid?"

"Nope, saying your human. While I don't remember getting drunk over Lily, I do remember Michael talking about Paddy sobering him up when Elizabeth left. Figure you're more like Michael than either Matthew or me."

He went on into the kitchen.

Daniel stood in the doorway and watched as Jackson deftly stirred his sauce, started the spaghetti water, put a loaf of bread in the oven to warm and got a tossed salad out of the refrigerator.

"No dessert?"

Jackson gestured to the array of liquor and mixers on the counter. "Figured this would serve."

"So Ashley called Lily and Lily called you and—," he started out, each word infused with hostility.

"Just to start us off with the truth," Jackson interrupted. "Ashley did not call Lily and Lily did not call me. Matthew stopped by to show you Madison Michelle's latest pictures," he held up his hand when Daniel opened his mouth.

"He called me and said something was wrong. You were driving your crew and swinging a hammer as if you were intent on murder or something. I then called Lily and said I was hanging out with you tonight here and that she and Eleanor were on their own for dinner. If I was sober enough I'd be home, otherwise I'd see her in the morning."

Daniel turned on his heel, stomped back into the living room and flounced on the couch. "Flounced, I just flounced on the couch, you —," he stopped short of cursing knowing Jackson had done nothing to deserve his anger.

He sat up, head in his hands, elbows on his knees. Neither had his crew. He hoped they didn't all quit. It would serve him right it they did but they were a top-of-the-line crew and had been with him for years. *I hope they give me a break.*

"Here," Jackson held out a glass with ice and whiskey and—Daniel sniffed the glass—sour mix. "Maybe this will sweeten your mood."

Daniel took a sip and choked. "What? Did you just wave the cap from the bottle of mix over the glass?"

"It's half and half," Jackson replied.

"The hell it is," Daniel growled taking another sip. "I'll be falling down drunk before dinner."

"Water should be boiling in a few minutes and dinner will be served in less than ten. Just don't chug it down and you'll be fine."

"I'll set the table," Daniel offered.

"Great, just put plates and silverware on the counter. We'll do this buffet style except dish up out of the pots."

"What no freshly grated parmesan cheese or the perfect blending of sauce to pasta?"

"Freshly grated cheese is in the fridge."

The water boiled and Jackson slowly added the pasta. "The bread is half garlic and half just butter. I brought enough cheese so you can add it to your bread, your spaghetti, and even your salad if you want."

"You do know you've spoiled me," Daniel pulled the dish of parmesan cheese out of the fridge along with the pasta salad. "I can tell if parmesan isn't freshly grated."

Jackson tested the pasta, determined it al dente or perfect and quickly drained it. He dumped the steaming noodles into the sauce and gently stirred them together. Pulling the pan of bread from the oven, he announced, "Dinner is ready."

Daniel added the parmesan cheese to the bread, spaghetti and tossed salad. He did not add it to his drink which was refilled once before dinner was over.

"Man, I don't know how you do it," Daniel said patting his very full belly. "It seems so effortless when you're working in the kitchen. I can cook the basics but usually open a can or box. It's easier even if it doesn't taste as good."

"It relaxes me. And I remember mother being so grateful whenever my dad cooked breakfast or grilled something for dinner. You'd think he'd given her diamonds." He leaned back in his chair, a soft grin on his face. "Now my Lily and mother are alike that way. I sometimes wonder if my cooking was the deciding factor in Lily consenting to marry me."

"The women in The Circle are so different. I knew Lily wasn't a fan of housework or cooking," Daniel said.

"And neither is Diana. The joke amongst them is that both of them would go without new clothes to have someone come and clean house for them," Jackson said and smiled. "That is a true statement when it comes to Lily."

"I remember Lily talking about Hunter and Logan helping her out when she was in that accident," Daniel said. "Sophia loves her garden and cooking. She's always dropping something by for Ash and the kids."

"I remember being right here in this room with Lily, Diana and Sophia when I realized that if I didn't win them over, I'd never have Lily in my life. They come first and we men come next."

"Doesn't look to me like you come in second with Lily," Daniel remarked. "And Ashley's kids come first."

"I don't kid myself, if one of them called, Lily would be out of the house in a minute. Look what they did when Elizabeth—,"

"I know what you mean. They are a formidable group. You do know we're called 'The Second String' don't you?"

Jackson laughed. "Yeah, I heard about that. But it isn't because of me. It's you, Matthew, Logan—,"

"Don't forget your mother. Without Eleanor I don't know what we'd have done until the others could show up."

They finished dinner, cleared the table, loaded the dishwasher and turned it on before refreshing their drinks and heading back to the living room.

"I'm listening," Jackson said, his gaze locked with Daniel.

"And I'm supposed to talk?"

"That's the idea," Jackson said, taking a sip. "You talk, I listen and then we solve the problem."

"What problem?"

"Stalling will only get you drunk before the problem is solved. But I'll play along for now. The problem you have so you beat yourself and your crew up today. That problem."

One of the things he always liked about Jackson was his loyalty which translated into his showing up and being there when you needed something. *Guess now is one of those times he's showing up whether I asked him to or not.* Daniel rubbed his forehead where a dull ache was beginning to form.

"You said I owed Ashley the truth about why I've changed. She asked me what she and the kids had done. Actually pinpointed the change to when the kids were kidnapped."

He took a large swallow of the amber liquid, held it in his mouth while it warmed before letting it slowly trickle down his throat. The sweet and sour mixer dulled the taste of the whisky but not its effect.

Jackson didn't respond and when Daniel glanced over at him, his friend just sat there watching him, occasionally sipping his drink. Waiting, being there, staying until the problem was solved.

"Did you know angels have ears?" Daniel said, his voice shaky. "Ashley said my sister heard me say I was sorry and that I loved her. She said if she didn't hear my words with her human ears she heard them with her angel ears."

Tears flowed in a steady stream down his cheeks, dripped off his chin onto his shirt leaving blotches and dots like Rorschach paintings. What would someone see if they looked?

"It was a stupid fight that morning. Too many people living in a house with one bathroom." His voice broke with emotion. "I'd made up my mind to move out and had looked at an apartment at lunch. 'Show them' I thought to myself. Twelve hours later there wasn't anyone to show anything to."

Jackson removed the glass from Daniel's hand. In a steady quiet voice he asked, "And what does this have to do with Ashley, James, Anthony and Rose? I know you miss your family. I know you regret what happened. I know you even feel guilty that you weren't there, that you didn't die too."

Earnest, he leaned forward and continued, "I, for one, am very glad that didn't happen because then I wouldn't have known you, had you for a friend. I'm going to repeat what I said the other day at lunch. Don't let your fear of losing something keep you from having whatever it is. In this case, don't let your fear of losing Ashley and the children keep you from having a family of your own.

"You do know, my friend, there are no guarantees. I could lose Lily, god forbid, tomorrow. I almost did lose her in the accident and that was before we'd created what we have today. But I can tell you right here and right now, I wouldn't trade a minute of what we have for anything."

"Don't you ever worry about how you'd manage if anything happened to her?" Daniel stared at Jackson wanting to catch every nuance of his answer.

"Not really. I know I'd be devastated and wish I was dead too. But I'd have you to help me through it and now Matthew and Michael. Giovanni would come. And the women, the other women in The Circle would gather round me also. And then I do still have my mother.

"But you Daniel, you have all of us. And if you lost Ashley, you'd still have the children. Rose more than the boys needs you in her life. Can you imagine what it must be like for her to know her own father doesn't want her? I shudder at the thought of what she went through." Jackson sat back, sipped his drink and waited. He didn't have to wait long.

"When it's just the two of us, she calls me "Papa," Daniel said, a soft smile on his face. "I've told her not to but she ignores me." The soft smile morphed to a rueful one. "What am I going to do to her? Wash her mouth out with soap? Tell Ash? I try to ignore her but—,"

"And when she calls you Papa, do you feel sick like you're going to vomit?" Jackson asked.

"Of course not!" Daniel exclaimed, appalled at the idea.

"In your mind are you screaming at her to stop?" Jackson asked, his mild-manner at odds with the words.

"Jackson, what's the matter with you?" Daniel was on his feet and pacing. "No, I don't think things like that or feel sick. It's just uncomfortable because I know I can't give her what she wants from me," he said, tunneling a hand through his hair.

"Really?" Jackson's brow raised in a disbelieving arch.

"Okay, I'm afraid." Daniel sat back down, slouched in the couch corner.

"Tell me something I don't know," Jackson countered. "Tell me what you're going to do about it. How you're going to face it? How you're going to defeat the ghosts of your family?"

"I don't want to defeat the ghosts of my family. That's all I have left," Daniel said, tiredness coating the last words.

"I'm not asking you to forget them, Daniel," Jackson said. He stood and crossed the room, rested his hand on Daniel's shoulder. "I'm asking you to look at how to add another family and other memories to your life so when you are at the end, you have no regrets."

"You have no regrets?"

"If I think of things as happening in that 'right time' the women are always talking about, then no I don't."

He crossed the room and sat back down in the chair. "I'm going to ask you the most damnable question I know. If there was a way to move past your fear of losing Ashley and/or the children and claim them for your own, would you?"

Daniel studied the liquid, shifting in the glass as if the answers were just under the surface. "That is a damnable question."

He took a sip, knew he was at a crossroads. He could just see the look on Ashley's face if he told her he'd gotten drunk and in the process had made a decision. She wouldn't be pleased.

Setting the glass on a coaster on the table, he leaned back against the couch. Looking at the ceiling, no answer appeared. "Do you have any suggestions?"

"Only one," Jackson replied.

"Care to share it?"

"Keep talking to her. Keep searching for a way to make everything come together. Keep—well, you get the idea. One of the most painful times of my life was spent on this couch with Lily.

We used it as a marker to chart the progress in sorting things out between us. So many times I wanted to get up and leave but I didn't. Why?" He paused waiting to see if Daniel cared to hear the answer.

"Are you going to keep me in suspense?"

"Because I loved her and wanted her in my life. I knew I had to find a way through her defenses if that was to happen. As it turned out, she loved me too so in the end we got our most of the time happily-ever-after."

"You loved Lily and Lily loved you—,"

"And you love Ashley and the children and they love you."

"How do you know?"

"It shows, Daniel. Those children—,"

"But Ash has never indicated anything more than friendship. That's what she said she wanted back, our friendship."

"And you'd told her you loved her and wanted to marry her and adopt the children?"

"Well, no."

"Why with all she's been through and what she's dealing with now, would she profess her undying love for you?"

"You mean I have to go first?"

"Pretty much. And don't expect her to leap in your arms and smother you with kisses either."

"I'll have to work to win her over?"

"I'd be surprised if you didn't. How much work I don't know. But she is guarded and vulnerable. She will protect herself and her children. Just be prepared."

"I can do that. I was a Boy Scout. Made Eagle. That's our motto."

Daniel rose and took his glass to the kitchen. He dumped out the inch left in the glass. "Lots to think about and I think I'll do that better if I spend the night here. You're welcome to join me."

"Nope, I'm in good shape to get myself home. I've got a loving wife waiting for me and that's incentive enough. She'll be very pleased I'm home and sober."

Daniel watched his friend drive away. He washed up their glasses and put the leftover food away. *Something for lunch tomorrow. I'll take it all and give it to the crew. Maybe make up for how I treated them today.*

Climbing the stairs to the bedroom, he saw his sister, a smile on her face, at the head of the stairs. Or maybe he didn't. Because when he blinked, she was gone. Dreams assaulted him during the night but never turned into his worst nightmare. Upon waking, semi-rested, he dressed, gathered up the food, stopped and purchased a dozen donuts and a box of coffee before dropping by the job site.

"Peace offering," he said as he put everything down on a pick-up truck tailgate. "Be back later." He heard the murmurs and audible sighs of relief as he turned and strode back to his truck. "Might as well stop by and make sure the kids made it to school."

41 - THE JUDGE

*D*aniel walked into a tornado of panicked activity. Stupefied, he stood frozen in the doorway, winter winds blowing past him.

"Shut the door," Eleanor ordered.

Her sharp tone and frantic look was enough to prod him the rest of the way into the room, shoving the door closed in the process.

"What's going on?"

Ashley rushed out of the hall bathroom, a towel her only covering, gasped at seeing him and darted into her room.

Daniel's concern meter skyrocketed. "What is going on?" He asked in a near shout, enunciating each word, while standing in the middle of the hall at the entrance to the kitchen.

"The judge," Eleanor managed, wiping down the counter he'd just seen her clean as he came through the door.

"The judge what?"

"Emergency hearing at 1 p.m. I sent Jackson to find you when you didn't answer your phone."

"What?!" He reached in his pocket and pulled out his phone. It was charged, he unplugged it this morning. It was charged but it was off.

Swearing under his breath, he turned it on. As soon as it booted up, he saw five, no six missed calls from Eleanor and Jackson.

"I'm here now. Who does she want to see?"

"All of us."

"All? Even me?"

"All," Eleanor echoed. "And yes, even you and me. Lily, Jackson, of course Ashley. I suspect Ms. Muir will bring the children although I could be wrong. When Ashley asked about bringing them, the judge's response was 'no'.

"What with parking downtown being so scarce, Ashley and I want to leave around noon so I can drop her off and find a place to park. She is doing better but I worry about her stamina all the same." Eleanor looked around the kitchen. "That will have to do. I need to take care of myself. I cannot go to court looking like this," she said in a horrified voice, looking at her reflection in the windows.

Daniel was glad he'd taken the time to shower and shave that morning and had yet to get dirty and sweaty. He looked himself over deciding a pair of dress slacks and newer boots would be a better choice to wear to court.

Daniel dropped Ashley and Eleanor off in front of the courthouse and found a parking spot in a nearby garage. They arrived at the courthouse at ten to one and waited for twenty more minutes before being shown into Judge Peterson's chambers. The children sat to the side of the judge's desk. Anthony wore his normal sullen look, James looked nervous, but Rose looked triumphant.

He escorted Ashley to a chair next to the children and stepped away only to be told by the judge to sit in the chair on the opposite side of her desk. Eleanor and Lily with Jackson in between sat in the chairs in front.

"Perhaps I misjudged the situation," Judge Peterson said looking directly at him.

"I'm afraid I don't know what you're talking about, Your Honor," Daniel said.

Her smile did not ease his nerves in the least. A knock on the door announced more people coming to this meeting.

At the judge's welcoming response, the door opened and Ms. Lawford, with Art and his attorney stood waiting.

The judge assigned everyone their seating, having Ms. Lawford squeeze in next to Ashley and Art and his attorney next to her. Lily, Eleanor and Jackson moved their chairs closer to him and back a ways so they now all sat in a semi-circle around the judge's desk.

"It's been brought to my attention that all is not going smoothly at the house," the judge said, directing her remarks to Daniel.

"I'm not sure what you mean, your honor," Daniel replied, curbing the impulse to squirm.

"It seems you are not as engaged with these children as you were before you moved back to your home," Judge Peterson clarified.

"I see them every day, sometimes drop them off at school, check in with them in the evenings. Ask about their day, homework, school. I'm still not sure what the problem is." Tension in his posture, he shifted in the chair.

"As you know Ms. Muir has been seeing the children once or twice a week over the last eight or nine weeks. She's noticed a change in the energy level, I believe are the words she used in her reported. The children tell me you don't like them as much as you once did."

"That's preposterous," Daniel sputtered. "Of course I still like them, just as much if not more than before."

"I'm glad to hear that, Mr. O'Donnell." The judge turned to Ashley. "And how do you see Mr. O'Donnell's relationship with you and your children at this point, Ms. Carlyle?"

He watched her fidget, twist her hands together, pick at the hem of her top. "Daniel, Mr. O'Donnell has been," she paused as if trying to find the right words, "very generous and helpful. I can do the stairs but they tire me out so he and Eleanor, Mrs. Montgomery are the ones who see that my kids are settled in for the night.

"These past weeks he's been… ," her voice trailed off and she looked at him in desperation.

"Your Honor," Daniel began. "I lived in this house for five years; the first two spent restoring it. It's taken some getting used to is all."

"Do I understand you to say you want Ms. Carlyle and her children to remain in the house with you?" Judge Peterson asked, her voice deceptively calm.

"Yes, I very much want them to remain. The kids are doing well in school and are making friends in the neighborhood. Ms. Carlyle is still regaining her health. I think having a stable living situation where the kids are happy can only help. With the help of Mrs. Montgomery and Ms. Carlyle's other friends, we're making it."

"Through the end of the school year then?" The judge leaned toward him, her hands folded on her desk, her eyes searching his.

A peace settled over him, the stomach that was in revolt calmed, the steel bars in his shoulders and back melted. Was that his sister's voice telling him to go for it, he'd suffered long enough? "As far as I'm concerned, this is Ashley and the kids' home. While they can move if they insist, I hope they stay for a very long time." When he looked away from the judge, he saw Ashley's grey eyes filled with tears. Rose and James had silly grins on their faces. Only Anthony looked like he was going to cry.

"I'm glad that's settled then," the judge said. "Now on to the next item. I have considered the request from James and Rose to change their last name. While they will accept their mother's maiden name, Carlyle, their first choice is O'Donnell. I will not grant that without your permission and also Mr. Kenner needs to have his say.

"Mr. Kenner? Do you have any objections to Rose and James changing their last names?"

Daniel was glad looks couldn't kill or he and Ashley would for sure be dead, followed by the judge and Ms. Lawford. His attorney's hand on his arm seemed to settle Art a bit.

"If the girl wants to change her name, I have no objections."

The girl? Daniel gripped his chair to keep from reaching across

Eleanor, Jackson, Lily, Ashley and Ms. Lawford to grab the bastard by the throat and shake him. *The girl?*

The judge's voice had a hard edge to it. "Your daughter, Rose, is who is being referenced. I take it then that you have no objections to her changing her name?"

"None."

"Do you have any objections to my terminating your parental rights to her? Before you answer, let me tell you what that will mean. You will have no responsibility to or for her in any way. No child support, no say in her upbringing. You will have no contact with her until she is eighteen at which time, should she choose to have contact with you she can. If she doesn't, you still can't. That order severs any and all ties to her."

Art turned to his attorney and they had a whispered conversation. When he turned back to the judge he said, "I have no objections at all, Your Honor."

A sharp intake of breathes.

Then silence.

Judge Peterson was the first to recover. "I'll give you time to think it over, Mr. Kenner. We have a review hearing scheduled for March 18. If you do not change your mind, that will be my order."

"I won't change my mind," Art shot back. "I don't even think—"

"Thank you for the time to think it over, your honor," Mr. Treeland, Art's attorney interrupted. "If I might add, Mr. Kenner will not entertain a similar idea with regards to his sons, Art Jr. and Anthony."

"Art Jr.'s name was legally changed to James, at his request. I suggest your client get used to the idea that Art Jr. no longer exists." Judge Peterson scanned the room's occupants.

"I am continuing the order requiring Daniel O'Donnell live in his home as well as his legal guardianship of all three children. It is so noted that at this time Mr. Art Kenner objects to his son, James, changing his last name but does not object to his daughter, Rose, changing hers." She looked over at Daniel. "What are your objections to Rose using your last name?"

"I have none, your honor. I'd be very proud to continue as her guardian and have her carry my last name."

Rose jumped up and ran around the back of the judge's desk. She leapt into his lap, tugged one of his arms around her and snuggled.

James, Daniel noted, looked out the window. He swiped his face with the back of his hand.

Art stabbed a finger in his direction while glaring at Ashley. "I knew she wasn't my kid. He's been in her pants for years."

Daniel thought to deny the accusation that he and Ashley were intimate but thought twice before saying anything. Why dignify the remarks with a response. Although glad he wasn't the direct object of Art's fury, he paled knowing that hatred was turned on Ashley.

But when he looked in her direction, she wasn't even in her chair. She was squatting next to James, talking to him in a quiet voice, smoothing a lock of hair off his forehead, comforting him. Paying no attention to the a-hole she'd been married to.

Judge Peterson stated the terms of her order which included Rose using the last name of Carlyle. She explained that she would make a final ruling on March 18th regarding last names. She dismissed everyone except James and Daniel. Rose did not want to let him go but the judge stepped in and told her in this she had no choice. She must go with her mother.

A reluctant Rose dragged her feet, looked back over her shoulder and stopped just on the other side of the door. Ashley bent down and said something and Rose moved a bit farther. The door closed.

"I'm going out of a limb here," Judge Peterson said to James. "I can see your disappointment in having Mr. Kenner's last name. I've asked Mr. O'Donnell to remain because I think I know his answer but I want you to hear it.

She stood and turned to Daniel. "I think this young man needs to hear from you what place he has in your life." "This is off the record." She motioned to the court reporter, who picked up his machine and left the room.

Daniel walked around until he stood in front of the last chair on the other side of the room. The one still occupied by James whose face was a mixture of misery and nonchalance. A lump caught in his throat blocking words. *How could I have closed myself off to him?*

Standing in front of the young man he opened his arms.

"Come here." When James didn't move, Daniel tugged his arms pulling him up. He slung an arm around James' shoulder and tucked him against his side. Looking over at Judge Peterson he said, "This is one of the finest young men I've ever known. I'm honored to be his guardian and if you ever see your way clear to change his last name, I'd be more than proud to have him use O'Donnell."

James turned into Daniel, clung to him, tears soaking his shirt. He did nothing but hold him until the sobs subsided.

"You'd want me too?" James asked, his voice shaky, the words muffled.

"You bet. Rose is coming into the business with me. She swings a mean hammer already," Daniel told the judge with a grin. "And you, my man, will follow in Jackson and Giovanni's steps and be a world-class architect."

Judge Peterson handed James some tissues. He wiped his face, blew his nose and tossed them in the trash can.

"I didn't know James wanted to be an architect," she said.

"He's happiest when hanging out with Jackson making teeny tiny models and studying blue prints. Doesn't much care for hammers and nails but that's alright. Rose does."

"And Anthony?" the judge asked.

"Anthony hasn't quite figured things out yet. I think it's a loyalty issue. He can't like construction or architecture or cooking or horses because those are activities the husbands of his mom's friends do. He can't like teaching or writing or helping others much less dancing because that's what the women in The Circle do."

"So he's a bit lost right now?" Judge Peterson asked, a frown knitted her brows, concerned laced her voice.

"He wants to be with Art more than anything. I'm not sure he can sort things out for himself if his fantasy of what it would be like to live with Art remains just that—a fantasy."

Walking out of the judge's chamber, his arm still around James' shoulder, he met Ashley, Rose and Anthony. *My family.*

"Where is everyone?" he asked.

"We've been invited to Jackson and Lily's," Ashley answered. "Jackson's fixing steak. I said we'd stop and pick something up but Jackson was definite that we won't."

"Let's not upset the cook this time. I hear he has a freezer full of homemade ice creams. What would top that?"

Rose wanted to be carried. He said 'no' but held her hand as they left. James walked with his mom and Anthony hung off to the side. "Hey man, what're you doing way off over there?" Daniel asked and gestured him to move closer. Anthony stalked over but before they reached the parking garage he'd lost his antagonistic stance.

A couple of blocks along, he had both boys wait with Ashley while he and Rose went on to get his truck.

"You should carry me," Rose said.

"Nope, you should carry me."

She laughed, her giggle lightening the last dark spot in his heart.

42 - THE PROPOSAL

Sunday, February 20, 2005

The Court Order had given Daniel three days to change his mind, three days to object but he did neither. Yesterday, The Circle met and his house was full of women, children and men. Today Matthew and Diana had invited the children to spend the afternoon, promising they'd be back before eight; tomorrow was a school day.

Lily and Sophia had taken Ashley out for a few hours which gave him time to create the setting he wanted. Champagne flutes on a silver tray, a bottle of sparkling apple cider cooling in a matching ice bucket, fresh fruit and brie on a flowered china plate. Silver serving pieces and silverware on a lace cloth that covered the coffee table in front of the fire place. He'd debated about candles and settled on a fire instead. Plush cushions surrounded one side of the table, just the right height to sit on while enjoying a feast.

In the oven, hot hors d'oeuvres: crab cakes and parmesan-artichoke stuffed mushrooms. A fondue pot with warming pan underneath and a basket of cubed bread graced the side of the table closest to the fireplace.

Hearing a car in the back, he quickly lit the paper pausing only to make sure it caught before closing the screen and heading to the back entrance.

~

ASHLEY WAVED at Lily as Sophia backed around. The few hours at The Grotto were just what she'd needed. The quiet winter garden was conducive to meditation and reflection and the thoughtful conversation she'd with her friends was an added bonus. Waving again as Sophia drove away, Ashley stood on the back deck a feeling of contentment settling in her stomach.

Relaxed. Not a word she'd use to describe herself in recent months. She pulled her coat close, tucked her hands in the opposite arm's pit and gazed at the winter garden. Already there were crocus pushing bright yellow, blue and lavender buds through the cold earth. Potted winter pansies added another splash of color as did another planter of flowering cabbage.

Lily and Sophia say not to worry. Everything will work out. While that helps immeasurably, talking to the judge Wednesday— Tears blurred her vision. She blinked rapidly to clear it.

The backdoor opened but the chatter she associated with her kids was missing. Turning around, she saw Daniel, his face wreathed in a welcoming smile, his hand held out in invitation. "Come on in and get warm."

Ashley kept her gaze on his as she crossed the deck to the back door. He stood to the side so she could enter. The smells of food and fire warmed her. Daniel helped her off with her coat and escorted her into the living room.

"Where are my kids?"

"Rose is helping Diana with Madison Michelle and James and Anthony are helping Matthew with a project. They'll be home before eight."

"What have you done?" she asked puzzlement in her voice, questioning on her face.

"Fire and food to celebrate you've turned a corner. I know you've gained weight and are stronger. Well, that didn't come out exactly right," he hurriedly added.

Since the meeting with Judge Peterson, Daniel had been attentive to her and involved with the children. He'd changed his schedule so he either took them to school or waited with them in his truck for the bus to come. "Don't want them waiting in the cold."

She'd decided not to mention they'd been doing just that for a couple of months already figuring if he wanted to do this, her kids benefited.

"Hope you're hungry," he said gesturing to the table. "Be right back." He strode out of the room, returning shortly with a plate of crab cakes and parmesan-artichoke stuffed mushrooms.

"Smells wonderful." She took a deep breath of the delicious odors. "Did Sophia do this?"

"Nope, wanted to surprise you by putting this together myself."

An arched brow communicated her surprise. "You made all this yourself?"

"Don't sound so incredulous," Daniel said, a mock frown on his face.

"Okay, I didn't know y'all were this good of a cook."

"The deli at the bottom of the hill did the cooking. I followed the instructions, opened the bottle of sparkling apple cider, got out the silver, china and crystal."

"And it looks much better because of all your hard work," Ashley teased.

"Better than on paper plates?" he joked. "Be right back." He dashed from the room returning moments later. "Forgot these, the finishing touch," he said putting two damask napkins on the table. "Will you join me?" He gestured to the cushions with a courtly bow.

Still confused about what was going on, Ashley did join him. The food smelled so good and now that her appetite was better she was hungry.

Daniel put bits and pieces of everything on a plate and handed it to her before filling a crystal flute with the sparkling cider. He placed a napkin with a silver fork and spoon centered on it to the right of her plate and the flute on the left. Moving the fondue closer to them he gestured to the different colored forks. "Which one?"

She chose the green one. *Life, new growth, new beginnings.*

Daniel picked red. Taking her fork he speared a cube of bread, dipped it in the cheese sauce and handed it to her.

Savoring the chewy bread coated with the fondue was treat enough but being waited upon made the event special.

"Very, very good," she moaned as she accepted another piece. "I love fondue."

"Good. Hoped you did. It's one of my favorites and I don't get it very often. Do you think the deli has the right mix of cheeses?"

"Mmm." Ashley nodded, her eyes half closed in pleasure.

"Don't forget the crab cakes and mushrooms. I can put them back in the oven to keep them warm," Daniel offered.

She shook her head. A sip of cider cleaned her palate. Tasting the two dishes, she sighed. "Excellent. I think I like the crab cakes best but the artichoke and parmesan stuffing in the mushrooms is wonderful too."

He kept her glass filled, coaching her to eat a bit more. "I don't have anything for desert," he apologized.

"This has been heavenly. A wonderful meal and I've eaten so much I'm as stuffed as the mushrooms." She laughed and put her hand over the flute. "No more, Daniel. I'll burst if I take one more sip or eat one more bite."

The heat from the fire, a full belly and an amiable companion; Ashley couldn't remember the last time she and Art had done anything like this. *I don't think we ever did. That picnic with Art in the bandstand in the town square back home is the last time a man has waited on me.*

Resting against the front of the couch, Ashley watched the multi-colored flames dance. *There's more yellow in this fire than any other color.* As if reading her mind, Daniel got up and added a couple of pinecones to the fire. In minutes blue, green and red colors melded with the yellow mesmerizing in the way they blended and parted coming back again—the same colors but in a different pattern. *Reminds me of The Circle. We're all different and yet at the core the same. And every time we come together is a little different than the last.*

"Sure you don't want more?" Daniel asked.

Too full and content to speak, she shook her head.

When he began to clear things up, she started to get up. "No you don't," he admonished. "You are the guest of honor and as such you stay where you are. I'll get this. Won't take me long."

Ashley subsided against the front of the couch, her gaze once again on the fire. Her fingers stroked the dragonfly pendant around her neck. A niggling doubt poked up from her dreamy reflections. She stopped herself from completing the thought although she knew what the rest of the words would be.

Daniel rejoined her, sitting close enough that their shoulders touched. "You okay?"

She nodded.

He put his arm around her and scooted closer so they were side by side, hips and thighs touching. Coaxing her head onto his shoulder, he shifted a bit and settled.

Ashley thought back over the past week. Confused by what was happening now, she tried to figure things out but nothing really made sense. *I know he can't really commit to a family but I know he will do everything in his power to keep James and Rose from going to Art if something happens to me.*

"Hey, Ash." Daniel's voice calling her name pulled her out of her ruminations.

She glanced up. His warm brown eyes searched hers. "Hmm?"

"I've been thinking," he started. He shook his head as if clearing those thoughts. "What I want to say—that is what I want to ask." Shifting to his side, he faced her.

Her heart stuttered. The serious look on his face bordered on grim.

"We should get married. No, that isn't what I meant to say. Well, it is but... ." He leaned forward and placed a warm kiss on her cheek. "We'd make an awesome family, you, the kids and me."

Stunned. For a minute she sat there stunned into silence. When words came they were accompanied by a slow shake of her head. "No, Daniel. No, I won't marry you. No, we would not make an awesome family." Ashley stumbled to her feet and marched out of the room.

An unbelieving Daniel sat on the cushion. *She said 'no'.* The fantasy he'd manufactured—of Ashley's bright smile, throwing her arms around his neck, kissing him, all the while saying 'yes, yes, yes' vanished. The empty doorway mirrored the emptiness enveloping him. He was alone in the quiet.

The quiet broken by the closing of her door.

43 - WHAT NEXT?

*H*e proposed. *Daniel proposed.* His words filtered through the early morning haze as her brain came awake. How could she feel both angry and sad and happy at the same time? It didn't make any sense. Late into the night when sleep eluded, she wondered if her answer should have been "yes." But her stomach told her something was off.

Should she have said yes? *No, I did the right thing. I may love that man and my kids may adore him, but I'm not willing to marry him just because he asked. Not even for my kids will I do that.*

Ashley dressed in her dragonfly sweatshirt and her Pink Ribbon shoes. In her pants pocket she tucked a small dragonfly embroidered bag with healing stones: amethyst, angelite, citrine and phenacite.

The kids were off to school and Ashley was having a cup of tea when Eleanor arrived. Although she'd been cleared to drive, she still had occasional bouts of light-headedness and was grateful Eleanor was willing to be her chauffeur one more time.

Ashley knew she always carried a book in her bag, something to pull out and read whenever she wasn't busy doing something else.

"What are you reading?"

"*Love & Magick*, an anthology of short stories written by three authors of romance who were unknown to me. I find reading anthologies an excellent way to experience new authors and new genres. The first short story is very well done and I am looking forward to reading the others," Eleanor said showing Ashley the book.

"Can't mistake that book for anything other than a romance," Ashley said as Eleanor returned the book to her bag.

"And," Eleanor said, changing the subject, "in case it has missed your notice, Lily remarked this morning that Diana mentioned that your Rose has all the makings of an excellent mother's helper. She was immensely helpful last night."

"She sure was talking a mile a minute about Madison Michelle" Ashley smiled at the mental picture of Rose, her face and hands animated, as she talked non-stop about the baby. "Why that baby is the most awesome baby in the entire world according to my daughter."

~

ARRIVING AT THE VALET PARKING, Eleanor turned the car over to the attendant. Walking into the medical office building evoked strong feelings of hope and anxiety in Ashley. She reached into her pocket and felt her bag of protection. The tightness in her shoulders eased but her stomach still swirled.

I owe everyone so much. She was keeping track of it all and would pay The Circle back. It didn't matter everyone said this was a gift and didn't need to be paid back. For Ashley, putting money into The Circle's account was a marker she was healthy.

This appointment with Dr. Burton was her two month checkup since her last treatment. Eleanor sat with her in Dr. Burton's office, her book out when Dr. Burton came in.

At her doctor's questioning gaze, Ashley nodded and said "Eleanor has been through all of this with me."

"Overall, things are looking good," Dr. Burton said. "You've gained five pounds in the last two months. Keep doing what you're doing and you'll get your strength and endurance back as well as gain another ten pounds.

"We're going to keep a closer-than-usual-eye on everything, Ashley because, since you chose not to have a mastectomy, it's possible the cancer will return."

Ashley heard the words. The double whammy of numbness and fear struck. She could only nod to let Dr. Burton know she'd heard because speaking wasn't possible. For an instant it was August and she faced the choice to have the mastectomy and lose her husband or to have the treatment and keep her marriage. Obviously her decision to go for treatment backfired. Or did it? *Art would have left me no matter which way I went. I can see we're better off now without him.*

"I'm grateful for all you've done for me," Ashley told Dr. Burton, a quaver in her voice.

As she and Eleanor strolled back to valet parking, Ashley avoided looking at Eleanor and kept the conversation light and superficial. On the drive back to the house, Eleanor seemed quiet and thoughtful. She didn't come in for a cup of tea as was their habit. Ashley worried. *Should I ask her not to say anything about what the doctor said?*

"I am stopping by Diana's on my way back to my place. I just have the feeling she needs my help this morning," Eleanor said. A warm hug and a kiss on the cheek and she was gone.

Tired from the trip to the doctor's, Ashley napped. When she woke, she had enough time to wash up and get an after-school treat together before the kids got home.

Today they didn't dash in the front door but instead, piled out of Daniel's truck and raced each other for the back door. At second glance only James and Anthony were racing.

Her eyes filled with happy tears at the sight of Rose walking with Daniel, holding his hand looking as happy and content as Ashley'd ever seen. When she looked at the man, he looked happy also.

The back door flew open and James and Anthony spilled in, pushing and shoving, shouting as to who was first.

"I've got cookies and hot chocolate if anyone wants some."

"I do," the boys chorused.

"Then wash up," she reminded everyone.

James was changing, his voice deepening or shifting from his young boy voice to his young man one within a single word. He was growing up so fast. He'd turned thirteen in December. No longer a boy, fast becoming a man. In five years he'd be eighteen and off to college. She promised herself to enjoy these years knowing they'd be gone in a dragonfly-flash.

The three kids sat at the table.

"You each can have two," she said, as she set the plate of cookies down. The tray with their cups of hot chocolate was lifted from her hands.

"I'll take these," Daniel said, his actions following his words.

"It's hot so take a sip first," Ashley warned.

Daniel relaxed against the island, a mischievous grin on his face. "Do I have to go to school to get cookies and hot chocolate?"

"Perhaps," she said, a mock sternest in her tone. "You at least have to ask politely."

"May I please have two cookies and a mug of hot chocolate, Ms. Carlyle?"

"Because you asked so nice, Mr. O'Donnell, you may," Ashley said and put a plate with cookies and a mug of hot chocolate in front of him.

"All these for me?" Daniel said, tugging the plate closer to him.

"And me," Ashley said, snatching up one of Sophia's chocolate chip cookies.

Rose left the table and came to sit on a stool next to Daniel. She leaned into him, her hand wrapped around his arm. "Are you okay, Mom?"

James and Anthony's heads swiveled in her direction and Daniel seemed more alert.

"I'm fine, Rose. Dr. Burton said I'm doing just fine."

"Madison Michelle takes naps. I don't like naps," Rose announced.

"And you don't have to take them, Sweet Pea, unless you become a Snap Dragon," Daniel teased.

Hearing her daughter's laugh was infectious and she laughed too. "A snap dragon? Why they are one of my favorite flowers."

"You like them better than sweat peas?" Daniel asked.

"Mom, you like roses bestest," her daughter said obviously affronted by their nonsense.

"I like you bestest," Ashley said, coming around the island to tickle her daughter in the ribs. Hastily she added. "You are my favorite daughter." Crossing to the small table she kissed Anthony's cheek, "You are my favorite Anthony and you, James are my favorite—,"

"I know Mom, I'm your favorite thirteen-year-old son."

"That you are," she said, reaching across the table to pat his shoulder. "I've the best three kids in the whole world."

Ashley relished this moment, storing the memories of this light-hearted, happy time.

Daniel watched her, gauging something. She hoped he didn't propose again. *If there's a next time, my answer will still be 'no.' I want the love I see Lily, Elizabeth and Diana have and I know he can't give me that.*

Remembering Lily saying the feeling of love wasn't enough. There had to be more: loving actions, loving words. *I believe Daniel can do the actions and words but I don't believe he has the feelings. It all has to be there if it's going to work.*

44 - AFTERMATH

In the relative scheme of things, three weeks isn't that much time. Knowing that intellectually helped. Grateful, overflowing with gratitude, thankful, blessed were the words that permeated her prayers each night and were whispered to herself upon waking. Another thing to be grateful for? The subject of marriage was not brought up.

The old Victorian was three times the size of the house she was used to keeping up. She now did the stairs, the laundry, the cooking and kept track of the kids' school work. She was exhausted.

March 18th was Friday. The hearing with Judge Peterson loomed. Rose was anxious and becoming obstinate unless Daniel was there. Understanding her daughter's emotions didn't make it easier to deal with. James was withdrawn and Anthony hyper. She saw him muttering to himself but when she said anything he replied "Nothing, Mom." She knew her middle son well enough to know that always meant 'something'.

She and Daniel were polite to each other, at times even friendly but there was an undercurrent of unease. It was as if they both wished that awkward evening never happened, as if the words were never spoken.

~

FRIDAY MORNING ARRIVED TOO SOON. Lily was the only one from The Circle who could attend. Well, of course Ms. Muir was there and Eleanor. Hunter had classes, Sophia did also and Gabby was away again on business. Diana would have been there but the babysitter backed out and she didn't want to leave Madison Michelle with someone new and untried nor did she want to deal with a fussy baby during the hearing. Ashley did understand.

Daniel drove the five of them to the Courthouse and parked in the garage a block over. Rose refused to get out of the truck unless he carried her. He looked to her for help, she shrugged her shoulders. When he leaned in and spoke quietly to her, she wished she could hear the words because Rose's stubborn 'you can't make me' look softened, her arms uncrossed, and albeit with great reluctance, she unbuckled her seat belt and got out of the car. He did not carry her, but he held her hand every step of the way.

Even in the Courthouse he held her hand. Even as they went through security—well, there were a few seconds because the guard would not bend, even for a seven-year-old. He said something more and Rose, head held high, marched through, turned and fixed her gaze on him. As soon as he cleared the security screening, she was at his side.

Ashley had more problems getting through security than Daniel. She had a metal pendant on a chain. But also tucked in a pocket was a metal dragonfly. Then she wore a belt with a metal buckle. By the time she and her purse, yes, there were metal items in it also, got through the others had cleared security.

Lily, Eleanor and Ms. Muir were sitting on benches outside the courtroom. Relieved to see a friendly face, she eagerly hugged Eleanor and Lily and warmly greeted the social worker.

They entered the courtroom and Anthony raced ahead when he saw Art, throwing his arms around his dad and chattering animated about something. Art looked over Anthony's head, speared James with a look and totally ignored Rose.

If looks could kill—yes, a trite saying but one that was so true. How could this man who once found strawberries for her in November because they were her favorite fruit look at her with such hatred? But if she was dead from Art's glare, Daniel was cremated.

Glancing at Daniel showed her he was very aware of the man at the table before the bench. A vein ticked in his temple and his stride shortened. He stepped so he partially blocked Rose and her from Art's stare and he put his hand on James' shoulder. At that gesture, Art started out of his chair. A word from his attorney and the guard moving quickly, settled Art down.

If Daniel had been cremated, his ashes were now blowing around in hell—that is if Art had his way.

They found their seats. The boys sat between Ms. Muir and Lily, Rose was sandwiched between Lily and Daniel who still had not let go of her hand. Eleanor was next to Daniel.

Ashley sat on Ms. Lawford's right glad again for the buffer of attorneys between Art and her.

"All rise."

Judge Peterson banged her gavel and everyone was seated.

"Please clear the courtroom and hang the 'closed session' sign on the door," she instructed the bailiff. Once that was done she asked Art whether he wished to voluntarily relinquish his parental rights to Rose.

"Not if that bastard gets her," he shot back.

His attorney immediately spoke to him at a volume Ashley couldn't hear.

"Your Honor," Art's attorney said, rising to his feet. "My client obviously has strong feelings that Mr. O'Donnell has alienated his family from him. Therefore, while he does not wish to provide a parenting role in his daughter's life—,"

Art jumped up. His attorney attempted to push him back in his seat. The guard stepped up and stood behind him waiting for the judge's instructions.

To Ashley's surprise the judge said, "Go on Mr. Kenner."

"She is my wife," he stabbed his finger at her, "and they are my kids. He," his lip curled in distain as he pointed at Daniel, "he isn't fit to be around my kids. He's tried to turn them against me and succeeded with all but one. He's had an affair with her," again his finger aimed toward her, "for years. He's interfered with my trying to provide for my kids."

The judge raised her hand. "And how did he interfere with you providing for your children?"

"He moved them to his house."

"And was that before or after Ms. Carlyle was served with an eviction notice for non-payment of rent and had also received notices that the water and power were being turned off?"

"I would have taken my kids. I did try to take them but he interfered. She was dying. They needed to be with me!"

"Mr. Kenner, I have no doubt you believe or believed that your ex-wife was dying. But I'm looking at her right now and, to be honest, she looks better today than at any previous hearings. I have a report from her oncologist who states that at this point she is cancer free."

"Yeah right. That's what the doctors said the first time," Art said, in a mocking, derisive tone.

"Do you have another point to make, Mr. Kenner, before I rule?"

"I want you and everyone else to listen to me. I can be a good father to my kids. He shouldn't be anywhere near them."

"Mr. Kenner, you are in jail. Just how are you being a good parent to your children? Are you calling and talking to them? Are you writing them?"

Art sat down. His fisted hands on the table and the scowl on his face left no doubts he could not answer the judge's questions with "yes."

Ms. Lawford stood and waited for Judge Peterson to recognize her.

"You have something to add, Ms. Lawford?"

"I do, Your Honor. I would like the record to show that at no time has my client been intimate with or had an affair with Mr. O'Donnell. You may wonder why we've not spoken on this issue before and the simple reason is, we've not wanted to dignify Mr. Kenner's false accusations by responding. Why am I speaking now? Because I've finally convinced my client it is important to have the record show there has never been any relationship between my client and Mr. O'Donnell other than friendship."

"The record now shows Ms. Carlyle denies having an affair with, and I'm assuming that also means denying Mr. O'Donnell is the biological father of Rose?"

"That is correct, Your Honor," Ms. Lawford said, before sitting down.

"Moving on. I have the report from Ms. Muir who has continued, at the court's request, to visit with the children individually and as a sibling group, both in the home, at school and in a neutral public setting. I believe from her report, they have a favorite ice cream place." Judge Peterson smiled in the children's direction.

"It is the order of this court that Arthur Kenner's rights to the child Rose Amanda Kenner aka Rose Amanda Carlyle be terminated and that Daniel Charles O'Donnell remain her legal guardian responsible for her care and up-bringing along with her mother Ashley Ann Carlyle.

"It is further ordered that Arthur Kenner will pay child support for James and Anthony Kenner in the amount of $300.00 each. That support will be due to the County Child Support office by the 10th of each month. Support order goes into effect thirty days after his release from jail."

Mr. Treeland's hand was on Art's shoulder and he was quietly but animatedly saying something. The murderous look on Art's face firmed. His mouth opened but before a sound was emitted the judge spoke.

"Say nothing, Mr. Kenner or I will hold you in contempt of court. Anything you wish to say, say it through your attorney."

Judge Peterson banged her gavel, stood and before turning away from the courtroom added, "Mr. O'Donnell and Ms. Carlyle, in my chambers now."

⁓

Ms. Lawford was asked to wait outside. Rose's threatening tears did not sway the judge. She would talk to Mr. O'Donnell and Ms. Carlyle in her chambers—alone. Yes, it was all very irregular, however, she was the judge and this was how she wanted it.

It was clear Daniel had no idea what was going on and neither did Ashley. They sat side-by-side in front of the judge's desk, waiting for her to take off her robe and sit down.

"Now," Judge Peterson began. "There is no court reporter and no one to hear what we discuss. I want the truth from you both although we all know neither of you are under oath and therefore can lie if you want.

"Are you still of a mind to adopt Rose?" she asked Daniel.

"I am," Daniel responded in a clear, firm voice.

"Do have any objections to Mr. O'Donnell adopting your daughter?"

"No, Your Honor, I don't," Ashley said looking over at Daniel.

"I will tell you why I'm hesitant to finalize an adoption. Society has adjusted to divorce and also bio-parents never marrying as well as step-parent adoption. However, not only do the two of you have no legal connection to each other, only one of you has a biological connection to Rose.

"You may both love these children and want what's best for them. You may both have similar ideas as to how to support them in your role as parents. You may both believe you'll be able to work any disagreements out with no harm to the children." Judge Peterson leaned forward and let a moment of silence fill the air.

"I know in Rose's case and I'm fairly certain when it comes to what James desires is to have you, Mr. O'Donnell as their legal father and you, Ms. Carlyle as both their biological and legal mother."

She rose and, hands clasped behind her back, paced the floor behind her desk. "In the reports from Ms. Muir and my conversations with Ms. Hughes words like 'fond of' 'respect' 'care about' are attributed to each of you speaking about the other. However, from their observations," she spun on her heel, marched back to the desk and let the silence build before she added, "they each used the word 'love' as in you love each other as well as the children."

The judge leaned forward, both hands flat on the desk top. "I want you to know what Ms. Muir's report says and that Ms. Hughes concurs. Ms. Muir's report states whatever the prior difficulties were, they are resolved. The children, even Anthony wants Mr. O'Donnell in their lives, although Anthony also wants to live with his father when he is out of jail." She straightened and sat. Her piercing gaze focused on one and then the other before she resumed speaking.

"Please be clear about this. I am only encouraging, not ordering, the two of you to talk in a complete and truthful manner with each other about the children's future as well as your own."

She turned to Ashley. "I know Mr. O'Donnell has said you and the children are welcomed to stay in his home for as long as you want. At the time he made the offer, you did not respond so I don't know if that is what you want. I also don't know if the two of you have thought about or talked about life when the children are grown and on their own."

She consulted her calendar. "I'll see you back in my chambers at four Monday afternoon to finish this discussion."

Judge Peterson stepped from behind her desk and strode to the door. Opening it, she stood to the side. "Thank you for listening. I'll see you Monday," she said, her friendly tone matched her smile.

Ashley stumbled to her feet, numbness and panic warred in her stomach. Glancing over at Daniel, who still sat in the chair, she saw a stunned look in his eyes. He was as blown away by what the judge said as she was.

As soon as they were through the door, it closed behind them. Rose grabbed Daniel's hand in a death grip. James and Anthony's worry was evident. Only Lily and Ms. Muir were relaxed.

"Did y'all know what was going to happen?" Ashley asked the two women, her tone accusatory, her stance wide, her hands on her hips.

"Since we don't know what happened, that's an impossible question to answer," Lily calmly replied.

Daniel was talking quietly to Rose who let go of his hand and glommed on to Lily. Rose's hand rose toward her mouth. James rested his hand on his sister's shoulder and she took his hand instead.

"Let's step down the hall and talk for a minute, okay?" Daniel asked Ashley.

Ashley nodded and they walked shoulder to shoulder down to the end of the hall, still within sight although outside of everyone's hearing before either one spoke.

"Lily and Ms. Muir put her up to it," Ashley started.

Daniel held his hand up and shook his head. "I don't think they put her up to anything. She's a judge with a mind of her own. Here's what I'm proposing." At her arched brow, he smiled. "Let's go get a marriage license." He rested his thumb on her lips and she resisted, just barely the urge to either bite it or kiss it.

"Tomorrow we'll—maybe they can spend the night with Lily and Jackson or Diana and Matthew or maybe...." He paused and took a deep breath. "One thing Judge Peterson got right is we need to talk.

"We need to have an honest conversation about how we feel about each other. We both know we love those three." He gestured towards the group at the other end of the hall intently watching them. "There's nothing that says we ever have to use it, but if we do decide by the end of the weekend we want to be a family, warts, foibles and all, we can ask the judge to marry us on Monday."

"Monday," Ashley's voice squeaked. "Monday?"

"Hear me out," Daniel said, his eyes searching her grey ones. "I didn't say we'd get married Monday. I said if we decided over the weekend that was the best course for us to take because of our feelings for each other as well as for the kids that would be an option."

His mischievous grin reminded her of better times, of the friendship and laughter they'd shared. She was surprised and yet she wasn't that tension had not struck. No iron bars across her shoulders. No queasy stomach. No free-floating anxiety. *Maybe?*

"Promise me you won't say anything to anyone about this if I go along with this madness?" Ashley implored.

"I promise, if you can think of a way to ditch Rose," Daniel said and laughed.

"I've got that covered," she said. She turned away and walked back down the hall.

"Judge Peterson wants Daniel and me to take care of some business while we're here in the court house so we need y'all to go on. Daniel's treating all of us to dinner. You kids get to pick the place.

"Lily and Ms. Muir will take you there and Daniel and I'll be along shortly." She turned to Lily, "you've got Daniel's cell phone number so you can let him know where y'all are."

Rose pouted but went along when Lily said she could call Daniel and tell him where they were. As soon as the group was in the elevator and the doors closed on the debate as to where they'd eat, Ashley and Daniel looked at the directory at the top of the stairs. "One floor down," Ashley said, pointing to the room number.

"Are you up to walking down the stairs or do you want to take the elevator?"

"I think I'd better do the elevator. It's already been a long day and we've dinner to get through."

There was no line and the form was fairly simple. They stepped away and called their doctor's offices for the medical information to be faxed as soon as possible. Daniel paid the fee. When they left thirty minutes later, the marriage license was tucked in her purse.

"Hope we can find it again," Daniel quipped as they left the building.

"I'm sure we will when I dump it out on your head," Ashley rejoined.

He held her hand at one point, his hand rested on the small of her back at another. They made their way back to the parking garage and his truck. Rose had called to say they were eating dinner at Burgerville and she wanted a real chocolate peppermint milk shake not a kid's size.

She listened as Daniel joked with Rose. Her giggles warmed her heart. The man beside her was the best thing that had happened to Rose in a very long time. Maybe it would work out between them.

The cold started in her bowels and spread outward. Doubts that had simmered for the past six years boiled. *I'm still bald and scarred; I'm only a fair housekeeper and not even that great a cook.* She sat next to him in the cab of the truck as he drove through traffic. He seemed relaxed, okay with the events of the day.

Glancing out the window she saw a couple walking down the street. Arms around each other's waist, they looked lovingly at each other. She said something and he laughed, his head bent and he kissed her cheek. She snuggled into him. They turned a corner and the couple was gone. *A very different picture than when Daniel and I walked to the truck.*

45 - HONESTLY, I DO

The food was devoured. Her kids ate like they hadn't eaten in a week. She nibbled, avoided eye contact with Daniel and limited her answers when Lily or Ms. Muir asked a question. Once home, Daniel followed the kids upstairs. The deep rumble of Daniel's voice, the cracking sound of James', Anthony's tone followed by Daniel's no-nonsense response. *I wonder what that was all about?* Rose piped up, Daniel answered. *Maybe I can go upstairs and help out.* Her mind was willing but as she stood at the bottom of the stairs, she knew physically she'd used all her energy up with the day's events.

Back in the kitchen she prepped the coffee maker for Daniel's morning cup and took a package of Sophia's cinnamon rolls from the freezer. His footsteps on the hardwood floors announced his arrival.

Ashley turned toward him. He leaned against the door jam, rumpled, in need of a shave, his hair tunneled from his fingers. "You look beat," he said.

"I'm a bit tired,"

"Ash, you look like you're about to fall down. We have the weekend to find the time to talk."

Leaning against the counter, she said, "I mentioned to Lily that you and I needed some time to talk this weekend. She offered to come over tomorrow night and fix dinner for the kids. Well, Jackson would do the cooking. They'd stay and entertain the kids if we needed them to."

"If they did that, we could go out to dinner." Daniel still slouched against the doorframe but his intent gaze never wavered.

"This isn't something I want to talk about in public." A mild panic surged, its energy standing her up; a bit of panic but no queasiness. She steadied herself with one hand on the back of a barstool.

"We'll work it out Ash. We've got the time." He straightened. "Thanks for getting my coffee ready. I'll see you in the morning."

His footsteps retreated down the hall, his measured tread up the stairs. All was quiet.

Ashley waited until her heartbeat slowed. *He's as kind and caring as he's ever been. But... .* She set out his thermos and a plastic container for his cinnamon rolls.

In the hall bathroom, she brushed her teeth and prepared for bed. Pulling the covers up, she curled on her side, knees tucked to her chest. *May we find our way through this time and may our highest good be served.* Her hand sought the small stone with the painted dragonfly under her pillow. Clutching it tightly, she repeated her prayer until she slowly relaxed and sleep claimed her.

SUNDAY EVENING, the kids were in bed a bit early because tomorrow was a school day. Saturday had been busy. Instead of them leaving when Lily and Jackson came over, they stayed. A whispered conversation in the hallway, they agreed it would draw attention to them. Not only would the kids have questions, they'd want to go. And, surmounting that hurdle still left them with both the reality that, upon their return, Lily and Jackson would want to know what happened.

So at nine Sunday evening, they sat in the living room in front of a fire. She had a cup of tea to fiddle with, Daniel had a soda.

"I can't do this," she whispered. At his startled look, she added in her normal tone, "not here."

"Where then?"

"Kitchen." She led the way to the chairs in the bay window. After putting her tea on the table, she got down a small plate. Adding four of Sophia's peanut butter chocolate chip cookies to the dish, she picked up two napkins and returned to her seat.

At his quizzical look she explained, "Just in case one of us raises our voice, the kids are less likely to hear us from here."

Settling into her chair, she warmed her icy hands on the tea cup and waited. After a few moments of silence she said, "One of us needs to start."

"I think first we need to decide what we want to talk about," Daniel said, tapping a finger against his glass of soda.

Her heart beat a rapid tattoo. "Judge Peterson said the kids' future and our own."

"But there is more to it than that. We can even love each other," Daniel said, his eyes never leaving her face, "but that doesn't mean we can make the kind of family together we want."

"What kind of family do you want?" Ashley asked, now eager to hear his answer.

"More of a partnership between the parents in taking care of the kids." He leaned forward, his whole being told her he was earnest, serious about what he said. "Major decisions about the house, vacations are made together and where appropriate include the kids. For example I wouldn't get James a car at sixteen unless you agreed."

Ashley bristled. "Whether we're a family or not, Daniel, James will not get a car when he's sixteen unless he helps pay for it and has a job to pay for his own gas and insurance."

"See, that's what I mean. Major decisions are made together which means we'd talk about it first."

Even when her marriage to Art was at its best, they didn't have the kind of true partnership Daniel talked about. Her circle sisters all had that kind of partnership in their marriages. Her chest swelled with excitement and anticipation as a vision of sitting down, right here in the kitchen and talking things over with Daniel formed in her mind. "I can agree to the partnership piece."

"What would you like to see?"

His tone was neutral as was his posture but Ashley knew he was concentrating on her. She paused to sort through her words and feelings, noting he waited without fidgeting. "I want to know what's going on financially. I want to have a budget and a separate bank account for the house."

"Not a problem."

"Insurance. The kids need to have insurance and with Art in jail and all, it runs out the end of this month."

"Not a problem. And if we marry, you'll be on my insurance also."

"And if we don't come to an agreement to marry, the kids and I'll move into the little house at the end of the school year."

Silence greeted that statement. Ashley busied herself refreshing her tea from the kettle on the stove and waited for him to say something. He didn't.

Returning to her place at the table, she looked him straight on. Her stomach churned, her head pounded louder than her heart which was doing its own thundering noise but she forged on. "I understand about your reluctance to commit to a family given what happened to your family and all. And I know I'm not the pretty girl I once was." A wry smile twisted her lips. "I've got scars and stretch marks everywhere."

This was harder than she thought it would be because he did nothing. His face set in neutral lines, he made no moves or said anything but an air of intentness surrounded him, while she talked.

He listened.

"I won't be in another empty marriage. I know love isn't enough. I believe Art really did love me in the beginning but when the fairy tale turned into a nightmare, he left. Maybe not physically at first but he left me and then the kids. I won't go through that again."

The uncomfortable silence wrapped around her. She'd gone first and he'd said and done nothing. All that was left was to wait, to hear him say he couldn't make that commitment, he loved her kids and was fond of her but—.

"Done?" Daniel shifted forward, arms on the table, hands folded, the soda moved to the side as if it needed protection.

Ashley's throat tightened, her hands gripped her cup. She glanced down expecting the china to crack from the pressure. The need to look at him as he talked was compelling. She raised her head connected with his brown eyes. What did she see there? Compassion? Caring? Something more? The urge to look away was strong. She resisted.

"I had the chance to do a bit of soul searching after I told you about my past," he began. "Actually that isn't true. I did a lot of soul searching. Jackson helped." His smile was more a grimace and she saw the memories of that time flicker across his face.

"The night you didn't come home?"

"Yeah, it was that night." He shifted, tunneled his fingers through his hair and went on. "Fear of something bad happening can keep us from experiencing all kinds of things was his general message. He reminded me that he and Lily's path wasn't paved with flowers, that they had some hard times and had to face things about themselves and each other. In the end, he assured me it was worth the journey."

"They love each other," Ashley pointed out. "And we all saw it long before either one of them recognized it."

"That's what he told me."

"That we saw it before they did?"

"No, Ash, that all of them see us as a couple, as two people who love each other, who are already a family in all but the legalities." He was so earnest, leaning forward, reaching for her hand.

"But how can that be?" She drew back from his touch. "You don't love me."

"I've loved you for a long time, Ash. Loved you from afar, stuffed it, ran from it, denied it but it made no difference. In the end, I still love you. I've never told you and never would have because you were married."

"But you said you could never be part of a family," she said, her voice broke on the words 'never' and 'family'.

"I did say that. I didn't say I didn't love you because that would be a lie. When Judge Peterson first started hinting about us getting together, I was so afraid. When I picked the kids up in New Mexico, I was terrified. What would I do if something happened to one of them? I didn't think I'd survive.

"Jackson said it would be hard, would be devastating. That if something happened to Lily he'd be lost, but he knew I'd be there for him. The Circle would be there and so would Matthew and Michael, Giovanni and, of course Eleanor. The point was he wouldn't go through the pain of her loss by himself. He would survive and in time have some semblance of a life for himself if for no other reason than she would want that for him."

"Is this what you talked about that night?

"I'd decided to get drunk but never made it that far because Jackson started talking. He assured me that if I owned up to my feelings for you and the kids and something happened, I wouldn't be alone.

"After he left and I thought about what he said I knew part of my truth was when my family was killed, I was alone. I wasn't in a relationship with anyone and I had no family close by. In the morning I'd been a part of a big family and by night I was alone. Two of my mom's brothers and one of my step-dad's sisters came to the funeral. They left in less than a week. I was alone. That's what I've really feared. Having a family and then suddenly being alone.

"I do love you and I do want to marry you and adopt Rose and James if that is allowed. Well, Anthony too but I don't foresee he'll ever agree to that."

Ashley's folded hands rested under his left hand. The warmth of his touch filtered through the cold that permeated her body: from her hands, up her arms, across her shoulders, down her spine. He'd said the words. Said he loved her.

It was a time for honesty. Honesty with herself and with him. Her turn to speak her truth. She did love him. She also denied it. Why was she worried he'd abandon her? He'd walked beside her through this cancer treatment, carrying her when she couldn't walk on her own, being there when she needed his physical strength and mental strength, his determination. In so many ways they were a family. Sharing his bed was all that was left. It terrified her she'd be seen lacking.

"I'm so frightened," she admitted, taking her cup in her hands. "I want a marriage where we are honest with each other, even though we are frightened about how the other one will react to what we say."

She touched her dragonfly pendant. The cool metal warmed. Images of dragon and damselflies flickered in her mind's eye. Taking a deep breath, her words rushed out on an exhale. "There's a possibility the cancer will come back."

Ashley concentrated on her hands wrapped around the tea cup. "I didn't choose to have a m-mas-mastectomy. I was afraid Art would leave me." She laughed in that hollow way that's more like a sob. "He'd already left, already stopped supporting us, already crossed me off as dead."

Her hands shook so hard she put the tea cup down rather than spill the contents. "N-n-now, I'm terrified that if you were to see me naked, you'd turn away."

Daniel sat in numbed silence. He loved her and she just told him she could die sooner rather than later.

Ashley, the woman he loved, sat, head bent, tears dripping off her chin compelled him to speak.

"So when you told everyone Dr. Burton said everything was looking good, you lied?" he asked, his efforts to keep his tone reasonable failing because the last word was tight.

"No," Ashley said lifting her head to look at him. "Everything does look good now it's just that the recommended treatment for recurrent breast cancer is a m-mastec-mastectomy. I couldn't face—" She looked away, looked away out the window, looked for the words that wouldn't come, words that weren't there.

Reflected in the window's glass, she saw two people.

Daniel's face filled with anguish.

Her face filled with sadness.

He reached out, his hand overlay hers. "Here's the deal then," he paused.

She turned at his silence.

In his brown-eyed gaze she saw the warmth and his commitment. "I'm not going to lie and say this is good news but I'm not turning away."

He chuckled. "And as to your fears about my seeing you naked? Think about it. I've seen you with your head in the toilet, with no hair, with puke stained shirts. Actually I have seen you naked, Ash. The towel you had around you when the shower drain plugged up didn't cover much at all. If you think I'm going to gag at the sight of you naked, in my bed, writhing under my touch, you are so very wrong."

"Writhing under your touch?" Astonished, she spat the words back at him. "You are so full of yourself," she said in disgust.

"Is that a challenge?" he asked, a grin on his face. "There's a bed nearby. Want to see who's right?"

Ashley glowered. "I will not participate in a contest when it comes to making love. I will not—,"

His raised hand stopped her mid-rant. "I am wrong. I was trying to tease and failed. Our love making will not be a contest." Daniel stared into her eyes, such a serious expression on his face her breath caught in her throat.

What an unusual situation. When Art was sorry he did something extra nice rather than apologize out loud. And, he was right. He'd seen her at her worst and still never turned away.

"I'm glad to know we'll be mutually pleasing each other should we get to that point," Ashley said. Dragon and damselflies danced in her peripheral vision. "I do love you, Daniel. And more than that, the kids love you too. Anthony may not admit it and he may not want to change his name but I know he loves you."

Daniel rose, took the two steps to stand next to her. A gentle tug and she stood next to him. "In less than fifteen years, even Rose will be grown. While I'm glad the kids love me, what's more important is that you do. We have decades ahead of us after they are grown and gone." He bent and placed a chaste kiss on her forehead.

Ashley rested her hands on his chest, so familiar but not. He'd held her cradled against him as he carried her to bed when she was too sick and weak to walk. Would he be able to carry her now that she'd put a little weight back on? She leaned against him, let him bear her weight. His finger tipped her head and the chaste kiss on her forehead turned into a foray, an exploration of her cheeks, chin, throat, neck and finally her mouth.

Kissing him back her heart beat strong in her chest, her lungs breathed life giving air and, to her surprise, her breasts tightened. Her body responded to his touch with a sensual force that rocked her back on her heels. Daniel's arms held her tight, warm firm lips trailed heat everywhere they touched. She thought he might touch her, stroke her, caress her body more but he didn't. Lost in the sensations he wrought, Ashley struggled to find functioning brain cells when he stopped and stepped back.

"Ashley Ann Carlyle will you do me the distinct honor of becoming my wife?" He stared straight at her, searching her face for her answer.

He was so serious. It touched her heart. He leaned forward, "I have a marriage license upstairs and a judge who'll do the honors tomorrow," he whispered in her ear creating a shiver of awareness.

"Daniel Charles O'Donnell I will do you the distinct honor of becoming your wife." She smiled up at him and winked. "Just so happens I also know a couple of people who'd jump at the chance to be our witnesses."

"Looks like we have a plan." He kissed her nose. "We've waited this long, how about we wait until after we're really married to consummate it."

"Okay." She was actually pleased she felt disappointed.

"Plans for a honeymoon?"

"I don't—."

"Here's the deal. The kids have Spring Break starting next week. Let's call around and see if we can get a place for all of us. It'll be a family honeymoon with special times for just us, because I'll invite Logan to come along and she and the kids can take in the sights while I show you the stars."

"And tomorrow night?"

"Tomorrow night I'll sleep down here. Until you get your strength back and can easily do the stairs. We can decide then if you want to keep this as a spare bedroom or turn it back into the sitting room for the lady of the house."

An arm around her waist, Daniel walked her to the bedroom door and kissed her long and passionately.

He stepped back, his hands on her shoulders, his brown eyes locked with hers. A flare of doubt flashed. She'd seldom seen him so serious.

"I want us to make an appointment with your oncologist when we're back from our honeymoon. You are more than your breasts, Ash. If it guarantees we'll grow old together then have the mastectomy. I'll be right there with you."

Breathing was difficult. Her heart stuttered in her chest, tears streamed down her face. All her life she'd been told how pretty she was, or how beautiful, or how great her figure was, or how she looked like an angel with her long platinum blond hair. Daniel loved her unconditionally—with no hair, with her head in the toilet, with puke stains on her shirt, so weak she couldn't walk on her own. In her heart she knew he would love her through whatever their future held.

Daniel's hands slid down her back. He stepped closer. His head bent and he kissed her forehead, her cheek, her nose and finally her mouth.

She couldn't breathe, but this time it wasn't from shock it was from his passionate kiss.

"I love you more than I have words for," she said her arms wrapped around his waist, holding him tight.

"If I don't head upstairs right now," he started, stopped, shook his head. "I'm a grown man. I can wait."

"I'm a grown woman. I can wait, too," she said. "One more kiss so I don't forget you tonight?" Ashley rose on her tiptoes, her arms around his neck, she pressed her body to his and felt his erection firm against her belly.

When they broke apart, she smiled. "I'm pretty sure I won't forget you."

"Good, because I know I won't forget you."

Daniel turned away and strolled down the hall, a tuneless whistle on his lips.

Brushing her teeth, Ashley touched her kiss swollen lips. *Tomorrow I'm getting married.*

Snuggled down in bed, she started her list which included calling all her circle sisters and inviting them to her wedding.

46 - THE WEDDING

When she heard Daniel in the kitchen, she struggled awake. A frantic whispered conversation and they had a plan. He waited with her until the kids tumbled in for breakfast. Holding hands, it was awkward yet sweet, telling the kids they were getting married that afternoon.

Rose jumped up, grabbed Daniel's other hand and beamed. James gave them thumbs up. Anthony's face initially shone with a bright smile, he quickly snuffed out. While he wasn't thrilled, he was not opposed.

THIS WAS the shortest time frame The Circle had ever had for pulling a wedding together but they made it. Jackson started his spaghetti sauce and checked his ice cream toppings to make sure there was enough for the wedding feast. Diana's babysitter was able to come at two-thirty which gave her time for a shower to make sure she didn't smell like baby puke. At two months, Madison Michelle had developed the knack of spitting up on her mom or dad just before they left to go someplace.

Hunter called her seven o'clock students and cancelled tonight's lessons. She let her two o'clock students out fifteen minutes early. Gabriella informed her supervisor she was taking two hours of vacation time and leaving at three. Matthew and Daniel were letting their crews off at three so they had time to clean up and get to the Courthouse by four.

Eleanor had arrived at eleven and insisted on a quick shopping trip. Amazingly they found an ankle length dress in a greyish blue that enhanced her eyes. The sleeves were long and lace edged the neckline, cuffs and hem.

"Very elegant," Eleanor pronounced. They found a dress in a complimentary color for Rose and bought new dress shirts for James and Anthony. Loaded down with their purchases, they were back at the house before one.

"Time for you to pamper yourself with a soaking bath and maybe a nap," Eleanor announced as she fussed around the kitchen. "Do not worry. If you fall asleep, I'll wake you at three."

Jackson came by and picked up Daniel's suit. "He'll meet you there. And plan on dinner afterwards at our place. Everything's taken care of." He disappeared out the back.

Ashley did pamper herself and she did take a nap. She fussed with her makeup hoping to distract anyone from noticing her hair was barely more than an inch long. Swiping makeup off for a third time, she stared at her reflection. *Maybe I'm not supposed to wear any.*

Hunter showed up and sat her down. Minutes later she stepped back and called Eleanor. "How does she look?"

"Like a bride."

The kids bounded in from school. Ms. Muir had picked them up at two o'clock. With few complaints, they took baths and dressed in their new clothes. Rose was delighted with her new dress and twirled around and around. The boys grumbled but underneath it all, James was pleased and Anthony resigned.

And that was that. At three-thirty Ashley was ushered into Lily's car for the drive to the Courthouse. "Just in case there are traffic or parking problems we've plenty of time."

At the Courthouse, Jackson herded the boys to one end of the hall where Daniel and Matthew waited. At the other end, her circle sisters clustered around her, words of congratulations and "it's about time" said with love and hugs.

Judge Peterson's secretary came out to announce the hearing was running a little late. The initial invitation to wait in her chambers was rescinded when the secretary counted the number of people present.

Ashley sat on the bench outside the court room with Lily on one side and Hunter on the other. Rose was walking in the halting wedding march step down the hall to Daniel and then back to her. No point in telling her to stop or sit down. Rose was ecstatic and that's what mattered most.

It was closer to five when everyone was asked to come into the courtroom. Judge Peterson stood in front of the bench, tables and chairs for prosecutors and defendants pushed aside.

Daniel held his hand out and Ashley took it.

"I see you've come to a decision," the judge said, a brilliant smile on her face. "I am performing a wedding, am I not?"

"Yes, your honor," they replied in unison.

Rose planted herself between them until the judge told her she needed to stand on her mother's other side because that's where the maids of honor stood.

With Eleanor and Ms. Muir along with her circle sister's around her and her sons, Jackson and Matthew flanking Daniel, they were ready.

When the last I Do was said and the bride was kissed, Judge Peterson turned to Ms. Muir. "I'd like an adoption home study on my desk at your earliest convenience." She turned to Rose who was once again, standing between them. "Will you Rose Amanda have Daniel Charles O'Donnell as your lawful father? Will you honor and obey him?"

Rose stood tall and in as solemn a voice as Ashley had ever heard, said clearly "I do."

"Do you Daniel Charles O'Donnell take Rose Amanda as your lawful daughter? Will you promise to take care of and protect her?"

His hand rested on Rose's shoulder. "I will and I do."

Daniel's hand left Rose and reached out for James, his other for Anthony. "And for the record, your honor, I will do my very best to take care of these boys. They are already the sons of my heart."

"They remain in your legal custody. I gather you would willingly adopt both of these boys?"

"In an instant," Daniel replied.

Ashley left the courtroom with Daniel's arm around her waist, Rose skipping ahead of them, James on Daniel's right side and Anthony? Well, Anthony dragged his feet, matched by Matthew so he wasn't really alone.

"Hey, you two," Matthew called over to them in the parking garage. "This one's coming with us. See you at Montgomery's" Ashley glanced over and saw Anthony in a lose headlock, with Matthew giving him a Dutch rub. When Matthew let him go, Anthony had a goofy smile on his face and readily went off with them.

"He'll be okay," Daniel said to her in a low voice. "We'll all make sure of it.

Knowing she wouldn't be facing the challenges that were sure to come with her middle son by herself was a comfort. She reached out and wound her arm around Daniel's waist. He leaned down and gave her a quick kiss on the lips.

"Don't either of you say anything. You will see me kissing your mom from time to time and I don't want to hear any groaning, or 'eewws' or anything like that."

"Will I want to kiss a boy when I'm bigger?" Rose asked Daniel.

Ashley hid a smile and kept silent.

Two steps later he answered. "You will when you are thirty. Believe me, before that age, you'll think it's icky."

The others laughed and kept on walking to their vehicles.

ASHLEY SAT in the chair next to the fire listening to her circle sisters catch up on each other's lives. She drifted off from time to time thinking about the night ahead. Eleanor and Gabriella were staying with the kids and she and Daniel had reservations at a posh address— Elizabeth's and Michael's Fremont house. They had the house to themselves for their wedding night.

She looked around at the familiar faces. *Who will be next?* With a certainty she knew another one of them would be loved by and would love another this year. *Who?* Of the three yet to be married, none of them were involved or showed any interest in a particular person much less the state of matrimony themselves. *Giovanni continues to be interested in Gabriella but I don't know. She shows no interest in him at all.*

Sophia's Jonathan had been gone four years and she showed no interest in dating or remarrying.

Hunter caught her eye and winked. *With Logan graduating this June and going off to college in the fall, her life is in for a huge change.*

Daniel appeared in her line of vision. Her gaze traveled up his long legs past the telltale sign of activities to come, on up his chest to his face. His eyes were warm and inviting. His hand outstretched.

"Shall we, Mrs. O'Donnell?"

"Remember I'm still Ms. Carlyle to everyone but you."

"As long as you're mine, Ash, I don't care what name you go by."

Wrapped in a hug, his breath feathering her cheek, Ashley stood on her tiptoes and kissed him. "What are we waiting for, Mr. O'Donnell?" she asked, her voice husky with invitation.

Daniel scooped her up, laughed when she squealed and headed for the door. Jackson strode ahead and opened it, ushering them out with a gallant bow.

Jackson stood with the door open, the laughter and joy of the newlyweds filtered back in. When the truck's doors closed, he did the same with the front door.

Across the room his Lily was talking to Ms. Muir. She glanced his way and smiled that welcoming one of hers that warmed his toes. Diana and Matthew were visiting with Hunter and Logan. Eleanor and Gabriella were rounding up the kids. They still had school tomorrow.

Jackson heard the truck engine come to life. His friend was a lucky man. Perhaps not quite as lucky as he was, but lucky enough.

Ten minutes later, Daniel pulled into the Murphy's' driveway. Another five minutes passed before he and Ashley made it out of the cab. Both had clothing in disarray.

"House," he managed.

"Bed," she added.

The tumblers in the lock gave easily and they were inside in seconds. Clothing strewn from the front door to the bedroom left a trail even the most bumbling detective could follow.

In the passion of the moment, neither Ashley nor Daniel paid any heed. Tomorrow was another day. Tonight was theirs to enjoy, to treasure as they embarked on a journey to last them the rest of their lives.

LEARN MORE ABOUT THESE BOOKS

Get the Latest News about New Releases, Special Events, Special pricing/sales

You have just finished reading **Ashley: Dragonflies and Dreams** the fourth book in the Sacred Women's Circle series.

Be the first to learn about future releases, any pre-release pricing or sales and special events by signing up for my mailing list here. I do not spam and you are free to unsubscribe at any time.

For More Information on The Sacred Women's Circle series check out:

My website: www.JudithAshleyRomance.com
My blog: www.JudithAshley.blogspot.com

A REQUEST

If you enjoyed reading about *Diana*, I'd be grateful if you would spread the word by telling friends and family, posting on social media and writing a review. Any and all of the above will be greatly appreciated and are a perfect way to support me..

ABOUT JUDITH

What do you do if you see visions and hear voices? If you're Judith Ashley, you write these stories down.

It helped that her visions and the voices were of seven women creating a sacred women's circle, a haven from whence they deal with the issues and struggles many of us face in everyday life.

It also helped that Judith experiences firsthand the healing power of supportive relationships and spiritual practices.

Judith's Prayer for you: *May your dreams manifest in "right time" and may you know the peace of unconditional acceptance, support and unconditional love.*

http://judithashleyromance.com

facebook.com/JudithAshley.Romance

twitter.com/JudithAshley19

bookbub.com/authors/judith-ashley

WINDTREE PRESS

For more books from the heart in fiction and non-fiction please visit
Windtree Press

http://windtreepress.com

www.ingramcontent.com/pod-product-compliance
Lightning Source LLC
Chambersburg PA
CBHW071725190726
48292CB00003B/612